This book is to be returned on or before
the last date stamped below.

WITHDRAWN

Also by Anna Kendall from Gollancz

Crossing Over
Dark Mist Rising

CROSSING OVER

BOOK ONE
of the Soulvine Moor Chronicles

✦

ANNA KENDALL

The right of Anna Kendall to be identified as the author
of this work has been asserted by her in accordance with the
Copyright, Designs and Patents Act 1988.

First published in Great Britain in 2010 by
Gollancz
An imprint of the Orion Publishing Group
Orion House, 5 Upper St Martin's Lane,
London WC2H 9EA
An Hachette UK Company

This edition published in Great Britian in 2011
by Gollancz

1 3 5 7 9 10 8 6 4 2

A CIP catalogue record for this book
is available from the British Library

ISBN 978 0 575 09427 7

Typeset by Input Data Services Ltd, Bridgwater, Somerset

Printed in Great Britain by Clays Ltd, St Ives plc

The Orion Publishing Group's policy is to use papers
that are natural, renewable and recyclable products and
made from wood grown in sustainable forests. The logging
and manufacturing processes are expected to conform to
the environmental regulations of the country of origin.

www.orionbooks.co.uk

For Jack

1

The first time I ever crossed over, it was market day and I was a little boy, barely six years old. I had spilled goat's milk on the linsey-woolsey that Aunt Jo had spent weeks weaving, the linsey-woolsey that she was going to sell at market. Hartah beat me unconscious, and I crossed over.

No. That is not true. I must have crossed over earlier, in dreams. There must have been times when my infant self lay asleep, restless and feverish from some childish illness, pain in my head or belly or throat. That's what is required – letting go, as in sleep, plus pain. Not great pain, but Hartah doesn't believe that. Or maybe he just likes beating me.

That first time, eight years ago – the milk staining the bright green wool, my aunt's gasp, her husband raising his head from the table with that look in his eyes and I . . .

'Roger,' he said now, 'you will cross over today.' Again Hartah raised his head, this time looking at me over the rim of his mug of sour ale.

My neck and spine turned cold.

It was barely dawn. We sat alone in the taproom of an inn somewhere on the Stonegreen Road. It wasn't much of an inn. Three trestle tables of rough wood on the cobbled floor, two ladders leading to 'rooms' above that were no more than lofts with dirty straw as pallets. The beams overhead were so blackened and ill cared for that soot dropped onto the tables. Still, last night my heart had surged with gladness when our wagon pulled into the stable yard. During the summer we almost never slept indoors. But now the first leaves had begun to turn colour and the air smelled of rain. Hartah must have hidden a few pennies, or stolen them, to pay the innkeeper.

'Today is the Stonegreen harvest faire,' Hartah said. 'You will cross over.' Before he could say more, the inn door opened and four men entered. They were loud, laughing and joking, but no louder than the clamour in my head.

I can't, I can't, I can't, I won't—

But I knew I would.

'Brought your ram, then, Farlowe?' said one of the men. 'Puny beast – no prize for you, I wager!'

'Seventeen stone if he's a pound!'

'Pound of sagging skin and weak bones!'

Rough male laughter and cries of 'Ale! Ale before the faire!'

The innkeeper's wife came from the kitchen, Aunt Jo trailing meekly behind with Hartah's breakfast. She didn't meet my eyes. She knew, then, what Hartah would make me do this day, and how he would make me do it.

'Ale! Ale before the faire!'

'You shall have it then,' the innkeeper's wife said, a frothy mug in each hand and two more balanced on her meaty forearms. 'And breakfast too, if you're with money, you scurrilous lot! Good morrow, Tom, Philip, Jack. Henry, where's that pretty new wife of yours? When I was her age, I was never left alone in bed of a faire morning. Or did you wear her out before dawn?'

The youngest man blushed and looked proud. The others roared and teased him while the woman set down the ale. She was broad, red-faced, merry – everything my aunt was not. Aunt Jo set a wooden trencher of bread and cheese – no meat – in front of Hartah and backed quickly away. So cowed was she that she didn't even realize he would hardly strike her here, in front of men among whom he hoped to be selling later in the day. Her thin body shuddered.

I felt no pity. Never once had she protected me from him. Never once. And there was no bread and cheese for me. Probably Hartah's stolen coins were only enough for one.

The oldest of the laughing men glanced at me. Casually he flipped a penny onto the table. 'Here, boy, water my horse and his burden, the one with yellow ribbons, there's a good lad.'

The penny landed midway between Hartah and me. I saw the muscles of his great shoulders shift, as if he meant to reach for it. But the older man watched us, and so Hartah merely nodded, as if giving permission. As if he were some sort of gracious lord. Hartah! Hatred burned behind my eyes. I snatched the penny and went outside.

The day was soft and clear, traces of the gold and orange sunrise still in the sky and the rough grass smelling of last night's rain. I fetched water from the stable yard well both for the horse and for the ram tethered in the cart, its horns bright with yellow ribbons. More wagons drew up to the inn, farmers arriving for the faire. Their cart-wheels groaned under loads of vegetables, sheep, baskets, children. 'The caravan comes! I saw it!' a child shrieked, leaning so far over the side of his wagon that he nearly fell out. 'I saw it!'

'Hush your noise,' his young mother said fondly. She wore a lavender dress and lavender ribbons in her hair, and her hand strayed to stroke her little lad's soft curls.

Bitterness ran through me like vomit.

Hartah would make me do it. He would make me cross over, lying concealed in the back of our worn and faded faire booth. That was why we had come here. And to make it happen, he would beat me first, as he had all the other times.

I was no longer six years old. I was fourteen, and as tall as Hartah. But I was skinny – how could I be otherwise, when I got so little to eat? – and narrow-shouldered. Hartah could lift a cask of new ale on each shoulder and not even sweat. But now I had a penny. Could I run away on that? On a single penny and the memory of my dead mother in her lavender dress?

No. I could not. Where would I go?

And yet I dreamed of escape. Sometimes I gazed at Hartah and was frightened by the violence of my desire to do him violence. But Hartah had told me and Aunt Jo of finding the bodies of lone travellers on the roads of The Queendom, set upon by highwaymen, robbed and gutted. After such stories I huddled in my thin blanket and went nowhere.

My stomach rumbled. I took the penny round the back to the kitchen and exchanged it for breakfast, which I gobbled standing up in the stable yard.

A girl leaned against the well. There were other girls here now, climbing down from wagons or trailing behind their families into the inn. They wore their best outfits, wool skirts dyed green or red or blue hiked up over striped petticoats, black stomachers laced tight over embroidered white smocks, ribbons in their hair. This one was no prettier, no more bright-eyed, no better dressed than the others, although she wore black lace mitts on her hands. But she watched me. The rest of the girls looked through me, as if I were a patch of air, or else their eyes narrowed and their pink lips turned down in disgust. *Dirty. Weak. Homeless.*

But this girl watched me thoughtfully, her heavy bucket of water dangling from one hand and weighing

4

down her shoulder. Something bright and terrifying raced through me. *She knew.*

But of course that was nonsense. Nobody knew about me except my aunt and the bastard she had married, and sometimes I think even my aunt doubted. He can do *what*? Does he merely pretend? But Aunt Jo said so little, serving Hartah in such cringing silence that it was impossible to tell what she thought except that she wished I had not come to her on her sister's death. That wish was evident every moment of every day, but even so she didn't wish it as fervently as I.

However, there had been nowhere else for me to go. My mother dead, my father vanished before I had any memory of him. Aunt Jo would never talk of either, no matter how much I begged. And now, all these years later, still nowhere else for me to go.

The girl nodded at me and walked off with her heavy bucket. Her long black braids swung from side to side. Her pretty figure grew smaller as she walked away from me so that it almost seemed as if she were disappearing, dissolving into the soft morning light. 'There you are,' Hartah's voice said behind me. 'Getting breakfast, are you? Good. You'll need your strength this afternoon.'

I turned. He smiled. A mouth full of broken teeth, and eyes full of pleasure at what would come later. Slowly, almost as gentle as a woman, he reached out one thick finger and wiped a crumb of bread from beside my lips.

2

By noon the faire was in full whirl. Stonegreen was bigger than I had realized. The inn where we had slept was five miles back down the road, and there was a much better inn beside the village green, along with a blacksmith's shop, a cobbler and the large moss-covered boulder that gave Stonegreen its name. The boulder reached as high as my shoulder, and someone had planted love-in-a-mist all round it. A placid river, bordered by trees, meandered by half-timbered cottages thatched with straw. The straw too had grown green with moss and lichens. Around the cottages grew hollyhocks, delphiniums, roses, ivy, cherry and apple trees. Behind were neat herb gardens, well houses, chicken yards and smokehouses – all the sources of good things that exist when women hold sway over prosperous households. I smelled bread baking and the sweet-sour odour of mulled ale.

The faire was held in a field at the other end of town from the green. There were booths and tents where local people sold crops, livestock, meat pies, jellies, cloth woven by wives and daughters, ale and ribbons and carved wooden toys. In other booths, merchants from as far away as Glory, the capital of The Queendom, offered pewter plate, farm tools, buttons. A third group, neither local nor from Glory, had come in a caravan of red and blue painted wagons that travelled all summer to country faires. I had seen the caravans before. There would be a fire-eater, puppeteers, jugglers, fiddlers, a show of trained fleas, an illusionist, a wrestler offering to take on all comers. Children ran among the booths and couples strolled arm in arm. Fiddlers and drummers played, boothmen bawled out their wares, animals for sale bleated or lowed or clucked. I saw no soldiers, which of course was a good thing.

'Here,' said Hartah, and my aunt and I began unloading the tent from our wagon.

Our booth, unlike most others, was completely closed. The stained and faded canvas displayed only a small group of stars arranged in the constellation the Weeping Woman. Sometimes people entered thinking we were some sort of chapel, but Hartah was good at spotting those and sending them away none the wiser. Others, recognizing the ancient pattern of stars and their hidden meaning, entered alone. They conferred with Hartah and, later, came back for their answer, also alone. Hartah could neither read nor cipher, but he was not stupid, he took care, and it had been a long time since we had been denounced as witches. These were prosperous days in The Queendom, and even I at fourteen knew that prosperity lessens suspicion of witchcraft. People were not desperate. It is the poor and desperate, so accustomed to danger, who most fear what they cannot see.

Although, of course, we were not even witches.

As I tugged on the heavy canvas I thought again about running away. I could do it. Boys my age did it, didn't they? They found work as farm hands or stable boys or beggars. But I knew nothing of farming, not much about horses, and I was afraid of not only highwaymen but of starvation. And in a few months winter would be here. Where did beggars go in winter?

The truth is, I was a coward.

'Look lively, Roger,' Hartah growled. 'Your aunt works faster than you!'

And she did. Aunt Jo scurried around like a scrawny whirlwind, afraid of Hartah's fists.

When the tent was up, he shoved me inside it. A rough table was set in the corner and draped with a rug that fell to the ground. Under this, unseen but hearing all, I would crouch for several hours, as the faire goers came with their requests. We would not get the happy men, women, and children carrying their fairings, drinking their ale, winning prizes for their seventeen-stone rams. We would get the other people found in every village, every city, every flower-bedecked cottage in every queendom. The people that the happy ones tried not to notice, lest it ruin their pleasure at the faire. The ones who were beset, grieving, afraid. My people.

And so it would begin again.

The first time I ever crossed over I was six years old. Now I was fourteen and it was the same, ever the same, always the same.

All morning I lay cramped beneath my table, listening. Then at noon, when the sun beat hot on the heavy canvas, the tent flap was fastened close and Hartah pulled me out. He smiled. 'You ready, boy?'

'Hartah ...' I hated that my voice quavered, that I brought my hand feebly to guard my face, hated that I was too frightened of him to fight back. His fist smashed into my belly. All the air left me, and I gasped with pain. He hit me again, in the chest, the groin, all places covered by clothing where my bruises would not show. The sounds of the fiddles and the drums and the shrieking children hid my cries. I was not an infant now, crossing over in an infant's mindless letting go; I must choose this. Pain plus choice. I willed it so, and even as my body fell to the ground, it happened.

Darkness—

8

Cold—
Dirt choking my mouth—
Worms in my eyes—
Earth imprisoning my fleshless arms and legs—

But only for a moment. I was not, after all, actually dead. The taste of death lasted only for the brief moment of crossing, the plunge through the barrier that no one else could penetrate, not even the Dead themselves. A heavy barrier, solid and large as Earth itself, and just as impossible to bore all the way through. Except, for reasons I did not understand, for me.

I tried again to cry out and could not for the dirt clogging my mouth. I tried to flail my arms and could not for the lack of muscle and flesh over my naked bones. Then it was over. The dirt gone, my bones restored, and I had crossed over into the country of the Dead.

A few of the Dead sat on the ground, doing what the Dead do. I ignored them as I took my bearings. There, in the near distance, the gleam of water. It might be the river beside Stonegreen.

The country of the Dead is like our country but weirdly stretched out and sometimes distorted. A few steps in Stonegreen might be half a mile here, or two miles, or five. Or it might be the same. Sometimes our rivers and forests and hills exist here, but sometimes not. The country of the Dead is vaster than ours and I think it changes over time, just as ours does, but not in the same way. It is our shadow made solid. Like a shadow, it shrinks and grows, but from some unseen influence that is not the sun. There is no sun here.

There *is* light, an even subdued glow, as on a cloudy day. The sky is always a low featureless grey. The air is quiet, and I could again breathe easily, all hurt gone from my chest. Pain does not follow me when I cross over. It is merely the price of passage.

In the cool calm light I walked towards the water. Before I reached it, I came to the big moss-covered boulder that on the other side had marked the village green. The boulder looked exactly the same, although without Stonegreen's surrounding cottages and shops and fields. Without the road as well. There are no roads here, just the untrampled grass of an everlasting summer. The steps of the Dead leave no marks.

Five of them sat cross-legged beside the stone, holding hands in a circle. They like to do that. It's always hard for me to get the attention of the Dead, but when they're in one of their circles it's impossible. They sit for long stretches of time – days, years – never talking, and on each of their faces is the calm absorbed look of men aiming an arrow, or of women bent over a difficult piece of needlework. I passed them by and continued on towards the river.

An old woman sat there, alone under a great over-hanging tree, her bare toes dangling in the water. She wore a rough brown dress and a white apron, her grey hair tucked under an old-fashioned cap with long white lappets. The old are the only Dead who will – or perhaps can – talk to me, and most often it is the old women who are good talkers. I sat beside her on the bank and said, 'Good morrow, mistress.'

Nothing. She didn't yet realize I was there. What do the Dead see when they see me? A wisp, a shimmer in the air? I don't really know. I squeezed her arm hard, just above the elbow, and shouted, 'Good morrow, mistress!'

Slowly she turned her head, squinted her sunken blue eyes, and said, 'Who's there?'

'I am Roger Kilbourne. At your service.'

That tickled her. She gave a cackling laugh. 'And what service d'you think you could render me, then? You've crossed over to bother us, have you not?'

'Yes, mistress.'

'What the devil do you want now? Go back, lad, it is not your time. Not yet.'

'I know,' I said humbly. 'But I would ask you some questions, my lady.'

She cackled again. '"Lady"! I was never no lady. Mrs Ann Humphries, lad.'

This was a piece of luck. Not an hour ago – if hours were the same here, which I doubted – I had lain under the table while another woman of that name had sobbed in Hartah's tent.

'My mother ... taken from us just this last winter ... Her lungs ... I know it's wicked to be doing this but I miss her so much ... The only one who ever really cared what becomes of me or my children ... My no-good husband ... drink and debt, and ... my mother my mother my mother ...'

My mother, in a lavender dress. But I would never find my own mother here. The Dead didn't wander far from where they crossed over. And neither Hartah nor Aunt Jo would tell me where my mother had died, nor how. Of my father, my aunt would not speak at all. I have given up asking.

I said, 'Mrs Humphries, today I met your daughter and namesake, Ann.'

'Oh?' she said, swishing her shrivelled feet to make the water roil. 'Look at the white stones under the water. See how they seem to shift shape.'

This is what the living do not understand about the Dead, and what I must never tell them. The Dead, unless they are very freshly crossed over, do not care about those they have left behind.

They remember the living, yes. Memory crosses over intact. The Dead know whom they have left, know who they themselves are. They perfectly recall life; it just no longer interests them. It's as if life was a story they heard once about an acquaintance of an acquaintance, a tale that unaccountably stayed in memory but without any personal connection. Without passion.

What does interest the Dead? For all my crossings, I still don't know. Of course, I'm never here for very long, and only the elderly will talk to me. Yet I have the impression that the Dead are absorbed in something of which they never speak, not even to each other – unless words like Mrs Humphries' mean more than they seem. 'Look at the white stones under the water. See how they seem to shift shape.'

The Dead will stare at stones for years. At trees, at flowers, at a single blade of grass. What is shifting in their minds, under what unimaginable waters?

Mrs Humphries had forgotten me. I pinched her hard. If I went back to Hartah without information, my second beating would be worse than my first. My pinch didn't hurt Mrs Humphries – nothing hurts the Dead – but it did remind her that I was there.

She snapped, 'What now, boy?'

'Tell me about when you were a girl.' And I held my breath.

Childhood is the one thing that will sometimes get the elderly Dead to talk. Their adult selves, their long lives, the families they left behind – these mean nothing to them now. But themselves as small children, that will sometimes animate them. Sometimes, anyway. Perhaps it is because little children, in their simplicity, are closer to what the Dead are now. I don't know. None of the actual children here have ever talked to me, or even seemed to see me.

Mrs Humphries gave her little cackle and her old eyes brightened. 'I was a rapscallion, I was! You would scarcely credit it, boy, but I was a pretty child, with hair like new-minted gold. But I wanted black hair, like my friend Catherine Littlejohn, so I—'

A family story, undoubtedly told and retold many times. It led to other stories. A prize chicken had been stolen from the Littlejohns and slaughtered for the Feast of the Winter Solstice. A nobleman, one Lord William Digby, had once ridden through Stonegreen and given Ann, that pretty child, a coin as gold as her hair. I listened carefully, watching the stones shift shape under the water. And all the while rage built in my heart that Hartah made me do this thing, come to this place, note with such desperation these trivialities from a woman months in her grave. A woman I would never see again. A woman who was dead, when I was not. I only felt that I was. Here, and there.

3

I delayed crossing back over for as long as I could. Always I feared the dirt in my mouth, the flesh gone from my bones, the maggots and the cold and the darkness. What if one time they didn't pass? What if I became trapped in that terrible moment between life and death, forever awake in my rotting grave?

And I did not want to return to Hartah. To my fear of staying, my fear of leaving.

So I loitered by the mossy green boulder and watched the Dead, and tried to get another one of them to talk with me. None would. They sat holding hands in their circles, or they sat alone, gazing at a blade of grass. One of them, a gentleman or even a lord in his velvet breeches and doublet, a short sword on his hip, lay full length on the grass. He stared straight up at the featureless grey sky. He never even blinked. I wanted to kick him, but what if this should be the one time when a kick aroused a younger Dead? That sword was as real and solid as everything else here.

Some of the Dead wear strange dress, clothing I have never seen on my travels with Hartah. Crude fur tunics. Armour with red plumes on odd-shaped helmets. Long white robes. The old ones speak languages I don't know, when they speak at all. But wherever or whenever their lost lives, they all behave the same.

Listening.

Watching.

Waiting with unimaginable patience. I don't know

14

what they wait for, what their calm gazes see. And they do not, or cannot, tell me.

When I had lingered as long as I dared, I took a sharp stone from my pocket. I rested my left hand against the Stonegreen boulder and drove the stone as hard as I could into my hand, harder than necessary. It does not take nearly as much pain to leave here as to come. But I wanted to inflict pain, and I could not inflict it on Hartah, so I cut my hand and crossed back over into the land of the living.

'. . . and dyed her hair black, like her friend Catherine Littlejohn's,' Hartah finished. The woman in the tent burst into tears.

Again I lay under my table, but I already knew that this time I was not needed. The woman sobbed, 'Oh, it *was* my mother! No one else could know those things, not all those details, not like that. Oh! And she said she's safe and happy . . .'

'Yes. And that she loves you very much,' said Hartah. For these occasions he used a voice that Aunt Jo and I seldom heard: low, slow, completely scrubbed of his usual snarl. He sat far away from the women – our customers were usually women – both to not make them uneasy with his great bulk and to give himself an air of mystery. Hatred of him filled my mouth like rancid meat.

'My good mother! Oh, thank you, good sir, I can never thank you enough, this is a gift beyond price!'

But of course there was a price. Hartah exacted it, plus a promise of silence, from Mrs Ann Littlejohn, born Humphries. He did the same with Catherine Carter, born Littlejohn, and with Joan St Clare and her young cousin Geoffrey Morton. They had all lived in Stonegreen their entire lives, the Humphries and Carters and Littlejohns and St Clares, as had their parents and grandparents before them. Their family secrets were shared secrets, and the dead Mrs Humphries had known them all.

'A good day's work,' Hartah said to me after the last customer had left the tent. He meant his work, not mine. Already he had forgotten the beating he'd given me this morning, blotted from his mind as completely as the grave blotted love from the minds of the Dead.

'May I go?' I tried to keep anger and fear from my voice.

'Yes, yes, go – who needs you now?'

Outside, long shadows fell across the faire field. Dusk gathered on the horizon, soft and blue and smelling of the night to come. Farmers drove their wagons, lighter by what they'd sold and heavier by what they'd bought, down the Stonegreen Road towards home. The cottagers of Stonegreen lingered at the remaining booths and at the ale tent, not wanting their brief holiday to end. Several, men and women alike, were drunk. They staggered about, singing and laughing, their merriment echoing from group to group. I found my aunt sitting in the shade of Hartah's wagon. With no money to enjoy the faire, she had probably sat there most of the day. Wordlessly she raised her eyes to mine.

'A good take,' I said. 'We will eat.'

She didn't smile; all smiles had left her years ago. But she laced her hands together on her skinny belly as if in thanksgiving prayer. I couldn't stand to watch. Grateful prayer, for a crust of bread and slice of cheese! I stalked away to the river and found myself standing under the same great overhanging tree where I had sat with Mrs Humphries in the country of the Dead.

Under the tree, staring at the dappled shadows on the river, stood the girl from the inn yard this morning. The girl with the long black braids. 'You're back,' she said, and I froze.

'Where did you go all day?' she continued. 'I didn't see you anywhere at the faire.'

She had looked for me. *She* had looked for *me*. And she didn't know where I'd been. So why had she looked for me? I couldn't think of anything to say and so stood there, wordless, like the oaf that I am.

'Oh!' she cried suddenly. 'What's wrong with your hand?'

The bruise where I had hit myself with the sharp stone. It had bled a little, the blood had crusted over, and around the angry wound my flesh was puffy and red, rapidly turning purple. Foolishly I covered it with my other hand, clasping both in front of me. Then I realized that the gesture was exactly what my aunt had done, and I scowled ferociously.

The girl didn't notice. She'd darted towards me, picked up my clasped hands, pulled them apart. She had removed the black lace mitts she'd worn in the morning, and the long white sleeves of her smock fell back over her arms.

'Did you cut yourself on– Oh!' Immediately she put her left hand behind her back. But I had seen.

'Don't tell,' she whispered softly, childishly, and the fear in her eyes loosened my tongue as nothing else could. I understood fear.

'I won't,' I said. 'I won't tell, I never would. But you should be more careful. Not that it signifies – I assure you it doesn't! Not to me! It means nothing!'

She nodded unhappily, tears in her eyes. The eyes were deep brown. Brown eyes, black hair – she should have looked drab, like a painting without colour, but she did not. She burned bright in my gaze, a beautiful girl with one tiny flaw that signified nothing. Or, to some, everything.

I babbled on, trying to find words that would reassure

17

her. 'Only the superstitious say it matters. Only the ignorant. Why, I've heard tell that Queen Caroline has the
same thing! And she is the queen!'

'The queen is a whore,' the girl said flatly, and I blinked.
This girl spoke her mind freely. Spoke her mind, did not
take enough trouble to hide the tiny sixth finger on her
left hand, the same mark rumoured of Queen Caroline.
The mark of a witch.

'Be more careful!' I blurted, and looked around to see
who else had heard her call the queen a whore. No one
was near. 'Take better care, my lady!'

'I am no lady,' she said, giving me the same smile as
Mrs Humphries when I'd called her a lady. Would all
women react with the same pleased amusement to my
honouring them so? But I didn't want to honour all
women. Only this one, standing here with my injured
hand still in her own small white one. She said, 'My
name is Catherine Starling. Cat.'

'I'm Roger Kilbourne.'

'My father farms at Garraghan.'

I didn't know what or where Garraghan was, and
I had no information I wanted to offer about my aunt or
Hartah. But I didn't need to speak. With a toss of her
black braids, Cat said, 'I don't believe in witches, anyway!'

'You must be careful who you say that to.'

'I know. I am careful. I can trust you, I knew that right
off this morning. You don't believe in witches either, do
you, Roger? All that foolishness – putting curses on people
and sickening cattle and talking to the Dead! Faugh!'

I said nothing.

She brought her left hand from behind her back and
joined it to her right, still holding mine. 'I'll tell you what
I do believe in, Roger,' she said with that luscious smile.
'I believe in stars and flowers and sweetmeats and my
doll!'

I saw it then. Her beauty had misled me, as had her pretty voice. She didn't stumble over her words like the poor creature Hartah had kicked in the last town; her head was not too large nor her eyes blank. But her wits were not all present, and the mind in her head was younger than her near-woman's body. It didn't make me think less of her. It made me want to protect her, keep her safe from those who would make her childish tongue and sixth finger into excuses to hurt her. The warmth of her hands felt like the best thing that had come to me all summer.

Before I could answer, another voice, high with fear, called, 'Cat! Where are you!' An older woman burst through the trees to the riverbank. 'There you are! You know you are not supposed to– She wandered off, sir, I hope she has not troubled you.' At the sight of my hand in Cat's, the woman stopped cold.

She was Cat's mother: the same brown eyes, black hair, pretty features, although this woman's hair was tucked up under a cap and her face was tense with worry. I hastened to reassure her.

'No trouble, mistress, none at all. We were just talking. She is fine.'

Mrs Starling looked from me to her daughter, trying to assess the situation. I saw her take in my old clothes, too small for me at ankle and sleeve; my dirty hair; the hole in one boot. I saw her decide that whatever I had seen, I could have no influence anywhere, and so was no threat. But she was kind.

'Thank you, sir. Cat must go now; we start for home. Come, daughter.'

'Bye, Roger,' Cat said. 'See you again!'

That would not happen, I knew. Not only because Cat was obviously the child of a prosperous farmer, but because she was beloved by at least one parent, who

19

would do everything to keep her safe. I watched her go, and in my breast warred a strange and bitter mix of regret, jealousy and desire. I wanted Cat to stay. I wanted to go with her. I wanted to *be* her, sixth finger and all.

A sixth finger and impaired wits would be lesser afflictions than what I bore.

Slowly I left the leafy riverbank and went back to Hartah's wagon.

4

We spent the night at the same rough inn five miles from Stonegreen, and for once there was dinner for all three of us. I gobbled the bread and cheese, not knowing when I would get more. Even Aunt Jo ate well, sitting on the wooden bench as far away from Hartah as she could, her eyes cast down. Firelight turned one cheek rosy, which looked grotesque on her thin lined face. Would my mother, had she lived, have looked like this? No. My mother, in my childish memory of her, had been beautiful.

Why, I thought at Aunt Jo, *won't you tell me where and how my mother died, you pitiful woman*? Aunt Jo raised her head. For an instant her gaze met mine. She looked away.

'Good food,' Hartah grunted, and belched.

In the morning the air had turned much colder. In another few weeks there would be frost on the grass. Hartah, to my surprise, turned the wagon south. As the sun warmed the day, he seemed in a very good mood indeed, whistling tunelessly. I rode in the back of the jostling wagon, sitting on the folded faire tent, and watched a fly crawl across the back of Hartah's neck. After several hours of wordless travel, I risked a question addressed to his and my aunt's back.

'Where are we going?'

'To the sea.' He laughed. 'I have a desire for sea bathing.'

He barely bathed at all. I could smell him every time the wind shifted.

Over the next few days there were fewer villages the farther south we went, and so fewer chances for harvest faires. The land grew wilder, less fertile. Fields of harvested crops gave way to pastures for sheep and then, as the ground became rockier and steeper still, to goats. After several days in the slow creaky wagon, we turned east. For the last time we spent the night at an inn, a rough place full of rough men who did not look like farmers or herders. There were no women. Hartah paid the last of his money for a tiny room up under the eaves and left Aunt Jo and me there.

'Bar the door,' he said, 'and don't open it until you are sure it's me.' He went back downstairs and did not return for hours. My aunt slept restlessly on the sagging bed. Rolled in my blanket on the floor, I could hear her light sighs, see her body twitch in the starlight from the tiny window. Did she dream, even as I did?

Let there be no dreams tonight.

There were not, and the next morning Hartah was cheerful. 'A good place for information!'

Aunt Jo looked at him and then away.

After that there were no inns, and we slept in or under the wagon, eating provisions Hartah had bought in Stonegreen. His good mood subsided, replaced by a restless tension I didn't understand. But he didn't hit me or Aunt Jo. He hardly noticed us until one night, over a campfire built beside a rocky landslide that barely blocked the cold wind, Hartah looked at me directly. His eyes flickered red and gold with reflections from the flames, like a beast. 'How'd ye like to be rich, Roger?'

For some reason I thought immediately of Cat Starling, back on her prosperous farm. Of her clean black braids, her carefully ironed petticoat. I said nothing.

'Scared ye, have I?' Hartah jeered. 'So much the better. There's fearful work for all of us ahead, and all of us will share the spoils. That's only right. You're a great one for right, ain't ye, Roger?'

Anything I said might provoke him. I stared at the fire. Hartah took another swig of the brandy he'd brought from Stonegreen.

'That's good. Stay silent, boy. Silence is what'll be needed, mark my words. But you'll stay silent or swing with the rest of us, eh? You'll see that. I know.'

I had no idea what he was talking about, nor did I care. As long as he left me alone, as long as he kept his fists on the brandy and not on me. When he again raised the bottle, I slipped down into my blanket and prepared to sleep.

But then I glimpsed Aunt Jo's face, her eyes wide and horrified, her withered lips parted in a silent scream.

The next day I could smell the sea on the wind, although I couldn't yet see it. We left the main road and climbed a muddy track up into hills even wilder, cut with deep ravines and falls of rock. The horse, old to begin with, faltered and strained. I thought the poor beast might drop dead in her traces, but still Hartah urged her on. The wagon wheels groaned, even though the load now consisted only of its driver. Aunt Jo and I walked behind. All of our provisions were gone except a half-loaf of hard bread, and Hartah had dumped the ragged faire tent into a ravine. When I dared to ask him why, he laughed and said, 'Rich men don't need such sorry lodgings!'

We reached the top of the track with the horse still alive, pulling the wagon into a thick wood of old oak and wind-bent pine. Here the tang of salt air was strong. In a clearing beside a swift hillside stream sat a crude wooden cabin, its log roof sealed with pitch.

'Hallooooo!' Hartah called. Two men came out of the cabin, one young and one about Hartah's age. The older leaned on a wooden staff, one of his legs bent and useless. He hobbled towards us.

'So you've come.'

23

'We have,' Hartah said.

'Is this your boy?'

'Yes.'

'Well, see that he does his share of the work.'

'He will.'

The younger man stared at me, scowling. He looked about seventeen or eighteen, wide-shouldered and handsome, with yellow hair falling over bright blue eyes. I found myself wondering if Cat Starling would have liked him, would have kissed him.

'Then come,' the older man said.

'Are the others—'

'Soon.'

Hartah said to Aunt Jo, 'Make camp. There, under the trees by the creek. Don't come near the cabin, or you'll wish you hadn't. You too, boy.' He and the yellow-haired youth strode into the cabin, the lame man limping after them.

My aunt and I drew the wagon under the trees, tethered and watered the horse, made a fire. There was nothing to cook. As I gnawed on my share of the bread, hard and mouldy, three more men arrived in the clearing. None had families with them. They disappeared into the cabin.

My aunt handed me her piece of bread. She had not touched it. When I looked at her in surprise, I gasped. Never had I seen a face like that. Whiter than frost and her eyes just as frozen, wide open and fixed in terror.

'Aunt . . . what—'

Abruptly she turned her head and vomited into the weeds. Thin strings of brownish-green bile retched from her mouth. In truth, I was surprised anything came up at all, we had eaten so little. Even more surprising, vomiting seemed to hearten her, or at least to return her voice.

'Go, Roger. Go now. What they plan . . . you must not . . . Run!'

I stared at her across the dying fire. Never once had

24

she told me to escape Hartah, or tried to protect me from him. I said, 'What are they planning? What's going to happen?'

'Go. Go. Go.' She was moaning now, like an animal in a trap, as she rocked back and forth by the fire on her skinny haunches. How could I go, leaving her like this? She was my aunt, my mother's sister, and I could not leave her here alone with whatever she feared so much.

No. That was not true. The truth was harsher, more shaming: I was afraid to run. To go off into that wild country without weapons or money or food. And Hartah had threatened to ... if he came after me and caught me ...

I felt shamed by my own cowardice, and shame turned me angry. 'You've lost your wits! I can't go! Be quiet or I'll—' I stopped, appalled. I sounded like Hartah.

Aunt Jo stopped too. No more moaning, no more rocking. She sank onto her blanket, her face turned away from me, and lay quietly. But one more sentence came from her side of the fire, and it was clear and cold as sea air.

'Your mother died at Hygryll, on Soulvine Moor.'

I went still. It seemed the whole world had gone still: leaves didn't rustle, wind didn't blow, embers didn't snap in the ashes of the fire. *At Hygryll, on Soulvine Moor.* After years of refusing to tell me anything of my parents. *My mother.*

'Where is Soulvine Moor?' I demanded. 'And how? How did she die?'

Aunt Jo said nothing, rigid as stone.

'*How?* And what of my father? Aunt Jo!'

But Aunt Jo would say no more. She lay as stiff and unresponsive as if it were she and not her sister who had died at that unknown place. Unknown now, but I would find it. Now that I had a name, I would find it. And for the first time ever I would cross over with gladness.

25

My mother, in her lavender dress . . .

It was a long time before I could sleep. I watched the stars between the branches of the trees. I watched the clouds drift in and cover them. Towards morning it began to rain. I crept under the wagon. The cold rain didn't matter; tomorrow I would go. My aunt had told me to run, and now I had a reason, a place to run to. Tomorrow I would go, and I would find the place my mother had died, and I would cross over and find her.

But towards morning Hartah woke me, and everything came crashing down.

'Boy! Get up, curse you, get up now!'

I started awake, sitting up so fast that I hit my head on the bottom of the wagon, a sharp crack that sent spears of light through my brain. Hartah seized me by one arm and pulled me from beneath the wagon.

The little clearing was bedlam. Men ran around cursing. A couple were hitching Hartah's old horse to a wagon that must have arrived in the last few hours. The rain still fell, a slow cold drizzle that soaked through my wool tunic as if boring inward. Through the grey curtains of rain the men's lanterns gleamed fitfully, illuminating now a clenched face, now the load upon the wagon bed, which was unseen beneath a tarpaulin.

'Come!' Hartah roared, dragging me with him.

Someone else yelled, amid a row of curses hot enough to blister rock, 'She be too early! She be too early!'

We ran behind the cabin and then kept going. There was a second track here, leading steeply downward. As Hartah and I descended in the darkness, I tried to keep my feet on the muddy ground, desperately looking by the light of Hartah's swinging lantern for firm footing amidst the streaming water. The smell of salt grew sharper. I could hear a wagon close behind me, the horse led by someone.

26

We left the trees and the wind hit me so hard I almost fell. All at once I could hear the sea surging below.

At the bottom of the track we reached a tiny pebbled beach. The sky was pitch black, but as lanterns came down with the men I saw that the beach lay between steep cliffs and the sea. The pebbles were dotted with large rocks, and even larger ones jutted from a wild sea. Dark waves rose and crashed on the boulders, some sending spray inland to dash against the cliffs. Rain fell steadily.

'There!'

'Hurry, damn you!'

'She be too early! Too early!'

'We can still do it.'

Do *what*? The yellow-haired youth pushed me out of the way, so hard that I fell on the rocks. I staggered up, dazed; no bones seemed to be broken, but I shrank back against the cliff, peering desperately around. No way back up to the cabin except by the one track, and men stood there, swinging their lanterns.

Yellow Hair pulled the tarpaulin from the wagon and tipped it. Such strength! A load of dry firewood spilled onto the beach in an enormous pile. Someone lit a brand soaked in oil and tossed it onto the wood, which flared instantly. Dry, cured, oiled – someone had prepared the wood with great care. The flames mounted high into the windy sky, a great bonfire.

And all at once I saw a light far out on the surging dark sea.

She be early! We can still do it—

No. No. They were going to—

I had heard of such things. I hadn't wanted to believe them. It was like witches or sick-curses, too monstrous to be believed. But here, here and now, my uncle—

Three lights flashed in rapid succession out on the dark sea, and the men on the beach shouted.

27

'She sees us!'

'She's coming in—'

'Get ready!'

The ship's crew thought the bonfire was a guide-light, the kind made to lead vessels towards safe harbour. She was sailing blind, out there in the wild storm, and this fire would lure her towards the rocks. How far out did the rocks extend from the beach? How soon would the captain realize what was happening?

I didn't know. I had never been on a ship. And there was nothing I could do.

Time passed. I don't know how much time. The rain lashed me as I huddled against the cliff, and out there on the sea the ship fought the storm. Her lights seemed to come closer, then to recede. In the rain and darkness I couldn't judge distances. I couldn't judge anything.

But enough time passed for the clouds to lighten in the east, over the top of one cliff, and hope seized me. If it got light soon enough for the ship to see the danger . . .

It did not. Even over the hammering waves I heard the crash as the ship ran into the rocks and splintered. Her lights bobbed wildly. A few moments later they went out.

The men on the beach screamed in joy.

Dawn approached. As the invisible sun rose behind the angry clouds, the entire horrifying scene came into view. The ship lay on her side about a quarter-mile out, breaking up as the sea pounded her again and again. Figures struggled in the surf, trying to get ashore. Some disappeared beneath the chaotic water, and didn't reappear. Others reached the beach, dripping and exhausted and bruised, their clothes torn ragged by the rocks. And my uncle's men rushed to meet them.

I saw the yellow-haired youth grab a sailor by the neck, push him down and drive a knife square into his back.

It was no contest. For every survivor from the wreck,

there was a killer on the beach. Blood streamed along with the rain, turning tide pools red. The men moved in a frenzy, silent now but all the more terrible for that, flashing their knives in and out of living flesh.

After a while no more figures staggered ashore.

Cargo began to wash up then, great casks and wooden boxes, dashed against the rocks in their passage. The men dropped their weapons – knives and swords and spears would have endangered them in that slippery sea – and waded out to grab the casks and boxes before they could split open. Stumbling, cursing, gripping the slippery rocks for balance whenever possible, the wreckers retrieved what they could, half carrying and half floating the cargo ashore. The sun rose higher behind the clouds, and I could see sticky red on the discarded blades.

'You!' Hartah roared at me. 'Help! Fetch in cargo!'

A box was tossed abruptly up by the waves, coming down on a rock just yards from the beach. The wood splintered and broke. Cloth spilled from the box, immediately sodden with saltwater. Red, gold, blue – the rich silks and velvets and brocades swirled in the water or clung to rocks even as my clothes clung to my body. The dyes began to run, staining the water colours that no sea ever was: red . . . yellow . . . cobalt blue . . . *lavender* . . . I stumbled towards the water until a hand on my arm stopped me.

'Roger! Go!'

My Aunt Jo had materialized on the beach. She must have come down the muddy track, come after everybody else had left the cabin, come to tell me where my mother was. I couldn't think. My back to the cliff, I stared at her, dumb, amid the wreck and the rain and the cloth dyeing pebbles fantastic colours.

'Go!' She thrust something at me, and without thought I took it. Hartah's knife, plucked from the bloody sand. She wanted me to take it, to run away while there was

29

still a chance. A chance to find my mother's death place, to cross over and see her again.

My feet finally moved.

A huge cry, and Hartah loomed before us. Some of the ruined cloth from the wreck clung to him, dripping blue velvet draped lopsided over his shoulders like a mockery of a cape. In his hands he held a metal-bound wooden box. From somewhere behind me, someone cried, 'Soldiers! Run!'

Rage blossomed on Hartah's face. His head jerked up, searching the cliff for soldiers. Rain streamed down his red nose, across a bruise on one cheek. Always rage must go somewhere. He screamed at Aunt Jo, 'I told you to stay above!' He raised the box and brought it down hard upon her skull.

Her slight body crumpled onto the rocks.

Without thought, I slid Hartah's knife between his ribs and twisted it.

His big body went rigid. One arm raised to grab me, and I stepped back, pulling out the knife. Instantly blood gushed from his side – so much blood! It pooled among the rocks, mingled with the rain, splashed when Hartah fell to his knees and then, after a long terrible moment when time itself seemed to stop, onto his face beside Aunt Jo.

The knife dropped from my slack fingers.

'Soldiers!' someone screamed again, and then they were pouring down the track, slipping in the mud, dozens of them in the rainy dawn. There was no other way off the beach except out to sea, where the ship broke up even more with each crashing surge of the waves. Some of the wreckers fought back, but it was hopeless. Only two of us were taken prisoner, me and the youth with the yellow hair, and there was no way Cat Starling would ever, ever have kissed either one of us.

5

I lay face down on the ground in the clearing above the beach, hands and feet bound, my mouth shoved against the wet dirt. The yellow-haired wrecker lay beside me, similarly tied. The rain had slowed. Soldiers dressed in rain-sodden blue milled around, and shouts sounded continuously as horses, Hartah's old nag among them, hauled wagons up from the beach. Every so often a boot kicked me in the leg or the belly, and painfully I brought my bound arms up to shield my head as best I could.

What would these soldiers of the queen do to me?

All my life Hartah had told tales of soldiers torturing prisoners, but even in my fear I knew I would not be tortured here. The soldiers didn't need to force a confession. They would hang us on the evidence of their eyes.

'A priest!' the yellow-haired man cried. 'It is my right to see a priest before I die!'

Two pairs of boots stopped on the muddy ground, inches from my head. 'He's right,' said a voice. 'It's the law.'

'And did they have law in their minds when they wrecked the *Frances Ormund*?' demanded another voice, rougher than the first. 'Sir.'

The *Frances Ormund*. That must be the name of the ship. Again I saw the bodies on the beach, the tide pools red with blood, Hartah and the others shouting in triumph as they snagged the cargo washing ashore. The killings. And I had killed too. The knife sliding so easily between Hartah's ribs, like butter into good cheese. And, just before, the heavy wooden box smashing down onto my aunt's head.

My mind shuddered away from both images, and from the knowledge that I was a murderer. And yet I did not regret killing him. The thought astonished me. I, who had shrunk from killing a rat that had crawled into the wagon, a snake in the house, when we had a house. But it was true. I should have killed Hartah long ago. And I should have no fear of death now. After all, I – of all people – knew that both he and I would continue on across the grave, in the peaceful country of the Dead.

But I did not want to go there. Not like this, not for ever. What had Mrs Humphries said to me? *It is not your time. Not yet.*

The first soldier said, 'Nonetheless, Enfield, I am bound by the law.'

'Sir, these scum don't deserve the law! Begging your pardon, sir, but ten hands dead, with only two survivors! And a woman aboard, the captain's own wife!'

'I demand a priest!' the yellow-haired youth screamed. A boot hit him hard in the side. He gasped and writhed on the ground.

'Enfield,' the other voice said, but without warning. All at once I was seized by the arm and hauled to my feet.

'Sir, let him at least see what he's done before he hangs! Let him face the survivors!'

The officer made no objection. Enfield dragged me to the cabin. As we went, one soldier spat in my face. Over a high limb of a great oak, two more soldiers threw a pair of nooses.

The inside of the cabin was dark, lit only by a single lantern on a small table. Two people sat in wet, bloody clothes. One had a crude bandage wrapped around his temples; he sat with his head in his hands, moaning. The other was a woman.

She was neither young nor old, with grey streaking the salt-crusted hair that dripped onto her torn gown. Her face was swollen, either from her battering in the sea or from tears. Grief dulled her eyes. Enfield thrust me before her on my knees.

'This, Mistress Conyers, is what killed your husband and wrecked the *Frances Ormund* – this!'

She looked at me. I steeled myself for the blow. Instead she said, with a kind of hopeless wonder, 'But he's just a boy.'

'Worked with the wreckers, mistress. The foulest vermin there is. He'll hang with the other.'

Her brow furrowed painfully. I could see that she hadn't taken it in yet: the wreck, her husband's death, her own freakish survival. She was like those newly arrived in the country of the Dead, bewildered by where she found herself, unable as yet to make sense of this new terrain.

She said, 'How old are you, boy?'

All at once I found my voice. I wanted to live. Two nooses swung outside, and I was not yet ready to live in that other country. And I looked – so skinny, so underfed – younger than I was, despite my height. I fell to my knees.

'Eleven, mistress. And I did not wreck the ship! My uncle brought me there. He made me come. I didn't know – I didn't know!'

Enfield snarled, 'A blubbering coward as well as a wrecker.' He seized me, but I tore myself from his grasp and stayed on my knees.

'Please, mistress, I swear to you, *I did not know*! And my aunt was there too – my uncle killed her as well. Look for her body – it's skinny and frail. She didn't enter

33

the sea, she wasn't killed by anyone coming ashore – she was my mother's sister!'

Again Enfield grabbed me, this time much harder. But the dazed, grieving widow raised her hand. 'No, wait, please . . . please.'

'Mistress, he'll say anything to get himself off! He's lying!'

'Was . . . was . . .' It seemed hard for her to weave her thoughts. 'Was there a woman's body on the beach?'

I thought Enfield would lie, but somewhere amid the vengeance in him also lay truth. As it did in my story, if he but knew it. After a long pause, he said, 'There was.'

'Murdered?'

'Her head was bashed in,' Enfield said reluctantly. 'But this bastard might have done it himself!'

'No,' I said. 'Aunt Jo was the only one ever kind to me.'

And now, when she was dead, I saw that this too was true. My aunt had never protected me from Hartah, no. But she had shared with me what food she had. She had told me to run from this very clearing. She had lost her life coming down to the beach to tell me, yet again, to run. *'Go, Roger. Go now.'*

And I had treated her with rage, with contempt, because I was too afraid of Hartah to direct those feelings at him.

Tears pricked my eyes. For Aunt Jo, for my lost mother, for myself. Then shame flooded me – fourteen was too old to cry! *Eleven* would have been too old to cry. All I could do was hang my head, but I knew both Enfield and Mistress Conyers had seen.

She said wearily, 'Let him live. He's just a child.'

'He is not! This is an act and he a coward, a lying—'

'Let him live. It is my right.'

Enfield bellowed, pulled me upright, and dragged me

outside. He was not going to listen to her; he was going to hang me. But all he did was hold me fiercely and force me to face the great oak.

One noose dangled, empty, from the high tree. The other lay around the neck of the yellow-haired youth. His whole body trembled and his eyes rolled wildly. He shouted something, but the words made no sense. Three men on the other end of the rope pulled, and the young wrecker was jerked off his feet into the air.

He went on jerking for what seemed for ever, kicking desperately. The men knotted the far end of the rope around another trunk. The rope chafed the tree bark as the hanging man struggled for air. His face distorted as he swung, kicking and kicking and kicking . . .

Eventually the kicking stopped.

Enfield drew his knife and cut my bonds. He shoved me to the ground, where I lay looking up at him.

'Now go,' he said. 'Run. It *is* her right.'

But the dead man had had the right to a priest, and they had hung him without any priest. Looking at Enfield's face, I knew I would not get twenty feet into the woods before he, or one of the others, spitted me on a sword. Or worse. Mistress Conyers would never know.

Her gown, bedraggled and drenched and torn though it was, had been made of richly embroidered velvet.

She had been the wife of a ship's captain.

Enfield obeyed her, as long as he was in her sight.

I got to my feet. But instead of running into the woods or towards the track from the clearing, I ran back into the cabin and threw myself again at Mistress Conyers' feet.

'My lady! Please – if I go, the soldiers will kill me! Take me with you!'

Outrage finally brought some colour to her face. 'How dare you? My husband—'

35

'I can bring you news of him from the country of the Dead!'

'Guards! *Guards!*'

I did the only thing I could. I threw myself against the corner of the table as hard as I could, aiming so that the corner would hit my forehead. Pain shot through me like fire, great sharp lightning bolts of pain piercing my head, and the room went dark.

I crossed over.

6

I stood in the same clearing, although the cabin was gone. Nine of the Dead sat cross-legged in a circle, holding hands. I had appeared in the middle of their circle. They ignored me, or didn't see me, or didn't care. I stepped over them and started through the clearing towards the track down to the beach.

There was no track.

The sea lay below me, calm and grey beneath the eternally calm sky. I stood at the top of a steep cliff, much steeper than it had been in the land of the living. There was no way down. Far below, tiny figures moved on the rocky beach, although there was no sign of a ship, either afloat or wrecked on rocks.

Was one of those figures Hartah? Was another my Aunt Jo?

I pushed the thought aside; otherwise I could not act. I had to get down to the beach *soon*. Always the newly Dead had a period of disorientation when they could be talked to and would answer, but that period was very brief. I had to get to the beach while the Dead from the *Frances Ormund* were still bewildered, still not reconciled to their new home. Otherwise there was no chance that any of them – who were young sailors, not gossipy old women – would notice me at all. Frantically I thrashed my way through the woods at the edge of the cliff. No paths down. The beach disappeared from my view, and I stumbled back to the clearing.

The hanging tree stood before me, its leaves unmoving

37

in the quiet air. I shuddered. 'Where is the track down!' I screamed at the circle of Dead. None of them as much as glanced up.

I ran back to the cliff edge. Two of the newly Dead had waded out to rocks and sat cross-legged on them, quietly contemplating the water.

Time was running short. If I threw myself off the cliff, I would surely die – that is, if I *could* die here. But if I didn't get down there soon, Enfield would just as surely kill me in the land of the living.

I cried out, a great echoing howl of despair. One of the tiny figures on the beach looked up, shading his face with his hand. The next moment he flew through the air to stand not far from me at the top of the cliff.

I don't know who was more surprised, he or I. A rough sailor, he wore a brown jerkin with leather belt and torn pantaloons. Saltwater dripped from his clothing, his untrimmed beard, his greasy hair. He screamed, drew a knife from his belt and charged towards me.

'Stop!' I shouted before I knew I was going to say anything. And he did.

'How did ye do that? How did you bring me to ye?' he sputtered. 'And where be I?'

He didn't yet realize that he was dead. Was that why he had been able to soar through the air and up the cliff? I had never seen any other Dead do anything like that – what else could they do?

My mind raced faster than it had ever done before. This was my chance, probably my only chance. He repeated, 'Where be I?'

I said, 'You are in my queendom!'

He eyed me, fear and doubt warring in his eyes. 'Ye don't look like no prince!'

My clothing was as poor as his, and not much drier. I said, 'No, of course not. This is The Queendom of . . . of

Witchland, and I am an apprentice witch. How else could I have flown you up the cliff?'

Fear routed doubt. The sailor threw himself at my feet in the weeds and rocks. 'Witchland! Oh spare me, sir – my lord . . . spare me!'

'I will spare you if you tell me all you know of the ship that brought you here, its voyage and its captain.'

The sailor, still on his belly, peered up at me with the expression of a dog that expects to be beaten. I realized then what I should have seen at first. His beard had hidden most of his face, but his flat nose and big head, the slur in his voice, his confusion at being asked three questions at once. This man was like Cat Starling, but without her beauty. His was the mind of a child, and it was as a child that he could not grasp where he was, what had happened to the ship, or why the murderous seas had turned calm in the space of a heartbeat.

'Rise,' I said, as lordly as I could manage. 'Good. Now, tell me, what was the name of your ship?'

'The *Frances Ormund*.' He turned his eyes towards the sea and grimaced in bewilderment – where had the ship gone?

I did not want him thinking, remembering, realizing. 'Look at me. No, directly at me. Good. Now, who was her captain?'

'Cap'n James Conyers.'

'Good. Where was she bound?'

'For Carlyle Bay.' It seemed to steady him to have only one short question at a time, questions he could answer with certainty. The fear had not left his misshapen face, nor the knife his hand, but I sensed that as long as I kept his attention focused on me, he would not panic. The knife had a curved blade, wickedly sharp, and a wooden handle carved like an open-mouthed fish.

I said, 'How many hands aboard the ship?'

'Eleven, and the cap'n, and Mistress Conyers.'

'What was your cargo – no, don't look down. What was your cargo?'

'Gold from Benilles and cloth from ... I forget.' He hung his head.

'It's all right,' I said. Cloth and gold – a rich cargo, a small ship, a light crew. A good choice for wreckers.

'Oh!' he said, brightening. 'And we brung a man from Benilles – someone important, he was! With medals on his chest!'

The man, his medals and his importance had all been devoured by the hungry sea.

'What is your name?'

'Bat.'

'No other name?'

'No, sir. Bat be all I carry.'

'And what kind of captain was James Conyers to you, Bat? A fair master?'

This question was too complicated. Bat looked at me hopelessly.

'Did Captain Conyers ever have you flogged?'

'When I fouled the line. The cap'n, he give me three lashes. But they was light. He tell me that I ... I be trying as hard as I can, and that be *true*.'

'Did he—'

But Bat had found his tongue. 'The cap'n have the bosun flogged for stealing, and we put him ashore at Yantaga, we did. No pay, neither, and lucky he warn't sent to no gaol. The cap'n, he stood on deck when the big storm came, and he won't let no man leave his post, and then afterwards he said ...'

I heard all of what the captain said, what the captain did, what the captain was. This simple-witted man stood before me, salt drying on his ruined clothes, and painted a picture of an idol, a man such as I had never known.

Fair. Kind. Intelligent. Capable of doing anything. How much was true, and how much blind devotion?

Bat finished with, 'But where be the cap'n now? I can't leave my post!' Panic took him. 'Did you witch my cap'n?' The curved knife in his hand twitched.

'I did not.' More figures had emerged from the sea to wander the beach below. One might even be Captain Conyers. 'Bat, come with me.' I tried to make my voice as full of authority as I could – I, a skinny and fearful murderer fighting for his very life, which in this country hardly even existed. But Bat followed me.

I led him to a stump halfway between the cliff and the clearing. 'Sit there. Wait for me or the captain or the first mate. One of us will come.'

'Aye, sir.' He sat. I had no doubt that he would wait there until the end of time, if necessary. I left him.

Behind some thick bushes I tried to make myself fly through the air, as Bat had done. I willed it, I jumped, I closed my eyes and tried to command myself. Nothing. Apparently it was not enough to merely be here; one had to also be dead.

I bit my tongue, enough pain for a return, and crossed over.

'He's reviving,' a woman's voice said. I lay on the floor of the cabin. Mistress Conyers' face, weary and grieving and disgusted, sagged above me. 'Guards, take him outside and set him free.'

'No, wait!' Beyond shame, I clutched the sodden hem of her velvet gown. 'Listen to me! I—'

'Out!' Her voice rose to a shriek. She was not, I sensed, a woman giving to shrieking, but here and now ... Her husband lay dead in the roiling sea, his ship wrecked on the rocks, her life in ruins. A soldier seized me, not gently.

I blurted, 'Captain Conyers bought you roses in

Yantaga! When you put into port to put the bosun ashore for theft – yellow roses, masses and masses of yellow roses!'

The soldier had me halfway out the door. Mistress Conyers said, 'Wait.'

'Mistress—'

'*Wait.*' And to me, 'What do you know of yellow roses at Yantaga?'

I knew what Bat had told me, no more. But her face had gone white, and so of course there was more. With women, there is always more. I stabbed wildly around in my mind for something to say, to give her, something that might preserve my life.

'The roses were a . . . an offering. Between you two. For something important.'

Her eyes filled with tears. To the soldier she said, 'Leave us.'

'Mistress, it may not be safe to—'

'Leave us!' And there it was, the tone of authority I had tried for with Bat and could never, not in this land nor that other, achieve as she did. She was born to that voice. The soldier dropped me and stalked out the door.

'Who are you?' she said. 'How do you know these things?'

We stared at each other across the dim space, lit only by one lantern and the grey light from the small window. The other survivor moaned in a corner. The cabin smelled of male sweat, of rodent droppings, of my fear. But I had no choice.

'My name is Roger Kilbourne. I know these things because your husband just told me while I lay unconscious. Mistress, please believe me, please let me convince you. I can tell you more of your voyage on the *Frances Ormund*, much more . . . No, please hear me out! I am not lying or conniving or trying to play on your grief. I don't

42

know why I am this way, and I want nothing from you except my life. Please listen to me. I can . . .'

I had never said it aloud to anyone except Hartah and my aunt, and then only when I was a child, too young to know that some things are better left unsaid.

'I can travel to the land of the Dead.'

7

She believed me. Hartah had always said that only
country folk believed in my ability, never the city-bred
nor those above us, and I had found that true. But Mistress Conyers was a rare creature, one of those few who
look squarely at the evidence before them, who weigh it,
who can accept even that which is distasteful or frightening if it also seems true. After I told her all I had learned
from Bat, Mistress Conyers accepted that I could cross
over. She also accepted that if I was not to be killed, she
must take me away from the soldiers filled with lust for
revenge over the *Frances Ormund*. She believed me, she
took me with her, and then she disliked me intensely for
both those things.

Witchcraft.

Child of ship wreckers.

We left late in the afternoon. The rain had stopped and
the sea had gone from raging to grumbling. Those bodies
that could be recovered lay under wet blankets in the
backs of wagons, along with such cargo as could be fished
from the waters. Mistress Conyers and I rode in a different
wagon from the corpses, and I stuck close to her. Soldiers
in rain-soaked blue glared at me with murder in their
eyes. The body of Captain Conyers had not been found.
His widow and I did not talk.

We stayed close to the coast, heading always downhill,
away from the mountains. In the early dusk of autumn
we reached a large inn on the coast. A rider had been
sent ahead, and we were met at the inn by a large party

of men who had ridden hard and fast to arrive just as we did. These, it turned out, came from Captain Conyers' brother's estate, somewhere inland. The queen's Blues left us then, perhaps to make their own camp for the night. With them they took the other survivor from the *Frances Ormund*. With relief, I watched the soldiers ride away. These new men were armed and booted like the others, but they had no reason to hate me. Not unless Mistress Conyers should give them a reason.

Should I slip off now, disappear into the gathering night? To go where, to eat what, to live how? Here I was being well fed, for the first time in a long time. My head still hurt where I had thrown myself against the table in the cabin, but I had a clean bandage for the wound. And I remembered all too well Hartah's stories of high-waymen, robbers, lone travellers gutted and left to die.

So I stood in a dim corner of the stable yard, a place where the wooden side of the inn met a high field-stone wall, and watched the commotion. Men carried chests from the *Frances Ormund* into the stable; I had no doubt they would be well guarded tonight. The corpses stayed on the wagons, which were drawn behind the inn. Among the new arrivals a woman dismounted, having ridden as hard as the men. She carried a cloth bag into the door where Mistress Conyers had been taken. All the horses trembled with hard use, lathered with sweat. They were watered, rubbed down, fed and housed in either the stables or, when there was no more room, in a paddock. The well winch creaked continuously as bucket after bucket was drawn. Inn servants rushed about, calling to each other. No one noticed me.

Eventually good smells of cooking wafted on the soggy air. By now it was full dark. I made my way to the kitchen, stood behind a table and bent my knees to look shorter.

'What d'ye want?' a harried servant snarled at me.

'I am Mistress Conyers' page,' I said, with as much dignity as I could manage. Certainly my clothing looked no worse than the widow's: just as torn, just as covered with dried salt.

Instantly the woman's expression changed. 'Oh, I'm so sorry, sir, I didn't know. Won't you step into the taproom? Matty will bring ye something to– Matty!' A bellow that could startle rocks.

'I prefer to eat here,' I said loftily, 'away from the soldiers.'

'Yes, of course, just as you like, sir.' She dropped me a curtsey. Pages in rich houses usually came from quality. The woman scurried to set a small table by the fire. On it she put a meal such as I had not had since . . . No. I had never had such a meal.

Thick soup with little crusty meatballs floating in it. Warm bread with new butter. Golden ale. And an apple tart, the crust rich and flaky, the apples sweetened with honey and spices. I ate it all. When I finished, my belly felt full and my blood swift in my veins.

'Sir,' the serving woman said timidly, 'if ye've finished, perhaps ye'd like to take your mistress's dinner up to her? It's ready, finally. Matty will light the way.' Another curtsey.

I took the heavy tray and saw that my own dinner, which I had thought so wonderful, wasn't a button on Mistress Conyers'. Roasted goose, the skin crisp and the scent so rich I could barely notice the currant jam, the red wine, the dozen other dishes, most of which I could not even name. It didn't matter; I had had mine.

I followed Matty, who held a lantern high through dark corridors and up stairs. At a heavy door with an unsmiling man in armour seated outside, Matty knocked. The door was opened from within by the serving woman I had seen riding in with Conyers' men.

Mistress Conyers sat in a carved oak chair beside the fire. She wore dry garments, a plain gown of dull black and a black cap: mourning clothes. She had been crying but now her face looked set and grim. When she saw who carried her dinner, she said, 'You!'

'The cook asked me to carry this to you, mistress,' I said. It was impossible to bow with the tray; I might drop it. 'As your page.'

'You are not my page!' she said so fiercely that the serving woman started. 'Leave us, Alice.'

The woman went swiftly, closing the door behind her. The room was spare but clean, and the wide bed looked comfortable, its hangings fresh and colourful. A table, two chairs, and a bright fire in the hearth banishing damp and chill. I had no idea where I would sleep tonight. I set the tray on the table and then stood awkwardly, my hands dangling at my sides, not sure what to do next. I needn't have worried; Mistress Conyers took charge of the situation.

'I don't know what you are,' she said, 'witch or charlatan or scoundrel. I don't know how you know the things you said about my husband, or why you were with those men who wrecked ... who wrecked ...' She turned her face away, but in a moment had regained control of herself. 'I don't know if you talked to my dead James or not. He—'

'I did talk with him! And he said he loves you very much!'

I was no better than Hartah, exploiting her grief.

She continued as if I hadn't spoken. '—was a good man, the best of men, and I don't need you to tell me either that he loved me or that his soul resides now in a better place than this. I want you to go, boy. Innocent or guilty, witch or not, I want you out of my sight. I cannot stand to look at you. Go.'

47

'Where will I go? I have no family, and I'm only eleven years—'

'You are not.' She stared at my chin, with its downy covering of hair, and at my Adam's apple – things she had not seen in the dim light of the cabin. My lie had come back to prove me a liar.

I cried, 'But I have no place to go! No people, no trade, no money—'

'Is that what you want from me? Money?'

Mistake, mistake.

'I'll give you money,' she said contemptuously. 'Then go.'

'If you give me money, mistress, it will be stolen from me at the first inn I stop at, or by the first ruffians who pass me alone on the road. And what will I do when it's gone? Please, mistress, from compassion—'

'The same compassion you showed my husband and his crew?'

'*It was not me!*'

She studied me. Perhaps she thought my desperation, too, was an act. But always before I had had the protection of Hartah's big fists, even if they were sometimes turned against me. I had had his ready knife, his connections with other scoundrels like him, his knowledge of cheating and lying, counterfeiting and stealing. This pampered lady with her superior virtue, what did she know of the life I'd been forced to lead? Her money and her birth kept her safe. At that moment I almost hated her.

She said, 'I do believe it was not you who wrecked our ship, and with it our fortunes. But nonetheless I still don't want to look at you.'

'Then find me a job on one of your estates, some humble job where you never see me!'

She laughed, a sound so bitter that I was startled. 'You

don't listen, do you, Roger? Your uncle's wreckers have taken everything I have. If I am not careful, I will be as poor as you. There is no estate.'

'I don't understand ...'

She rose, poured herself a glass of wine from the tray and retreated to stand with her back to the fire. It threw her face into shadow. Her fair hair, washed now and curling under her cap, made a halo around her unseen features.

'You are very young,' she said, her voice quiet now, and weary. 'And I can see that you have not lived much in the great world. My husband is – was – the fourth son of a minor baron. His brothers inherited such "estates" as there were. James had his own way to make in the world, and he invested everything he had in the *Frances Ormund*. Our cargo from Benilles and Tenwarthanal, plus the passage money from a nobleman we were carrying to The Queendom, would have let us rent a house somewhere, buy another ship, finance another voyage. Now I am ruined.'

'But the cargo ... I saw the chests carried in.'

'A little gold, enough to pay what we owe. The rest was cloth and spices, all spoiled by the sea.'

'But your family—'

'Cast me off when I married James against their wishes, ten years ago. And my brother, now head of the family, will help me only grudgingly and meanly. He belongs to the old queen. Now do you understand what devastation your uncle created? And why I cannot stand the sight of you?'

A long silence. Finally I whispered, 'Yes.'

She came closer to me then. As her features became clear, I saw the sad bewilderment on them, and something else as well, the same thing I had seen about her in the inn. This woman, whatever her personal sorrows,

49

was incapable of unfairness. In the flickering light she studied me carefully.

Finally she said, 'Can you really cross over to the land of the Dead?'

'Yes.'

'You could be burned for that, as a witch.'

'Yes.' My heart began to pound.

'Burning is a terrible death. Much worse than drowning.'

'Yes.'

Another long pause. Then, 'I'll tell you what I will do. A courier leaves from here tomorrow for court, because all shipwrecks must be reported to the royal advisers and recorded with the Office of Maritime Records. I will send you with him, with a letter of introduction to an old servant of mine. She is neither important nor influential, but perhaps she can find something for you to do at court. If you are wise, you will tell no one of your ability, nor attempt to use it there. That is all I can do.'

'Thank you, mistress!' I was overwhelmed. No one had ever shown me this much kindness. Clumsily – I had never done it before – I fell to one knee in an attempt at a courtly bow.

'Oh, get up,' she said tiredly. 'You make as bad a courtier as you do a prisoner. I'm going to write the letter now so that I never have to lay eyes on you again. Ask Alice to send downstairs for pen and ink.'

I opened the massive door. Alice waited patiently on the other side. As she scurried down the stairs, I wondered what would become of her if Mistress Conyers had really lost all she claimed. How poor was a person who could still send a servant running for pen and ink? Mistress Conyers' poor was not my poor.

Seated at the table, Alice again sent from the room, Mistress Conyers abruptly stopped scratching her pen across the paper and looked up at me. 'Can you read?'

'No, mistress.'

'Can you cipher?'

'Only a little, in my head.'

'Can you do *anything* of practical use?'

If I said no, she might withdraw her offer of help. Wildly I sought for something plausible, unskilled but needing muscle. 'I ... I can do laundry, my lady.'

'*Laundry?* A boy?'

'Yes.'

'Very well.' She finished her letter and, having no seal, folded it tight. 'My old servant is named Emma Cartwright. She's serving woman to one of Queen Caroline's ladies.' Her lips curved into a sad half-smile at some sweet, lost memory. 'I have not told her anything about you except that you are willing, biddable and strong.' She gazed at me doubtfully.

'I am strong, even though I don't look it!'

'Yes. Well. At court you would do well to stay clear of the royal family, in the unlikely chance that your paths should ever cross. There are many strange things at court these days. Many there would consider you a witch. Say nothing to anyone, including the courier who will take you there. His name is Kit Beale.'

'How will I find him?'

'Sleep in the stable. He will find you.'

'I thank you, mistress, for all you're doing for—'

'I don't want your thanks. What I want is to never see you again. Now go.'

'Yes, mistress. Where ... where will *you* go?'

She turned away, gazing into the fire. 'I don't yet know. And at any rate, it's none of your concern.'

No, mistress. It's just that ... that I wish you well.'

'Go!'

This time there was no mistaking her tone. I went,

clutching the paper I could not read, the paper that would keep me from aimless begging on dangerous roads, the paper that would save my life.

Or so I thought then.

8

I slept in the stables, as instructed, along with a dozen Conyers servants. We lay in the loft, atop and beside thick mounds of hay fresh from harvest. Below, the horses stamped, adding their own scent to those of hay, wool, leather and male sweat. I would have liked a place beside the sloping loft wall, but those were taken. So I lay in the middle of the men and listened to their sombre chatter.

'Be turned off now, most likely. Master had promised me to Cap'n Conyers when he made shore.'

'Where will ye go?'

'Where will *she* go?'

'My cousin at an inn at—'

'My father, who might take ye on—'

'The *Frances Ormund*—'

'The wreck—'

'My sister's husband, he farms near Garraghan—'

'The *Frances Ormund*—'

I sat up straight, trying to see in the gloom who had mentioned Garraghan. Cat Starling's father farmed at Garraghan. But in the dimness of the loft I could not tell which man had spoken, and even if I knew, what good would it do me? Cat Starling could not help me, even if the man took me to her, which he would not do. And the man 'promised to Cap'n Conyers' was now bereft of his future master and his expected livelihood, thanks to Hartah and his wreckers.

I lay down again, beset by thoughts of Hartah, of Aunt Jo, of the sailor Bat, who did not know he was dead, of what I did know – that I had murdered. But exhaustion wrung my body, and eventually I slept – only to wake to the man next to me shaking my shoulder and others cursing in the darkness.

'What? What?' Dazed, I put up my hand to shield my face from Hartah's blow.

'Ye cried out in yer sleep,' the man said, disgusted. 'Get away from me, boy, I need my rest! Go!'

Others also yelled at me. *Go, go, go* – from my aunt, from Mistress Conyers, now from these men. There was no one on this Earth – or that other – who wanted me nearby. I groped for the ladder until I found it, and lowered myself over the edge of the loft. The men, grumbling, settled back into the hay. At the top of the ladder I whispered to the man who'd woken me, 'What did I say?'

'"Bat." Ye were afraid of a bat. Now go and let me sleep!'

Bat. I had cried out the dead sailor's name, perhaps in some dream. Never before had I called out at night; Hartah would have beaten me for disturbing him. Did my sleeping mind feel more freedom now that Hartah was dead? Or did more things haunt my dreams since the wreck? What else might I call out another time – and who might hear me?

I made my way to the bottom of the ladder. During the night the clouds had cleared and a nearly full moon shone through the open stable door. The air was cold and sharp, the silence broken only by the restless stamping of horses. I curled up in a corner, on a pile of not-too-clean straw, but no more sleep came.

At dawn a man entered the stable from the inn and stood over me. 'Are you Roger Kilbourne?'

'Yes.'

He thrust a hunk of bread and some meat at me. 'Then

eat breakfast. We start for court shortly. Faugh, lad, you smell! Wash at the well or you don't ride with me.'

'Yes, sir.'

I did as he told me and hurried back to the stable yard. The courier had just finished saddling his horse. 'At least you'll ride light, lad. There's naught to you but bones and eyes. Here, put this on. You can't go to court in those bloody and torn clothes.'

It was a tunic of green wool, clean and whole, and I guessed it was his own. He was just as thin as I, but four or five inches shorter. The tunic was too short but fit everywhere else. Almost overcome by this simple kindness, I stammered, 'Thank you, sir.'

'I'm not "sir", I'm a courier. My name is Christopher Beale – call me Kit. By damn, you know nothing of court life, do you?'

'No, sir – *Kit*.'

'Then the skies alone know what will happen to you there. Come on.'

He swung easily into the saddle, then reached down a hand to me. The truth was that I had never before ridden a horse. But I sensed that I would now have to do many things I had never before done, so I grasped his hand and half-climbed, was half-pulled up behind him. I almost gasped; we were so *high*.

Kit twisted in the saddle to look at me. 'You've never ridden pillion before?'

'N-no.' The height was dizzying. I clutched his waist.

'And what is it you're going to be at court?'

'A l-laundress.'

He stared at me a moment longer, shook his head, and we cantered off. I hung on for my life. But after a few minutes the rocking of the animal between my thighs came to seem more natural, and I lost some – not all – of my fear of falling off.

We rode all day before coming to a wide river. There was a fishing village here, large and prosperous, but we didn't stop. Kit turned the horse west, on a wide well-used road along the river. Just beyond the village we stopped and dismounted to let the horse drink. My knees bowed outward, and when I tried to walk, I nearly fell. Kit grinned.

'You'll get used to it. Or maybe not. A laundress, did you say?'

'Yes. Does . . . does the court lie along the coast?' I knew it did not, but I wanted to get Kit Beale talking, so that I might learn from him as much as possible. He shook his head and gave me a superior smile.

And yet I could tell you things about the country of the Dead, and then you *would be the ignorant one.*

Kit said, not unkindly, 'No, lad, no. Don't you know the lay of The Queendom, your own homeland? Look here.' He drew his sword and began to sketch in the dust of the road. 'See, here is the coast. We came up from the south, the wild coast, from just before the border with the Unclaimed Lands. This river here—' he drew it with the tip of his sword '—is the River Thymar. The palace is in the capital city, Glory, on a large island far upriver, just before the Lynmar joins the Thymar. The Queendom is one huge valley. We're surrounded by mountains to the south and west, hills to the north, and the sea to the east. The valley we're in is all flat fertile land. Easy riding.'

'Where is Hygryll?'

'Hygryll? I don't know it, but the name sounds like the south. Maybe in the mountains of the Unclaimed Lands.'

'It's on Soulvine Moor.'

All at once his eyes grew cold. 'What business could *you* have with Soulvine Moor?'

'Nothing. I just heard the name once.'

'You'd do better to never have heard it. That's no place for men to go, lad.'

'Why?'

Kit shoved his sword back in its sheath. 'We go now. We've tarried too long already.'

'Why is Soulvine—'

'Be quiet,' he snapped, and I was.

He said nothing to me that night, nor the following day's ride to the capital. Not one single word. I had closed off my only source of information.

Although I knew that Glory, the capital of The Queendom, lay inland, that did not mean that I could ever have imagined the city itself. Hartah had kept us to villages, small and isolated, where there was less chance of encountering soldiers. And yet as Kit and I first approached the capital, it looked to me almost like a village, a vast village of thatched huts and numerous greens, all set between fields now busily being harvested of their crops. I saw no shops of any kind. As Kit had sketched in the dust, the whole was ringed in the far distance, south and west, by mountains, those in the west sharply high against the blue sky and those in the south hidden in soft haze. To the north, the country rose gradually in gentle hills.

In fact, The Queendom was a series of rings nestled inside each other. The widest was the distant, three-sided curve of mountains and hills. Then came a vast ring of plains, fields, pastures, and – although I could not see them now – the smaller villages through which Hartah had wandered. Closer in was this sprawling web of connected villages, curiously devoid of shops or alehouses, which circled an island in the wide River Thymar. And on the island was the capital city of Glory.

The entire island was ringed by a high thick stone wall

that came right to the water's edge. Soldiers patrolled the ramparts. Huge iron gates, now all raised, were set into the wall. Wide stone bridges connected the riverbanks to the island. Other gates had no bridges but instead docks, to which barges came and went on the placid waters of the river. In some places the circling island wall seemed to project out *over* the river, which I didn't understand.

The only thing visible beyond the city wall was a single slender tower, soaring several storeys high and dotted with narrow slitted windows. An open section near the top held immense bells. Above that was a flat roof surrounded by a parapet.

'Don't gape like a fool,' Kit said. 'You're not even inside yet.'

We were stopped at the land side of a bridge, where a guard dressed in blue read a paper that Kit handed him. The guard glared at Kit's green tunic, then at his face, and Kit glared back. As the horse clattered over the stone bridge, I glanced back over my shoulder. The guard in blue made a gesture at us, one so filthy that in any farming village it would have started a fight to the death.

The Blues and the Greens. Even in the countryside we knew of this, the scandalized talk of every faire and alehouse. I said, 'Kit, what—' but my words were drowned out by the pealing of the bells in the tower. They sang a sweet song, but it was *loud*. When the clamour stopped, we had passed under the iron gate and I forgot my question in astonishment at Glory.

Never had I imagined such a place.

Another ring, but nothing like the villages outside. Stone walls ran crazily through the city, carving it into small spaces crammed with tents. The tents held people, shops, livestock, alehouses – everything I had ever seen in the world, all crammed into spaces too small to hold them, all yelling and reeking. Children shrieked, running among the legs of adults; chickens cackled; songbirds in painted cages trilled; adults cried out to each other; a fiddler played with a wooden box at his feet to receive coins. Everything seemed for sale: food and copperwork and live ducks and cloth and chamber pots and leather goods and ale, and at least half of it smelled.

'Redpea soup! Good redpea soup, made fresh this morning!'

'Chickens! Live chickens!'

'Lemme go, Gregory, it's not your turn!'

'Lavender and herbs!'

'That was my pot, you oaf! Mine!'

'Empty your chamber pot here, will you!'

'Grain for bread!'

'I saw it first!'

'Redpea soup!'

My senses reeled. Kit smiled.

'Flooded your brain, has it, lad? We'll be inside soon.'

Inside *what*? 'Is it all like this?'

'Everything outside the palace. The law says no trade for three leagues around Glory except within the city itself. There's not much room left on the island, and the old queen decreed that no stone or wood structures are allowed here. Except the palace, of course.'

That explained all the tents. I saw now that the stone walls, which probably surrounded the palace, were all connected, a single vast structure with sections that shot out in all directions like a huge rigid grey plant sprouting stone branches. Some of these branches were short and wide, some long and narrow, some curled gracefully back on themselves like tendrils of stone, some led to other structures, round or boxy or triangular – there was no pattern to it, no plan. And no windows anywhere. Not one. The palace was another ring, although irregular in the extreme, within the circle of the city. What must it

59

be like inside, at the heart of all these rings?

Kit shouldered his way through the crowded narrow streets, leading the horse, which barely managed to get through but seemed accustomed to the smelly din. People shouted at Kit and he shouted back. Over his shoulder he called to me, 'Much of this rabble goes home off the island at night!' I said nothing, stunned by the noise and reek and lack of space to move.

We edged our way towards a wooden gate set into the palace wall. Kit showed his papers to yet another guard, this one dressed in green. The gate was opened, and we stepped inside the palace.

I blinked. Everything was different.

9

We stood in a large stable yard, open to the sky, very clean and very quiet. The thick wooden gate shut out all noise from the city. The very cobblestones seemed to have been scrubbed of dirt. A stable boy rushed forward to take Kit's horse and lead it into a closed stable at one side of the yard. Kit and I walked to the other side, the crunch of our boots on stone the only sound, and through a second, less solid gate.

Another courtyard, planted with bushes and boxed in by stone walls with many wooden doors, all painted green. Servants went in and out of the doors. I said timidly, 'I have a letter of introduction to one Emma Cartwright, a serving woman to—'

'You go nowhere until you've bathed,' Kit said with disgust. 'You *are* a savage, aren't you? There, to the left, that's the labourers' baths. I'll be here when you're done.' He strode though a door on the right. Almost I ran after him – what would I do if I were left alone in this strange place? But I did as I was told and went through one of the doors on the left.

More strangeness! The room – perhaps more than one room – had been built out over the river, and the floor removed except for a wide ledge around all four walls. A new floor, wooden on stone pilings, had been built two feet under the water, so that the Thymar flowed right through the room. A few men bathed, naked, in the clean water. I remembered that we had passed a section of the Thymar downriver where it had abruptly turned reeking

61

and foul; the city's sewage must be sent there. Here, upriver, the water was clean for bathing, and perhaps farther upriver, cleaner yet for drinking. It was an ingenious system.

I removed my clothing and piled it on a shelf against the wall. Other shelves held bars of strong soap. I scrubbed myself clean, pulled back on the tunic Kit had given me and cleaned my boots in the water. Since I couldn't bear to put on my smelly small clothes, I wadded them up and left them in a corner, going without underclothes. There was also nothing I could do about my filthy trousers, but the tunic hung to my hips, hiding the worst. Having no comb, I ran my fingers over and again through my wet hair until it held no tangles.

Kit waited in the courtyard, wearing fresh clothes. No riding clothes these, but a tunic of green velvet, white silk hose and green shoes. His dark hair gleamed and he had a silver earring in his left ear. I saw that despite his slight stature he was handsome: a manly little man.

He looked me over and sighed. 'I suppose you'll have to do. Come.'

More courtyards, and my astonishment grew until I thought my eyes, my brain, could take in no more.

Each courtyard was more sumptuous than the last. Wide, quiet, bright with trees and late-summer flowers, ringed with buildings of painted grey stone. Then buildings faced with smooth white marble. Finally, buildings faced with mosaics of pearl and quartz, all in subtle shades of ivory and cream, all in subtle patterns that changed as the light moved over them. Small fountains appeared, falling in graceful, tinkling arcs. All was subdued, quiet, with a balanced and graceful beauty I had not known existed in the whole wide world. Even the people we passed, dressed in fine green clothing, moved with quiet grace. A few nodded to Kit.

Kit said, 'Close your mouth, Roger.' He seemed to grow more and more tense the closer we got to ... wherever we were going.

Almost I wished I were back with Hartah, with Aunt Jo, jostling along in our wagon. This was too strange, too different. I could never belong here.

Kit said, 'Here I leave you. The quarters for Queen Caroline's ladies are over there, through that gate. Present your letter of introduction to the guard. I must report the wreck of the *Frances Ormund* to the Office of Maritime Records, and give the news of the hanging of the one surviving wrecker. May all their souls burn for ever.'

I could have told him they were not. I could have told him that the wreckers, along with their victims, sat on the beach and the rocks, contemplating the quiet sea. I could have told him his educated belief that souls burn or else go to paradise was much farther from the mark than was the countryside belief that they endure in their own land. I told him nothing.

'Worse luck that it had to be me,' Kit said gloomily. 'Never a Blue courier about when you need one.'

That was his only reference to the peculiar situation that I – that the entire Queendom – knew existed at court. Kit Beale walked away. With Mistress Conyers' letter in my sweaty hand, I moved towards the bored guard to meet the unknown Emma Cartwright, she who held my fate in her hands.

She was much older than Mistress Conyers, stout and wrinkled, just as clearly born a servant as the other had been born a lady. Emma Cartwright wore a plain gown of dull green, her hair in neat grey braids wound around her head. But her eyes were piercing. 'Did you read this letter, boy?'

'I can't read, mistress.'

63

'Ah. And Mistress Conyers thinks you should work in the court laundry.'

'Yes.'

'A boy. As a laundress.'

I said nothing, because what could I say? And was I supposed to kneel? Kit had laughed at me for trying to kneel to him – was this the same? My ignorance shamed me.

We stood in a small cheerful chamber hung with a tapestry of noblemen on a hunt. Unlit wood was stacked neatly in the fireplace. A pretty carved table held a bottle of wine, several pewter goblets and a bouquet of flowers. Embroidery, rather badly worked, lay tossed on a three-legged stool. A polished door led to a bedchamber beyond; I could see that in one corner someone had dropped a painted fan behind a brass water bucket.

Mistress Cartwright sighed. 'Very well. I'll ask Joan Campford, who runs the Green laundry. Although why Lettice should mix herself in your affairs—'

I was startled to hear this servant use what must be Mistress Conyers' given name: *Lettice*. Then all at once I grasped the situation. Emma Cartwright must have known Mistress Conyers when she was quite small; perhaps she'd even been little Lettice's nursemaid. That was why Mistress Conyers trusted her. And so—

The door burst open and a girl rushed in. 'Emma, you must help me!'

For a long moment I stood frozen, and then I dropped to my knees. No doubt *this* was a lady. She was also the most beautiful girl I had ever seen.

She was small, with long brown hair, its colour mingled cinnamon and copper and nutmeg and bronze – more gleaming shades than I could count. The hair flowed loose from beneath a little jewelled cap that framed huge eyes of bright green. The skirts of her gown, green silk with a low bodice and full sleeves, were held up in both hands; she'd been running. Her pointed little chin quivered. She ignored me.

'What is it, my lady?' Emma said.

'The prince! I – Oh, here he comes! Tell him I'm ill, dead, anything!' She dashed through the door to the bedchamber and slammed it, seconds before a youth appeared in the outer doorway. Emma sank into a low curtsey.

'Mistress Cartwright, summon Cecilia, please.'

I disliked him immediately. His peremptory tone, his rich clothing, his handsome and sulky face. He looked not that many years older than I, but was much more filled out. Well, why not – he ate well every day of his life, the bastard!

Then I realized I was silently cursing a *prince*, and the blood rushed to my face. How did I dare? I bent my head even lower, but I needn't have worried. The prince no more noticed me than he would a piece of furniture.

Mistress Cartwright said, 'Your Highness, I would summon her except that she is ill and vomiting in her chamber.'

His scowl deepened. 'Vomiting? I saw her just moments ago and she was fine!'

'Yes, Your Highness. It came on quite suddenly, and she rushed away lest she disgrace herself in front of you. I'm afraid she ate too eagerly of the roast swan at dinner. Lady Cecilia has a delicate digestion.'

I peered sideways at the prince. He looked uncertain.

Mistress Cartwright said, 'If Your Highness would like to wait until I get her cleaned up, her soiled gown changed, and her mouth washed with—'

'Oh, leave it! Let her rest. But tell her I shall expect her at the masque tonight!' He turned and stomped off. Mistress Cartwright closed the door softly behind him.

Instantly the inner door opened and Lady Cecilia ran to her serving woman, hugging her. 'Thank you, thank you!'

'What happened?' Mistress Cartwright looked grim.

Lady Cecilia laughed, a high sparkly laugh that went on a bit too long. 'He tried to kiss me again. And I slapped him and ran away!'

'Did you encourage him before that, my lady? Were you flirting again?'

'Maybe a little.' She smiled, the most enchanting smile I had ever seen. It tilted the corners of her green eyes, showed off her small white teeth. Her skin looked soft as swansdown, and as white. I felt light-headed, which must have caused some slight motion because all at once she noticed me. 'And who is this?'

'A new servant. My lady, this is a dangerous game you're playing with Prince Rupert, I have *told* you that. You cannot—'

'O Emma, I can manage myself, and the prince too. It's all in fun. He knows he must leave on his wedding trip in the spring, and he knows I serve his mother the queen. He would never try more than a kiss, nor I a slap.' She giggled, still smiling down at me. 'Rise, new servant. Do you have a name? And what will you do here at court?'

'Roger Kilbourne, my lady. I'm to be a laundress.'

'A laundress! How funny!'

Standing, I was much taller than she. All at once I was grateful that the tunic Kit gave me came at least over my hips. My member felt hard as stone. And for a lady born! The light-headedness increased.

'You ears are the most interesting shade of red, Roger,' she said. 'Are you blushing? You would look well in a doublet of that shade.'

It was incredible. She was *flirting* with me, as she must have flirted with the prince. Did she flirt with every man

66

then? Apparently so. I was not used to being a man anyone flirted with. I was not used to being a man. I was not used to any of this – I, Hartah's unwilling and underfed slave. Her eyes sparkled like diamonds – no, like emeralds – no, like ...

Mistress Cartwright said, 'That's enough, my lady. Go inside and rest; you are supposed to be sick from eating too much roasted swan. Roger, I will take you now to Joan Campford.'

'Goodbye, Roger of the Red Ears,' Lady Cecilia said.

I would never see her again. Or if I caught a glimpse of her, it would be at a distance, riding or dancing or feasting with the queen's ladies, flirting with the prince. And she would not remember my name.

Wordlessly I followed Emma Cartwright to the palace laundry, where my new life was supposed to begin.

10

Heat from the constant fires, three of them going day and night, and from the pressing irons. Steam choking the air. Soap so harsh it raised blisters on my hands and arms up to the elbow, to join the skin burns from every careless error with a hot iron. A perpetual ache in my shoulders from hauling cold water from the river. Cold and heat, strong soap and stronger stains, fire and water. This particular laundry – there were others in the palace – cleaned and dyed the clothing and bedding of soldiers, servants and couriers. Queen Caroline, like her mother, insisted on cleanliness throughout her palace. They were both famous for that.

At the end of the first day I thought I could not stand the work. By the end of the second day I knew I could stand it but didn't want to. By the end of the second week I had accepted my fate. It was not all bad here. Joan Campford, although she ran her laundry like a captain of the guard, was not unkind. I had three good meals every day in the servants' kitchen, nourishing food such as I had seldom enjoyed before. The other laundresses, all older women, made endless jokes about the boy doing women's work, but no one beat me. So I became resigned. That's what hard and ceaseless work is designed to do: require all your energy so that none is left over to think of another life.

Except that I did think of other lives. As I hauled water and boiled sweat-soaked tunics and pressed clothing, I thought ceaselessly of Hartah, of Aunt Jo, of the *Frances*

Ormund, of what I had done on the rocky little beach, of Lady Cecilia, of my mother among the Dead 'at Hygryll on Soulvine Moor'. Worse, I dreamed of them all. And in my dreams, as I had done in the hay loft of the inn, I called out.

'Wake up! Wake up, curse you!'

The boy who slept on the next pallet in the apprentice chamber, shaking me roughly awake.

'That's the second time tonight! Who can sleep with you caterwauling like that?'

'Not me,' said another voice, equally annoyed. 'I am sick of hearing about Frances Ormund! Who is she, your sweetheart? Go lie with her and not with me!'

Frances Ormund. Fright took me. What had I said, and what might I blurt next in my sleep, perhaps alongside someone who understood what he heard? Blindly I groped my way from the apprentice chamber to find somewhere else to sleep. The best I could do was the servants' kitchen, under one of the long trestle tables where we took our meals.

A few hours' fitful sleep, and another hand shook my shoulder. 'What are you doing here? You can't sleep here!'

Groggy still, I half opened my eyes. A girl crouched under the table beside me. From some dream or some madness, I thought she was Cat Starling. Before I knew what I was about, I had pulled her to me and kissed her.

She punched me hard on the nose.

'How dare you use me like that! Who are you? Guard! Guard!'

'No, wait – please!' My nose was on fire, the agony bringing tears to my eyes. 'I'm Roger Kilbourne the laundress! Please, don't call the guard!'

She paused, a safe distance from me. 'A boy laundress?'

'Yes, I – I'm sorry I kissed you, I was dreaming and ...
I'm sorry!'

But I was not. It was the first time I had ever kissed a girl, and despite the pain in my nose – had she broken it? – I could still feel her soft lips under mine. She was Cat Starling, she was Lady Cecilia, she was a kitchen maid in dark green gown and white apron, in the pearly dawn. Again my member was stiff. Was this going to go on the rest of my life, this madness about girls? How was I going to bear it?

'What are you doing here?' the girl demanded. 'If you're a laundress, why aren't you sleeping in the apprentice chamber?'

'I was. They made me leave. I ... I cry out in my sleep and it disturbs them. I meant you no harm!'

Severely she studied me. There was about her none of Cat Starling's simplicity of mind, none of Lady Cecilia's flirtatiousness. This was a girl used to hard work, with no nonsense about her. Well enough to look at but not beautiful, her fair hair bundled into a knot, her eyes a light, judgmental grey. Small burns and cuts covered her hands: kitchen injuries.

'I believe you,' she said. 'Now leave.'

'I will. But my nose ... I think you may have broken it ...'

'You deserved it. Oh, all right, sit there and be still.'

She brought me a cloth dampened with cool water. I held it to my nose, watching her as she fed the fire and began to knead bread left to rise overnight in the warmth of the banked fire. Other servants arrived, glanced at me, and then ignored me. A few men drifted in from the stables and sat at the other end of the table, chatting idly and teasing the women, a full hour before breakfast. I realized that the palace held life beyond the laundry chambers.

'I'm new here,' I said to the girl. Her strong arms, bare to the elbow, kneaded the bread. 'I'm Roger Kilbourne.'

'So you said.'

'Who are you?'

'Why should you care?'

'So I will know to tell the queen who broke my nose. I understand she keeps careful record of all crimes.'

The girl stopped kneading, stared at me and laughed reluctantly. I was astonished at myself. Where had the courage come from to tease this girl – to tease any girl? With Cat Starling I had felt protectiveness, with Lady Cecilia I had been tongue-tied and oafish. The only quick wit I had ever shown was in dealings with the Dead.

She said, 'What do you know of the queen?'

'I have never seen her.' I knew only what everyone knew, plus too much about the orderliness required by this exacting monarch. Endless clean linen from the laundry, to match the washed cobblestones, the spotless rooms, the careful record of shipwrecks. Endless clean clothing: green for the young queen's household, blue for the old, brown for the stable, grey for those who gardened anywhere in the palace.

The girl said, 'May Her Grace live long,' and something moved behind her eyes, something that gave the commonplace words a meaning I did not understand. 'Now let me work.'

'All right, but will you tell me something first?'

'Maybe.'

'What is your name?'

'Maggie Hawthorne. Now go away!'

Yet another person telling me to go away.

'Maggie Hawthorne, if I sleep here under the table at night, will anyone beat me?'

She gazed at me in surprise. 'No, of course not. But

71

I am first here in the morning, and if you misbehave again, *I* will beat you.'

I didn't doubt she could do it. I nodded gratefully, nursing my painful nose. And since she didn't tell me a third time to go away, I stayed and waited for breakfast.

The palace housed two rival queens.

Not, of course, that I ever saw either of them. Queen Eleanor, the old queen, should have relinquished her throne to her daughter when the princess reached thirty-five. So had the custom always been in The Queendom. No one monarch should rule too long, lest power become too entrenched and so corrupt. Queens always abdicated when the heiress to the throne reached thirty-five.

But Queen Eleanor had refused. Princess Caroline was not fit to rule, she said. The queen's duty to her country made it impossible to pass the Crown of Glory to a daughter who was – what?

Unstable in her mind, said some rumours.

A witch, whispered others.

A poisoner, said still others. The princess's consort, dead right after the birth of her youngest child and heir, and so suddenly in the bloom of health ... *a poisoner and a whore*.

No, said those loyal to Caroline. *It's all the old queen's vanity and love of power. She merely seeks excuses to hold the throne longer.*

And so she had, since the army had backed her against her daughter. Queen Eleanor controlled the Blues. That had not stopped the princess from having herself crowned, although not with the Crown of Glory, which her mother kept in her own possession. The old queen could have had Queen Caroline removed from the palace, but she had not. And so both queens lived in separate areas of the vast structure, each with her own guards and servants and loyal courtiers.

Rumours continued to fly, and in the inns and taverns and farmhouses across The Queendom the common people argued, or snickered, or just waited, shocked and fascinated to learn what might happen next. *As good as a masque*, said the irreverent and bold. The harvest had been good for several years, the land at peace, barns and larders and still rooms crammed with stores for the winter. Who ruled in Glory mattered little compared to a full belly, a snug cottage and a warm fire. Let the two queens skirmish over who sat on which elaborately carved chair.

But within the palace it meant everything.

'You here again?' Maggie said, as she said every morning.

'Why did you wake me?' I crawled, frowzy and irritable, from under the trestle table in the kitchen.

'You cried out in your sleep, Roger. You were afraid of a bat.'

Bat. The simple-minded sailor who did not realize he was dead, whom I had left to wait for his lost captain at the top of the cliff above the sea. Again I felt the terror of that night, saw the yellow-haired youth die in his noose, choking and kicking the air. Saw my aunt's skull crack open as Hartah hit her with the brass-bound wooden chest. Felt the knife slide into Hartah's flesh, easy as a bird wing slicing the air.

'What is it, Roger? You look . . . I don't know.'

'It's nothing.'

'You *always* say that. Bats can't hurt you, you know. You needn't be afraid.'

'I'm not afraid of bats!'

'But you said—'

'Don't you have work to do?'

73

'I was doing it,' she pointed out, 'until you called "Bat! Bat!" like some halfwit.'

'Can this halfwit have some breakfast?'

She brought me bread, hot and crusty from the oven, with new butter and stewed apples, and I lingered as long as I could in the fragrant warmth of the kitchen.

In the laundry the back-breaking work went on, but I saw that my body was filling out, getting stronger and bulkier. The good food and hard work added muscle and bone. Joan Campford, kind under her slave-driving severity, made me new trousers and small clothes. I never saw Lady Cecilia, nor any of the nobility, in my round of laundry chambers, servants' kitchen, servants' baths. I was on an endless narrow track, like a donkey treading his small circle to turn a millstone.

Maggie and I became friends, talking and laughing in the early-morning kitchen. She told me of her older sister, married and sharp-tongued and bitter, and of her brother Richard, a soldier with the Blues. I said, 'But you are with Queen Caroline and the Green—'

'Hush,' Maggie said, glancing quickly around. However much the rival queens were discussed in the countryside, people were more discreet within the palace. I could easily imagine that both camps informed on the other. Maggie continued, 'I was glad to get any place in the palace. Otherwise I must have lived with my sister.'

'Can I have more cheese, Maggie?'

'You're always so hungry.'

'True enough,' I said humbly. 'But it's partly because you make such good cheese.'

'Katherine made this cheese.'

'But yours is better.'

'I don't make cheese. Don't you know the difference between a cook and a dairymaid?' But she was smiling,

74

and she brought me a meat pie, rich and spicy, which I devoured in four bites.

But the other side of Maggie's friendship was her grasping desire to know everything I did, thought, was.

'Who is Mistress Conyers?' she asked one morning.

'No one.'

'Everyone is someone, Roger. You called her name in your sleep. Who is she?'

'A woman of the quality who was kind to me once.'

'A woman of the quality? Were you born on her lands?'

'No, no. She has no lands.'

Maggie eyed me suspiciously. 'Quality without lands?'

'They were lost.'

'How? When?'

'You ask too many questions.'

She flared, 'Who usually talks to me first? Almost every single morning?'

'I do, Maggie,' I said humbly. 'But I can't help what I say in my sleep. All I can do is ask you to not tell anyone else.'

She said slowly, 'Sometimes, Roger, I think you are not what you seem to be.'

To that I had no answer.

So I said the one thing I probably shouldn't, but the question had been on my lips a dozen times these past weeks. 'Maggie, what is Soulvine Moor?'

Quickly her gaze raked the kitchen. The other servants, busy with their work, paid us no attention. 'Don't say that aloud here! What's wrong with you?'

'I—'

'Be quiet!'

I had never seen Maggie frightened before. Always she was calm, competent, relentlessly in charge. I whispered, 'I'm sorry. I'm so ignorant. But please tell me . . . I need to know!'

'Why?'

'My mother died there.'

Maggie went stiff, and then her whole body shuddered, a long spasm from her neck clear down her spine. She gazed at me with horror in which mixed a kind of sadness.

'Roger, never, ever tell anyone that. You did not say it to me. I did not hear it.'

'But—'

'I did not hear it!'

She turned and walked away from me, leaving her bread half-kneaded on the table – Maggie, who never left a task without finishing it. I caught her arm. 'Maggie, don't go!'

She jerked her arm free and glared at me but said nothing.

'You have to talk to me!'

'I don't have to do anything.'

People were starting to look at us. Again Maggie turned away, but something brought her back. Her tone didn't soften, but a strange note crept into it. 'Roger, you can't help your ignorance, I know that. You can't even read, can you? Just try to stay silent and do your work.'

My work. Pressing irons, dye vats, buckets and buckets and buckets of water. That's all she thought I was: Roger the Laundress. All at once I couldn't bear Maggie's low opinion of me. She was my only friend in the palace, and to her I was an oafish laundress, my hands often green with dye. And she would not tell me what I needed to know about Soulvine Moor. I *had* to make her tell me more. Anger, shame, desperate craving to make her talk all churned in my mind, turning it to mush, the mush flavoured with my instinct that Maggie could be trusted.

I moved very close and whispered in her ear. 'I can cross over into the country of the Dead.'

Maggie jerked away from me. She stared, incredulous,

and then disgust settled over her features. She shook her head.

'I had not figured you, Roger, for a liar. Ignorant, but not a liar.'

Again she shook her head, and walked away, her back very straight. The rest of the day she stayed away from me, and when she entered the kitchen the next morning, she had another maid with her. And all the mornings after.

I was more alone than ever before, alone in the palace nested inside the teeming city nested inside the vast village nested inside the circle of fields and plain and hills and mountains. Winter gave way to the sharp freshness of early spring. I had been at court for six months, scrubbing and boiling and ironing and dyeing and hauling. And I might have gone on like that for ever, except that the prince's wedding, once again, changed all.

11

'More water! More water, boy!'

I had hauled water since dawn, until my shoulders felt as if they would fall off, and it was now almost dusk, and still Joan Campford wanted more water. The open courtyard of the laundry chambers seemed a solid mass of rushing women, skirts hiked up to keep them off the wet stone floor.

'More water! We need more water!'

Pots boiled, cloths flapped in a fitful wind, and I had never been so tired in my life. To make it all worse, spring had given way to a sudden unseasonably late cold. Water I hauled from the river to the boiling vats was near freezing, the courtyard fiery near the boiling pots, and the roofed ironing chambers steaming like wet wood on a new fire. I was always too cold, too hot, too achingly weary.

'More water!'

'I can't bring any more water!'

Words I hadn't even known I was going to say, anguished words. Joan Campford stopped and looked at me, really looked. Her broad red face softened. 'Aye, ye've done good work, boy. Did ye get anything to eat today?'

'No.'

'Go to the hall and eat. We can manage without ye for a bit.'

'Thank you!'

I stumbled through the corridors to the servants' hall, which was even more frenzied than the laundry.

Prince Rupert's bride, Princess Isabelle, had arrived two days ago from her own queendom beyond the northern mountains. She brought with her an enormous train of soldiers, servants, courtiers, ladies. They all must be fed, housed, waited on, and their cloth – bed linen, towels, garments, horse blankets – kept clean. Naturally, I had seen none of the strangers, who did not visit the laundry. But meals for our own servants had been suspended as all the kitchens raced to keep up with feeding Princess Isabelle's retinue and entertaining her court. Everyone snatched scraps of food as we could and kept working. Nor had I been able to sleep in the servants' kitchen; I'd lain on my old pallet with the apprentices and hoped I was too exhausted for dreams that might make me cry out in what passed for sleep.

By now I wished the royal couple in the country of the Dead.

But this madness would go on only two days more. Tomorrow was the wedding, and the next day Princess Isabelle would take her new consort back to her own queendom. The laundresses gossiped that the princess's mother was dying, and very soon Princess Isabelle would be Queen Isabelle. It was a good alliance for Prince Rupert, even if his bride was a full six years older than he. Meanwhile, tonight was a great masque, which had required that endless bolts of cloth not only be ironed but also that they be dyed yellow, the colour of the princess's court. That had proved a messy business. My hands, face, hair were streaked with yellow. Even my feet had ended up bright yellow.

The servants' kitchen was frantic with dinner prep-arations. Maggie, her fair hair greasy and falling around a face smudged with flour, scowled at me. 'Roger! Why are you here?'

'I'm starving.'

'Why are you *yellow*?'

'Dye.'

'Why are you swaying like that?'

'I'm exhausted.'

'We're all exhausted.' But her tone softened, sounding almost as she had in the days before I had mentioned Soulvine Moor and so lost her prickly friendship. She snatched a meat pie from a table and thrust it at me. 'Here. Don't tell – these are for Her Plainness's table.'

'Is the princess very plain, then?'

'I didn't say that – no, I *didn't*. Now go away, can't you see we have enough people here already?'

It looked like half the palace was here: the rushing, shouting cooks and maids and serving men were packed as thick as chickens in a crate, and just as agitated. It reminded me of my own brief glimpse of the city outside the palace walls in the summer. How long ago that seemed.

I gobbled my pie, too tired to savour the exquisite taste, and fell asleep in a corner piled with empty crates smelling of vegetables.

Music woke me. I leaped to my feet and for a long moment I thought I must be dreaming. This did not happen in servants' halls!

Lords and ladies streamed into the hall, accompanied by their musicians. All save the musicians were masked, their faces covered with fantastic devisings of feathers, silver, jewels, cloth-of-gold, beads and fur. Laughing, calling, dancing, staggering – they were clearly drunk. The few servants sitting at tables, eating dishes left over from dinner – what time was it? How long had I slept? – leaped to their feet and then sank into curtseys and bows.

'So this is where that vile tart came from!' someone screamed. More calls, derision, laughter. Their bright silks and velvets and satins filled the hall with green. All green

– this was the young queen's household, then. A courtier seized one of the serving maids and swung her, terrified, into a dance to fiddle and flute.

'Have you never seen a kitchen before, Hal?'

'Hal sees only bedchambers!'

'I have never seen a kitchen. I thought food grew ... grew ...' The man turned aside, tore off his mask and vomited over a table piled high with fresh bread.

'Ugh!'

'Put him in one of those crates!'

'Put him in the stewpot!'

But that drunken remark, which I did not understand, silenced a few of the courtiers and all of the servants. The servants' faces twisted with disgust or fear, and then immediately stiffened again. No one, not even the kitchen steward, knew what we should do. The fiddling and dancing and laughter and shouting went on.

'Give Hal some more ale!'

'Give him a kitchen wench!'

'Ale! Ale!'

'The queen!'

Instantly the musicians stopped playing. Courtiers and servants alike sank to their knees. Silence descended like hard rain, and the old queen came into the hall.

She was alone save for her personal guard of two Blues. Queen Eleanor, sixty years old, had ruled for forty-one years, since the death of her mother in a hunting accident. She wore a gown of pale blue silk embroidered with darker blue at the hem. The gown, like her simple silver crown, was austere and quiet and expensive. Her face was deeply lined, her hair white as an egret's wing. But she stood straight and tall, and power emanated from her like steady heat.

No one moved or spoke.

When the old queen did so, it was in a low voice

that carried into every corner of the hall, into every apprehensive ear. Her gaze swept over the courtiers. 'None of you belongs here.'

I realized then that I was still standing, frozen beside the vegetable crates. I tried to sink to the floor without calling attention to myself.

The queen's voice rang out imperiously. 'Caroline.'

The rustle of skirts moving forward; this lady had not knelt. She removed her mask of green feathers over cloth-of-gold. 'Yes.'

So this was the young queen!

Her mother said, 'You especially do not belong here.'

'This is my palace. And this is my merriment, before my brother must leave us.'

Queen Caroline, thirty-seven years old, was beautiful. Also dangerous, in some way I could feel but not understand. Her body curved lusciously under a tight green bodice, but so did many others among the ladies. The difference lay in her eyes, black with silver glints, as if something shining were submerged in dark water. The difference lay in the set of her white shoulders, the thrust of her lovely breasts, the very intricacy of her coiffure, black as her eyes, braided and puffed and set with jewels in contrast to the old queen's smooth white hair.

The two women stared at each other. I could see both their faces clearly. The old monarch stared at her daughter. Although neither queen grimaced, hatred crackled between them. And neither lowered her chin nor blinked.

Queen Eleanor said icily, 'A strange merriment, to terrorize the kitchen servants on the eve of your brother's wedding.'

'It is my choice,' the young queen said, 'and mine to make.'

'It is not. Rupert!'

The prince unmasked and came forward. He wore green, not blue, perhaps to go unnoticed among Queen Caroline's household. But even I knew that to wear his older sister's colours and not his mother's was a deadly insult. He looked just as handsome as when I had seen him chase Lady Cecilia, all those long months ago. He stood, sullen, beside his sister, one hand upon her shoulder.

The old queen said, 'Rupert, return to your bride, who awaits you upstairs. Your manners are deplorable.'

'Yes, Mother,' he muttered. This was not the imperious prince who kissed ladies-in-waiting. This was a pouting boy, ordered by his mother to behave or else take the consequences. What consequences? I could not imagine.

Prince Rupert skulked from the hall, followed by the old queen and her Blues. When they had gone, Queen Caroline said to the silent company, 'Unmask.'

Everyone obeyed, but still no one spoke, not even those who were most drunk. They had seen their young queen reprimanded in front of her court and the palace servants. No one dared say anything until she had spoken.

Queen Caroline's black eyes glittered. But she did not flinch. In a strong clear voice she said, 'My mother was never able to recognize merriment – just think what a gloomy time my father must have had while getting me upon her!' And she laughed.

The court too exploded into bawdy laughter. She had disarmed the old queen's haughtiness, somehow turning Queen Eleanor into a comically prissy old woman. Courtiers guffawed and chattered. The young queen stood amidst them, smiling. She was not far from me, and despite myself I looked for her famed sixth finger. Yes, it was there on her left hand, not a whole finger but just the stump of one, held bent inward to hide it as much as possible, and it seemed as if—

Among the unmasked throng I glimpsed Lady Cecilia.

The sight of her struck me like a blow. I stood, took a step towards her. My arm was caught from below and Maggie pulled me back down to my knees. 'What are you *doing*? She has not given us leave to rise!'

Where had Maggie come from? She must have worked her way, on her knees, through the kneeling servants and over to my vegetable crates. But this thought, and Maggie's presence, only flitted across my mind, which was turned to mush by the sight of Lady Cecilia.

She too wore green, soft silk billowing into stiffer, elaborately embroidered skirts. Her shining brown hair was braided and puffed as exquisitely as Queen Caroline's, and her bodice cut as low. A fancy mask of green-dyed feathers dangled from one little hand. But whereas the queen looked mature, luscious as a ripe pear, Cecilia was a little green berry. Her slim waist and small breasts started my heart thumping. Her face sombre, she leaned against a courtier, a good-looking youth whom I instantly hated. Her eyes swept across me without recognition.

But in all the milling nobility another pair of eyes found mine. Queen Caroline moved across the kitchen floor and stood before me. 'Rise,' she said.

Confused motion among the servants on their knees – were they all supposed to rise, or just me? A few staggered to their feet, the rest did not. The queen ignored them all.

'Boy, why are you yellow?'

My throat would not produce sounds.

'Yellow is the colour of the Princess Isabelle. You are of my household, not hers. So why are your face and hands yellow?'

'I ... I ...'

'Are you trying to insult me, boy, by wearing the colour of another royal?'

'No, Your Grace!'

'Then are you a fool?'

'I . . . I work in the laundry! We dyed the cloths for—'

'I think you must be a fool. And so you will be my fool.' She beckoned to a courtier, who sprang to her side. 'Robin, bring this fool to my rooms at midnight.'

'Yes, Your Grace,' he said, but he did not look pleased.

'You will find him in the laundry,' she said. Clapping her hands, she cried, 'Come, let us go now to the dancing! Servants, you may rise, and we thank you for your hospitality. The steward shall give you all Amelian wine to toast my brother's marriage!'

A ragged cheer went up from the younger servants. Amelian wine was the rarest and choicest of vintages, and very expensive. The queen's court swept from the hall.

Maggie said, 'O Roger, why does she want you?'

I was too stunned to answer. Only one thought raged in my dazed mind: maybe Lady Cecilia would be there too, in the queen's rooms, at midnight.

12

'Where is the queen's new fool?' a voice said loudly in the darkness of the apprentice chamber. Boys woke and cursed – until they saw who stood in the doorway, lamp raised high. Then some clambered out of bed and dropped to one knee, although there is nothing sillier than a bow made in a nightshirt. Others pretended to still be asleep. A murmur ran over the room, low as wind in grass and just as hard to locate: *Lord Robert, the queen's favourite, Lord Robert* . . .

I scrambled from my pallet, still in my one suit of clothes; I had not put on the nightshirt that Joan Campford had made for me from a worn bedsheet. But I had it rolled beside me, along with my change of small clothes, my wooden comb and a little knife for shaving: all that I owned in the world. I didn't know what to expect from this night, and after I saw Lord Robert, I knew even less. Why had he come himself instead of sending a page? At least he had known to look for me in the apprentices' chamber and not the laundry as the queen had told him.

'I'm here, my lord!' I called, and the high, squeaky voice did not sound like my own.

'Then come with me.' He sounded impatient, and yet there was a note of amusement too. I didn't see anything amusing. I trailed after him, my little bundle in my hand, and the others watched me go.

By the torchlight in the courtyard, I could see him better. After the queen and her courtiers had left the kitchen, Maggie had told me about Lord Robert Hopewell.

In her shock over my summoning, her coolness had vanished. Lord Robert was perhaps forty, tall and well-built. He had courted Queen Caroline when they were both young, but she had chosen instead another lord, far less strong, less handsome, less intelligent, as consort. Maggie had not said why, although from the way she pursed her lips, I imagined that she had a theory. Maggie always had theories. The queen's consort had given her two sons and then a daughter to rule after her, Princess Stephanie, now three years old. Shortly after the heir's birth, the consort had died of the sweating sickness. I had the impression from Maggie that nobody much missed him. But this too was not spoken aloud. Since then, Lord Robert had again become the queen's favourite.

He led me from the servants' portion of the sprawling palace through courtyards I remembered from my visit, so many months ago, to Emma Cartwright. Wide, quiet courtyards, their trees and barely budded bushes now white in the cold moonlight, ringed with buildings of painted grey stone. Then buildings faced with smooth white marble. Finally, buildings faced with mosaics of pearl and quartz, with small fountains playing among them. On this trip, however, there were no people. And we went further than the quarters of the ladies-in-waiting – was Lady Cecilia in there, fast asleep under Emma Cartwright's stern guardianship?

We went all the way to the courtyard of the young queen.

It was magnificent: bright with torchlight, tiled with green mosaics, set about with gilded branches of red berries in tall exquisite green urns. Soldiers dressed in green tunics stood guard. They flung open doors for Lord Robert and we passed through a large dark room empty save for benches against the wall. Then another large room, also dark, but this one furnished and hung with tapestries. Finally a much smaller room, where candles and fire burned brightly, and the queen sat alone at a heavily carved table set with wine and cakes.

She still wore her masquing gown, low-cut and sumptuous. Her white breasts gleamed in the firelight. But she had taken down her hair and it fell in rich dark coils around her face and shoulders.

'I have brought him,' Lord Robert said. 'Although I still don't believe any of it.'

'Thank you, Robin,' the queen said. I dropped clumsily to one knee. 'Rise,' she said. 'Are you frightened, boy?'

'Of course he's frightened,' Lord Robert said, grinning. 'For one thing, he's dyed yellow. No man can be at ease when dyed yellow.'

'But he can't help that,' she said sweetly. This midnight she was all sweetness, a different woman from the one I had seen crackling with hatred for her regal mother. 'He must do whatever work the laundresses demand of him. Is that right, Roger?'

'Y-yes, Your Grace.' She knew my name.

'But you have no reason to be nervous here. No one will hurt you.'

How many times had I heard that sentence from Hartah, always followed by '*if you do as I say*'? But she had no need to utter the rest of the sentence aloud. She was a queen. Everyone did as she said.

'Well, since he is here, give him some wine,' Lord Robert said, pouring himself a goblet.

'No, not yet,' she said. 'Roger, how old are you?'

'Fourteen, Your Grace.'

'Just a little older than my oldest son,' Queen Caroline said. 'Percy is eleven. Can you read, Roger?'

'No, Your Grace.'

'And where is your family?'

'All dead, Your Grace.'

'Like the crew of the *Frances Ormund*.'

I almost staggered and fell, held upright only by my hand on the corner of the table. She knew. Somehow she knew about the wreck ... and *what else*?

'You talk in your sleep,' she said gently, but her eyes raked my face. 'And I have people who report to me everything that happens in my palace. Did you know that, Roger?'

'N-no, Your Grace.' I had guessed that she had spies, but not that they would report on lowly laundresses. Maggie? Joan? No, it would have been one of the other apprentices whose sleep I had disturbed night after night. What else had I said? Lord Robert lounged in a chair, his expression somewhere between disapproval and amusement.

'Ordinarily, of course, I would not find it interesting that a laundress – even a boy laundress – called out the name of a ship foundered by wreckers. It was a public event, after all, and word spreads. But you have called out other things too, Roger. Soulvine Moor. Hygryll. Lord Digby.'

Lord Robert looked up sharply from his wine. The amusement disappeared.

'What do you know of Lord Digby, Roger?'

Old Mrs Humphries, sitting under a tree by a river in the country of the Dead, prattling of her childhood. I said desperately, 'Your Grace, I know only that he once rode through the village of Stonegreen and gave a gold coin to a child.'

Robin said, 'Bruce Digby never gave anything to anyone.'

'Lord *William* Digby!' In my agitation I scarcely knew what I said. All sweetness had vanished from the queen's face. She had so many faces, this queen; she was change-able as weather. Now neither firelight nor candlelight brought warmth to her chill marble.

She said, 'The grandfather? And how could you know that, Roger? He died long before you were born.'

'The child told me, when she was an old lady. It was a family story!'

'And is Soulvine Moor too a family story?'

I could only gaze at her in despair.

'I think, Roger, that it was not Lord William Digby whose name you called out, but that of Lord Bruce. And—'

'No, no, it was not!'

'You dare to interrupt me? And I think that calling out "Soulvine Moor" and "*Frances Ormund*" was not by happenchance, either. Nor was calling out "my lady Frahyll".'

I remembered Lady Frahyll. Another talkative old woman, another country faire with Hartah's booth. But that town had boasted a manor house, and the lord's mother had recently died. A harmless, babbling old dame, too old and too dead to preserve the distinctions of rank. She had told me happily about the people of the country-side, and I had saved myself a beating from Hartah.

'Frahyll is not a common name,' the queen said. 'It bears the tortured syllables of southern names, names from the Unclaimed Lands or even from Soulvine Moor. Names like Hygryll. Like Hartah. You call out "Hartah" often, Roger. Is he too dead?'

I was mute with terror.

'Roger, can you cross over to the country of the Dead?'

Lord Robert said impatiently, 'That is impossible. I have told you and told you, Caro, crossing over is a super-stition. A belief among the ignorant country folk, who still believe that spitting at frogs at midnight causes thunderstorms.'

The queen ignored him. Her gaze, black flecked with submerged silver, never left mine. Terror held me mute.

She could torture me, burn me for a witch . . .

'Think carefully, Roger, before you answer me. I will have the truth, and there are ways of obtaining it. They are not pleasant ways. I don't want to have to use them on you but—'

'For sweet sake, Caro, he's just a boy!'

'—but I will if necessary. I am not a cruel woman, Roger; I am a woman who wants to rule my country well. Who faces obstacles to my rule, obstacles you cannot begin to imagine. Who will do whatever is necessary to rule well, for the greater good and for the sake of my daughter, who must rule after me. Do you understand me?'

'Y-yes.'

'Then I will ask you one more time. Answer truthfully, and answer with full awareness of the consequences. You are not stupid. I can see that you are not stupid. Roger, can you cross over to the country of the Dead?'

'Yes,' I said.

'Show me.'

'Caro—' Lord Robert began.

'Show me now. Here.'

I said wildly, 'I must have . . .' I couldn't say it, but I had to say it. 'I must have pain. I can do it myself.'

'Then do so.'

I laid my little bundle on the polished table and unwrapped it. Lord Robert, now looking elaborately bored, smiled condescendingly at the plain nightshirt made from a bedsheet. I took my shaving knife and plunged it into my thigh. Pain burned along my nerves. Even as I made the necessary effort of will, I heard the queen cry out as my body toppled, and dimly I felt Lord Robert, cat-fast, catch me as I fell.

Darkness—

Cold—

Dirt in my mouth—
Worms in my eyes—
Earth imprisoning my fleshless arms and legs—
For the first time in half a year, I crossed over.

The palace was gone. Only the river remained, wide and calm as in the land of the living, but the ring of jagged western mountains had vanished; they must be farther away here. Everything had stretched out. The island was so huge I could not see across it, and trees dotted the vast plain on the opposite bank, where there had been farms and fields. Trees and groves and ponds and the Dead.

There were many more of them than there had been in the countryside, but the huge plain didn't seem crowded. Perhaps – and it wasn't the first time I'd had this idea – the very Earth expanded to accept however many died. More of the Dead were well-dressed than in the villages where Hartah had set up his booth. Silk gowns, burnished armour, old-fashioned farthingales, brocade cloaks and doublets, all alongside strange white robes or crudely stitched clothing of leather and fur. People had lived by this river for a very long time.

No matter what they wore, these Dead behaved like all the others: sitting in circles, gazing at the grass or sky, doing nothing. I tripped over a soldier in peculiar copper-coloured armour and went sprawling. He said nothing, just went on staring at the featureless grey clouds. Scrambling to my feet, I saw blood on my hand where I had just cut it on a stone, blood on my leggings from the knife I had thrust into my thigh. I was the only one here who could bleed. And yet I felt no pain. That would not recur until I went back.

Frantically I raced among the silent groups. I needed an old person, preferably a woman or a newly arrived Dead – someone who would talk to me. '*I will have the truth, and there are ways of obtaining it. They are not pleasant ways ...'*

A man suddenly materialized a few yards away. One moment he was not there, and the next moment he was. He wore a long white nightshirt of rich cream-coloured linen and a woollen nightcap, and on his shrivelled finger was a ring set with three huge rubies in intricately wrought gold. He gazed at me wildly. 'Where am I!'

I thought quickly. 'You are safe, sir.'

'I died! I am dead!'

'Yes, sir. And I am your guide in this place, sent to greet you.'

'I am dead!'

'Yes. And I am your guide. You must come with me.'

I think it was the yellow dye on my face that convinced him. He stared at me, shuddered, and followed.

I led him to a little grove where no one else sat. He looked at his arm, withered but without pain, and said wonderingly, 'My illness is gone.'

'It's over, sir. And you must answer questions for me.'

He nodded, still too bemused to question my completely false authority. That state of mind would not last. I must move quickly.

'What is your name, sir?'

'Lord Joseph Deptford.'

'And your position at court?'

'A gentleman of the bedchamber to Prince Percy. Although since I became sick ... Who are *you*, boy?'

'I told you, sir: I'm your guide in this place. For the sake of being judged fairly, you must answer just a few more questions. What was your last illness?'

'Weakness in the heart. I—'

'Is the young prince difficult to attend?'

'He– Now, see here, boy—'

'I cannot take you to my master without this information! Is the prince difficult to attend?'

'He is impossible,' the old man said flatly. 'He pulls my beard and whispers treason about his grandmother, anything his mother wishes to hear, and— Enough! I will answer to your master in person! This impertinence is over!'

I left him among the trees, free now to discover that for him all impertinence was over. In a moment he would lapse into the tranquillity of the Dead. My little knife had been left behind in the queen's chamber, but there were sharp stones enough by the river. I whacked one against a burn on my hand from a boiling laundry pot, and I crossed back over.

I lay on the hearthrug before the fire, the queen sitting on the rug beside me in a puddle of green silk skirts, in all her glorious unbound hair. Lord Robert still lounged at the table, drinking wine.

'That was quick,' the queen said. 'Did it happen?'

'Yes, Your Grace.' I sat up, a little dizzy, and a part of my mind thought how weird it was to be sitting on the floor with a queen, like two children playing at dice.

Playing at death.

'Well, tell me,' she said. Then, more ominously, 'Convince me.'

'I spoke to a Lord Joseph Deptford. He died just now, minutes ago, in a white nightshirt and blue woollen cap. He was a gentleman of the bedchamber to Prince Percy, and he told me—' Was this wise to say? Nothing was wise to say. '—that the young prince is difficult to attend. He pulls the old lord's beard.'

Lord Robert laughed and said, 'True enough. But easy palace gossip, for all that. And even if that old fool Deptford did die tonight, that could be a lucky guess. The whole palace knows he is ill.'

'Lord Robert could be correct,' the queen said to me. 'What else have you?'

'Only ... only ...'

'Out with it, Roger!'

To even utter the words might bring me death. To not utter them certainly would. I closed my eyes and said, 'He told me that the prince whispers treason about his grandmother. Because it is what he believes that Your Grace would like to hear.'

Lord Robert's goblet crashed to the floor, splashing wine onto the queen's skirts. She breathed out slowly – '*Aaaaahhhhhh*' – like a sigh. Then she leaned over and kissed my cheek, and it was a mother's kiss, tender and gentle and terrifying as spring buds.

13

The queen gave me two new suits of clothes, both green and yellow velvet with green ribbons at the knees. She gave me a place to sleep, a tiny alcove off her presence chamber, where no one could hear me cry out. 'For I cannot have you closer, Roger,' the queen said. 'You're a boy, but a boy nearing manhood, and I am a widow. I don't want to give my enemies food for scandal.'

I felt my ears burn. But she meant it, despite the whole court knowing that Lord Robert was her lover. He went openly in and out of her privy chamber, a little amused smile on his face, sometimes snapping his fingers at me or giving me a whistle, as you might a dog. Yet he was not unkind to me, not meaningfully.

'You must keep the yellow dye on your face,' Queen Caroline said. 'It makes you different from other fools. And it's a splendid joke on that stiff-necked prig my brother was forced to marry. Yellow – the colour of her court!'

Her brother Prince Rupert and his plain bride had left court the day after the wedding. None of us would likely see them for several years.

'Your Grace,' I said desperately, 'I haven't wit enough to be a fool!' A fool must stay close to the queen, making sharp and funny comments on the personalities and doings of members of the court. I knew none of the members of the court. I could not make sharp and funny comments. I would fail.

'Of course you have wit enough to be a fool.'

'Could I ... could I be a page?' A page's duties I thought I could manage.

'Pages are high-born, like my Alroy. They are also ten years old. No, you must be my fool.'

'I am not funny enough to—'

'Then become funny,' she said sharply. 'I need a reason to keep you close by, a reason that no one will question.'

'Yes, Your Grace.'

I stayed in my alcove, sleeping off my laundress exhaustion, until the day after the wedding. Then, for the first time and dressed in my new clothes, I accompanied the queen as she received in her presence chamber. I took the place she indicated, to the left and below the queen's tall chair on its raised dais. Sitting at her feet.

'Listen to everything,' she whispered to me. 'Learn, so that you will better know whom to approach and what to ask when I send you to cross over.'

'It doesn't happen like that. I can't—' But she didn't want to hear it. She waved her hand and the guards threw open the great doors.

I was terrified. *Be funny*.

The presence chamber was the first room of the queen's suite, the largest and barest room, furnished only with her throne upon a dais and benches along the walls. Next came the outer chamber, where she was attended by her ladies. This too was of a good size, richly furnished with tables, chairs, space for dancing and the presentation of the masques that the court so loved. Then the privy chamber, where I had crossed over for her, with its heavily carved table and green hearthrug. Last was the queen's bedchamber, which I would of course never see. The presence chamber was where her public events took place because the palace's real throne room was still in the control of the old queen. To my dazzled eyes, the presence

97

chamber was intimidating enough; what must the throne room be like?

Queen Caroline's advisers entered, a procession of three old men tottering behind Lord Robert. Women, who create life, must rule. But men, who defend life, must advise. Thus is the balance of the world preserved. The queen's green-clad advisers each bowed before her and then stood to the left and right of the throne. None of them so much as glanced at me, crouching at the foot of the steps to the dais in my yellow face dye and green and yellow velvets. I was just another piece of furniture, like the steps themselves but less useful.

The queen said, 'Let the petitioners come.'

There were not many. I thought that the wedding feast, the masques and dances, had tired everyone so that their business with the queen must have been postponed. Later I learned that I was wrong. The petitioners were all in the palace throne room with the old queen.

Where the power resided.

Queen Caroline's lips tightened. She barely opened them to say to the first man, 'Why do you come before me?'

'Your Grace, I am in a land dispute with my neighbour, Mistress Susannah Carville.'

'And what is the dispute?'

'We each claim the fields on the right bank of the River Ratten.'

I blurted out, 'All lands are the queen's, except when they are rotten!'

There was total silence. Then the petitioner said, 'The right bank is, of course, Your Grace's as well! But the use of it is in dispute between Mistress Carville and me.'

'Continue,' the queen said. She shot me a disgusted glance. I had not been funny. I had failed.

Almost I wished myself in the country of the Dead.

98

*

Over time, I became a little better at being a fool. Sometimes someone would laugh at my jest. A very small laugh. The queen, however, became no better at being sought out for anything important. Minor land disputes, minor points of law, minor appropriations of money for minor building. Queen Caroline settled them all with justice and knowledge. This was a side of her I had not seen before, much different from the woman who had threatened me with torture, or the one who each morning asked sweetly how I had slept. She was a just and equitable queen to her subjects beyond the palace.

Nonetheless, it seemed to me that she was hardly queen at all. The palace teemed with the old queen's Blues. Queen Caroline had her own Green guard, but it was tiny in comparison. And no one ever petitioned her for anything to do with the army. Courtiers' gossip whispered about the new navy – The Queendom's first – being built in Carlyle Bay, at the mouth of the Thymar River. However, in the presence chamber I heard nothing of any ships. I listened and I learned, but the truth is that I did not really care about the ships, or the army, or the endless land disputes.

I had enough to eat, enough sleep, sometimes ale or wine to drink.

The queen did not send me on any more journeys to the country of the Dead.

My jests as fool were becoming sharper, more knowing.

But best of all, after the day's work – which did not seem like work at all to one who had laboured for Hartah, had sweated in Joan Campford's laundry – I was with the queen's ladies. With Lady Cecilia.

'Are you here again, Roger? I see that you are. And yellow as ever!' And then her pealing laugh, always brighter and higher than the laughter of the young queen's other ladies. Always Lady Cecilia walked more quickly, danced more animatedly, smiled more widely, played the lute more passionately before tiring of it and tossing it aside. Her very needle, as the ladies sewed, darted faster in and out of the rich cloth, although the results often left much to be desired.

That's how they spent their days of attendance upon the queen: sewing or reading aloud or playing music or following her in walks around the various courtyards within the vast palace. When the queen was about her 'business of state' in the presence chamber – the meagre amount of business the old queen allowed her – I don't know what the ladies did. I sat at the foot of the queen's throne, making my feeble jokes while the time dragged by.

The nights were another matter entirely.

Then the men, the courtiers in their green silks and velvets and slashed satins studded with jewels, joined the ladies. Queen Caroline was there too, in the outer chamber lit by candles in great branching candelabra. They all gambled at cards and dice; they danced to lute and pipes and flute; they rehearsed and presented masques. They drank wine and ate sugared cakes. They flirted – how they all flirted! Nominally the ladies were under the charge of Lady Margaret, an older woman with a long horse-like face and sad intelligent eyes. But Lady Margaret could not keep the bevy of young, pretty, richly dressed girls from their endless romantic gossip. While the queen was sometimes serious, talking alone in a window embrasure or beside a warm fire with Lord Robert or one of the older men, the ladies were never serious. And Lady Cecilia least of all.

'Yes, my lady, I am still yellow.' How I longed to appear before her dressed in something other than my fool's cap and crazy green-and-yellow tunic!

'And still a fool?'

'A fool to follow you around, my lady.'

'That you are!' She gave her high trill of laughter, only there was something wrong with it. It was too high, too trilling. Her eyes were too bright.

'Is something wrong, my lady?'

'Why should anything be wrong?' she said, her smile vanishing. A second later it was back, too wide. 'Don't be impertinent!'

'I'm sorry, my lady.'

'You should be!' She tossed her head, her huge green eyes glittering at me, her small chin raised. I knew she wasn't really angry. She was flirting, as she would have flirted with anything male that sat beside her, from a fishmonger to Lord Robert himself. And she was so beautiful! The candlelight flickered over her hair, and it shone in so many shades of brown that I couldn't count them: nutmeg, molasses, bronze, cinnamon, almost-but-not-quite-gold. But her face was too pale.

'Where is everyone tonight?' Lady Cecilia said impatiently. 'The chamber is half empty!'

'I don't know, my lady.' I too had noticed the emptiness. Each week there were fewer courtiers in the queen's rooms. They had gone, I guessed, to the old queen's chambers in that part of the palace I had never seen. Did the deserters dare to attend Queen Eleanor while wearing the young queen's green? Or did they change their clothes with their loyalties?

Cecilia said, 'We have barely enough people to dance! I want to dance!'

'But you must wait for the queen to command dancing.'

'Of course, of course!' Restlessly she shifted on her stool. It was right after dinner, early in the evening. Bright fires burned in the two great hearths at either end of the chamber. Lady Cecilia and I, with two other of the youngest ladies, Lady Sarah and Lady Jane, sat on cushioned stools close by the fire. The others stood in clumps around the room, talking to the courtiers, waiting for the queen to declare the evening's entertainment. Lady Margaret sat on the other side of the hearth, reading a book. Cecilia stuck out her pink tongue at the heavy volume, slid her eyes sideways to meet mine and giggled.

The queen sat in a far corner with a sour-looking man I had never seen before. He was dressed well enough in black velvet with a black satin sash, but his face was weather-battered and his hair unfashionably short. He didn't look like a soldier, nor an adviser, nor a courtier, and I had never seen anyone at court wear black. He and the queen leaned close to each other in earnest conversation. Lord Robert occasionally glanced at them from his own conversation with Lord Dearborn.

Lady Sarah said, 'Cecilia, there are other things in life besides dancing.'

'I think she knows that,' Lady Jane said slyly, and Lady Sarah gave a bark of laughter. I didn't understand the jest, nor Cecilia's sharp reply.

'Hold your foolish tongue, Jane Sedley! And you too, Sarah!'

'And who shall make me? Your yellow cavalier?'

I said, trying to be witty, 'Green wood burns hotter than yellow.'

Lady Jane and Lady Sarah looked and each other and burst into more laughter, which grew wilder and wilder. They held their sides and roared. Tears sprang to Cecilia's eyes. She jumped to her feet and rushed off.

She had nowhere to go except to the other side of the room. I followed her, bewildered about what I had said to make the others laugh like that. Cecilia stood in an empty window embrasure, leaning out over the velvet-covered seat, her face pressed to the thick glass. Outside, a few flakes of unseasonably late snow fell into the empty courtyard.

'Lady Cecilia—'

'Oh, leave me alone!'

'If I said something to offend you—'

'Of course not! What do you mean? Why should I be offended?' She whirled so suddenly to face me that I had to step back. 'I have no cavalier, green or yellow or bright orange!'

'I know you don't,' I said. A memory came to me: Prince Rupert scowling in a doorway, demanding Cecilia's presence.

'Then why did you say I do?'

'I didn't! I was making a jest. Green wood ... it was but a jest.'

'It wasn't funny.'

'I know,' I said humbly. 'Please forgive me.' I started to go down on one knee. She grabbed my hand and pulled me up.

'Stop! You can't kneel to me while the queen is in the room! But you didn't think about that, did you?' She peered at me. 'You really are just an ignorant savage.'

All at once her mood changed, with that quicksilver speed that now, I belatedly realized, had in it something of hysteria. 'I know! I shall be your teacher! I shall teach you to be a courtier – to play the lute, and gamble, and ... oh, all sorts of things! It will be the greatest amusement!'

'My lady ...'

'And we shall start now! With the lute! Come!'

'We can't now,' I said with enormous relief. 'The queen is calling for dancing.'

Queen Caroline had just raised her hand to the musicians who waited obediently in a corner of the room.

'The jereian!' she called. Ladies began to form one line, gentlemen another facing them. Those not dancing crowded back to the walls, I among them. The queen's fool did not dance; not even Lady Cecilia was mad enough to think that. She skipped away to join the line of ladies, and the dance began.

Like all the court dances, it was slow, stately, sedate. More suited to the old queen than to Queen Caroline. I remembered the drunken masquers tumbling into the kitchen on the eve of the prince's wedding, and knew there was wildness caged among these courtiers, just as there was in Cecilia. It was troubling. But why didn't Queen Caroline introduce other, more vigorous dances? They existed; I had seen them at faires, among villagers exhilarated with holiday, with ale, with a day's freedom from labour.

But I did not understand the queen. She contained mazes, labyrinths. Crafty, kind, passionate, ruthless, just, deceitful – she was all of these. The one thing that never changed was her determination to obtain the throne that should already rightly have been hers. I had no doubt that she would do nearly anything to that end – as she had once told me herself.

The queen chose to watch, not dance. She sat on a big carved chair beside the fire, Lord Robert beside her on the stool that Lady Jane Sedley had vacated. I scurried to take my place at the queen's feet, now that the sour-faced stranger had left the room. From here I could watch Lady Cecilia move her graceful little body in and out of the figures of the dance, weaving slowly forward and back, her slim waist swaying and her green skirts changing colour in the flickering firelight.

'Enough,' the queen said. She raised her hand and immediately the musicians stopped playing. 'I find I do not want dancing, after all. I am weary. Goodnight.'

It was still very early. Courtiers and ladies gazed at each other in bewilderment. The queen turned to walk through her rooms, and the ladies of the bedchamber picked up their skirts to scurry after her. Cecilia was not one of these. She stood with a disappointed pout in the middle of the room. 'Could we not dance anyway ...'

But of course they could not. Not without the queen. Some courtiers, the older ones, left the room, including a reluctant Lord Robert. I knew he would be back later, much later, alone, to be admitted to the queen's privy chamber. And then Lady Margaret left, one hand on her belly. 'If you will excuse me ... The pork at dinner ... Will not you young ladies retire as well?'

'It's so early,' murmured Lady Jane.

'So early ...' 'Not at all tired ...' 'So very early ...'

With a sad smile, Lady Margaret walked from the room, her hand still on her aching belly. The younger courtiers' eyes sharpened. They would stay, and without the sharp and intelligent eyes of Lady Margaret upon them. Or the eyes of their queen.

I didn't know what I was supposed to do. Usually the queen retired very late and her ladies at the same time, and I went to my alcove to sleep. But Lady Jane was right – it was far too early to sleep. Should I stay here? What should I do?

Learn all you can, the queen had told me once. *Nobody notices a fool.*

I would stay. I wanted to stay. Lady Cecilia was here.

'Let us wager!' Lady Jane cried. She seized a pair of dice in a golden cup.

'I'll wager with you, pretty Jane,' said Lord Thomas Bradley, 'but not for a coin.'

'For what then?' Lady Jane asked, widening her eyes with mock innocence. 'A kiss?'

'Oh, I think more than a kiss.'

'How much more?'

'A game is no good unless the stakes are very high. Such as ... everything.'

Lady Jane smiled at him over her fan. '"Everything" against what? What do you put up for your side of the wager?'

'My best mare.'

'Done, my lord!'

I was shocked. This did not happen in the queen's presence. Queen Caroline liked gambling, and she was good at dice and cards. Nor did she cheat. I had watched Hartah cheat often enough to know it when I saw it. If the queen lost, she smiled and paid up. Nor did she try to keep her ladies from flirting and kissing. But I had been at court long enough to know that an unmarried lady must stay a virgin. It was one thing for the queen to take Lord Robert as a lover; she was a widow, and a queen. But her ladies must remain chaste until marriage, to preclude all doubt about who fathered their husbands' eventual heirs. So why was Lady Jane Sedley laughing like that at Lord Thomas and eagerly sitting down to wager with him for 'everything'? Or had I mis-understood?

I had not. More pairs of courtier and lady formed, sitting opposite each other at different small tables, the dice between them. Those not willing to gamble, or perhaps unchosen, clustered with excited envy around the players.

Lady Cecilia stood in the middle of the floor, her expression tense but otherwise unreadable. She was not one to join watchers, to be left out of whatever amusement presented itself.

Sudden jealousy tore through me like a gale. If she paired with one of these young lords to wager her chastity, if she lost, if she went with him to some secluded chamber ... I couldn't breathe. All at once I could feel again Hartah's knife in my hand, sliding into his flesh, and I knew I could do the same to any man who wagered with Cecilia for her sweet and untouched body. Stupid, irrational, *insane* ... Who was I to have such thoughts? Yet I had them.

A handsome minor courtier, Lord Dillingham, walked towards Cecilia. His sword gleamed at his hip. He grinned at her, but she, for once, did not flirt back. Instead she rushed forward and grabbed me by both hands. 'Roger! I shall wager with you! For a silver coin with Her Grace's image stamped upon it! Come!'

Jane Sedley, seated opposite Lord Thomas, looked up and gave a derisive laugh. But before I knew it, Lady Cecilia and I were seated at one of the little tables, people crowding around to watch this new amusement. One of the queen's ladies, wagering with the queen's yellow-faced fool!

But Cecilia faced me quietly, all at once as sedate and sober as Lady Margaret herself, and laid a silver coin upon the table. 'The game shall be fifty points,' she said. That was an incredibly high number; a single game would last all night. We began, and she stayed sedate, barely talking, her eyes only upon the dice. After a while the watchers, disappointed, drifted to other tables. No flirting, no bawdy jokes, no forbidden crossing of the boundaries of rank. We were too dull.

Bewildered, I threw the dice and counted points, as I was told. What was Cecilia doing? Was she secretly as shocked as I at the licentiousness of these young ladies and gentlemen, and so choosing this method of preserving her chastity? But surely she could have just announced that she preferred not to play, or even retired for the night? One other lady, besides Lady Margaret, had done that. What was truly happening here?

We played on. Cecilia never looked at me. Finally a great shout arose from one of the other tables: someone had won. Or lost. Under cover of the babble that followed, Cecilia bent her head over the dice and said, 'Roger, are you my friend?'

How to answer that? A lady-in-waiting could not be friends with the queen's fool. But I let my heart answer.

'Yes, my lady.'

'And friends do favours for each other, do they not?'

'Yes.' My stomach grew cold.

'I need a favour from you, Roger.'

'I am in attendance on the queen.'

'Not always. Not right *now*. Please ... please. It is very important.'

She raised her head and I saw that tears gleamed in her green eyes. Tears, and fear. I would have gone anywhere, done anything, to erase that look from her lovely face.

'Go out the kitchen gate – you came from the kitchens, didn't you? The queen found you that night in the kitchen?' Some private memory twisted her face with grief. 'Go into the city. Ask your way to Mother Chilton, it's not far. Tell her you need a "milady posset". And you must go masked, and in plain clothes.'

I reeled with all these instructions. The only thing I found to say was, 'What's a milady posset?'

'Never you mind. It's merely a thing that I need. O Roger, don't fail me now!'

'But you have other friends – men with swords ...'

'I cannot tell any of them! Oh, for sweet sake, smile; Sarah is looking at us.' Cecilia trilled with laughter. She cried loudly, 'You have won, you swine!' She pushed the silver coin across the table to me.

Lady Sarah strolled over, smiling maliciously. 'So the fool won! A good thing you did not make Jane's wager with him, Cecilia. For now Jane must pay up.'

Lady Jane stood and pushed over the table, stamping her foot in its high-heeled slipper. But even I could see that her anger wasn't real. Was she really going to allow her chastity to be won in a dice game? Or was Lord Thomas not the first?

The queen, whatever her own reputation, would not approve of this. Neither of the queens.

The courtiers, making bawdy jests, crowded around Lady Jane and Lord Thomas. Lady Sarah turned to watch. I felt another, larger coin thrust into my hand, and then Cecilia flounced away towards the others, crying, 'Jane! I will be your lady of the bedchamber!'

The coin in my hand was gold.

I put both in my pocket and slipped out the door from the outer chamber to the presence chamber. If Cecilia saw me go, she gave no sign. In my alcove I drew the curtain and stood there, shivering in the dark. The tiny space had neither fire nor candle. But usually I was there only when asleep, and Queen Caroline had given me three warm blankets. I wished I could crawl under them and never come out.

What was I going to do?

I couldn't bear to see Cecilia so unhappy. Was she sick, and the milady posset a cure for some illness? But then why not tell the queen and ask for a physician? Was the posset some herb that brought temporary – if deluded – happiness? Such things existed, I knew. But ale or wine would do the same thing if enough was drunk, and it didn't cost a gold piece. I had never even *seen* a gold piece before.

What was I going to do?

Slowly I took off my green and yellow fool's suit. At the same time I faced the truth. I was afraid to go into the city alone.

Slowly I drew on my old rough trousers and patched boots.

I was a coward.

I pulled on the tunic that Kit Beale had given me.

I had always been a coward. When I stayed under Hartah's beatings, when I begged Lady Conyers to keep me by her, when Queen Caroline threatened me with torture if I didn't do her bidding. A coward.

With my knife I cut off a section of a blanket, cut two holes in it to make a mask, and thrust it into my pocket. I put on my hooded cloak, a gift from the queen.

I was going out into the city. For Cecilia.

110

14

The queen's room emptied soon enough; the lords and ladies all went to put Lady Jane and Lord Thomas to bed. That whole business shocked me still – a lady, allowing herself to be gambled for like a whore! There was so much different about the court than I had, vaguely, imagined when I arrived here with Kit Beale. Even Queen Caroline, why had she retired so early? Who was the sour-faced man in black whose conversation had so upset Her Grace?

I crept through the darkened presence chamber. Just before my hand touched the doorknob, I realized my mistake. Green guards stood on the other side. If I, the queen's fool, walked past them in rough dress, the queen would know it within minutes. So, I was beginning to realize, would everyone else in the palace, which was a web of spies. If the queen had me searched, the gold piece would be found. Then what of Cecilia's secrecy?

I went back to my alcove, put my fool's garb back on, tightly rolled my old clothes in my cloak and walked back through the presence chamber. This time I opened the door.

'Good morning, queen's men!' I said, and kicked up both legs like a frisky colt.

One of the guards smiled. 'It is evening, fool.'

I looked amazed. 'Are you sure? No, It's eight o'clock of a morning! I heard a cock crow!'

'Then your ears are full of candle wax.'

'The better for noises to slip inside!'

He laughed and gave me a mock kick, his boot just connecting with my arse. The other guard watched sourly. 'Get away from me, fool. I have no liking for halfwits.'

'Ah, but I am but a quarterwit, so you must like me! Shall I bring you breakfast from the kitchen?'

'I mean it – get away with you.'

I skipped out of his boot reach in mock fear, pantomimed extreme hunger and scampered off.

Immediately I was lost in the intricate maze of the palace. I couldn't remember the route by which Kit Beale had brought me, and I had not left the queen's chambers in weeks. Now that I thought of it, neither had she. Did she never go beyond the palace, outside to the city or the countryside? Was that her mother's doing?

By asking servants, I found my way to the kitchens. Now I knew where I was. The laundry was in this part of the palace, as was my old apprentices' chamber. Dinner was long over and only a few kitchen maids remained, scrubbing pots or preparing for tomorrow. Among them, preparing dough to rise overnight for tomorrow's bread, was Maggie.

'Roger!'

'Hello, Maggie.'

'You did indeed become the queen's fool! I had heard that.' Her tone was not entirely approving. The other girls stared at us, and Maggie snapped at them, 'Get back to work!' They did. Maggie was in charge here, just as she had once taken charge of me. Fed me, befriended me, laughed with me. It was good to see her, despite her disapproving glances at my yellow face and bizarre clothing.

She pushed a lock of hair off her sweaty face. The kitchen was very warm. 'What brings you here, Roger?'

I kept my voice low. 'I need to go out of the door where

112

the kitchen barges bring food from the farms.'

'Why?'

'I just do.'

'Is this queen's business?' Her voice too was low, but she kept her face calm and her strong arms busy mixing dough.

'Yes, but I cannot say what. And you must not, either.'

A pause in mixing, soon over. 'O Roger, what have you got yourself involved in now?'

I didn't answer. Let her think my errand was an important matter on behalf of the queen. Maggie would help me all the sooner. Cecilia's sad face filled my mind.

She said, 'It's not connected with the navy, is it? Please say you are not involved in that mess!'

What mess? What about the navy? How could a kitchen maid know more than I about matters of state? But I already knew the answer to that. Queen Eleanor kept all military matters away from her daughter's side of the palace. And lords and ladies did not gossip about weighty matters, lest they be overheard and mis-interpreted. They could trust no one. Lower servants, however, could gossip about anything, as long as they did so in whispers, because no one in power cared what they said, or thought. The palace servants – all except me – often knew everything.

I said, 'It is not about the navy. But I must go soon, and I must change first and go unseen.'

She sighed. 'Wait a short while. Sit there and eat, as if hunger alone had driven you here.' She went to the hearth and poured me a bowl of soup left over from the servants' dinner. It had cooled and I was already full, but I ate it with a great show of famine.

When Maggie had dismissed the other girls, I went into the larder and changed into my old clothes. They were far too tight; I had filled out since becoming the queen's

113

fool. I put the piece of blanket over my face, my eyes and mouth at the crude holes. When I emerged from the larder, Maggie made a choking noise somewhere between a scream of laughter and a grunt of exasperation. I pulled my hood up over my head so that it hung over my forehead.

'This way,' she said, shaking her head. Another small courtyard open to the sky, this one stacked with empty crates and jars and smelling of old vegetables. After the warm kitchen, its coolness was welcome. Maggie unlocked a door set into the wall and the scent of the river rushed in. The water flowed lazily just a few feet away, and stone stairs led down to poles at which to tie up barges. No barges floated there now. Between the river and the palace wall a narrow path curved away in both directions.

'You can go either left or right,' Maggie said.

'Which way to Mother Chilton?'

She grabbed my arm, pulled me back inside and slammed the door. 'Why are you going to *Mother Chilton*?'

'I cannot tell you that,' I said with as much dignity as I could muster, which wasn't much.

'The queen would not have business with that witch!'

'She is a witch?'

'Yes. No. No, of course not, there is no such thing. Mother Chilton is a healer. But Roger ... what have you done now?'

'I have done nothing.'

'Then who has?'

Her grey eyes looked steadily into mine. I didn't answer. Finally she said, 'Turn left. Go three alleys over and turn right. Look for the tent with a picture of two black swans drawn near the bottom. Wait, you'll need a lantern.'

When she'd given it to me, I said humbly, 'Thank you, Maggie. I could not do this without you.'

'I suspect you should not be doing it at all. I'll wait here to let you back in. Don't be long!'

'I won't.' How could I promise that? I couldn't know how long I would be. I went out through the open door, holding my lantern.

In the autumn Kit Beale had told me that the city was mostly deserted at night, the keepers of the shops and booths having gone back home to the surrounding villages. In this cold spring it seemed completely deserted. Tents provide little shield from cold. But within a few of the cloth buildings, lanterns gleamed, and I heard laughter from what seemed to be an alehouse. Still, I did not like to be here so late, with the kinds of people who stayed out at night. My teeth chattered as I scurried along, and not with cold. In the third alley I had to stoop to find the two black swans drawn at the very bottom of a tent. A crude drawing, pretending to be the mischief of a child. Cecilia had blithely assumed that I could easily carry out her wishes because she was used to people carrying out her wishes. But without Maggie I would never have found this place. Never.

A bell pull hung outside, and I pulled it. After a few minutes of bone-rattling chill, the tent flap was pushed aside and a voice said, 'Come in, then.'

I went inside.

An open fire burned in a brazier in the centre of the tent, sending its smoke through a hole in the roof and its light flickering on the canvas walls. Dozens of poles stood against the walls, their butts jammed into the bare earth, and each pole dripped objects tied with string to big nails. Bottles, plants, feathers, hides, bits of wood, bulging cloth bags of all sizes, things I could not name. Besides the poles there was room only for the brazier, a pallet of straw and blankets and a table with a single chair. On the chair sat not the crone I'd expected, but a woman neither young nor old, fat nor thin, pretty nor ugly. She wore a grey dress and grey cap. No one would ever glance at her twice; in fact, I had the sensation that I was not really seeing her at all. And yet she was solid enough, sitting there in her unadorned chair, her face pale in the dim light.

'What do you want?' she said, not unkindly.

'I'm looking for Mother Chilton.'

'I am Mother Chilton.'

'You?'

'A faint smile. 'Me. What are you after, lad? Unmask.'

'I cannot.' And then, inanely, 'I'm sorry.'

She stood and moved close to me. Now the fire was behind her and her face in shadow. With one firm hand she turned my chin to the fire and stared through the blanket holes into my eyes. Her own eyes were colourless, an even pale gleam that seemed to reflect all light, keeping none. Her breath drew in sharply. 'Who are you?'

'I told you, I cannot—'

'Do you come from Soulvine Moor?'

The question completely undid me. Soulvine Moor, which Maggie had chided me for even mentioning? Soulvine Moor, where my mother had died? I gasped, 'What – what of Soulvine Moor?'

'Are they ready, then?'

'Ready for what? Mistress, I come for ... for a milady posset!'

A long moment, and then she laughed, forced and bitter. 'I see. A milady posset.' Her hand dropped from my chin and she moved away. 'Get out!'

'I can pay!' Desperately I fumbled in my pockets until I found the gold piece. I held it out to her.

'A milady posset,' she repeated. 'And I asked you–

Well, why not. All right. Sometimes none of us knows where we are. Or who. Sit there.'

I did, afraid to disobey. She moved briskly about the tent, taking things from bags, putting vials and bowls upon the table. Her body shielded whatever she was doing. Presently there was a crisp odour, like apples combined with something else, and she handed me a vial stoppered with wax.

'Have her drink this all at once, then eat nothing for a day. She will feel no sickness. And I don't have to tell you, do I, that she should lie with no one for at least a week?'

My ears grew warm. My lady Cecilia did not lie with men; she had proudly refused to play the court's bed-wagering game. Mother Chilton gazed at me with amusement and handed me the vial. But there was speculation in her amusement, and I got out as fast as I could.

Maggie let me back in by the kitchen-barge door and locked it behind her.

'Did you get what you needed?'

'Yes.'

'Good. I suppose. Roger, be careful. These are strange times.'

She seemed less angry at me than before, less impatient. She was glad I was back safe, which made a little warm fire in my heart. I risked questions. 'How are they strange times, Maggie?'

'Wouldn't you know better than I? I only know what I hear of gossip, or am told by my brother, the soldier with the Blues. *You're* the one beside the queen.'

I said slowly, 'I sit at her feet. I make jokes about matters I don't understand. I hope desperately that my joke will fit its subject, at least a little. And that it will be funny, at least a little. I dye my face yellow. I make inane movements like dancing backwards and pretending to fall down. And all the while I'm afraid that I will do something wrong, something that will displease the queen. Always I'm afraid, Maggie. Sometimes I wish I were back here, carrying water in the laundry, sleeping under the trestle table.'

She took my hand. Hers was warm, rough with work. 'We are the same age, and yet sometimes I think I am much older than you.'

She would not think that if she had known the things I had seen and done. The wreck of the *Frances Ormund*, the knife sliding into Hartah's flesh ... I had not trusted Maggie with my past, however much I trusted her in the present. I said, 'I need to know as much as I can learn in order to merely survive, and yet I know nothing. You hear more in the kitchen, from the servants who wait at table and the bargemen who come from outside, than I do among the courtiers. They must guard their tongues around the queen, and I am always around the queen. So please please tell me – how are these strange times?'

'The two rival courts in the palace cannot go on for ever,' Maggie said, her voice low. 'There are whispers – well, there always were – but my brother tells me that the rumours grow more intense, both in the army and in the villages. The old rumours.'

I remembered Cat Starling's flat words: *The queen is a whore*. 'Why do the rumours grow more intense now? Because of Lord Robert?'

'No. Well, maybe a little. Consort Will was much beloved, you know. He was so generous to the poor, and he travelled all about the countryside, listening to people. I was not yet working at court when he died, but I remember villagers whispering that the queen had him poisoned.'

'Poisoned? Her own husband? I don't believe it. He was no threat to her rule.' I realized all at once that we were talking treason. If anyone overheard … But we were two young servants in a cold and deserted kitchen courtyard beside a pile of vegetable crates and slop buckets, and there was no one else around.

'Some say,' Maggie continued, 'that she had already taken up again with Lord Robert, and so wished her husband gone.'

'Why does she not marry Lord Robert now?'

Maggie shrugged. 'Perhaps she does not wish to share power, not even with a consort. Some say she waits for a better alliance through marriage, a foreign prince, after the old queen dies. Some say …' Maggie raised the lantern, looked fearfully around, and put her mouth close to my ear. 'Some say she is a witch.'

All at once pieces fell into place in my mind, like tumblers clicking into a lock. The queen's readiness to believe that I could cross over in the face of Lord Robert's amused disbelief. Maggie's horror that time in the kitchen when I asked where Soulvine Moor lay. Mistress Conyers, telling me to avoid the notice of the queen. But I knew that there were no witches. I alone knew this with certainty. I had crossed over to the country of the Dead, had talked to the Dead, had even talked to old women burned as witches. They had not been that. But common people believed in witches, and were terrified of them, and an army was made of common soldiers. No one was more superstitious than a soldier – I had seen it again and again at faires. And I knew all too well that a statement need have very little truth in it to be believed.

I said slowly, 'Agents of the old queen have put about rumours that Queen Caroline is a witch, haven't they? Amongst the army and in the countryside. Queen Eleanor has fanned the flames of gossip and fear against her own daughter, in order to keep her crown.'

'How should I know?' Maggie whispered. 'But the

119

army is as close to the old queen as feathers on a chicken.'

Now I understood why Queen Caroline had so few petitioners. Such hatred and manoeuvring between mother and child! My own mother in her lavender gown, so tender and caring in the few memories I had of her.

'Maggie, what's on Soulvine Moor?'

But, despite all she had already said, there were places Maggie would not go. She stared at me mutely, and all at once I realized that the hand holding mine had turned icy and her teeth chattered.

'You're freezing! I'm sorry, come back into the kitchen. I cannot thank you enough for all your help.' I led her back inside. 'Just one thing more – what is a "milady posset"?'

Maggie stopped just before the closed door to the kitchen. She flung my hand back at me and screeched, all at once careless of listeners, 'A *milady posset*? Is that what you went to Mother Chilton for? A *milady posset*?'

'I—'

'For whom? Look at me when I speak to you – *for whom*?'

'I can't say.'

'I'll bet you can't! And to think I trusted you – that I even thought ... A milady posset! You're a filthy animal!'

'Maggie, don't—'

'Don't tell me what to do! And get out of my sight! A *milady posset*!'

She flung open the door and darted through to the kitchen, slamming it behind us. Before she could run off, I grabbed her by the shoulder. 'What is it for? What?'

'Don't pretend you don't know! Who was she, some whore brought in for you, that you stupidly believed was clean and now take pity on? Were you the only one who had her? And to think I helped you!' Maggie tore herself free of my grasp and ran out of the kitchen, leaving her dough half-kneaded on the table.

And I understood.

Lady Cecilia had the crawls. She had bedded with someone, and he had given it to her. Men could carry the disease but did not fall ill of it. Women did. Untreated, the crawls could even make it impossible for women to ever bear children. Bawdy jests overheard at country faires had told me that girls greatly feared the crawls, which turned them red and itching in their . . .

Cecilia. My shining lady.

Who was he?

In the larder I changed back into my court clothing. I stole a kitchen lantern, lit it and made my way back through the labyrinth of courtyards, scarcely seeing them. Anger and hatred burned in me. For him, who had taken her. For her, who had played me for the fool I was. All the while I adored her, worshipped her, would have given my life for one kiss from her, Cecilia had been lying with one of the courtiers, perhaps allowing herself to be won in a game like Lady Jane.

No. The truth came to me so suddenly that I stopped cold beside a winter-empty planting bed, my feet as rooted to the ground as the tree whose bare branches arched above. It was not some random Lord Tom or Sir Harry. If it had been, Cecilia would have done whatever the other ladies did in such circumstances. It had been someone she could not admit to. It had been the prince.

I saw her again, running to Emma Cartwright the day I had arrived at court, hiding in her room from Prince Rupert. I had thought then that her hiding was genuine, when I didn't yet know her. Cecilia lived for admiration, for being petted, for love. She had been teasing him, as she teased me, as she teased every man at court. But Prince Rupert had bedded her, and the other ladies knew.

121

(*'Cecilia, there are other things in life besides dancing.' 'I think she knows that!' 'Green wood burns hotter than yellow'* – the prince had favoured green to please his sister.) Emma Cartwright had left court shortly after I arrived – dismissed because she knew too much? Did the good Mistress Cartwright know that Prince Rupert carried the crawls, and that he had undoubtedly given them to his new bride? That knowledge might have cancelled his wedding to Princess Isabelle, might have endangered The Queendom's political alliance with the bride's rich realm. No wonder Cecilia had been nearly hysterical. The crawls from a prince, with a royal marriage hanging in the balance and the danger of wrath from two queens.

It was at that moment, in the dark of a cold spring night, that for the first time I understood what life at court truly was. I had been a fool; I was a fool still. But now I knew. Nothing was as it seemed. Everything was for sale, and everything was judged by how it affected the web of power.

My new knowledge turned me careful. I extinguished my lantern. In the dark I fumbled towards a flower bed, took Mother Chilton's little cloth bag from my pocket, and buried it. It was an easy matter to rearrange some ornamental green stones to disguise the freshly turned earth.

After a long time standing there, thinking, while my toes grew stiff and the hairs in my nose froze, I moved on. I passed the guards with a jest and made my way through the deserted presence chamber to my alcove. I drew back the curtain.

And there, waiting for me in the darkness, stood the queen.

'Where have you been, Roger?' she said.

'Where have you been, Roger?' the queen repeated when I did not – could not – speak.

With the kitchen lantern at the end of my suddenly slack and terrified arm, I could scarcely see her face, only the gleam of light on the green satin of her gown. 'I … I went to the kitchen … I was hungry!'

'So you told the guards. And what else? No, wait, not here. Follow me.'

I stumbled after her, wondering if I was to be led to some dungeon, to some instruments of torture that would … But the queen led me through the outer chamber to her privy chamber, the room where I'd had my first audience with her. The door to her bedchamber was closed, as ever. In the privy chamber Lord Robert sat beside a bright fire, with a goblet of wine before him on the ornately carved table.

The queen closed the door and leaned back against it. Her face was kindly, her eyes warm. She smiled at me. 'Now, Roger, tell me where you have been and whom you have spoken to. And leave no detail out.'

How much did she know? I had to protect Maggie, protect Cecilia. Why protect Cecilia? Because I loved her still. And I could no more deliver her into the hands of the queen than I could a butterfly to the pin that would fix it, squirming, on a board.

'I was hungry,' I said. 'I went to the kitchen to get something to eat. I have a friend there, a kitchen maid, and ... and we lay together. In the courtyard where the barges bring vegetables to the palace.'

The queen stood so that she could see both me and Lord Robert. From the corner of my eye I saw him give a tiny nod. So he already knew where I'd been, and with whom. Her web of spies – or his – must extend itself even farther than I had guessed. If one of those spies had overheard Maggie and me ...

The queen studied me, still with that kindly smile on her beautiful ruthless face. Finally she said, 'I believe you. You have grown taller and fuller since you entered my service, Roger, and I can believe you would lie with a maid. Nonetheless, after I retire, Lord Robert will search you to make sure you carry no messages, to anyone. And you will not leave my rooms again without permission, do you understand?'

'Yes, Your Grace.' Relief flooded me, so strong that for a shameful moment I thought I might cry.

All at once the queen came towards me, took both my hands in hers. She stared deeply into my eyes, her voice low and soft. 'In the coming days I will need you, Roger. No one else can do for me what you can, and your gift makes you a treasure beyond price. The Queendom is in grave danger. I am determined to protect it, and to someday hand the realm intact to my daughter. I will do whatever I must to protect my realm. Do you believe that?'

And I did. Her dark eyes so earnestly searching mine ... The queen was beautiful, but I knew I was not responding to her beauty. Cecilia filled all that part of my mind. The queen was a skilled actress, but I didn't think she was play-acting about this. She was genuinely concerned about the future of The Queendom she was not being allowed to rule, and she would do whatever was necessary to protect it. She would flay me alive if that would help. She would even do the same to Lord Robert, if she had to. Did he know that?

In one night my mind had travelled over too far a distance. I was bewildered, frightened, weary. The world was not as I had thought it.

'Yes, Your Grace,' I said. 'I believe you care for The Queendom.'

She dropped my hands. 'Good. Robin, give him some wine, search him and send him to bed. This is a tired lad.'

Lord Robert rose. The queen walked towards her bedchamber, but in the doorway she turned and looked back over her shoulder at me. 'Your kitchen maid, was this your first time?'

'Yes,' I said, and she smiled at me roguishly and shut the door.

Lord Robert's search was swift, not gentle and very thorough. Sometime during its course I realized that he – a lord of The Queendom, the queen's adviser and lover – was afraid of me, because of what the queen had called my 'gift'. She was not afraid, but he was.

No, the world was not as I had thought it.

Lord Robert found nothing in my clothing, on my person. 'Go to bed,' he said roughly, 'and don't ever do this again.'

The next afternoon Cecilia came with the queen's other ladies to the outer chamber. Queen Caroline had spent the morning closeted in her inner chamber with Lord Robert and a series of couriers, all of whom looked as if they had ridden hard to arrive at the palace. Some of their clothing looked strange, and no one knew where they had come from. She sent word early that her ladies need not attend her and so they had not. Nor did I, and I spent the whole long morning alone in the vast presence chamber or the outer chamber, staring out the open window at the courtyard. Sometime during the night the cold had finally released its grasp, and it was spring. But the soft air and sweet scents didn't move me.

Not even hunger moved me. I didn't dare go to the kitchen for anything to eat – not after the queen's warning – and nothing was brought to me, so my stomach clenched and growled. Breakfast and dinner were carried in to the queen. The smells of roasted meat and steaming soup filled my mouth with hopeless water.

I made myself a vow during those long hours at the window. I had been uninterested in the larger life at court for too long; I would be so no longer. If I could not choose my fate, I could at least meet it with less ignorant eyes. I would observe, I would ask questions, I would learn.

Finally, when the afternoon was nearly gone and the shadows long in the courtyard, the ladies-in-waiting and their courtiers burst into the outer chamber in a great flock, chattering and tired and happy. 'We rode as far as the mountains, fool!' Cecilia called cheerfully to me. 'A wonderful ride!'

'Yes, my lady,' I said. She was smiling, her skin warmed from the sun, her hair still damp from a bath. Never had I seen her look more beautiful. Hysteria shone in her green eyes like fever. My stomach rumbled.

'Now we must have music! Music and dancing!'

The others took up the cry: *Music! Dancing! Music!* Only recently had the queen given permission for dancing to occur when she was not present. The ladies and courtiers were young, alive, oblivious to whatever the queen may have been doing all day, although they would leap to her service the second she required them. Although were they really so oblivious, so heedless and carefree as they seemed? All of them – everyone at court – were such skilled actors. Except me.

Musicians were sent for. Under cover of all the bustle, Cecilia said to me, 'Roger?'

I said, 'It is buried under the tree in the fish-fountain courtyard, on the side of the tree facing the fountain. Organize a game of hide-and-seek or hide-the-coin, and you can easily retrieve it. Drink it all at once, eat nothing for a day and lie—' my voice faltered '—with no one for a week.'

'Oh, I thank you so—'

'Was it Prince Rupert?'

She stiffened beside me, then rose and flounced off, her satin skirts swishing. But a moment later she was back. Lips so close to my ear that I could smell the scented soap on her damp hair, she whispered, 'Don't think less of me; I could not bear it,' and again she was gone.

My chest contracted in on itself, held, had to be forced to breathe again. Why should Lady Cecilia care what I, the queen's fool, thought of her?

I watched her move through the slow sedate figures of the court dance, her restless charm confined to one step forward, two back, a slight dip of the head. Wrong, wrong. The wrong dance for her, the wrong man, the wrong contrast between the courtiers' gaiety and the ominous absence of the queen.

Just as darkness fell, the door to the privy chamber opened and the queen stepped out. Instantly dancers and musicians fell into deep curtseys. The queen gazed at them bleakly. She wore a gown of such deep green it looked almost black, and the dark colour turned her skin chalky white. It made her look older, unlike the woman who had questioned me at midnight, let alone the one who had roistered with her court in the kitchens on the day she had found me there. It occurred to me now that never since had I seen her join her courtiers with that same abandon.

Had she come to the kitchen that night only for me?

'Roger?' she said now. 'Come, fool.'

I rose and moved through the kneeling courtiers towards the privy chamber.

'Resume dancing, then,' Queen Caroline said, smiled at them all, and closed the door. She turned to me. 'It occurred to me that you must have eaten nothing, Roger, since yesterday. Sit, eat.'

There it was again: kindness in the woman who had threatened me with torture, remembrance of the small amid whatever great concerns consumed her. Lord Robert sat at the other end of the table, now covered with a green-embroidered dinner cloth that hung to the floor, his face as bleak as hers. His fingers curled loosely around the stem of a wine goblet. When he raised the goblet to drink, the green stones of his rings flashed in the firelight.

I loaded a plate – it was a royal order, after all – with meat and fruit and bread and cheese, and devoured it all. I drank two goblets of wine. The queen and Lord Robert talked only of trivial things: the change in the weather, the shoe that his horse had thrown, Lady Margaret's cold, a favourite hunting dog about to whelp. The fire burned low, throwing the room into shadow. After my heavy meal and heavier thoughts, I felt sleepy. When I slumped low in my chair on the far side of the table, the queen said, 'Roger, you may go now and—'

The door was flung open with the force of a gale and soldiers burst in.

Blue soldiers, not the queen's Green guard. The sleeves above their armour were blue, the ribbons on their helmets blue, the arms on their shields ... Their short swords were drawn. Before I knew I was even going to move, I had slid down in the chair and slithered under the table, where the long cloth hid me.

Lord Robert leaped up, his hand going to his sword. But then a woman's voice rang out.

'Caroline.'

I knew that icy voice, although I had heard it only once. The old queen. The door slammed shut. Beneath the edge of the cloth I could see the hem of her blue gown, the heavy boots of her soldiers. I felt Lord Robert hesitate. Then he went around the table, between the two queens, and knelt. 'Your Highness,' he said, giving her not the title of a reigning monarch but of a royal family member.

She ignored him. 'Caroline, what have you done?'

'I have done nothing.' As much ice as in her mother's voice, and much more rage.

'I think you have,' Queen Eleanor said. 'Your couriers come and go from the harbour at Carlyle Bay, and other strange couriers ride in from the west. And your lover here—' it was impossible to convey the contempt in those three words '—has called upon the lord high admiral himself.'

Queen Caroline said, 'I would know what happens in my queendom.'

'*My* queendom, Caroline. You are not fit to hold it, and could not hold it if you had it.'

'I was crowned well over a year ago!'

'A sham without my presence, and without the Crown of Glory, and you know it. I would give you The Queendom if I thought you could hold it, but you cannot.'

'Because you have turned the army against me. You know I could rule, but you want to keep all power for yourself!'

'And so I shall, for the good of The Queendom. I will not see it descend to civil war. And you will keep your fingers – all eleven of them – off my navy. Do I make myself understood?'

The young queen said levelly, 'Mother, are you planning to send both the new navy and the army to attack Benilles? To take The Queendom into war?'

Dead silence.

I had heard of Benilles – where? Then it came to me: Bat's voice in the country of the Dead, about the *Frances Ormund*: *Gold from Benilles and cloth from ... I forget*. Had Captain James Conyers' cargo included information as well? So perhaps it had not been by mere chance that the old queen's Blues had interrupted Hartah's wreckers. The soldiers had been waiting in that desolate place for something that did not happen because my uncle's wreckers foundered the ship and Captain Conyers drowned.

Queen Eleanor said, 'Caroline, if you interfere in matters that do not concern you, you will regret it.'

'If you plunge The Queendom into a war we cannot win, you will regret it.'

I wondered, cowering under my table, which of the two women had the greater capacity for hatred.

The old queen said, 'Keep to your music, daughter, and your wild young court, and your powerless lover. As of tonight, you will receive no visitors except these. I will have guards at the doors of your presence chamber. Since it was not enough to restrict you to the palace, I will also restrict those you may see. I have spoken.'

A swish of the blue gown as she turned, a slam of the door behind her soldiers.

The young queen said, 'I will—'

'Hush, Caro,' Lord Robert said in a tone that would have silenced an earthquake. 'The first thing you will do is dismiss your fool before he hears even more than he has. Roger, go.'

I crawled out from under the table, just as I had done so many times in Hartah's faire booth. And, like those times, I held information I did not want. But I made a rapid decision. 'Your Grace.'

'I said go!' Lord Robert thundered.

'Your Grace, I know something more of Captain Conyers and the *Frances Ormund* and Benilles. I learned it from a sailor of the crew and from the captain's widow.'

She stared at me, white-faced, her mouth still twisted with anger at her mother. I knelt before her and told her that Bat had said 'someone important' had been on board the ship, someone 'with medals on his chest'. Mistress Conyers had mentioned passenger money from a nobleman, suggesting a sum large enough to make a difference to her husband's fortunes. And Queen Eleanor's soldiers, a large number of them, had already been gathered in this remote corner of The Queendom.

When I finished, she said, 'Roger.'

'Your Grace?'

'Rise and look at me.' Lord Robert watched us closely from across the room.

'Do you realize you have just confessed to participating in a deliberate wreck?'

'Yes, Your Grace.'

'And that such a crime is punishable by hanging?'

'Yes, Your Grace.' I saw the yellow-haired youth choking in the noose, kicking the air.

'Then why have you told me?'

'Because I thought you might wish to know. Because it might . . . might be useful to you to know. And you are my queen.'

She was silent. Her black eyes, with their glints of submerged silver, searched mine. Lord Robert said dryly, 'And because he knows you value his "gift" too highly to kill him, and may in the future remember his willingness to aid you.'

'That too,' I said, and the queen smiled.

'You did well to tell me,' she said. 'I won't forget it. Roger, say nothing of what you heard tonight.'

'I will not, Your Grace.'

'You may go.'

In the outer chamber I was immediately besieged by courtiers and ladies. 'What happened in there, fool? What did the old queen say to Her Grace?'

What? What? What? The word echoed in my head, as if from a drum instead of being whispered from a dozen eager throats. They were like a bunch of ravens, feeding on carrion.

I said, 'Her mother told Queen Caroline that the expenses of her household were too high.'

Lord Thomas said, 'The fool is lying.'

Then Lady Cecilia cried, 'Oh look, the moon has risen full! Let's all play a game of hide-the-coin among the courtyards! Such fun! Come, all of you, I shall go out and hide the coin first!'

She caught Lord Thomas by one hand, Lady Sarah by the other, and it was true that the moon had risen full. Its light shone through the window, lying silver on her bright face and on the hard, polished stone floor.

16

A week later I sat at the queen's feet in the presence chamber, listening to the few petitioners who came to her and not to her mother. They were all peasants or farmers, allowed in because the Blue guards posted just beyond the door didn't think they were worth keeping out. A peasant's stolen cow, a farmer's field in dispute. One of the queen's advisers had fallen asleep, his beard stirring with his light snores.

In the courtyard beyond, someone screamed. Not a woman, a man.

The queen's own guards leaped in front of the dais, shielding it. But no Blues were attacking; the ones stationed at the door looked as startled as everyone else. Another scream – a woman this time – and a shout. Then running outside, people rushing and calling, and the captain of the Green guard ran into the presence chamber and up to the queen, not even kneeling.

'Are you unharmed, Your Grace?'

'Yes, Captain, I am. What has happened?' She looked towards the door.

More Greens marched into the room and took up posts around the queen. The Blues at the open door looked at each other, clearly mystified and without orders, their hands on their swords.

'I asked you – *what has happened*?'

The captain knelt then, just as yet more Greens closed the doors to the presence chamber, shutting the Blue guards without, and barred it. The captain said, 'Your

133

Grace, Queen Eleanor has ... The queen is dead. Long live the queen!'

'*Dead?*'

'Yes, Your Grace.' He did not raise his eyes but I, crouched on the bottom step of the throne and looking up, could see them. I saw no fear – he was a captain of the guards – but I saw doubt. Much terrible doubt.

'Did she—'

'Just now, Your Grace. She was with her advisers and she slumped to the floor and– The physicians are with her now. She– I—' He looked for certainty, and found it in duty. 'There is unrest in the palace, Your Grace.'

The queen said sharply, 'My children?'

'I have already secured the nursery; the princess and her brother are safe. But you must stay here until my men have secured the entire palace. Your privy chamber would be better yet.'

For the first time I realized why the privy chamber, and presumably the bedchamber beyond, had no windows.

'I will go to my privy chamber,' the queen said, 'but only to dress. And as soon as possible, Captain, I will go to the throne room. Clear and secure that first. And if you can spare the men, have them bring to me my ladies of the bedchamber and Lord Robert Hopewell.'

'Yes, Your Grace.'

'Roger, come with me.'

She swept from the presence chamber, leaving behind her the grim-faced guard and the peasants still on their knees. One of them, his back to me, whispered something to his friend. In her privy chamber the queen told me only, 'It is not safe for you out there,' before vanishing into her bedchamber and closing the door.

I didn't know what to do. I went cold, then hot, then cold again. There was no wine. I sat at the carved table, and then on the floor. I poked the fire, which did not

134

need poking. I could not settle, could not think.

No. That is not true. I could think, but only of one word, the word the peasant had whispered to his friend – had dared to whisper there, in the queen's own presence chamber.

Poison.

The queen is dead. Long live the queen!

I will do whatever I must to protect my queendom. She had said that to me.

The queen is dead. Long live—

Finally the door was flung open and Lord Robert entered; at the same time that the queen emerged from her bedchamber. I fell to my knees. She had changed without aid from her ladies, who were ... what? Delayed? In hiding? Slaughtered by the Blues? *Cecilia* ...

'Caro,' Lord Robert choked out.

She did not answer. She looked magnificent, dressed in a gown I had not seen before. It was so embroidered with green jewels that the green velvet underneath could scarcely be seen. Her full skirts swept the floor and lengthened to a train behind. Long lace-and-satin sleeves fell almost to her fingertips, hiding the bud of the extra finger. She wore an emerald necklace and earrings and her rich black hair hung loose down her back, her bare head ostentatiously awaiting a crown.

Lord Robert ignored all that. He grabbed her hands, causing the sleeves to fall back over her white arms.

'Caro ... Sweet palace of the heavens, Caro, *what have you done*?'

Poison, the peasant had said.

'Please escort me to the throne room, Lord Robert,' she said, and at her tone he jerked and then – finally, belatedly – knelt.

'The queen is dead,' he said in a voice as rigid as Queen Eleanor's. 'Long live the queen.'

'Roger, you will stay here,' she said. 'I will need you later. Bar the door and open it to none but myself or Lord Robert. Do you understand?'

'Yes, Your Grace.'

'Open the door, Lord Robert.'

He did, and trailed her out, and now I could hear the great bells in the tower begin to toll, as slow and stately as the court dances required by the old queen, sending the news to The Queendom of death, and change, and triumph. I didn't know how much time I had.

If the Green soldiers could not secure the palace, would the queen return to her privy chamber or wait in her presence chamber? Might she bring her ladies in here, for safety, if guards brought them to her? Most important of all, how long had the old queen been dead?

If I was going to do this at all, it must be now. Before I could change my mind, I seized a carving knife from the table and jabbed at my arm. Pain sprang along my nerves, making me drop the knife. I willed myself to cross over.

This time I was close by the river, almost in the water. A large group of soldiers sat together on the grass, all dressed in the same leather armour and crude sandals, as if they had died together. Like the rest of the Dead, they bore no injuries or maiming. The whole group ignored me. From their old-fashioned garb I guessed that they had been there a long time. For all I knew, they might stay there for ever.

The western mountains had disappeared altogether, as if the valley now stretched larger than in my previous visit, and the river seemed even wider and slower. I was still on the island, however. Running along its banks, in and out of groves of trees, I searched for the old queen. Circles of the Dead, more Dead lying on the grass or gazing at rocks – *where was she*?

I found her wading ashore from the river, sputtering

136

and angry. Water dripped from her blue silk gown and from her crown, the simple silver circlet she favoured on her white hair. Even wet, Queen Eleanor had a terrifying dignity. Even furious. Even dead.

I dropped to one knee. 'Your Grace!'

'Who are you? Where am I?' And then, a moment later, 'I am dead.'

No use lying, not to this woman. 'Yes, Your Grace.'

'And you are . . . you are my daughter's fool! With the stupid yellow dye on your face!'

'Yes, Your Grace.'

'What happened, boy? Are you dead too?'

I thought quickly. 'Yes, Your Grace.'

'And this is the country of the Dead.' She turned thoughtful then, and I saw it begin: the contemplative remoteness of the Dead. In a few moments I might not be able to reach her at all.

Desperately I said, 'Were you poisoned, Your Grace?'

That caught her attention. 'What?'

'Were you poisoned by your daughter, Queen Caroline? Did any messenger visit you last night or this morning? Was there any strange person in your chambers? Did anything happen that might have been poisoning?' I did not know what I was looking for.

'Caroline,' she said vaguely, as if trying to remember the name. It was happening right before my eyes. She was detaching from the living. She was no longer subject to those loves, those hatreds, those ties.

'Your daughter, the new queen! Who may have poisoned you and now has your queendom! Your Grace!'

Gracefully she sat down on the grass and stared at a flower. I had lost her. This was one old woman I could not jar into jolly stories of childhood.

I smacked my fist against my thigh. To have taken this risk for nothing! I must get back now. I must—

Two soldiers materialized a short way off. They wore Queen Eleanor's blue. My body blocked her from their view, but one cried, 'The whore's fool! Seize him!'

He rushed towards me, sword drawn. The other, not so quick in mind, looked around him dazedly. I stepped aside and pointed. 'Your queen!'

That stopped the attacking soldier. He fell to his knees and bowed his head. 'Your Majesty! Are you safe?'

She, of course, said nothing. Not for a long moment. But then she looked up at me and said simply, 'Yes.' A moment later she had relapsed into the calm of the Dead.

The second soldier came uncertainly towards me. 'What is this place? What ... They said Queen Eleanor was dead.'

I saw it come to him then. He looked down at his own belly, as if expecting to find it run through with the sword of a Green, and then looked again at me. I couldn't help but be moved by his bewilderment.

The kneeling soldier sprang up. 'None of your fool's talk, boy! Where are we? What witchcraft did the whore use on us?'

Here, then, was my story, handed to me like meat on a golden plate – the same story I had once told Bat. If I could use it to make these soldiers believe I was not Queen Caroline's ally but her victim, they might not harm me. Swiftly I said, 'You have caught me out! Yes, the young queen used her sorcery to bring us all here to Witchland – I saw her do it! She crooked her sixth finger and chanted her spells and ... and flew through the air and brought us all here! Me too, for daring to say fool's rhymes that displeased her. And she has ensorcelled Queen Eleanor! Look, the queen breathes and yet cannot speak, cannot see.'

The soldier cried out in superstitious fear and outraged fury. He waved his drawn sword, but there was no one to run through – until three Green soldiers appeared beside the river.

There must be fighting in the palace. Men were dying. And now there would be fighting here as well.

The two Blues rushed towards the Greens, who drew their weapons. And I saw what I had not thought possible: the Dead fighting each other to kill. Only it did not, could not, happen. One soldier got the advantage and slashed brutally at another's head. The blade passed right through flesh and skull and bone, and the man stood on his feet still, unharmed.

That stopped them all.

I dared not go closer. I could be harmed, even if they could not. From beside the queen I called, 'In Witchland, no one can die. Look how many the witches have brought here! And she can summon us back whenever she chooses. It has been done to me before!'

The Blues looked wildly around. The three Greens had already retreated out of earshot; soon they would be tranquil and motionless. The Blues didn't understand, but they believed me. In the face of the senseless, men will seize on any belief that promises sense.

The less quick of the Blues said uncertainly, 'Ye have been here before, fool?'

'Yes. Come here, to your queen, just you.'

He came. I said to him, very low, 'What happened to her? Did she drink or eat anything, or—'

'I don't know. I wasn't there. But my captain, he said she clutched her belly and cried, "Poison! My daughter!" But ye say it was not poison, it was witchcraft? I don't know.'

'It was witchcraft,' I said firmly. 'Look at her! She's not dead; she breathes and sits. You walk and talk. You are banished in Witchland until they summon you back. And so are these others.' Two more Blues had appeared in the river and were staggering, dripping, to shore. 'You must tell them! I hope I don't—' Deliberately I broke off my sentence, bit my tongue hard and crossed over.

My tongue bled into my mouth. I writhed on the hearthrug and then all at once I was weeping. But was I weeping from pain, or from knowledge?

In truth, I had no certain knowledge. The old queen had cried out that she had been poisoned, but she might have cried that even if her death had come from a failure in her heart. She might have clutched her belly anyway, believing her daughter to have poisoned her no matter what the fact. And the *Yes* that the old queen had said to me – the last thing she would ever say to anyone – might have meant anything.

But I believed that Queen Eleanor had been answering my question. *Yes*. Yes, she had been murdered, and Queen Caroline was what rumour had called her: a poisoner.

The queen is dead. Long live the queen.

I don't know how long I lay on the hearth, my thoughts in chaos. Queen Caroline had always roused in me so many contradictory emotions: fear, admiration, anger, respect. Now my feelings towards the queen reduced themselves to only one: the desire to survive her patronage.

Eventually I rose and washed the blood from my mouth with cooling water. Some time later Lord Robert's voice bellowed on the other side of the door. 'Fool! Open!'

I unbarred the door. He and Queen Caroline stood there. Her ladies and courtiers clustered at the other end of the outer chamber, some looking frightened, others triumphant. I fell to my knees as the queen swept through the doorway.

Lord Robert said, 'Only a few moments, Your Majesty. This is urgent.'

'So is this. Close the door, Robert. Roger, rise. Why is there blood on your chin?'

'I bit my tongue, Your Grace.' My words came out thick and garbled.

'Clumsy of you. And on your sleeve?'

'Drippings from my tongue, Your Grace.'

She took my face between her hands. I had to force myself to not recoil at her touch. *Poison.*

'I need you to go to the Dead. You must find a man called Osprey, the palace locksmith. A short squint-eyed man who died this evening. He wears the seal of The Queendom on his breast. You must ask him for the location of the key to the iron safe, where the Crown of Glory is kept. I need that key now, Roger, right this moment. I am going to the throne room and I want to be wearing the crown that my grandmothers have worn since time itself was young.'

I gaped at her. 'Your Grace; it's impossible. The Dead don't—'

'Don't what?' she said sharply, dropping her hands. 'Don't talk to you? You have declared that they do. You have shown me that they do. What is the difficulty?'

'It's ... it's the *country* of the Dead!' I said desperately. 'It's vast and ... and wild, and to find a specific person is so difficult. I probably wouldn't come across this Osprey if I searched for days, and you said you need it now, the Crown of Glory, now.' I was babbling from sheer terror.

'Try.'

One word, with so many unspoken words behind it. And in her eyes everything to justify my terror.

Hartah had told me what instruments of torture look like. What they can do to a helpless body. So for the second time I cut my arm with the queen's jewelled carving knife, crossed over, and – amazingly – found Osprey. Finding him did me no good. He had been dead too long, he was not old, and I could not rouse him. I shouted in his ear; I shook his shoulder; I lifted him bodily, dragged him to the river and threw him in. He lurched out, lay on the grass and gazed at the sky. He would say nothing to me.

'It's the queen's fool again,' a Blue soldier said. 'The witch bounces him back and forth.'

'Aye, and she racks his bones with pain,' said another. 'Poor oaf.'

There were more of them now, the dead soldiers. Some of the Blues stood guarding the unknowing old queen at the edge of the island. Others milled about, talked, kept their swords drawn. They did not know they were dead. They had believed me when I said this was Witchland, and they had repeated that belief to newer arrivals all too ready to believe it. Of course the young queen was a witch – hadn't that been rumoured for years? Of course she had sent them to Witchland! And that belief kept them animated, as alive as they would ever be again.

What had I done?

'Don't come closer, fool,' one soldier said. 'I'm sorry, boy, but the witch has you for fair, doesn't she?'

'Yes.'

'Then don't come near us!'

I did not. A little ways off a green soldier lay tranquil on the ground. The Blue followed my gaze. 'You see, fool, how evil is the witch-whore you are forced to serve! She magicks even the corpses of her own to Witchland. She dare not let their relatives find her mark upon their bodies, lest her witchery be plain to all. No, don't touch him; we do not know if this be a trap of poison, or worse.'

I did not intend to touch the Green, nor anything else. In despair, I crossed back over and faced Queen Caroline. Blood seeped from my cut arm, sticky on the velvet. 'Your Grace, I . . . I'm sorry. I couldn't find Osprey. I– It is such a big place! I had no time!'

She stood with her back to the fire and gazed at me

from hard eyes. From the other side of the door, Lord Robert called urgently, 'Your Grace!' I was near fainting from fear. To be run through with his blade, or burned alive, or ... I knew there were deaths even worse. And I had failed her.

She said softly, 'Did you *really* go there? To the country of the Dead?'

'Yes!' I stabbed about in my mind for something to convince her. 'I saw the old queen!'

Swiftly she crossed the room and seized my arm. 'What did she say?'

'I– Nothing that—'

'Don't lie to me, Roger! What did the old hag say?'

My life balanced on my next words. Only honesty would convince her – she was so good at detecting evasions. Might even implying that she had committed murder be construed as treason? Done if I spoke truth, done if I did not. Despairing, I choked out, 'She ... *she* said you ... poisoned her. That she felt it in her belly and clutched her belly and died. She cursed you.'

The queen laughed, a high hysterical peal that reminded me horribly of Lady Cecilia. But this was no Cecilia. In half a moment she had herself back in control and into another of her lightning changes of mood.

'You *were* there. I am sorry I doubted you. Those are exactly the lies my mother would utter, the old bitch. There, don't look so scared, Roger; no one will hurt you. You did your best, I know, and in the future there will be more for you to do, and you will succeed. There now, little fool, it's all right. Come along, and I shall allow you to see me take back my palace.' She gave my arm a quick caress and smiled at me. Then she opened the door to Lord Robert and forgot me.

And so, not daring to do anything else, I followed behind the young queen, who was now the only queen, into the part of the palace where lay the power of the living.

The palace had been secured. There seemed to be more Greens than the queen had commanded formerly, and this puzzled me until I studied their tunics. Some looked very new; others seemed ill-fitting. These soldiers must be former Blues, either recruited secretly ahead of Queen Eleanor's death or else newly turncoat this afternoon.

For the first time I saw the palace throne room. It was no more lavish than Queen Caroline's former presence chamber, and just as bare. However, it was so much vaster that I wondered how the palace could contain it. This, then, was why the city outside the palace walls had been squeezed into a narrow circle of jammed alleys and temporary tents. This enormous expanse of polished stone floor, vaulted ceiling two storeys above us, walls hung with so many candelabra that the windowless room seemed full of light. Despite the change in the weather, the throne room was cold; no fireplaces could take the chill off such a vast space. The only furnishing was a raised dais at one end, holding a carved throne. The queen, a white fur cape thrown over her dress of jewelled green velvet, sat on the throne and received her new subjects.

Queen Caroline's ladies watched, wide-eyed and pale, from the left of the throne, her courtiers from the right. One by one, the old queen's advisers came before her in the huge empty space, knelt and removed their blue robes. Each said, 'I swear fealty to Queen Caroline, and to her alone, unto death.' Then each, shivering with cold, was handed a new robe of green to put on over his undertunic. There were not very many advisers. Those who had refused the oath must have been imprisoned. By tomorrow, I guessed, they would be dead.

At a gesture from the queen, Lord Robert mounted the dais and knelt. She smiled at him, but her face was very pale, and only I heard the words she whispered to him. 'The army?'

'No,' he said.

Her face did not change, by what effort of will I could only imagine. Lord Robert resumed his place and the procession of advisers continued.

'I swear fealty to Queen Caroline, and to her alone, unto death.'

No loyalty from the Blue army. I realized what that meant. The word the captain had spoken – *poisoner* – was what the army believed of Queen Caroline. The Blues did not see her as the natural successor to Eleanor; they saw her as the unnatural murderer of their queen. And they would fight to avenge that murder. The Greens had been able to secure the palace only because the main part of the old queen's army was housed outside the city. The great gates to both the island and the palace had been shut and bolted and archers set on the ramparts. No one could either enter or leave.

We were at war, and under siege.

The procession seemed endless. After the advisers came Queen Eleanor's ladies and courtiers. These too were far fewer than I guessed there had once been. Some seemed to choke on their words. Then the physicians, musicians, stewards, couriers, pages. The boys, some as young as eight, knelt before the queen, who wore on her head only a simple circlet of gold. Tomorrow the safe would be broken open through hours of patient labour and the Crown of Glory claimed, but tonight the oaths went forward without it. Loyalty, like the palace itself, was being secured. And perhaps as precariously.

'I swear fealty to Queen Caroline, and to her alone, unto death.'

The serving men, the ladies' maids, the gardeners. How long could the Green guard hold the capital against the entire Blue army? But for tonight the queen sat on the throne and heard everyone in the palace promise to die with her if necessary.

'I swear fealty to Queen Caroline, and to her alone, unto death.'

Last came the cooks, the laundresses, the seamstresses, the stable boys and grooms, the kitchen maids, all kneeling in batches to swear. I saw Joan Campford, her rough red hands swollen with winter chilblains. And later it was Maggie, who sank to her knees with a grace and dignity that might almost have matched the queen's own. She did not glance at me. I wondered about her brother Richard, soldier of the Blues, but I could tell nothing from Maggie's face.

'I swear fealty to Queen Caroline, and to her alone, unto death.'

And then it was over, and nearly midnight. The queen's court moved their possessions into the rooms beside the throne room, the rooms that had been the old queen's. Everything was bustle and confusion. I found Cecilia, in tears as she followed the harassed steward to her new chambers.

'O Roger, it's all so different! I don't know what to do! I wish the old queen hadn't—'

'Hush,' I said quickly. 'It's all right, my lady.'

'Why does your voice sound like that?'

'I bit my tongue.'

'I can barely understand you. Oh, what will I do now?'

'You will go where you are told and serve Her Grace as you always have.'

'Yes.' Her eyes darted wildly around. 'I'm to share a

146

room with Jane Sedley. The ladies on ... on this side of the palace shared, because there were so many. And now we have with us the Blue ladies as well as the Green.'

'They are all Green now,' I reminded her.

'Yes, of course. Only it's so ... so strange!'

'My lady,' said Cecilia's serving woman, the young and timid girl who had replaced Emma Cartwright. Her arms were full of gowns. 'Where shall I put these?'

'I don't care! Roger, what will happen? They say the old queen's army is outside the gates and they will starve us out! Or worse!'

'Go to bed, my lady. Her Grace will need you in the morning.'

'I—'

'Goodnight, my lady.'

'Goodnight.' She went, and it was only later that I realized I had been giving orders to a lady. I, the queen's fool.

No one had thought to assign me a place to sleep. I found the queen's new presence chamber, which actually looked small after the throne room. I knew the single guard posted in the room. He looked grim and would answer none of my questions, but he admitted me to the deserted outer chamber. No guard here – I guessed they were needed to defend the palace if the Blues should attack. There was no curtained alcove off these rooms, but a great fire had burned in the fireplace at some point during this terrible day, and the embers still gave off a faint warmth. I curled up beside the ashes. My tongue hurt. My arm hurt. My heart hurt.

It was a long time before I could sleep. When I did, I dreamed I journeyed to Soulvine Moor. It looked exactly like the country of the Dead, and my mother sat there in her lavender dress, silent and unmoving, beside the old dead queen.

17

'We will run out of food.'

'The army has seized all the horses.'

'They will burn us all at once, in a huge fire where all the villagers can see.'

'The servants will hide the food from us.'

'We will have to eat rats. They did that in the old times during sieges.'

'They will take the city and burn us as traitors.'

The ladies and courtiers whispered among themselves. Now there was no dancing, no gaming, no flirting. The Blue army was camped along both banks of the river. Or so I was told by those who had climbed the stairs to the windy ramparts atop the city walls. Below, I attended the queen. She spent all morning with her advisers, and all afternoon moving around the palace.

'There is no meat left in the kitchens,' the people whispered to each other.

'The servants are hoarding the food somewhere.'

'My mother will be desperate for news of me; she's all alone in the country house.'

'My father—'

'My son and his family—'

'Burn us alive—'

'No fruit left—'

Only the queen remained serene. She did not ration the food left in the larders, the wheat stores, the cellars. No barges came to the kitchen docks, and in spring food always ran low, consumed over the winter. By the fifth day of the siege we ate bread and cheese and ale, but we ate fully. No one understood this, least of all me. Why didn't the queen count and ration the remaining food? We would run out soon enough, because of course the servants must be hiding some of it against starvation. I would have. I hoped Maggie was.

This was when I saw the cellars for the first time, along with everywhere else in the palace. I accompanied her every afternoon. 'Keep your eyes open, Roger,' she told me. 'Remember everything. I don't know what I may need you to do in the future.' She had dropped all requirements that I act the fool, or that I make witty comments. This was good, because all wit had deserted me.

Everywhere we went, the queen, magnificently dressed and accompanied by a guard of tall handsome Greens, smiled at her new subjects and studied them and let them wordlessly know that she ruled here now. To the still rooms. The laundries. The kitchens. The guard rooms and stables and servants' halls, of which there were more than I had known. The courtiers' chambers. Despite the siege, masons had been set to work in the palace, tearing up the blue tiles in the royal courtyards and replacing them with green. When they ran low on green tiles, they interspersed them with white or cream, creating intricate patterns. In the laundries blue cloth was dyed green: bed hangings, table linen, livery, cushions, saddle blankets. Seamstresses worked feverishly to create enough emerald-coloured tunics, gowns, doublets. In the royal dining hall even the blue glass plates, imported from some distant land, had been packed away in straw, replaced by delicate white plates decorated with graceful green vines. The queen, gracious and smiling and tireless, oversaw it all, and I went with her.

We went too to the royal nursery, where for the first time I saw the queen's heir, three-year-old Princess

Stephanie, with her six-year-old brother. The queen's older son, Prince Percy, had been sent away over the winter to be a page in the house of a Green noble, as was the custom. The little princess was thin and pale; she did not look strong. A grave grey-eyed child without her mother's beauty, she had her grandmother's long face and wide jaw. In fact, she looked so much like a sickly, miniature version of the dead queen that I was startled. What did Queen Caroline think of that? I couldn't tell. She kissed her children, held them, played with them, and I could not tell if it was genuine mother love, or the regard of a master chess player for her pawns.

I could not tell anything the queen might be thinking. She was as contradictory as ever: serene in the face of civil war, of siege, of starvation. Calculation in her eyes as she assessed her new realm. Kind to everyone in the palace, all those terrified servitors sinking into deep and reverential curtseys even as many believed that she had poisoned their monarch. The one place I did not go with Queen Caroline was the dungeons, if they existed. And if they did not, then where were all the advisers and soldiers who had refused to take the oath of fealty? Were they already in the country of the Dead?

No, I did not understand the queen. Beautiful, cruel, kind, ambitious and, most of all, unruffled. Even as the food ran out and the Blue army lined both banks of the river and the ladies-in-waiting whispered in terror.

'Starve us out—'

'Burn us all—'

'What is she *doing*?'

Then, on the sixth day, Lord Robert found us as we made our afternoon tour. We were crossing an exquisite courtyard, larger than most, with three circular flower beds. Tiny green shoots pushed up through the black soil of the beds. The air was soft and sweet. The queen had left off her furs and I my hooded cloak. My face had been freshly dyed yellow just that morning; my wit was no longer required, but my appearance as the queen's fool still was. Lord Robert was in full armour.

He knelt, straightened and said simply, 'They're here.'

She said sharply, 'Where?'

'Within sight of the palace, obviously, since the lookout on the tower saw them. How else would I know?'

'Don't speak to me in that tone, my lord!'

'I beg Your Grace's pardon.'

Tension crackled between them like heat.

He said, 'Your Grace, may I—'

'No. You may not. I need you here.'

'Your Grace, I am commander of the army! My place is out there, leading!'

'No one can be "out there" until the siege is lifted – you know that. And your place is beside me. Go observe from the tower, and bring me report of the battle.'

Battle? What battle? What was happening?

Lord Robert bowed stiffly and stalked off.

'Come, Roger,' the queen said. 'We return to my rooms.'

'Your Grace.'

'Yes? What is it?' She walked so swiftly that those we passed barely had time to fall to their knees, collapsing like so much scythed grain.

'You said "report of the battle". Who is fighting outside the palace?'

She spared me a glance, never breaking stride. 'Who do you think is fighting?'

I had begun this conversation; I must finish it. 'Not our Greens against the Blues; we have not enough soldiers. So—'

'Yes?' We entered the outer chamber and the queen's ladies sank to the floor in puddles of green silk.

'— we must have allies to fight with us?'

'You are waking up, Roger. Lucy! Catherine! I want you!'

The ladies of the bedchamber shot to their feet and followed the queen into her privy chamber. As soon as the door closed, the rest of the women seized upon me. Cecilia cried, 'Roger! What's happening?'

'There is a battle being fought,' I said.

'Is the palace being attacked?' Cecilia's green eyes were so big there seemed no room in her face for anything else. She looked drawn, even gaunt, and the clutch of her little hand on mine was icy cold.

'Not yet, my lady.'

'Cecilia,' Lady Margaret said, 'come at once. This fool can tell us nothing, and we have our orders.'

I said, 'What—'

'We are to get dressed in our best gowns and go to the throne room,' Cecilia told me as Lady Margaret turned stern with the other young ladies. 'A page ran to tell us so but he did not say why. Is the queen going to surrender? Will we all be taken prisoners by the Blues?'

'No, my lady.' Would we?

'Cecilia! Come!'

They bustled away. The outer chamber was empty except for two Green guards who looked as uneasy as me. I waited, as I had done so often before. Sometimes my whole life in the palace seemed to consist of either waiting or fear. Or both together.

If the queen did indeed have allies arriving, it could only be the army of her sister-in-law Queen Isabelle. Isabelle's mother had died shortly after the wedding, and Isabelle had been crowned. How many soldiers would she send? If the Blues defeated them and took the palace, what would happen to me? Would they think it worthwhile to hang a fool? And what would they do to the

152

queen? They could murder her and put Princess Stephanie on the throne, with a loyal Blue adviser to rule for the child. If there were any loyal Blue advisers left alive. And what would happen to Lady Cecilia? Surely they wouldn't charge a girl as foolish, as innocent, as lovable as my lady with treason? It would be like killing a kitten.

People killed unwanted kittens all the time.

The privy chamber opened. The queen wore the green-jewelled gown she had worn six nights ago to receive the oaths of fealty, but this time she had on her head the Crown of Glory, broken out of Osprey's iron keeping-box. Heavy beaten gold, the crown was set with jewels of every hue, a rainbow of the colours of every queen who had ruled The Queendom. Emeralds, sapphires, rubies, amethysts, diamonds. Onyx, beryl, opal, topaz. Jewels I could not name, neither the stone nor the colour. How could the queen's slender neck even hold up such heaviness? But it did, and she swept past me, her ladies scrambling to hold up her long velvet train, her guard falling into step before and after her. She looked as if neither defeat nor surrender could ever be possible.

'Come, Roger,' she threw at me over her shoulder. 'It won't be long now.'

We waited in the throne room, and it was clear from the faces who knew what we waited for, and who only conjectured.

The advisers knew. They stood in their long green robes to the right of the throne, a group of old men with carefully blank faces and apprehensive eyes. The courtiers and ladies did not know. Grouped at the left, the young men and women in all their finery looked like a flock of alert peacocks. Loveliest among them was Cecilia, in a robe of green silk that exposed most of her small firm breasts. She shivered, but not with cold. The vast throne room was chill as ever, but braziers must have been lit under the dais. Heat radiated from the throne as if the queen herself had fire within her. She sat straight-backed, head held high, and waited.

And waited.

And waited.

I grew stiff, crouched on the dais steps. Cecilia's gown rustled and swayed; she was shifting from one small foot to the other. Finally the door was flung open and Lord Robert, in full armour, strode into the room. The armour, like Lord Robert himself, looked clean and unused, not at all as if he had been fighting a battle. It seemed to take him for ever to cross that vast floor. His boots rang on the stone, the only sound. Queen Caroline half-rose, then lowered herself again to her throne, regal and imperious. Lord Robert knelt.

'Rise.'

'Your Grace. It is as you predicted. The countryside around the island is ours. The Blues gave way with only a brief fight, and the others stand at the west bridge.'

She didn't move or speak, but something flashed from her, like unseen lightning.

'It is my duty as commander,' Lord Robert continued, 'to tell you that this Blue retreat is only temporary. Their army is startled and confused, and they lost soldiers in skirmishes at the bridges. But the main portion of the Blue army was not there, and they will regroup and continue the siege. To bring the others inside—'

'Bring them in,' she said. 'Open the west gates to the city and the palace.'

Lord Robert snapped his fingers. A courier set off at an all-out run – running from a throne room, with his back to the queen! She said nothing, however, and her eyes gleamed as bright as her crown. Lord Robert moved to

154

stand with her advisers. He looked odd there, an armoured soldier in the strength of his prime amid the old men in their green robes. I saw his big hard hands clench into fists.

I was confused. The west gate? Queen Isabelle's army would have marched down from the north. To the west lay only inland villages rising to high jagged mountains. If there were queendoms beyond those mountains, I had never so much as heard their names. But I remembered all the strangers that had come and gone from Queen Caroline's former rooms, in the long weeks before the old queen died. They'd all had the look of hard riding, even though a few – clearly couriers – had been barely more than boys.

It was a boy that first entered the throne room.

No older than I, he walked alone across that vast expanse of floor, his head held high. No one spoke or moved or, it seemed, even breathed, and the only sound was the boy's boots ringing on the stone. Heavy boots, with strange metal caps on the toes. He wore no coat – unless he had left it outside the room – but only tunic and breeches of rough brown cloth and, on his head, a wreath of dead twigs, like a mockery of the flower wreath a girl might wear at midsummer. No sword or other weapon. As he approached the throne, we could all see that his forehead bore strange markings of red dye.

He came right to the foot of the throne steps, and *did not kneel*.

A murmur ran over the courtiers, like wind in a field. The boy turned towards them. Lady Cecilia, standing closest to him, shrank back, and I felt my muscles tense, ready to spring if he touched her. But instead he turned, walked to the left of the dais and faced away from the throne. He began to sing.

His voice filled the entire chamber. Powerful, sweet

and yet guttural, the song seemed to swell to the vaulted ceiling with strange words.

> *'Ay-la ay-la mechel ah!*
> *Ay-la ay-la mechel ah!*
> *Bee-la kor-so tarel ah!*
> *Ay-la ay-la mechel ah!'*

Now two more figures appeared in the doorway, and these were not boys but men. Warriors. They wore tunics of some shaggy fur, metal-capped boots and helmets topped with twigs. Each man carried a cudgel, thick around as my leg, and each had a strange metal stick slung across his shoulder. Knives at their leather belts, but no swords. The pair advanced, singing along with the boy in deep unmusical voices and beating their cudgels upon the floor as they advanced.

> *'Ay-la ay-la mechel ah!*
> *Ay-la ay-la mechel ah!*
> *Bee-la kor-so tarel ah!*
> *Ay-la ay-la mechel ah!'*

Halfway down the room, the two warriors parted. One marched to and along the left wall, the other the right, stopping several feet from the dais. Two more marched behind them, and two more behind those, and yet two more. All of them sang the guttural song, and pounded their cudgels upon the floor, and stood to line the walls. And still they came, more and more and more, until the entire length of the huge room was lined with warriors. And still more came.

And more.

And more.

They formed double lines down the room, triple lines,

four abreast. The noise was deafening. The queen's advisers glanced sideways at each other. And still they came.

> *'Ay-la ay-la mechel ah!*
> *Ay-la ay-la mechel ah!*
> *Bee-la kor-so tarel ah!*
> *Ay-la ay-la mechel ah!'*

Now the room was full of men pounding their cudgels on the floor, singing their wild rough song. Only an aisle remained, stretching from throne to door, and down it came six more boys with crowns of twigs and red-tattooed foreheads. Three beat drums and three played string instruments that sounded like cats being strangled. Behind them walked more men, two abreast, with short capes made of grey feathers. These wore their knives in elaborately beaded belts, with more beads braided into their long hair. The musicians – if you could call them that – joined the singer beside the queen's courtiers, and the warrior captains parted to join their men. The singing grew in intensity, the cat-strangling lutes were plucked faster, the cudgels beat in double time on the stone.

> *'Ay-la ay-la mechel ah!*
> *Ay-la ay-la mechel ah!*
> *Sol-ek see-ma taryn ah!*
> *Ay-la ay-la mechel ah!'*

A single figure appeared in the doorway and walked towards the throne. As he advanced, the warriors fell to one knee before him, as they had not knelt to the queen. Lord Robert's face darkened and his hand moved towards his sword. The chieftain was huge, a giant with sun-leathered skin and dark hair going grey, its braids twined with beads. His cape was made of feathers of every possible bird, of all possible colours. At the exact moment that the chieftain reached the dais, all noise stopped.

He gazed at the queen and went down on one knee. But he did not bow his head, and his gaze met hers with a proud vitality. He had the bluest eyes I had ever seen, as if pieces of sky had been beaded into his head. I couldn't look away from that fierce blue, and for a long moment neither could she. Whole rivers flowed between them.

Then he had risen and was saying something in his guttural language. A man stepped from behind the throne. I recognized him: the small sour-faced man in black velvet who had come to the queen all those weeks ago. He was no less sour-faced now. He knelt, rose and said, 'Your Grace, Solek son of Taryn comes to your court, as agreed, to offer the services of his army, for the payment agreed.'

Queen Caroline said, 'Tell him he is welcome to the court of The Queendom.'

The small man translated.

She continued, 'Lord Solek is—'

'They do not use that title, Your Grace,' the small man said.

He had interrupted the queen. One never interrupted the queen. But she let it pass, her eyes still locked with the stranger's. 'He is in my queendom now, with the title I choose to give him. Tell him that I will have rooms prepared for him and his captains in the palace, but that I deeply regret we are unable to house his entire army.'

After the translation the stranger gave a great shout of laughter, as startling in that formal room as a rampaging bear, followed by a short speech.

The translator said, 'The chieftain says that of course his men will camp beyond the island, and he with them.'

I thought of the villages that surrounded the island,

each with its own neat cottages, its little green, its sheep and chickens and pretty girls. These savage warriors – so many of them! and perhaps even more outside – were the roughest-looking men I had ever seen. They scarcely looked like men at all, with their shaggy fur tunics, huge cudgels pounding like hoofs on the floor, feathered capes and helmets. And what were those metal sticks each man wore on his shoulder?

The queen said, her voice now lowered so that even I, closer than anyone except Lord Robert, had to strain to hear. 'Eammons ... is there a polite way to tell him that the village cottages – and the village women – are not available to his men?'

'No,' Eammons said sourly. 'There is no way. It would be a gross insult.'

Lord Robert said to the translator, 'These savages will be of no use to us if they defeat the Blues but turn the queen's own subjects against us!' His voice held a strange satisfaction, which in turn angered the queen.

She rose from her throne and descended the steps. Immediately all of us – but none of the savages – fell to both knees. She stood beside the chieftain in her green gown, its train spreading up the steps behind her, as the translator hissed, 'Don't take his hand, Your Grace! For the sake of heaven, do not touch him!'

She did not. Beside him, she looked tiny, although she was not a small woman. In a low intimate voice she said, 'Translate what I say exactly, Eammons. *Exactly*, word by word. 'Lord Solek, I will speak frankly. Please forgive my ignorance of your customs. Your soldiers are manly and strong. My villagers are gentle. Does your soldiers' discipline and restraint match their strength and their ability in war?"

'Your Grace—'

'Translate!'

159

He did. Lord Solek's blue eyes darkened and his face went hard. I took a step back, away from that look. Lord Robert's hand went to his sword, but the queen did not flinch. Instead she looked up at him with a look I had never seen on her face – helpless, naked, feminine appeal. And then she curtseyed.

A gasp went up from the advisers, the courtiers. Lord Robert put out one hand, as if to yank her up from obeisance to anyone – she, the queen! But she had already straightened, her curtsey done but her beseeching look going on, eyes fastened onto Lord Solek, until he threw back his head and again gave that huge rough laugh. He turned to his captains and gave a long speech. When he was done, each captain raised his left fist aloft for a moment before letting it drop.

'He said,' Eammons reported, 'that his men will stay away from your villages.'

Lord Solek had said a great deal more than that. The promise of punishments if his savages did not obey? Of rewards if they did? And what had Queen Caroline promised in order to bring Lord Solek's army here in the first place?

She said, 'Tell Lord Solek that he is bid to come to dinner in my rooms at sunset. With whatever of his chiefs it is customary to bring. We have much to discuss.'

And still her dark eyes held his blue ones, and neither looked away.

18

The bustle over the dinner was enormous. It turned out that before the siege began the queen had planned ahead and ordered certain foodstuffs sequestered for this entertainment. But it was only the beginning of spring and there were no fresh vegetables or fruit, only dried. No fresh meat, only salted or smoked. And the appalled cooks had only a few hours to prepare. 'What do they even eat?' one wailed. 'They are savages!'

'I heard they eat roasted rocks,' quavered a frightened kitchen maid, and the cook slapped her.

The queen had sent me to the kitchens on an errand. She was closeted in her privy chamber with Lord Robert and her three most important advisers, none of whom looked happy. Lord Solek had marched out with his men, singing and pounding their cudgels on the floor as when they marched in. The pages had all been commandeered by the frantic steward, who was trying to have tables set up, entertainments arranged and precedence established in the same few hours that had upset the cooks. Ladies, courtiers and musicians went from victims of siege to performers in a masque that must be instantly created. The palace seethed with hectic activity and with terrified conjecture about the 'savages'. And I had been sent to the kitchens to tell the head cook that the translator, Eammons, had a delicate stomach and could eat only a few slices of chicken and a little thrice-ground bread.

'Chicken! There are no chickens left, boy! And where am I to get thrice-ground bread!' She reached out to cuff me, presumably because she could not cuff Eammons. I danced away from her and went to find Maggie.

She was frantically pouring wine over dried apples while kneading biscuits with her other hand. 'How am I to make a dessert without sugar?'

'You'll manage. Did—'

'Go away, Roger. I haven't time for you. No, wait. What news? No, wait. Why are these apples so *mealy*?'

I knew more about girls than I once had. Lady Cecilia was responsible for that. Deftly I elbowed Maggie aside and began kneading the bread myself, freeing her to concentrate on adding spices to the apples. I said, 'The savages are camped on the north bank of the river, in Fairfield and beyond. All the villagers have left Fairfield, the soldiers on the ramparts saw them flee. So far the savages have not harmed anyone. The Blues are camped on the plain beyond Darton Ford: they can barely be seen from even the top of the tower and nobody thinks there will be any more fighting until tomorrow morning at the earliest. What of your brother?'

'With the Blue army.'

'Have you heard any more than I just said?'

'Don't knead so hard, Roger; it's bread not stone! I heard only that the first battle hardly deserved the name. The savages marched in, and when the Blue archers let loose their arrows, the savages used their fire-sticks and—'

'Their what?'

'Don't stop kneading! Have you never before made bread? The savages have new weapons. Fire comes from the end of their metal sticks – fire and small fast projectiles they call *bullets*. A few men died and then the Blues ran away.'

I had never heard of such weapons. From her face, neither had Maggie. She whipped sweet cream as if it had sinned, her face pulled taut with wonder and fear. But, being Maggie, she kept talking.

'The Blues will regroup, everyone says so. Now you tell me: what has the queen promised the savages in return for their help in securing The Queendom?'

'I don't know.'

She looked at me straight. Her fair hair straggled down her face, and her grey eyes were serious. She looked pretty. Not as beautiful as my Cecilia of course, but still . . .

What was I doing thinking about girlish beauty *now*? I said, 'I really don't know what the queen promised. But I'm to be at the dinner, and perhaps I'll find out then.'

She stared at me. 'You're to be at the dinner? The dinner for the savage lords?'

'Yes.' And then it was all between us again: what I had told her about crossing over, about my mother dying on Soulvine Moor. She did not trust me. I could feel her withdrawal, sure as a swift tide.

'I have work to do, Roger.'

'I'm going,' I said coldly. Damn her, I was doing the best I could. And now I knew why Queen Caroline had looked so serene all the days of the siege. She knew what powerful new weapons her savage allies would bring. I wanted to go up on the ramparts or even climb the bell tower, to see the situation for myself, but I didn't dare. I still must go only where the queen sent me. I was still the queen's fool.

The dinner for Lord Solek and his captains took place in the queen's new presence chamber, which had been transformed. Gone were the cool blues and greys of Queen Eleanor. The stewards, rushing around shouting and cursing all afternoon, had remade the royal chambers. Green cloth hung on the walls, where cloth had never been before, gathered into draperies and festoons tied with jewelled green ribbons. Lest the place look too feminine, shields hung between the velvets and satins. The high table was draped in green damask, and at it sat the queen, Lord Robert, her three most trusted advisers, Lord Solek and three of his chieftains, and a translator. Also, to my surprise, three-year-old Princess Stephanie. Purple was the princess's colour and her gown was a miniature of her mother's but with a much higher neckline. She sat pale and grave, and on her lank hair was a small golden circlet set with a single amethyst.

The rest of the court sat at lower tables in the chamber, all below a hastily constructed platform on which the masque would occur. I, with the Green guard, stood behind the high table, reconciled to being unfed. 'I shall want you tonight,' the queen had said. 'Listen to everything.'

As it happened, there was little information to listen to. The queen and her advisers began by offering the usual compliments to the visitors, all through Eammons, but compliments seem to make Lord Solek and his chiefs uncomfortable, and no compliments were offered in return. So instead the queen fell into a game, asking the names of things in the savage language, repeating them prettily and teaching Lord Solek our words.

'And what do you call this, my lord?' She pointed to the wine in her goblet, turning the stem slightly to make the wine swish and the candlelight flash fire from her jewelled rings. The bud of her sixth finger she kept curled under, hidden in her palm.

'*Kekl.*' It was like the grunt of a boar, and just as wild. Lord Solek had eaten and drunk prodigiously, but he did not seem affected by the wine.

'*Kekl.*' From her, it was music. He gave his great laugh. The advisers smiled with strain. Lord Robert did not smile. He had not smiled all evening.

164

'And this?' A soft hand fingering the goblet suggestively.

'*Vlak.*'

'*Vlak*,' she repeated. '*Kekl* in *vlak*.'

He was charmed, almost against his will. The heat that I had felt between them from the first glance had been no more than that, the heat of man and woman. But now he gazed at her, almost puzzled, and I wondered what the women of his own country were like, in that unknown place far to the west across the distant mountains.

Lord Robert drank more.

'Wine,' Lord Solek repeated, making the word guttural. 'Queen Caroline.'

'Yes,' she said, and their eyes locked, watched by her uneasy advisers and his wary chieftains. It was a relief when the entertainment began.

Lady Cecilia was in it, and it was shocking. Not to the visitors, who watched in polite incomprehension, but to the court. Gone were the stately dances that the old queen had insisted on. Cecilia, Lady Jane, Lady Sarah, my lords Thomas and George and Christopher – all of them performed *village dances*, as if they were peasants. They sashayed and roistered and kicked jewelled slippers and polished boots. The women swished their skirts with abandon so that ankles and even knees were revealed, and the men swung the girls so high their feet left the floor. The musicians played the lively village tunes, although without the bawdy lyrics. There was supposed to be a masque too, but the players never got to it because after the second shocking dance Lord Solek leaped from the high table to the floor below and bellowed something.

Eammons choked out, 'He says he will ... will dance with Your Grace.'

Dead silence.

No one asked the queen to dance; it was her prerogative to do the choosing. Not even Lord Robert could transgress that rule. But that had been the old dances, the old court. And the savage chieftain stood on the polished stone floor, his hand outstretched towards the dais, his brilliant blue eyes both an invitation and a challenge.

Queen Caroline gathered her train over her arm and descended to the floor. To the musicians she said, 'Play.'

They were almost too shocked to obey. The piper's lips were stiff with horror; they could barely curve around his instrument. But somehow a tune was started and taken up. The queen and the savage danced.

He was quick, with an athlete's grace, and the peasant dances were of course much simpler than the endless complicated figures of court dances. Lord Solek did not do too badly. She flowed like water around him, looking small next to his bulk even in her high-heeled slippers, and when he swung her high at the end of the dance she seemed to float towards the ceiling. Then she was sliding down against his body until her feet were again on the floor, and again there was silence. No one dared move or speak.

'All dance,' the queen said.

Panic, but controlled panic. More courtiers and ladies scrambled up from the tables, down from the masque platform. The savage's three chieftains leaped up and each seized a lady, all of whom looked terrified. Lady Cecilia cowered in Lord Thomas's arms, as far away from the savages as she could get. And so they danced.

It went on for an hour. The little princess was taken away to bed by her nurse. The stewards brought more wine, more ale. The savage captains performed a 'dance' together from their own country, a brutal leaping towards each other, knives drawn, in a three-way mock combat that I thought any moment would become the real thing.

166

This was dancing? But when it was over, they laughed and clasped hands and knelt before Lord Solek, who cut each of them lightly on the left cheek with his own knife. Drops of blood dripped into their beards. All three laughed again, and the queen smiled. And not even I, who had studied her day after day, month after month, who had done for her what no one else in The Queendom could do, could tell if the smile was emotion or calculation. Or both.

Then the entertainment was over. The savages left the palace. Courtiers, ladies, advisers retired, and the servants began to clear the debris from the feast. Green guards admitted me to the queen's outer chamber, where I still slept on the hearth. I crept cautiously through the dark room, holding my candle aloft. But a sliver of light came also from the privy chamber beyond. The door was open a crack, and within Lord Robert was shouting.

'— bad enough that you promised him the princess for his barbaric son, but to also—'

'That is not your business.'

'— promise the ships and their captains, and—'

'I am doing what is best for The Queendom!'

'You are selling him The Queendom! Do you really think you can control him, after he defeats the Blues? We'll be left with nothing but his army of savages, which *he* controls! Those damn *guns*—'

It was a strange word; I had never heard it before. But I had heard the queen's tone before, and I knew that Lord Robert ignored it at his peril.

'I will not let anyone else control *my* queendom, Lord Robert.'

'And how do you think you can stop him? By taking him to your bed?

'How dare you!'

'You were sniffing at him like a bitch after hound spoor!'

The sharp crack of hand on flesh. She must have slapped him. Appalled, I crept quietly back towards the far door, extinguishing my lantern. In the dark I deliberately overturned a stool, cursing loudly.

'Who's there?' Lord Robert called. He flung open the privy-chamber door and peered, backlit, into the outer chamber.

'It's Roger the fool, my lord! I tripped while coming in.'

'The queen called, 'Come, Roger!'

I groped my way across the room and into the privy chamber, rubbing my shin and looking as foolish and unknowing as I could. Lord Robert glared at me. The queen looked composed, all her fury hidden. She said coldly, 'You are dismissed, Lord Robert.'

He had mastered himself, or her slap had mastered him. But he was not the actor she was, and the colour was high in his face as he made his bow and left. The queen smiled.

'What did you hear? Don't lie, Roger. Not to me.'

'I heard angry voices, but no words. And then I tripped over the stool.'

She studied me, and I could not tell if she believed me, or if she were just stowing away my lie for her own use in her own time. But all she said was, 'I have work for you now.'

'Yes, Your Grace.'

From the table she picked up small jewelled scissors, an elegant trifle for snipping thread. 'You will cross over and find one of the savage warriors dead from today's battle with the Blues. Only two were killed, both slain with lucky arrows from Blue archers before the Blues fled. From one of them you will find out two things.

First, you will say, *"Solek mechel-ah nafyn ga?"* And they will answer either *"Ven"* or *"Ka."* Listen while I say it again, and then say it back to me.'

Eammons must have taught her the words. How many words? Had the exchange of language with Solek at dinner been no more than pretty feminine play? It might be that she already understood much of what he said. Or not. We went over and over the words until the queen was sure I had them correct.

'Good, Roger. Second—'

'Your Grace, whatever those words mean, common soldiers . . .'

'Common soldiers know everything,' she said calmly. 'Just as kitchen maids do.'

Was that a reference to Maggie – even a threat? I couldn't tell. With the queen I could never tell. But I did not forget that this woman had poisoned her mother.

'Second, I want you to learn the secrets of that fire powder in the warriors' guns. How is it made? What must the tubes from which the projectiles fly be made of, and how?'

'Your *Grace*—'

She put her hand on my shoulder. 'This is important, Roger. The most important thing I have ever asked you to do. The fate of The Queendom may depend upon it. In a few more days more help will arrive for us, but meanwhile this will help me so much now. Can I rely on you?'

This was the queen at her warmest, her most persuasive. The threat and the warmth, all mixed together. I nodded, too frightened to find words. But she went on gazing at me, and so words were necessary. I tried to say, 'Yes, Your Grace,' but what came out was, 'What other help?'

She frowned, withdrew her hand and then laughed.

169

'Why not? It isn't really a secret. I'm sure conjectures are rife about the court. My brother's bride, Queen Isabelle, sends troops to reinforce Lord Solek's army. They are on their way already.'

Queen Isabelle. I had been right after all, or at least partially right. Queen Caroline had remained so calm during the siege because she had not one but two armies to oppose the Blues rising against her. And then I saw something else. Queen Isabelle's army, loyal to Queen Caroline through the marriage tie, would also ensure that Lord Solek could not take the throne for himself. She was not trusting in Lord Solek completely; she had other insurance. The Queendom did not really depend upon my report from the country of the Dead. However, she did not believe that either the savage chieftain – who, after all, did not know our language – or I would realize this.

It was the first time that I had ever thought, for so much as a second, that I had the upper hand with her.

'Are you ready, Roger? Then go now.'

She handed me the jewelled scissors. I thrust them into my soft underarm, just above the yellow velvet of my particoloured sleeve, and I crossed over.

Dirt in my mouth—

Worms in my eyes—

Earth imprisoning my fleshless arms and legs—

Then I was over, and something was very wrong.

19

As ever, the Dead still sat, or lay, gazing at nothing. But the *ground* was wrong. I was used to the way the country of the Dead stretched or shrank, so that what was close in the land of the living might here be miles off. But always the ground was the same, covered with low dense grass. Always the sky was an even featureless grey. Always the river meandered placidly, flat and slow.

Not now. The grass stood in uneven patches: some places high weeds, some low grass, some bare ground. The river had rocks in it and the water, flowing faster, eddied around the rocks in tiny bursts of white foam. The sky seemed darker. And beneath my feet the ground rumbled softly. What was happening in this place, where nothing ever happened?

Dazed, I began walking along the river. I saw no one I recognized. After a while the trees grew denser, making small groves and then patches of woods. The land grew wilder and I had to veer away from the water. I could not find the two dead savage warriors, and even if I had, they would have been sitting tranquilly, as unreachable as the rest of the Dead. In the land of the living the queen waited for my answer. What was I going to do?

All at once, a man jumped out at me from behind a thicket of bushes. I hit out at him and he hit back, his blow landing on my jaw, not hard enough to break it but hard enough to knock me down. It was a Blue soldier. As I lay panting for breath, he grabbed me by the arm and hauled me over to another soldier, who recognized me.

'Boy! Did the witch queen, that whore, send you back here again?'

It was the same soldier I'd spoken to on my last crossing. I stammered, 'Y-yes. She told me ... she told me to see how all goes in Witchland, until she herself can return.'

He spat, and his saliva made a little wet spot in the dirt. Had the Dead always been able to do that? But clearly this man still did not believe he was dead. The country of the Dead was filling up with people who, like Bat, did not believe they inhabited it and did not behave like the Dead. The rumbling of the ground, the wind and lightning and the darkening of the sky were all growing as the number of Blue soldiers increased from the battles on the other side. *I had caused this.* I, Roger Kilbourne, with the lies I had told about 'Witchland'.

'All here goes slow,' the Blue captain said to me. 'We have found no way to go back to The Queendom. Queen Eleanor remains under a spell, not eating nor sleeping nor talking. But there are more of us now, sent by the magic fire-sticks.'

'Fire-sticks?'

'Weapons that belched fire along with their magic, wielded by an army of male witches chanting foul spells.' He shuddered and spat again. 'It was a battle outside the city walls, won by darkest magic.'

The *guns*. Today's skirmish had been small; Lord Robert had said the major battle would take place tomorrow morning. And when those additional Blue soldiers died and arrived here, they too would be told this was Witchland. And so the number would grow of men who did not behave like the Dead because they did not know that they were.

'But we caught one of the witches,' the Blue said grimly. 'Just a while ago. And we will burn her.'

'You caught a witch?'

'Yes. Tell *that* to the witch queen when she snatches you back!' His face took on a strange expression, both horrified and sly. 'Does she strip you naked for her ensorcelling? And herself too?'

'No. Yes. No.' I scarcely knew what I was saying. They had caught a witch here, a woman, and were going to burn her? How? Who?

'Did the whore queen—'

'Can I see the witch?' I said. 'I could ... I could report back to the ... the whore queen that she does not have the control over Witchland that she thinks she does!'

He considered, nodded. The ground rumbled under my feet. 'Come then, boy.'

I followed him across the plain, away from the river, to another patch of woods. The leaves blew in a restless breeze, where there had never been breeze before. On the far side of the little woods were three dozen Blues, some standing and some sitting, none of them behaving like Dead. A captain held a writhing girl by the arms. It was Cat Starling.

'Let me go!' she shrieked. 'Let me go!'

Beside her was a great pile of dry wood, with a tall stake in the centre.

'Help!' Cat cried as I stood there, dumb. 'Help me, whoever you are! I've done nothing wrong! I – want – my – mother!'

'Tie her,' one of the Blues ordered.

The soldier dragged Cat, still screaming piteously for her mother, towards the stake. Another handed him two long strips of red wool. They had been torn from her skirt.

The Blue with me said, 'She has the sixth finger. Just like the witch queen who controls you. You'll enjoy this, boy.'

I found what brain I had left. 'Wait! I must talk with her first!'

The soldier scowled. 'Why?'

'To ... to ...' All at once country lore, heard at so many faires with Hartah, came back to me. And I thought too of Bat, from the *Frances Ormund*. '... to take the amulet from her! She will not burn so long as she has the amulet.'

'Aye, that's true,' said a Blue seated on the ground. 'My granny always said that. Their magic amulets protect witches from fire.'

'You're a brave man,' the soldier beside me said. He stepped back respectfully, and I walked to Cat.

'Give her to me.'

The captain did, and I wrapped one arm around her waist. She flailed and struck at me, but she was no fighter and I found I could hold her, although not without difficulty. That made her flail and shriek more. Under cover of her noise I spoke into her ear with all the urgency and authority I could.

'Cat Starling, a message from your mother – think of the river at Stonegreen. Think hard and wish yourself there. Do it *now*!'

She seemed to have not heard me. The soldiers looked at each other – was that suspicion on that face there? I was supposed to be looking for an amulet ... I thrust one hand into her blouse, between her breasts.

At the touch of her skin, I got an immediate and enormous erection. My member leaped like a startled dog. The effect on Cat was different. She brought up her nails and raked them across my face, crying, 'Mama!' The next moment she was flying through the air, faster than a bird, towards that distant place where Stonegreen should be.

The soldiers all cried out and fell on their faces. To tell

the truth, I shivered myself. Cat *looked* like a witch, flying away from us, even though I knew she was only a girl too simple-minded to know she was dead. Like Bat, who had flown up the cliff face because he wanted to. How much else could the Dead do? And when would these Blues discover it? One thing they could not do was kill each other again, but Cat hadn't known that. Her body would not really have burned. But I had at least spared her more terror.

How had she died, back there among the living? Burned there too, as a witch?

A Blue rose cautiously from the ground. 'Did you get the amulet, boy?'

'No. She was too quick for me.'

'Witches are,' another said grimly. He looked at my bleeding arm, my bruised jaw. 'Does the whore queen hurt you, boy?'

'Sometimes. I– Oh, she calls!' I put on the expression of a brave man suffering without noise, bit my tongue, and crossed back over just as the uneasy sky flashed with sudden, shocking lightning.

The queen sat at the carved table, holding a goblet of wine, her green-jewelled skirts spreading inches from where I lay on the floor. Unlike all my other returns, this time she seemed hesitant to touch me. She said, 'I watched, Roger, and all at once these long scratches appeared on your cheek.'

I put my hand to my Cat's scratches. My fingers came away bloody. So that was how it worked. Never before had anyone watched me while I sustained injury in that other country.

The queen said, 'Do you . . . do you want some wine?'

'Yes, please, Your Grace.'

I sat up slowly. My jaw ached where the Blue had hit

175

me and the touch of the goblet on my mouth hurt. But I drank all of the wine.

'Now tell me.' Her uncertainty had vanished, along with any concern for me. She was again the queen. 'What did the savages say to your question, "*Ven*" or "*Ka*"?'

I had listened carefully at dinner. *Ven* was yes, *ka* was no. I thought I knew what answer she wanted, and I gave it to her. 'They said "*Ven*," Your Grace. Lord Solek does ... he *does* seek your throne.'

Instantly she stiffened. 'How did you know that's what the words meant?'

Mistake, mistake. Muddled by the wine, by the pain in my jaw, by seeing Cat Starling again, I hadn't meant to reveal that I knew what Queen Caroline had asked the savage Dead, any more than I would reveal that I was making up the answer. But there was no help for it now.

'Your Grace ... at dinner with Lord Solek you named the word for "throne" to teach him, and he told you their word for "want" when he desired more ale. I'm sorry, I was standing so close ...'

'You have a good ear,' she said disapprovingly. 'I will remember that, Roger.'

'Yes, Your Grace.'

'And their answer to my question was "*Ven*." You are certain.'

'Yes, Your Grace.' My lies were multiplying like ants in spring. Once I would have been afraid to lie to the queen. But I didn't think this lie, warning her of danger from Lord Solek, would do me harm. She must anticipate that already. To say "*Ka*" would have been even worse. And she would not have believed me.

'And my second question? How is the fire powder made?'

'Your Grace, how could they tell me that? I pointed to their *guns*—'

'They have them still, over there?' It was the first time she had ever asked me anything about the country of the Dead except information about the land of the living. But her curiosity didn't last. It was a byway, and the queen's ambition kept her on the main road, always.

'They have their *guns*, yes,' I said. 'And they pointed to them and mimed for me that they do not make them, nor the fire powder. There are special craftsmen who do that, just as we have special craftsmen to do blacksmithing or to build ships.'

'That makes sense,' she said thoughtfully, and I breathed again. My jaw throbbed; I could feel it swelling. Cat's scratches burned on my cheek.

All at once the queen stood in a swirl of green silk. 'You've done well, Roger. Thank you. Here is a token of my appreciation.' She tugged a ring off her finger, a gold ring set with small emeralds, and gave it to me.

'Your Grace—'

'For you. Now go to bed. It's past midnight; you were gone longer than usual. The battle may begin as early as dawn, and I want you to watch it with me.'

'Me?'

'Who knows what you will learn? You are quicker than even I knew. Perhaps you aspire to take Eammons' place as translator.'

'No, no, of course not . . .'

'A joke, Roger.' But she was not smiling. Her dark eyes, with their flashes of submerged silver, measured me even as I stumbled from the room, one hand clutching the ring she had given me, my jaw bloating painfully with the blow I had taken in the country of the Dead. I was vulnerable there. I was vulnerable here.

I shut the door to the privy chamber quietly behind me, and went to another sleepless night beside the ashes.

20

The queen spoke truly. The battle began just before dawn.

I stood wrapped in my cloak on the palace tower. This was the only place on the island city taller than two storeys, and it was nothing more than the flat roof of the bell tower. The space was no larger than a small bedchamber, circled by a low stone parapet. A wooden trapdoor, now raised, covered the spiral stairs that led through the bell cavern and on down to the palace below. I stood jammed into the small area with Queen Caroline, a few advisers and the queen's personal guard of Greens.

No one spoke. A light breeze blew. The unrisen sun streaked the east with red, as if blood already flowed.

From here I could see the whole of the palace spread below, as I had never seen it before. Finally I saw that the shadowy maze of courtyards and buildings, so bewildering to walk through unguided, made symmetrical patterns. The whole was far larger than I had imagined, a vast and beautiful stone rose with too many petals to count. Every courtyard was now empty, the fountains stilled, the new green buds washed grey in the pale light. Soldiers of the Green stood atop the wall that enclosed the palace, with more soldiers on the ramparts circling the very edge of the island itself. Between lay the narrow ring of the tent city, as deserted as the courtyards. The great city gates were closed, soldiers posted at their bridges. Was Mother Chilton somewhere in one of those tents? Was Maggie in the kitchen, kneading bread for a victory feast if Lord Solek's army defeated the old queen's Blues?

And if the savage warriors did not win . . .

I could not think about that. My mind refused it. We who were closest to the queen would surely die, but I could not bear to think how. My mind could not keep its grasp on the possibilities, just as it was unable to grasp what lay beyond the stars now fading from the sky.

The last stars disappeared and the sun rose.

The Blue army stood massed on the northern plain, foot soldiers in the centre and archers to either side. The officers, on horseback, were scattered behind their cadres. A drum sounded a code I did not understand but which turned my blood to water: *Boom boom BOOM BOOM boom*.

The savages had crossed the river from Fairfield sometime during the night. They now stood on the Thymar's northern bank, directly below the city. Yesterday I had thought them so many, filling the throne hall with their chanting numbers and pounding their cudgels on the floor, but today they looked a pitifully small number compared to the Blues. They weren't massed in orderly rows either, but stood in uneven clumps, and as I squinted in the rising light, it seemed that many were *laughing*. Was that possible? Did men laugh at the start of battle? I had no way to know, but it seemed strange.

There was one cadre of Greens among the savages, Lord Robert's troops. He had left the rest inside the palace, where they would make a last stand to defend the queen if necessary. Lord Robert sat astride a huge black horse, a magnificent animal with green jewels on its bridle and the queen's emblem on its armour. His Greens stood behind him, silent and grim, their shields raised.

Lord Solek was there too, at the forefront of his own savages. Neither he nor they wore any more body armour than before, although they carried shields. The butt end of each man's *gun* rested lightly on the ground. To the left of the small army, I was surprised to see, stood the

179

musicians from yesterday, including the boy with twigs braided into his hair and two other young singers. As the sun streaked the sky with red that matched the paint on his face, he began to sing, and the musicians to play.

The weird instruments wailed away. The boys' powerful voices floated up on the dawn air. The savages chanted, marching forward in ragged lines, their guns held loosely in their hands. Across the plain, the drum changed rhythm – *BOOM BOOM BOOM* – and the Blues also marched forward.

The queen put both hands on the stone of the parapet, leaned forward and said something under her breath. A prayer? A curse? A threat?

The two armies marched towards each other.

When they were barely within bow range, the Blue archers fitted their arrows and let fly. A few struck savage soldiers, who went down. Lord Robert rose in his stirrups and waved his sword. I could not see Lord Solek, marching at the forefront of his men, but all at once a huge noise came, such a noise as had never rung on that plain. *Crack crack crack* ... The savages were making explosions with their *guns*.

Fire leaped from the end of each metal stick. Many *bullets* rang on the Blues' shields, hard enough to knock them down. As they scrambled back to their feet, a second wave of savages flowed to the front of their line and fired. I heard men screaming. Most did not get up. Smoke rose from the *guns*, forming a pall over the battlefield.

Now the savages broke ranks. A third wave parted, flowed to each side, and fired on the archers. The first wave of men had been doing something to their *guns*. Now they ran to the fore and fired again while the second group stood behind them and also did something to their weapons. Numbers of archers went down. Many of the savages dropped to one knee as they fired. And all the while, the shouting and yelling came from them, not all at once but from whoever was not firing, and the horrible music played beneath the island walls, and the savage boys sang as if to fill the world with harsh syllables.

The Blues broke. Whether it was by order or from fear, those left standing turned and ran. Their drums ceased. The savages pursued them – the big men were so fast! – and caught many. Knives flashed in the sun. Screams echoed across the plain, and the ground ran red.

I turned away. I, who could see, talk with, touch the Dead, was sickened by all this dying. I knew pain and fear, and easily I could imagine myself one of those on the battlefield.

The queen leaned farther over the parapet and watched it all, a tiny smile at the corners of her red lips.

The battle was quick. No, the battle went on for ever. Time itself was maimed and twisted, and still I could neither look closely, nor stay turned away. When the fighting was finally over, with some Blues escaped but more lying dead upon the ground, the savages marched back to the palace. Chanting, they carried their own dead – so many fewer than the Blues! – at their rear. Lord Solek marched in front. Way off to the side, Lord Robert with his Greens was in pursuit of the fleeing Blues. On the battlefield the bodies lay like abandoned dolls.

Finally – finally! – the boys stopped singing, the absence of their hoarse voices stilling the musicians as well. But nothing could silence the chanting soldiers.

'Come,' the queen said, standing very tall. 'My lords, come. To the throne room, to greet our victors.'

She had not named me, but I knew better than not to follow her. Still I lingered as long as I could on the tower roof. The great northern gate was already being raised to admit Solek's army, and in the distance, on the plain, the first of the villagers were running from hiding towards the fallen, who were their husbands and brothers and fathers. I could hear the cries of the grieving women, desperate and frantic, like birds lost far out at sea.

Inside the palace there was a repeat of yesterday's ceremony, gone terrible and bloody. Ladies, courtiers, advisers massed beside the dais. The queen sat tall on her throne. Lord Solek's army marched in, chanting, led by a chieftain negligently holding his broken arm. When Solek himself arrived, Eammons translated his words, delivered as simply as if he had been announcing that water is wet: 'We have won.'

But this time he did not kneel, and so Queen Caroline could not tell him to rise. Their eyes, one silver under black water and the other blue as sky, locked so fiercely that I had to look away.

'You have The Queendom's deepest thanks,' the queen said. 'And mine.'

I could take no more. No matter what it cost me, I could not listen to her words dance around her calculations, which must be paid for in other people's blood. Solek's army to defeat the Blues, and Queen Isabelle's army to defeat Solek's if he did not march her line. To gain Solek's help, the tiny Princess Stephanie sold into marriage before she turned four. And on the plain hundreds of Queen Caroline's own subjects dead or dying.

For the first time ever, I slipped away from the queen without her permission, sidling back along the edge of the dais until I was behind the crowd of courtiers, all eagerly pressing forward to watch the ceremony. I would watch it no longer, would help the queen no longer, would accept no more kindnesses from her, except when I must do these things to survive.

The wall behind the throne was hung with a tapestry of heavy embroidered silk. Noiselessly I slipped behind it, where a doorless arch gave servants access to the throne room. Someone followed me through to the narrow stone passage beyond the tapestry.

'Lady Cecilia!' I whispered. 'You should not be here!'

She caught my arm. 'What will happen now, Roger? Please tell me!'

'Nothing that will harm you, my lady,' I said. The light was dim, coming only from an alcove farther on. In the gloom I saw that Cecilia's face was ashen. Her teeth chattered, from either cold or fear.

'How can you know that? Will the savages take us all? All the women, I mean? Are we to be prizes for them?'

'No, no,' I said. 'The queen made Lord Solek promise that his men would leave our women alone.'

'That was the village girls. I mean us, the queen's ladies, are we to be marriage prizes? Like the princess?'

This had not occurred to me. Before I could answer, Cecilia sobbed, 'O Roger, I am so afraid!' She threw herself into my arms.

All thought fled my mind. She was so soft, so small, and she smelled so sweet. My arms were around her, her crying eyes pressed to my chest, and I held her. Just that: held her, and I wanted the moment to never end. Without knowing what I did, I lifted her face and pressed my lips to hers.

A moment of shocked stillness, and she pulled away. 'Roger!'

'My lady, oh, forgive me—' She could have me whipped, have me sent away from court—

But she was smiling. Tearfully, but still my kiss had wakened the coquette enough for her to mock me through tears. 'Really, I had no idea I was so irresistible.'

'I love you, my lady. I have loved you since the first moment I saw you.' It was true; never in my life had I meant anything more. I was dizzy with her, intoxicated with her.

Cecilia laughed. But a moment later she leaned close to me and whispered, 'Then if a savage comes for me, will you hide me? Will you, Roger? You must know all the palace hiding places.'

Would that I did! Were there hiding places, secret corridors? Of course there were, although I had never thought of this before. But this was a palace of secrets, of things hidden. Perhaps one reason the queen had kept me so close beside her was to keep me from discovering those hidden passageways, hidey-holes, escapes.

'I will serve you always, my lady!'

'How funny! You sounded almost like a courtier when you said that! You with that funny yellow paint on your face ... Hide me now, Roger. Show me where I can go to be safe from the savages!'

I would have given my left eye to be able to do that now. But I could not. So instead I tried to look important, and ended up merely feeling stupid. 'I ... I have an errand for the queen. I can't delay! But you will be safe, my lady, I promise you that! If it takes my life, I will keep you safe!'

She cocked her head to one side. 'I believe you, Roger.'

'Thank you, my lady!'

Why was I thanking her? I didn't know what I meant. Her nearness addled my brain. I blundered away down the corridor, towards the kitchens.

Maggie sat at the trestle table, her head in her hands. Only a few other servants remained in the kitchen. The fire was nearly out; nothing had been done about dinner. I stood beside her. 'Maggie?'

She looked up. No tears, but a depth of quiet suffering that Cecilia's hysteria could never match. That thought came, and was banished. 'Maggie?'

'My brother Richard,' she said. 'With the Blues.'

'I'm sorry. Maybe he escaped to—'

'Maybe. The others have already gone out onto the field,

all the servants, to find their dead. In a minute I must . . .
I thought that first I should . . . What do you want?'

I didn't know what I wanted, why I had come here, had
come to her. Before I could summon a fresh set of lies for
yet another girl, Maggie's eyes grew wide at something
behind me, and she leaped to her feet. I turned.

The boy with red twigs in his hair, the first singer, stood
in the doorway. Unarmed, he nonetheless stood without
fear. The few servants in the hall stiffened, and a middle-
aged cook hissed loudly.

The boy walked to Maggie, who was closest. He said in
a heavy guttural accent, 'Food. For Solek and queen.'

'We have nothing. No food,' Maggie said. And, indeed,
the kitchen looked as bare as if overrun by ravenous rats.
The siege, plus yesterday's feast, had all but emptied the
larders. Yet I guessed there was some food left in hoarded
stores. Queen Caroline planned too carefully to let her
capital starve.

'Food,' the boy repeated, but not demandingly. Up
close, he was extraordinarily handsome under the red
paint on his forehead and cheeks. Dark hair, eyes as blue
as Lord Solek's. He was taller than I, and broader. Did
Maggie notice that?

'No food,' she said. How did she dare?

The blue eyes searched her face, which had gone white
with defiance. His hand reached inside the shaggy fur
tunic to draw out something, which he held out to her.
'You eat,' he said gently.

It seemed to be a kind of dried meat mixed with berries.
The thing actually smelled good. Maggie stared at him.

'No food,' he said. 'You eat, girl.'

Something pounded behind my eyes. 'She doesn't
want your stinking savage rations!'

His gaze measured me, and I saw the moment he
dismissed me. Laying the food on the table beside Maggie,

he raised his voice loud enough for the rest of the frozen servants to hear. 'No food? We bring food. You eat.' He looked again at Maggie, then strode from the hall.

A man ran in from the opposite side, from the courtyard where the barges docked. 'The savages are letting us take our dead for burial. Walter ... I didn't find him. Maybe he got away!'

A middle-aged cook who'd just entered the hall spat, 'He was avenging Queen Eleanor, the true queen, and yet now he must run! Shame scars this day!'

Another woman shushed her, with a quick glance at me. Of course. The servants had all taken the oath of fealty to Queen Caroline, but not all of them had meant it. Some of the former Blues were blue still, despite their green tunics, and even some of Queen Caroline's most loyal servants had relatives among the Blues. Like this man, like Maggie.

The cook snapped, 'Begin work, all of you! Before long the queen will send someone for her dinner, and here the fire is nearly out! Bestir yourselves!'

I went out of the kitchen, leaving Maggie to her grief. I could do nothing to ease her. But I did not want to return to the queen, who had caused that grief. So I spent the entire afternoon prowling the palace, trying to discover secret passageways or hiding places. But, of course, if they were that easy to discover, they wouldn't be secrets. I found nothing.

But I learned much.

I wore my cloak, hood pulled low over the yellow dye on my face, and sat quietly in alcoves, pretending to wait for someone. In courtyards, pretending to weed spring beds. At docks, where barges held downriver by the siege were once again arriving with their loads for the palace. In the guardroom of the Green army. Even in the laundry, where Joan Campford gave me more yellow dye and treated me with a confused deference that upset us both. 'I never thought my laundress boy would be fool to the queen,' she said, shaking her head. 'Now get away with ye.'

At dusk, as the lanterns and candles were being lit in the palace, I made my way back to the queen's rooms, bracing myself for punishment for absenting myself. That was when I learned the most astonishing thing of all: there would be no punishment. The queen had not called for me, had not asked after me, had not even missed me. The presence chamber was empty except for the guards. In the outer chamber were no courtiers, only a little knot of the queen's ladies, sewing with a sobriety and earnestness totally foreign to all of them except Lady Margaret. With her sat Lady Sarah Morton, Lady Jane Sedley, two others. And Lady Cecilia, who did not greet me but whose eyes had lost none of their fright since this morning. No such fright, however, twisted the face of the wanton Lady Jane. She wore a small sly smile as she stitched away on a chair cushion, or what was supposed to be a chair cushion. Lady Jane, like Cecilia, was no needlewoman.

'Fool,' Lady Sarah said to me, 'what news?'

'It is nightfall,' I said, in my role as fool.

'I know that, idiot!'

'Then if you know, you don't need "knew".'

'No silly wordplay! Are the savage soldiers still in the palace or have they gone back to their camp!'

'Well, one is certainly here,' Lady Jane breathed, and rolled her eyes at the closed door to the privy chamber.

I said, 'Savage is as savage says.'

'He knows nothing,' said Lady Jane, her voice full of disgust. 'He's a *fool*, Sarah.'

Lady Margaret said, 'That's enough nasty chatter.' The others ignored her.

Lady Sarah said, 'The fool has eyes! And while we're stuck here, on guard—'

'Aye,' I said, 'He has I's, and you have you's, and they have theirs! Alas!'

'He knows nothing,' Lady Jane repeated, and turned her back on me.

She was wrong. I had learned much in my afternoon of prowling. No secret passages, but much else. I knew that Lord Solek's younger and handsomer soldiers had walked through the castle, learning it well but also making themselves agreeable. They had given away food – of which their army, on the move, could not have had very much. They had offered help. They had gestured admiration for much, and looted nothing. In the narrow ring of the city, to which shopkeepers were returning, the savages had bought items, paying in gold. Outside the palace, savages had helped carry the Blue dead to burial grounds, whenever grieving kin had permitted them to do so.

'Well, they aren't so bad,' reported the villagers and merchants loyal to Queen Caroline. 'Not as bad as some.'

'Their gold's as good as any.'

'They can *fight*,' said a young Green guard, not without admiration.

'Good discipline.'

'Fair dealing, at least so far . . .'

I saw a serving woman gaze after a tall young savage, and her admiration was not for his fighting or his gold.

But the queen's ladies, stuck all afternoon in the outer chamber, knew nothing of all this. They sewed and they speculated, equally badly. Cecilia's eyes were round with fright. When the outer door swung open, she jumped, gave a little cry and pricked her finger.

Lord Robert strode in, dirt and sweat and blood on his clothing. His boots rang on the stone floor as he made straight for the privy chamber.

Lady Margaret, the ranking lady-in-waiting, leaped up and said, 'Lord Robert!'

He neither looked at her nor broke stride.

'My lord!' she said desperately. 'You cannot see the queen just now!'

He stopped then, turning on her a look that made Cecilia shrink against the back of her chair. *I* would not have liked to face that black temper. Lady Margaret, usually so composed and acerbic, paled.

Lord Robert said, 'And who are you to tell me when I can or cannot see the queen?'

'She . . . she left orders. That no one is to disturb her.'

'Really.' He took a step closer to Lady Margaret. She stood her ground beside the frozen group of seated women, the hem of her green skirt trembling on the floor. Lady Margaret, trembling!

Lord Robert said, 'And what is the queen doing that she does not desire to be disturbed?'

'I . . . She did not tell me, my lord.'

'And whatever it is, is Her Grace doing it alone?'

Lady Margaret conquered her trembling. She looked straight at Lord Robert and said, 'Her Grace is not obligated to tell me what she does.' The unspoken half of her statement was clear: *Nor tell you, either.*

Lord Robert said, 'The queen will see *me*,' and started towards the door.

I called out, 'Lord Robert! She is with Lord Solek!'

Slowly he turned to face me. The ladies all stared, aghast. I said, 'She told me too that they must not be disturbed. They are settling the future of my lord's army. It is a . . . a delicate negotiation.'

He sneered, 'And what does a fool know of negotiations?'

'Nothing, my lord. I only repeat what I was told. They are discussing the army.'

189

It was the wrong thing to say. Lord Robert was supposedly the head of the queen's army. In three strides he was at the door and yanking on the handle. The door was barred from within.

Lord Robert's hand flashed to his sword. But a sword is no good against heavy oak. He kicked the door and bellowed, 'Caroline!'

I said in a low voice to the five women, 'Get out. Quickly. She will never forgive you for witnessing this, if she knows.'

Lady Margaret, oldest and quickest-witted, said, 'Yes! Come *now*.' She had to pull Cecilia to her feet, but the last of their green skirts disappeared through the door to the presence chamber, with Lady Margaret closing it behind them, a scant moment before the queen flung open the door on the opposite side of the room.

Her gaze swept quickly around the room, found only me, and rasped, 'Go.'

I did not have to be told twice. I scampered from the room, hunched over, trying to look as much as possible like some small animal, harmless and mute. In the presence chamber the queen's ladies huddled against the far door, too afraid of the savages to risk the open courtyard beyond. As I approached, Lady Margaret said sharply, 'Well?'

What to say? 'She ... sent me away.'

Lady Jane said, 'Was Lord Solek there?'

'Of course he was there,' Lady Sarah said. 'We already knew that. Only, why didn't Lord Robert challenge him? No, wait. Lord Solek must have already left the queen.'

'We would have seen him go,' Lady Jane argued. 'Unless ... Oh! There must be a secret passage from the queen's bedchamber!'

'*Enough*,' Lady Margaret said, and not even those two dared disobey her tone. Lady Margaret looked at me with new, reluctant respect. 'You did well, fool.'

Lady Sarah said, 'But did you *see* him? Will the savage and Lord Robert fight over her – later, I mean?'

I said, 'Lord Solek and the queen had matters of The Queendom to discuss.'

Lady Jane snorted with delicate lewdness.

Lady Margaret said, 'The fool is right. Lord Solek had to discuss the army with the queen, and that is what we will say to anyone who asks. Do you all understand that? *Do you?*'

One by one they agreed. Lord Solek was there on affairs of state. It was a meeting of negotiation, to which Lord Robert arrived late because he had been pursuing the retreating enemy. The three of them had discussed matters of The Queendom, such as the princess's betrothal to my lord Solek's son. The meeting among the three was about important affairs of The Queendom. Lady Margaret rehearsed them over and over.

But it was Cecilia who knew what really to ask. As the ladies finally dispersed, under heavy guard, to their chambers until next sent for, Cecilia caught my arm. 'Roger, what was the queen wearing when she opened the door?'

'Go to your chamber, my lady,' I said. She pouted and flounced off, escorted by two Greens.

The queen, barefoot, had been wearing nothing but a short shift, and her dark hair had tumbled loose around her bare shoulders.

The next day Lord Robert rode from the palace on his magnificent black charger, off to his estate in the country, and did not return. He had gone, Queen Caroline announced to her court, at her bequest, on an important mission of state.

21

'Roger, I have work for you,' the queen said.

That could mean only one thing. My spine froze.

Weeks had passed since the battle. Spring flowed into early summer, with roses budding in courtyards and crops pale green in fields. Lord Solek's savage soldiers were everywhere – how could so few of them seem like so many? They directed the Green guards, they marched through the spider's net of villages around the palace and secured them for the queen, they supervised the barges arriving at the palace, they controlled everything that happened in Glory. A few had learned some words of our language, but most managed with gestures and demonstrations of what they wanted. They were tireless, superbly disciplined, courteous in their rough way. They were – always, everywhere – *there*.

The queen kept me close by her, except when she was in her privy chamber with Lord Solek. She never mentioned what I had seen the night of the battle. She didn't have to mention it; we both knew it was worth my life to stay silent about the scene between her and Lord Robert. Much of the time, as Lord Solek received reports from his captains and directed his growing power over the capital, the queen sat with her ladies as they sewed or sang or gambled or danced. She said little, and did not join them in their forced revels. They had to be cheerful and amusing, for her sake; she did not have to cheer or amuse them, and she didn't. She sat quiet, thoughtful. Sometimes she didn't hear when Lady Margaret spoke to her.

Queen Caroline's beautiful face showed nothing, but I could sense her growing fear. This had not been part of her plan. Lord Solek was swiftly, surely, securing power over The Queendom. The queen had defeated her mother's forces, only to fall before those of her lover.

'Will she marry him?' Cecilia whispered to me as she sat in a window embrasure, supposedly sewing. Her cushion cover was a tangled mess; I could have set neater stitches myself.

'Marry him?'

She giggled. 'Well, they bed together, don't they?'

'I am never in the queen's bedchamber. Hush, my lady.' Quickly I glanced around. Cecilia had no discretion, and sometimes I thought she had no memory. Both Lady Margaret and I had warned her again not to speak of the queen and Lord Solek. But she was like a kitten: curious, wide-eye, playful, completely adorable. The scent of her made my head float and my eyes blur.

'Maybe she *should* marry him,' Cecilia said. 'He's very handsome. Those blue eyes.'

'Lady Cecilia, *please*!'

'Well, he is. And Princess Stephanie is not strong. The queen is old but not that old – he could maybe give her another daughter in case. Oh all right, Roger. You cautious old thing.' She patted my shoulder. Her touch was like wine. 'It's all right now, don't you see? We're at peace again and everything's all right. The queen– Oh, she wants us now!'

'Stay, she wants me,' I said, and rose to follow the queen to the high roof where we had watched the battle. Three or four times a day we did this, climbing the steep stone steps through the bell tower, just she and I and two Green guards, the same two I often saw drinking ale in the guardroom with one of Lord Solek's captains. That savage had a good ear for words; he was among the best with our language. 'I like to gaze at my queendom at peace,' the queen said to explain her frequent trips to the tower. I knew better.

Now she leaned on the stone parapet and called me to her. Her Green guards stood by the trapdoor to the staircase, a respectful distance away and out of earshot of whispers. She knew as well as I that her guards were Lord Solek's spies. The queen's hands gripped the stone hard. Wind pulled at her hair, her gown. She had lost weight, and there was a fierce desperation in her dark eyes. She said, 'Roger, I have work for you.'

'Y-yes, Your Grace.'

'You will cross over and see if the country of the Dead contains a new arrival, a messenger from my son's bride.'

'Your Grace, I have tried to tell you ... The country of the Dead is such a big place, to find one person—'

'Nonetheless, you will find him. He will be small, in order to ride fast, and he will be wearing yellow, the colour of Isabelle's court. You will ask him when her army will arrive here.'

'Your Grace, you are presuming that such a messenger was not only sent but also is now dead.'

'He must be dead, or he would be here. Or Isabelle's army would.'

And she needed them. Her need was in every line of her taut figure, her tense face. Only an army that she commanded could counterbalance the one led by Lord Solek, the bedmate who was usurping her queendom. Queen Isabelle's army, bound to Queen Caroline through Prince Rupert's marriage, would not have the *guns* of Lord Solek's men, but the Yellows had a reputation as the best soldiers in the world. If Queen Isabelle bore a daughter, that princess would be second in line for the Crown of Glory, after the sickly Princess Stephanie. Queen Caroline had a strong claim on her sister-in-law's army, in addition to the affection of her brother. And she had sent for the yellow army much earlier, had carefully timed their probable arrival as part of her grand design. So where were they?

Her situation was clear to me. Mine, as always, was not to her. To find one messenger in the country of the Dead – if he was even there! – would be impossible. I had lied to the queen before and got away with it – but what if another lie caught me out?

'You will cross over now, right here,' the queen said to me. 'Not in my privy chamber – right here on the tower. I have already told my lord Solek that my fool is given to fits.'

Fits? And she did not trust her own privy chamber. Were there spy holes? In her bedchamber as well? Things were even worse for her than I had guessed.

As if to confirm my fear, the queen said in a low voice that seemed torn from her against her will, 'He seeks to send Princess Stephanie to his barbaric country until her marriage. Roger, *men* rule there!'

My eyes grew so wide that the wind on the tower made them water. Men did not rule; they could not create life, only defend it. I – everyone at court – had assumed that Lord Solek acted on behalf of some unknown barbarian queen. But if *men* ruled ... And for a future queen to be sent away – unthinkable! A princess or queen left her queendom only once, on her marriage journey, to inspect in person the dowry her husband brought her. After that, her place was in her own palace, always. Princess Stephanie was only three; she would grow up not even knowing The Queendom that she must one day rule. Her loyalty would be to the savage realm, not her own. She might even forget her mother tongue.

'I cannot make Lord Solek understand,' the queen said, still in that same low voice, although we both knew that

Lord Solek understood only too well. 'Go now, Roger, and find Isabelle's messenger. Have a fit right here, right now.'

Have a fit! How did one have a fit? I had never even seen a fit. The queen's hand brushed mine; her fingers left me with a piece of gold. What good was gold to bring on a fit? All at once I was angry, furious at the way I was used. I was a tool, no more than her spoon or her goblet. A tool – just as she was to the savage who shared her bed and wanted her queendom.

There was no choice but to do as I was told.

I screamed and jumped up on the stone railing. The Green guards rushed forward, swords drawn, and pulled the queen away from me. I tossed the gold coin in the air, cried, 'I buy the sky! Why why why!' and jumped back down from the parapet to writhe on the stone floor. My hand felt in my pocket to work my little shaving blade free of its sheath, and viciously I cut my palm. Blood filmed my hand, and I crossed over.

I did not know where I was.

I stood among huge boulders, an outcrop such as I had never seen anywhere near Glory. Among the boulders grew scrubby bushes, leafless and misshapen things that sent out twisted twigs from twisted stems. I blundered into one. Its sharp thorns pricked my already bloody palm. The ground shook under my feet and the dark sky raced with clouds. My gut twisted. I had caused this devastation.

Noise came from my left. Careful to avoid the thorny bushes, I picked my way among the boulders until I emerged onto the plain beside the river, but a plain changed and misshapen as the bushes. Rocks were strewn everywhere, some small enough to kick, some as big as I was. More of the scrubby bushes spiked the ground, which rumbled under my feet. Amid this chaos the Dead sat or lay in their usual oblivion – but not all of them.

The noise came from two sources. The river ran more swiftly now, breaking and swirling against new rocks, sending up spray and sound. But most of the noise came from across the river. Blue soldiers, hundreds of them, dead in the recent battle with the savage warriors. The Blues were being drilled by their captains. They marched, shouted, brandished swords, stamped their boots. None of them acted even remotely as if they were Dead. One of them caught sight of me across the water. He cupped his hand to shout across the river.

'Witched fool! What news, boy?'

I could not have answered to save my life. When I stood, dumb as one of the inexplicable boulders, he yelled even louder. *'What news?'*

When I still did not answer, the soldier and the man next to him stepped onto the water and walked across its surface to my side of the river.

Dizziness took me and everything swirled and swooped. When I could see again, one of them had hold of my arm.

'His wits are returning, Lucius,' he said. 'Boy, ye be all right?'

'Of course he not be all right; he's witched, you idiot!'

'No worse than us, stuck here in Witchland. Fool? Ye be all right?'

'Y-yes.' Their boots were not even wet.

Lucius said, 'What news, then? Does the whore queen still hold the palace?'

'Y-yes.' I fought to master myself. 'But Lord Solek—'

Lucius let loose with a string of violent oaths. I had not heard such language since Hartah. 'The savage holds the palace for her?'

197

'Yes.' The truth was too complicated to explain, even if I had wanted to.

Lucius shook my arm, not gently. 'What, then? How do we escape from Witchland? Have you nothing good to tell us?'

'Leave off, Lucius,' his friend said. 'Don't shake the fool like that. He's on our side. He tried to get the young witch's amulet for us, remember?'

Cat Starling. What had happened to her after I left? I said, 'Have you taken the amulet from her since I was last witched here?'

'No one has so much as seen her. Is that what will send us back – the amulet?'

'I don't know yet,' I said. 'But the ... the witch queen keeps me close, and I hope to learn how to undo my own ensorcellment, and so yours. I work for that night and day. Meanwhile ...' I tried to fake a sob, and discovered it was not fake. There are many kinds of witching.

'Don't cry, fool,' Lucius said with disgust. 'You're nearly a man.'

'He's not crying – are you, boy? What can we do meantimes? We drill, you see, to prepare for the battle. When we go back, that savage will not beat us, no matter how many fire-sticks he brings against us, nor how the witch queen deforms Witchland to frighten us. We will defeat her and her savages. We fight for The Queendom.'

They all believed still that they were in Witchland, all the Blues whom Lord Solek's army had killed. I had said so to the first ones, who must have told the others as they arrived, and so none at all believed that they were dead.

The second soldier grew impatient. 'I asked you, fool, what can we do to aid our own freedom from Witchland?'

'You can ... you can continue to prepare for battle.' They expected more from me. Lucius's eyes darkened with anger. At the same moment, the sky rumbled and lightning flashed from one glowering cloud to another. I invented wildly: 'And you can make amulets that will be useful on your return. Each amulet should consist of five of the thorns on the new bushes that have appeared – you have noticed the new bushes?'

They nodded, listening carefully, anxious to miss nothing that might save them.

My stomach clenched, but I went on. 'Wrap the five thorns – and they must be five perfect thorns, not blemished – in a bit of cloth and wear it around your neck. The thorns will not hurt you in this place —' Truer words were never spoken, since nothing could hurt them in this place '—but once out of Witchland, they will impart a little of the witch power to each of you. This have I learned by stealth, and as a result of my own ensorcellment.'

Lucius nodded. 'I will tell the captain. Thank you, boy. We are in your debt.'

'Then you can help me now. I seek a messenger from Queen Isabelle, who married our Prince Rupert. The messenger was . . . was witched here. He will be a small man, a rider, dressed in yellow. He may be under the same spell as Queen Eleanor. Have you seen him?'

Both soldiers shook their heads. They thanked me again, and I watched as they walked on the surface of the water back across the swift river. Then I set out to find the messenger in yellow.

It was hopeless. The land had become so much more difficult to walk across, let alone to scan. Boulders, thorn scrub, groves of trees thicker than before and somehow menacing. Beneath my feet the ground rumbled. I scrambled away from the riverbank and towards the north, the direction of Queen Isabelle's queendom, frantically searching. I looked for a long time, becoming dirty and exhausted. Although even if he were here, I didn't see how I could find the messenger.

Instead, a dead Blue found me. He jumped out from behind a boulder several yards away. Unlike the other Blues I had seen here, he had lost his military discipline. His eyes were crazed and wild. He shouted something incoherent. Thinking himself in Witchland had unsettled his wits, perhaps never strong to begin with. Or perhaps dying had deranged him. He carried what he must have brought with him, seized from the enemy in battle: a *gun*.

He shrieked again, raised the thing and fired at me.

Something hard and hot – so hot! – struck my left arm, sending me falling back against the rocks. The sky gave a great *crack*! of lightning. I screamed; the pain was pure agony, searing my flesh like flames.

And then I lay on the stone roof of the tower; it was night, and I had other questions to torment me. I already knew I could be hurt in the country of the Dead, by the Dead. But what would happen to me if I were killed there? Would I return to my body in the land of the living, or would I lapse into the unknowing tranquillity of the Dead?

Now I had not one but two places where I could die.

The pain continued. It was too dark to see my arm, but when I made myself flex it, I could tell that the bones were not broken. This was a flesh wound only, but I had seen men die of flesh wounds that turned black and rancid. And the pain did not diminish, burning like acid along skin and nerves.

Cradling my left arm in my right, I forced myself to my feet. Where was the queen, her guard, anyone at all? How much time had passed? My eyes adjusted to the night, and I peered over the parapet. Most, although not all, of the courtyards were dark. So was most, but not all, of the narrow ring of the tent city. Above, the stars shone brightly, without a moon. Summer had barely begun; the night air was cold and sharp.

I tried the trapdoor that led from the tower roof. It was bolted from below.

Something must be happening in the palace, something that had drawn the queen away from the tower. She had forgotten me before, but never while I was on a mission for her to the country of the Dead. What if she had been murdered, as she had murdered her mother? What if no one came to the tower before morning? The courtyard was many storeys below, too far to jump. I didn't think I would freeze to death here, but I needed to clean the wound in my arm, bandage it.

Why did everyone always abandon me?

I leaned over the parapet and screamed, 'I'm here! I'm here!'

And then, 'I'm here, you bastards! I AM HERE!'

Nothing.

I don't know how long I stood there, clinging to the stone railing, shivering and cursing, my arm pure agony. Stars moved overhead, I know that. I grew light-headed, maybe feverish. And then, on a rooftop below the tower, two figures emerged. It was forbidden to all but soldiers to go onto the roofs at night. These were not Greens. In the starlight I could see their silhouettes clearly: a soldier of the savages and a woman. They embraced.

My voice was hoarse, but I called down, 'Help me, please! I am Roger, the queen's fool, and I am trapped on the tower by mistake! Please, send for help!'

Instantly the woman vanished, perhaps unwilling to be identified. The savage came to the edge of his roof, peering up at me. He looked a tiny figure, no more dangerous than a small pet dog that stands on two legs. Distance deceives, promising safety where there is none.

The savage called something that I of course did not understand, and then disappeared from the roof. Several minutes later, which seemed like hours, the door to the tower roof opened and a man emerged.

Lord Solek himself.

Behind him was Eammons, the translator, who said, 'What are you doing here?'

'I was forgotten! The queen—' I gasped as a wave of dizziness hit me.

Eammons said sharply, 'What about the queen? What did she say to you?'

There was something wrong with his tone. It held not only sharpness but fear. Of what? Something was wrong here, very wrong. With every last shred of strength in me, I summoned what wits I had. They were all that had kept me alive until now. They counselled caution, counselled evasion, counselled lies.

'Nothing. I ... Her Grace left and ... I wanted ... I wanted to be alone. So I came here. But I fell asleep and the tower was locked at dusk – I guess that is the usual way – and by now the queen must be looking for me.' I tried to look befuddled, foolish, out of my depth. It was not hard.

Lord Solek said something, and Eammons replied. Translating my words, I guessed. The savage chieftain gazed at me from cold blue eyes. Up close, he was even more terrifying: huge, hard, full of suppressed energy, like an enormous boulder about to fall and crush me. Then he shrugged, turned and strode off.

'Go back to where you belong,' Eammons said irritably. 'If you do this again you will be flogged, queen's fool or no. If she doesn't order it, I will.'

He will? Did Eammons, who now trailed Lord Solek and not the queen, have that much power? It was clear that Solek did; he now kept as close a watch throughout the palace as Queen Caroline had once done.

I, on the other hand, had no power, not even to stay upright. I staggered down the tower steps, far behind Eammons, who had hurried after his master. Every few steps I stopped and rested against the stone wall. Then, at the bottom, I collapsed.

Sometime later – that same night? – a page bent over me, shaking my good shoulder. 'Fool? Fool? Are you ill?'

'Mag– Mag—' I couldn't get the word out for the chattering of my teeth: *Maggie*. She was the only one I could think of who might help me, cure me, care what happened to me. But of course the page didn't know Maggie. He was only nine or ten, a scared little boy in royal service to a palace gone mad.

He said, 'Who?'

'Mag—'

'I'll get her!' And he was off, running into the courtyard, bringing the only person he knew who served the queen and had a name like what he thought he had heard. When next I opened my eyes, Lady Margaret bent over me, a green velvet cloak over her nightdress.

'Fool? Are you sick?'

'H-hurt,' I managed, and then I fainted, and knew no more.

22

I woke on a nest of blankets on the floor beside a strange hearth. A fire burned brightly. The room was small but richly decorated in green and warm brown, with a table between me and the door. Sunshine streamed in the one window through a curtain of light silk. On the window cushion sat an elderly serving woman, mending a petticoat.

'Where ...'

She rose, looked me over, and said a single word: 'Wait.' She left the room.

I sat up. I felt light-headed, but the pain in my arm was gone. It had been bandaged, and the bandages smelled of some faintly vinegary ointment. Carefully I got to my feet, trying to puzzle out where I was. A second door, ajar, led to a bedchamber. I glimpsed a narrow bed and a plain highly polished chest. Three books were stacked neatly on top, beside some needlework. The other door opened.

'Roger!'

The serving woman had returned, and with her was Lady Margaret. Some part of my mind realized that this was the first time she had ever used my name instead of calling me 'fool'. Clumsily I fell to my knees.

'Rise,' she said impatiently. 'How do you feel?'

'Better, my lady. Did you bring me here and—'

Lady Margaret interrupted me to speak to the serving woman. 'Leave us, Martha.'

'Yes, my lady.'

When she had gone, Lady Margaret said, 'Eat first. You've had nothing for two days. Sit there and eat that.'

As soon as she said this, I was ravenous. Nothing existed except the bread, cheese and wine on the table. I gobbled like a boar. Then, when my belly was full, Lady Margaret existed again, looking haggard. She was ten or fifteen years older than the other ladies and still in the queen's service because no one had married her, and she had never been a beauty. Still, I had not thought it possible that her long face could look this gaunt and drawn, and there were violet shadows beneath her eyes. I said, 'The queen . . .'

'Knows where you are. I told her that you had fallen ill from being locked all night outside on the tower during a fit, and that I would have you cared for. She sends her good wishes.'

But no regrets for having locked me out during my 'fit'. Nor any reasons for having left me there, where I might have died. I said dryly, 'The queen is well?'

'Don't be insolent, Roger.'

Lady Margaret was much shrewder than Cecilia; I must remember that. I bowed my head in repentance. Also to hide my anger. But her next words made my head jerk up to stare at her.

'I did not tell the queen that you were injured as well as ill, nor that the injury came from a savage's *gun*. Fortunately, it was but a flesh wound. But how did that happen while you were locked on top of the tower, Roger the Fool?'

We gazed at each other. I chose honesty, partly because I didn't think I could get away with anything else. Not with her. 'I cannot tell you, my lady. On the queen's orders.'

'There is much that cannot be told, these days.'

'Yes.'

She leaned close to me and lowered her voice to a whisper. 'You have been ill for two days,' she said, 'and so you don't know what has happened. I'm going to tell you, Roger, but only because I think it important that you know the truth and not the rumours swirling around the palace. And because I think you already know more about the truth of Lady Cecilia than does anyone else.'

'Lady Cecilia?' Now I was truly bewildered. I thought we had been talking about the queen.

'You were on the tower roof helping the queen look for the messenger from Queen Isabelle, weren't you?'

'Yes.'

'He arrived while you were in your fit.'

'He arrived? He's here?' Not among the Dead.

'He was here, but no longer. Nor is Isabelle's army, which will never come to the queen's aid.'

I was staggered. Queen Isabelle *must* come to the aid of her sister-in-law; that's what queens did. There was a marriage pact. And any daughter of Isabelle and Rupert would be second in line for the Crown of Glory. Queen Isabelle could not have refused to send her army.

'Why?' The word burst from me like the explosion from a savage's *gun*. And Lady Margaret had mentioned Cecilia . . .

All at once I knew, and the world turned sick around me.

'Yes,' Lady Margaret said, looking at my face. 'Queen Isabelle had a bout of the crawls. Her physicians say it has scarred her inside, so that she may never bear a child. She caught the crawls from Prince Rupert, who said he caught it from Cecilia.'

'It was the other way around! Cecilia caught the disease from him!'

'That not what Queen Isabelle believes,' Lady Margaret said wearily, 'nor Queen Caroline either. Rupert is her brother. She believes as she wishes – and so do you, Roger. You believe Cecilia, that foolish child, because you want her to be the victim. But the truth is more complex than that.'

'As if anyone here cared for truth!'

'Everyone here cares for truth,' Lady Margaret said, 'just not the same truth. And yours is this. You helped Cecilia obtain medicine for the crawls early in her infection, and she sent you for the milady posset because she knew what she was experiencing. Queen Isabelle did not know and waited too long, and has paid the terrible price. There will be no heir to her throne. Queen Caroline will gain no help from her, and is practically a prisoner in her own palace. The messenger with the news arrived while you were in your fit, and the queen rushed away from the tower. Somehow the door must have become locked behind you.'

'And Lady Cecilia . . .' I could barely get out the words. All those men who had refused to swear fealty to the queen, vanished to who-knew-where, dead, tortured . . .

'Cecilia escaped.'

'*Escaped?* How?'

'I don't know. No one knows. Someone warned her, just before the queen sent for her. I was with Her Grace; her other attendants had been sent to bed. I was there when the messenger arrived and the queen received him. She had only minutes before Lord Solek was alerted and joined us, and in those minutes the queen . . . I have never seen her that bad,' Lady Margaret finished simply.

I had. I could picture the scene: the queen raging, Lady Margaret trying to calm her, the messenger terrified for his life. Then Lord Solek striding into the room, so that the two women and the messenger must pretend that all was well, that this was a routine message from her brother. And, as soon as possible, the queen giving the order to arrest Cecilia, and take her ... where? To what punishment? I shuddered.

'My lady, did *you* warn Lady Cecilia?'

'No. I remained with the queen. So did Lord Solek, for some hours. Whoever warned Cecilia had time to do so. Cecilia has so many admirers; it could have been any misguided Sam Slip-Lip.'

'But who else would have known what the messenger said?'

'I don't know. But I think you understand what the palace is – spies, spy holes ... Still, it *is* strange that someone knew to warn Cecilia. There has always been something strange about Cecilia. But it is the queen I am afraid for. As are we all, with our supposed saviour as the gaoler. The savages have their fire-sticks, their poison-tipped knives, their brutality. I am afraid for the queen, and I cannot forgive him his treachery.'

I didn't care what she could or could not forgive him, nor that Lady Margaret remained loyal to her queen, still. She was one of those who, having given her allegiance, would never change it. I cared only about Cecilia. 'But how could Lady Cecilia have escaped the palace that night? The gates were barred!'

'I don't know. And neither do I greatly care. Cecilia brought this on herself, on all of us, and she deserves whatever she gets. But you should know the truth because it will help you better serve Her Grace.'

Lady Margaret actually thought I was going to do that. I was not. But I bowed my head again and said, with sincerity, 'Thank you for nursing me, my lady.'

'I didn't do it for your sake,' she said irritably, rising from the table. 'In truth, I didn't do it at all. The nursing was done by my woman and by your friend from the kitchen, a Maggie Someone.'

'*Maggie?*'

'You called for her so insistently that I finally sent a page for her. She nursed you like a sister. But now you seem well enough, and I am glad to have both of you out of my rooms. The queen has been asking for you. Go serve her, fool, with whatever it is you do.'

'Yes, my lady.' I rose, fortified by the good food, and left the ladies' chambers. But not to go to the queen.

I knew where Cecilia had gone, and where she might still be found.

The mid-morning kitchens bustled as if this were a normal day, a normal year. Stews bubbled in great pots over the fires. Bread baked in brick ovens. Chickens and rabbits turned on spits, dripping fat into the hot embers. No matter who held power, or who imprisoned whom, or who bedded whom, courtiers and soldiers and servants must be fed.

No one looked surprised to see me, who had so often been sent by the queen with orders for where and when food should be served. Only Maggie, trimming vegetables at one end of the long trestle table, raised glad eyes. 'Roger! Are you feeling better? You're wobbling a little.'

'I'm fine. Thank you for nursing me. Lady Margaret said that no true sister could have been more devoted.'

Maggie scowled at me; some people cannot stand praise. She snapped, 'You need more yellow dye for your face. It faded while you were sick.'

'All right. Maggie, I need more of your help.' I said it in a whisper, but not the keenest of the queen's spies, or Lord Solek's spies, or anybody's spies could have heard us over the din of the kitchen. 'I need to get out of the palace.'

'Out?' She looked blank for a moment, and then began wielding her little peeling knife as if it were a sword and

209

carrots were the direst of enemies. 'You're going after that titled little bitch!'

I was shocked at her language, her look. 'Lady Cecilia is not—'

'Everyone knows she disappeared two days ago! Ran off with some man in heat, probably, and you're going to– Oh, why are men so stupid!' And she burst into tears.

Now people *were* looking at us. I was dumbfounded. Did Maggie, like Lady Margaret, know that Cecilia was the reason Queen Isabelle's army would not arrive in The Queendom? There was no way Maggie could know that. But she was clearly in distress, and I put my hand on her arm. She shook it off so violently that I, still weak from my illness, staggered against the edge of the table.

'Don't touch me!'

'All right. I will not, if that's what you want. But I need to get out of the palace tonight without being seen, and you are my only—'

'No!'

'Maggie—'

'I won't do it! It's too dangerous! Go to her if that's what you want, but leave me out of it! '

All at once anger swept me. No one but me cared that without help Cecilia could be captured, tortured, killed. My lady, so playful and light-hearted and laughing – unlike Maggie! I stalked out of the kitchen to the laundry, where amidst the clouds of steam from the wash pots I stole a small packet of dye.

In the courtyard outside the ladies' chambers I pretended to collapse again. Two Greens picked me up, not very gently. 'You take his arms and I'll take his legs. Damn but the fool's grown almost as heavy as a real man!' They dumped me back in Lady Margaret's chamber, where her serving woman sighed, remade the nest of blankets by the hearth and sent word to the queen that I was still unwell. I stayed there all day, pretending to sleep.

In the evening, while the ladies were attending the queen and Lord Solek was at whatever revels he chose, I painted my face with the red dye I had stolen from the laundry. Into my hair I braided the twigs I had broken from the tree in the courtyard where I collapsed. From Lady Margaret's chest I took a green velvet cloak lined in fur and a white nightdress. I put them on, the nightdress fitting over my own fool's outfit only because it was so billowy. I pulled the cloak tight around me, put up the hood and made my way through the palace to the west gate. Two Greens guarded the gate. They had been Blues, had sworn the oath of fealty to Queen Caroline, and now served Lord Solek. They were the kind of men who would serve anyone for enough coins and enough ale. Unlike Solek's savages, who were kept under such strict discipline that no girl of The Queendom had been molested by any of them, these two were avoided by every serving woman in the palace. That's how I knew about them. Women talk, and ever since the night that Cecilia had sent me to Mother Chilton, I had been listening.

'Well, what comes *here*?' said the Green with the bristly beard.

The other nudged him, elbow hard in the ribs, and said uncertainly, 'My lady—'

But Bristle Beard's eyes were sharper. 'Not a lady, Dick – look at them boots!' He grabbed for me and I danced away. I let the hood of my cloak fall back, then snatched it back up.

'It's one of them fancy savage singers! In a shift!' Bristle whooped and grabbed for me again.

I said, trying to speak in a high-pitched version of the savages' guttural accent, 'I be—'

'We know what you be,' Bristle Beard said. Dick had abandoned his initial caution; he made kissing sounds in the air and grabbed me. To these rough idiots all the savage singers looked alike, and I had used the red dye liberally.

Dick pretended to kiss me, went 'Faughhh!' and pushed me to the ground. 'Sing for us, boy!'

'Sing a pretty girl's song or we'll treat you like a girl!'

'You but not me – I don't fancy male meat.' Bristle Beard kicked me.

I cried, 'I be go for Solek!'

That sobered them. Bristle Beard said, 'Let me see your pass.'

I shook my head as if I didn't understand and repeated, 'I be go for Solek.'

Bristle Beard said, 'He's supposed to have a pass.'

Dick was quicker. 'Yeah, but if he's dressed like *that* for Solek . . . who knows what those savages do when they be by themselves? Those singers are all flower boys anyway. I don't want no part of this.'

'So we—'

'Go,' Dick said to me, scowling. 'You can understand that, can't you, you sick dog? *Go*.' He unbarred and opened the gate. I scuttled through into the city.

It was dark and cool, although summer wound through the night air like embroidery through cloth. I was nowhere near the kitchens, where the food barges drew up to deliver and Maggie had let me out of the palace once before. But if I stuck close to the palace wall and circled to the right, I thought I would arrive there. This proved to be harder than I expected. The alleys lined with tents twisted and turned, sometimes away from the wall, sometimes towards it. Also, many of the tents had been torn down, replaced with wooden structures in various stages of construction. It was the old queen who had decreed that, on the island of Glory, only the palace be a permanent dwelling. Queen Caroline must have done away with that law, perhaps in an attempt to win her subjects' favour. My way was frequently blocked by piles of lumber and brick, by raw-wood houses lighted from within, once by a sty full of nasty-looking boars that snorted at me in the darkness and bared their teeth.

I felt weak from illness and ridiculous in my green velvet cloak and lady's nightdress. But I kept the hood drawn well down over my face, and few people were out on the streets to see me. Perhaps in the night my dark green cloak looked brown or black. No one stopped me, not even when I encountered two of Lord Solek's savages. They passed me without a glance and went into an ale tent. As they drew aside the flap, warmth and light and laughter spilled out. The queen might be a virtual prisoner in her own palace, her throne all but usurped, but for the common people there was peace and liberality.

Eventually I found the dim alley, and the tent with the picture of two black swans at its hem. I knocked on the door jamb, did not wait for an answer and pushed my way inside.

Mother Chilton sat in the same chair. It was as if she had not moved in all these long weeks since I came here last. The same fire burned in the brazier in the centre of the tent, sending its smoke through the hole in the roof and its light flickering on the canvas walls. The same poles hung with the same bottles, plants, feathers, hides, bits of wood, cloth bags.

This time, Mother Chilton rose as I entered. My disguise did not deceive her for a moment; she did not even comment on it.

'You've grown, lad. You're nearly a man.'

'I've come for—'

'I know why you've come.' She moved closer to me, and it seemed that as she moved, all the objects hanging from the poles moved too, yearning towards her. In her eyes swam strange colours, lights. 'You seek the Lady Cecilia, who sent you here before.'

'Yes. Is she safe? Is she here?'

'She was here. Here and gone. And she will never be safe.'

My breath stopped in my throat. 'Never? Why? And where has she gone? Did you help her escape from the capital?'

Mother Chilton did not answer me directly. Seen up close, her face was smooth cheeks, wrinkled forehead, and those eyes that were no colour at all. She said, 'So they are not yet ready in Soulvine.'

Once before she had mentioned Soulvine to me – '*Do you come from Soulvine Moor? Are they ready, then?*' On that visit I had been shocked that she would connect me with what no one else would even name. This time I didn't care. I only cared about finding Cecilia and protecting her.

'Where is Lady Cecilia? Did you help her?'

'I did, lad. But you don't know why. You know much, even more than you think, but you don't know what Cecilia is.'

'What is she?'

'A pretty, empty-headed tinder box that will ignite all.'

I said, with as much dignity as I could manage, 'I know she is not a great wit, but she is not empty-headed. And yes, she has "ignited" me, and I am not shamed by that.'

Mother Chilton did not laugh. She closed her eyes and an expression of great pain crossed her face, as if I had turned a knife in her bowels. I sprang forward to catch her if she fell, but she didn't so much as sway on her feet. But I think I swayed at her next words.

'I have sent Cecilia into the Unclaimed Lands. It is the only place the queen cannot reach her. Caroline studied the soul arts but she has no talent. Still, it is why the queen recognized *you*. I told Cecilia to go into the Unclaimed Lands but not to enter Soulvine Moor, not for any reason. It may be she can find some goat herder or scrub farmer to marry her, pretty little kitten that she is, and keep her safe. But you can't go after her, lad. I thought once that you came from Soulvine. You do not, and you've already caused enough disturbance in the country of the Dead.'

'You . . . *you* can cross over to the country of the Dead?'

'No,' she said, without explanation.

I seized on what mattered. 'You sent Cecilia south to the Unclaimed Lands *alone*?'

'She is not alone.' Mother Chilton put her hand on my arm, and a strange thing happened: my vision blurred. Almost something formed in front of my eyes, some picture. But no. It was gone. Mother Chilton withdrew her hand.

'You are not ready,' she said sadly. 'Lad, don't go after that girl. She was born on Soulvine Moor, and although Caroline brought her to Glory as a child, she is still a Soulviner. Do not go after her.'

'I must,' I said simply.

'You're a fool,' she said with equal simplicity, and I didn't know if she referred to my character, my post with the queen, or both. For a long moment neither of us spoke. The fire crackled in the brazier. Finally Mother Chilton said, 'Don't try to go about in daylight as either a girl or a savage bard. You can't even sing. Take off that ridiculous nightdress and scrub your face with this cloth. I will give you a cloak.'

I said sullenly, tired of being ordered like a child when I was on a hero's mission to rescue my love, 'The red dye won't wash away. It must wear off.'

She snorted and attacked my face with the cloth. It came away red with dye. She dragged the twigs, not gently, from my hair. I put off the green velvet cloak and pulled Lady Margaret's nightdress over my head. Mother Chilton slapped a poultice on my wounded arm, yanking back my sleeve to do so. Instantly, cool strength flooded through my arm. She took my court cloak and handed me a thick hooded cloak of brown wool lined with brown rabbit, by far the nicest I had ever owned.

'I . . . I cannot pay you.'

She said sharply, 'Give me that gold piece in your pocket.'

How had she known?

Before I could ask, she added, 'And give me Caroline's ring too. How stupid are you, to carry markers like those around with you? Give them to me.'

Markers? I put my hand in my pocket and clutched both my gold piece and the little ring set with tiny emeralds. I had planned to use both to bargain my way to Cecilia. If she took—

Of its own will, and without mine, my hand drew out of my pocket and laid both ring and gold piece on the table.

'How did you—'

'Here, lad.' She gave me a handful of silver pieces. I was too dazed to count them.

'How did you—'

'Hush. Go to the alehouse by the east gate and drink there all night. In the morning, when the worthless alehouse louts stagger out of the city to do what they call "work" in the fields, go out with them.'

'But how—'

'I said to hush!'

But I could not, even though I could barely get out my next words. 'I never, never believed in witches. Are you a witch, mistress?'

'Get out before I kick you out, lad. Your stupidity shames us all.'

'But I—'

'Get out!'

'Will you tell me one just more thing? How did Cecilia know about you in the first place, for the milady posset I mean, and why are you now helping her to—'

'Such stupidity will destroy us all yet,' she said despairingly, and then all at once I stood in the dark alley, and the tent door was laced tightly shut behind me. I blinked, and a shudder ran over me. So it was true and I had never known it: witches existed in the world. Or maybe Mother Chilton had merely babbled, and I had walked myself from her tent. Or maybe—

'Hello, Roger,' said a voice behind me in the darkness. I whirled around. There, wrapped in a grey cloak and somehow sounding scared and furious and determined all at once, stood Maggie.

23

'What are *you* doing here?' It came out harsh and accusing, my tone born of my own fear, my own unsettling doubts about what I was doing here.

'I'm going with you,' Maggie said in an un-Maggie voice, humble and beseeching. Nothing was as it should be.

'You're not. Go back inside the palace.'

'I can't let you go lurching around the countryside alone. You're too ignorant,' she said, and *that* sounded more like Maggie. But she was the second woman in two minutes to tell me how stupid I was, and I lost what remained of my temper.

'I have "lurched around the countryside" since I was six years old! With people you couldn't imagine, doing things you couldn't imagine! Damn it all, Maggie, leave me alone!'

She started to cry.

Her tears were not like Cecilia's, stormy and clutching, tears a man could comfort. She stood there in the starlight with her hands hanging limply at her sides, tears sliding silently down her face. Her nose began to run. But she didn't move, didn't go back to the palace.

'Maggie, I can't take you.'

Finally she said, 'You understand nothing.' Which was not true, and certainly didn't help. She added, 'I mean, nothing about me.'

'What don't I understand?'

'Anything!'

I stalked off towards the alehouse by the east gate. I could feel Maggie following me. There was a pocket in my new cloak, and I put my hand into it and fingered the coins Mother Chilton had given me. Ten silvers, more than I had ever seen together in my life. Five hundred pennies! I was a little afraid of so much money. Just before we reached the alehouse I bent over and, under cover of my cloak, I slipped nine of the silvers into my boot.

The alehouse was half tent, half newly constructed wood. A brazier burned brightly in the centre, warming all but the farthest corners. Queen Caroline had undone her mother's edict that tradesmen must leave the city at night, and the two long tables on either side of the brazier were full of people drinking and talking and laughing. Maggie and I took one of the small cold corner tables. Keeping my cloak and hood on, I laid my silver coin on the table, and the serving woman looked hungrily at it and so not at us. She brought two mugs of ale, two bronze coins and seven pennies.

Maggie said in a low voice, 'Where did you get the money, Roger?'

'That's my concern.'

'Then where do you think Lady Cecilia has gone?'

'I don't know.'

'Then how will you—'

'Maggie, you've been very good to me. Helping me, feeding me, nursing me. But I must do this alone.'

'No,' she said simply.

'Who are you to—'

'I'm coming with you. I'm dressed as a boy, Roger, under my cloak. I have cut my hair. I'm coming with you.'

A monstrous thought occurred to me. Appalled at myself, I said, 'Maggie, are you a spy for the queen?'

She stared at me, her face a mottled maroon. But she didn't attack me. She said only, 'I told you that you were stupid. Don't you know how much I hate the queen?'

I hadn't known. 'Why?'

'Because Richard was a Blue who died for his loyalty and bravery.'

So her unaccustomed tears had not been for me, after all, but for her brother. The thought was welcome. I said gently, 'You know now for certain that Richard is dead?'

'Yes,' Maggie had control of herself now, 'I finally heard. But that's not the only reason I hate the queen. She beds the savage lord who killed so many of us in The Queendom. She murdered her own mother – everyone says so. And she has treated you like a dog – no, less than a dog. Like a *thing*. You could have died up there on the tower roof. She is a monster, and I hate her. I cannot stay and serve a monster. Not any longer, now that I know what she really is. Queen Eleanor was right: her daughter is not fit to rule. I was serving the wrong queen.' She took a sip of her ale, her eyes anguished.

I realized then what made Maggie different from most people I had ever known: she could name hard truths. Not even Mother Chilton, with her anguished evasions, had done that. Maggie was domineering, stubborn and meddlesome, but she could name truth. Like Mistress Conyers. Like – perhaps – Queen Caroline herself.

I made one more attempt. 'You have a sister in a village somewhere – you told me once. You could go to her.'

'I also told you that my sister is a miserly grasping fishwife who screams at everyone, including her husband. I am not going there. I am coming with you.'

An unwelcome suspicion formed in my mind. I was willing to risk everything for Cecilia. Was Maggie then willing to risk everything for me because ... 'Maggie,'

I choked out, 'do you . . . Are you . . .' I could not say the words: *in love with me*.

A long silence spun itself out, fragile as cobwebs.

Maggie finally answered. Her voice held great carefulness. 'You are my friend, Roger. My brother is dead, my sister a shrew, and I can no longer serve a queen I despise. If I stay in the palace one night longer, I will go mad. I have nowhere else to go except with you.'

Nowhere else to go. I well understood that! Relief crept through me, warming as the ale. Maggie was my friend, she had nowhere else to go, and it had been deeply vain of me to suspect anything else. I would not entertain such vain thoughts again. Who was I, fool and murderer and homeless wanderer, that anyone should love me?

Still, I made one more attempt to dissuade Maggie from coming with me. 'You said in the kitchen that leaving the palace was too dangerous for you to—'

'I meant danger to *you*, idiot!'

'That's my concern, not yours!'

'It's mine now,' she retorted, sounding again like the Maggie I knew: competent and scornful.

'Well, come on, then,' I said ungraciously, and after that neither of us spoke again. We sat, drinking slowly, while the alehouse emptied as the night wore on. I spent sixteen more pennies, the last ten for the serving woman to let us sleep beside the dying brazier. In the early morning we joined the labourers streaming over the east bridge, the men and women who would work for daily hire planting and weeding the fields, then spend all they earned in the alehouses and cook shops of the city when night came. No one noticed us. We walked to the farthest of the village fields, where a cottage woman sold us as much bread, cheese and dried meat as we could carry, plus a goatskin water bag, in exchange for a silver. Then we took the south-east road towards the coast.

It was the same road I had ridden with Kit Beale, nearly nine months ago. Then it had been autumn and now it was early summer, and Maggie plodded beside me. Now, as then, I didn't know what I was going towards, or what would happen to me. But all else was different. I was different. And, every step of every mile, Cecilia filled my heart. With worry, with fear, with pain. With love, which was all three.

My arm hurt only a little. Whatever Mother Chilton had done to it, the *gun* wound seemed to be healing more rapidly than it had under Lady Margaret's nursing. I was still weak from my illness, and sometimes I had to stop and rest. Maggie had more strength than I. Still, I rested less than expected, and for that too Mother Chilton's poultice may or may not have been responsible.

Maggie said little all that first day. But when we had made our camp in a thicket well off the road, when we had eaten our bread and cheese and meat, she faced me across the glowing coals. It was cold after the sun set, and both of us wrapped our cloaks tight around our bodies. The moon was a thin crescent in the east, barely visible, and the stars shone high and clear.

'Roger, what will you do if you find Lady Cecilia?'

I didn't want to discuss Cecilia, not with Maggie. I said brusquely, 'Serve her.'

'As her fool?'

'No!'

'As what?'

'You cannot ever let anything rest, can you?' I said angrily. 'Lady Cecilia is in the Unclaimed Lands. She is not alone, but whoever is with her is only one person. Mother Chilton did not tell me who it is. Cecilia will need servitors, guards, a court.'

'You are neither a servitor nor a guard,' Maggie said,

'and you are certainly not a courtier.' She stared straight into the fire, scowling.

'She trusts me. And anyway you're going to need a home too, Maggie. You wanted to escape the palace, and you have. But what now? Lady Cecilia could maybe give you a place as her serving woman, or—'

'Be quiet!' Maggie said, with such fierce pain that I was astonished. It did not seem to me a fall in rank to go from cook to lady's maid, but I questioned her no further. I didn't want any more arguments. Maggie lay down and rolled herself into a ball with her back to me.

I dreamed, that night by the fire, that I was back in the laundry at the palace. I was dying cloth green, but then – in the manner of dreams – I was dying people, and not green but yellow. All the people were female, and all of them were naked: the queen, Cecilia, Cat Starling, Maggie. 'There,' I said, 'now you are all fools.' I woke with such a powerful bodily response that there was nothing to do but creep off into the bushes and hope Maggie did not wake.

All fools. Including me.

Maggie and I walked for several days while talking but little. She was sullen, seldom even looking at me. The Queendom was in soft spring, filled with new light and tender green, but the nights were still cold. The moon grew steadily until it was a full round circle, shedding a silvery glow over all beneath. The land around us became wilder, less fertile. Fields of new plantings gave way to pastures for sheep and then, as the ground became rockier and steeper still, to goats. Hills turned to mountains, with deep ravines and abrupt cliffs. Whenever anyone rode down the road from either direction, Maggie and I hid. But I realized that Hartah, with his gruesome stories of highwaymen and robbers and dangers to lone travellers, had lied to me. I saw no corpses gutted and rotting by the road. And, each day, fewer and fewer riders appeared. We had reached the edge of the Unclaimed Lands.

'Our food is almost gone,' Maggie said.

'There's an inn up ahead. We can get provisions there, and ask for information.'

'An inn? How do you know?'

'I know,' I said. And so we came to the last inn where I had ever stayed with Hartah and Aunt Jo. It looked the same, a rough place for rough people. Somewhere to the east lay the sea, and I noticed, as I had been too naive to notice before, the sheltered creek that would be so convenient for smugglers. Dense woods behind the inn would let a traveller approach or leave unseen from the road. *A good place for information,* Hartah had said. I took another of Mother Chilton's silvers out of my boot and put it in my pocket.

'Maggie, you must do exactly as I say while we are inside this inn.'

She said, reasonably, 'What are you going to tell me to do?'

'Say nothing. You can maybe pass for a boy if you keep your hood up, with all that dirt on your face, but not if you speak. And when we take a room upstairs, you must stay there with the door barred until you're sure the person knocking is me.' I hated that I was giving her the same instructions Hartah had once given me, but there was no help for it. In this, at least, Hartah had been right. This was no place for a woman. Aunt Jo had been old and shrivelled, but Maggie was young and, if not exactly pretty – no one was pretty, next to Cecilia – would still be in danger. And I, with my small shaving knife, could not defend her.

Who was defending Cecilia? It should have been me.

Maggie nodded. She pulled her cloak far over her face.

I said, 'Part the cloak at the waist so they can see your boots and breeches. They must think we are two boys.' She nodded again and did as I directed – a first.

Two men sat drinking in the taproom, with another carrying in mugs of ale from a room beyond. They studied us with cold eyes.

'We need a room for the night,' I said, holding out my palm with a silver coin on it. 'My brother has fallen and hurt his leg.'

Maggie began to limp.

The innkeeper looked from my coin to my face to my thick fur-lined cloak. His voice was genial and oily. 'Aye, lad. I've a fine room for ye, upstairs. My best. And mayhap a bit of supper?'

'No, thank you.'

'As ye wish. This way.'

I followed him upstairs. The same tiny room under the eaves, the same sagging bed. Maggie limped behind me. The innkeeper said, 'Thirty pennies for the night.'

That was outrageous, but I nodded. 'Fine. My brother must rest his leg, but I'll come down with you and have a mug of ale.'

His greasy smile broadened. 'As ye say, sir.'

Maggie, looking frightened, hobbled into the room. I heard her bolt the door. I followed the innkeeper to the taproom, let him bring me a mug of ale from the back room, let him charge me a ridiculous three pennies. The remaining seventeen lay on the table beside my mug. The other two men sat across from me, saying nothing. They were neither young nor old, dressed in patched brown wool, and neither had washed in a very long time. Their smell would have been even worse, except that the room was cold. Wind off the sea whistled between chinks in the walls, turning the small fire fitful. We all wore cloaks.

They would make their move soon – robbery at best, murder at worst – and I must make mine first. 'Warm in here, is it not?' I said.

No answer.

'Very warm.' I made a great show of wiping my fore-head and neck. And I waited.

Finally one growled, 'Where ye bound, boy?' His teeth were broken, brown as his cloak.

'I'm looking for my lady mistress.'

That got both their attention, and the innkeeper's as well.

'She fled her father's estate a few days ago, and forgot to tell me where to meet her.'

'Forgot? What d'ye mean, boy? Speak plain!'

'I am speaking plain.' I opened my eyes wide, looking as guileless as I could, and then clutched my stomach.

'You sick?'

'No, no, just something bad that I ate . . . Yes, she forgot. And she never forgets me. I'm her musician, you see, and she is very musical. Shall I sing for you?'

'No,' he growled, as I knew he would. 'What's your mistress's name?'

'Lady Margaret. Although I think she might . . .' I scrunched up my face, like a halfwit trying to remember something. 'I think she might use another name. I forget what.'

The innkeeper said, 'Your lady mistress runs away—'

'Not runs away – flees.'

'—*flees* from her father's home to the Unclaimed Lands? Not likely, lad.'

The other man at the table was now watching me more closely. He had as yet said nothing at all. I spoke directly to him. 'Have you seen her? She's small, with brown hair and green eyes and she's very, very pretty.'

There was a sudden silence among the three men. Finally the innkeeper said, 'She does not travel alone.'

'No.' Mother Chilton had told me as much, and then had not told me whom Cecilia was with, calling me stupid for even asking.

The man with broken teeth said, 'You're a fool, boy.'

'I am told that often,' I said with a big sunny smile. 'But in her haste my lady forgot me, and my brother and I must follow her. Do you know where she went?'

They all glared at me now. I knew I had not much time. The one with broken teeth said, 'She went inland, of course. Where else should one like her keeper go? She went towards Soulvine Moor, towards Hygryll. But you—'

I cried, interrupting him, 'Oh thank you! You see, I—' I knocked my pile of coins to the floor, dived under the table after it, and pulled a hair in my nose as hard as I could. When I rose again, staggering and without the coins, my eyes watered, my face had gone red, and I was sneezing violently. 'Oh ... oh, I'm afraid I ... Help me, please. My lady fled her estate because of the plague there and my brother ... Help us ...'

The men froze. The innkeeper breathed, 'Plague!' Then all three scuttled away from me.

'Help ...' I collapsed against the table.

One man drew his sword. The other said sharply, 'No! Don't go near him!'

'The coins—'

'Leave them, you idiot!'

All three left the inn, fleeing out into the night.

I went upstairs, collected Maggie, and we slipped away, making camp a few miles down the road in a deep thicket. First, however, I took food from the inn and another old, patched but still serviceable blanket. It would be cold going over the mountains to Soulvine Moor.

Where my mother had died. Where Cecilia had fled, in the company of ... whom? Where I might, at last, find the truth of both my past and future.

24

'We cannot go to Soulvine Moor,' Maggie said. 'We *cannot*.'

Morning, and Maggie and I faced each other across the embers of our campfire. Last night she had been too frightened to ask me much, but this morning she was herself again. Still afraid – if anything, she was more afraid since I had told her our destination – but since she was also Maggie, her fear led her to fight rather than cower.

I retorted, 'At least you said the name. In the palace you would not even utter "Soulvine Moor", as if the words alone could somehow harm you.'

'Not the words, you idiot! The people who might overhear them!'

That made sense. I had not known then how the palace was riddled with spy holes, with spies, with factions. I knew now. But we were not now in the palace.

'Tell me,' I said. 'Tell me what Soulvine Moor is.'

Despite the beautiful morning, she shuddered.

It *was* a beautiful morning. Overnight spring had turned to the first taste of summer. Golden light lay on the half-budded trees. Hawthorn leaves unfurled with that tender yellow-green seen only once each year. Birds sang. The woods smelled fresh and expectant, spawning life.

She said, 'Soulvine Moor is death.'

'No riddles, Maggie. Tell me true. Who lives on Soulvine Moor?'

'The ones who never die.'

'Witches?' I still wasn't sure what had happened to me at Mother Chilton's or what I believed about it.

'No. They burn witches there, as everywhere else. But they also ... They ...'

'Tell me!'

She shuddered. But no one could say that Maggie did not have courage. 'They don't die because they take the life from others. They murder them and steal their souls to gain their strength to add to their own. And so they live for ever.'

'Nothing lives for ever.' I, of all people, had cause to know that! 'How do they steal the souls from others?'

'I don't know. The ceremony is secret, known only to them. There are rumours, but no one really knows.'

'Are you sure this is not just a folk tale? A story meant to frighten children into being good, like the hawk man or the monster under the mountain?'

Her temper flared. 'How should I know? Do you mean, have I ever gone to Soulvine Moor to find out? I have not, and I am not going there now. If Lady Cecilia is in the Unclaimed Lands, then I will stay with you until you find her, but not afterwards. Do you hear me, Roger? Not afterwards! I will not stay as a serving woman to Lady Cecilia, as you so charmingly suggested days ago. I would rather live as a scullery maid, a pig tender, even a whore! Do you understand me?'

I was shocked. Maggie, a whore? Even though I knew she didn't mean it, the words gave me a queer feeling in my heart. It was not like Maggie to be so irrational. Nothing made sense.

But I didn't dwell long on Maggie's tantrum. As I scattered the fire and we returned to trudging along the rough road, my mind roiled with what she had told me. Soulvine Moor, from whatever terrible and fearful belief, killed intruders. To 'steal their souls'.

My mother, Aunt Jo said, had died on Soulvine Moor.

Had she been murdered? How?

No. I could not think that. I would go mad if I thought that. It was nothing but a folk tale anyway; no one could gain immortality by taking in the souls of others. Souls could not be taken in. They could only cross over to live on in the country of the Dead, if that could be called living. But here, in the land of the living, my Cecilia could be harmed.

'*She went towards Soulvine Moor, towards Hygryll,*' the man with the broken teeth had said. '*Where else should one like her keeper go?*' What keeper? What did I not know about Cecilia? Lady Margaret had said there had 'always been something strange about Cecilia'. But to me she was like a small stream, swift and light and clear to the bottom, babbling happily along in its little course. The man with the broken teeth had been lying, or mistaken, or cruel. Mother Chilton had not sent her to Hygryll – '*I told her to go into the Unclaimed Lands but not to enter Soulvine.*' Cecilia was somewhere in the Unclaimed Lands, and I would find her. I would.

And my mother?

Don't think such thoughts!

But there was only one way to stop the thoughts. I would do what I had intended to do over half a year ago, ever since Aunt Jo told me how my mother died. I would go as close to Soulvine Moor, to Hygryll, as was safe, and I would cross over. I would find my mother in the country of the Dead. Old women often talked to me there. My mother was not old, but she was there, and she would talk to me, her only child. From her I would finally have answers.

Having a plan cheered me. It was an idiot cheerfulness, since all difficulties still remained. But I had a plan: Find Cecilia. Enter her service, just to be around her. Then ask for a brief leave, go to the edge of Soulvine Moor, cross over and find my mother. I could do all that. I had done so much already! And the sun shone warm, the birds trilled in the fair morning, and I was away from the palace and its ruthless, contradictory, passionate and imprisoned queen. So my imbecile cheerfulness sang in my blood. I whistled as we walked, something I had not done for months.

Maggie trudged beside me, head down, saying nothing.

Information was not hard to come by in the Unclaimed Lands, not once we had turned away from the sea. Along the coast were the smugglers, the wreckers, the road that carried whatever travellers there were. But as the land rose in wild ravines and desolate moors, there seemed to be only one road, sometimes dwindling to a mere cart track, sometimes lost altogether so that, cursing, I had to search to find it again. The cottages were few and mean, and their inhabitants, once they set aside their initial suspicion of strangers, were glad of travellers to break the monotonous pattern of their days. Goat herders, hunters, farmers trying to survive on a couple of poor upland acres and a fierce independence, they gave us food and shelter in exchange for a few pennies and scraps of news. Nor did they seem surprised at two young 'brothers' travelling alone. Boys grew up quickly in this wild land. The food that Maggie and I were offered was scanty and sometimes almost inedible, but not once did we feel menaced as we slept among the ashes of the hearth – unless that place was already occupied by a flock of big-eyed children or by the family pig.

And nearly all of the upland folk had seen, or heard of, Cecilia.

'She be here yestreen a twelveday,' they said, and their accents were the same as Bat's, the seaman off the *Frances*

Ormund. 'A nineday.' 'A threeday.' We were drawing closer to her.

'How was the lady travelling?' I asked that first night. 'And who was with her?'

'On a donkey, she come,' an old woman told me. But when I looked closer, I saw that she was not old at all. Bent, slack-bellied, gap-toothed, she had no lines around her eyes. This woman was younger than Lady Margaret, younger than the queen, no more than thirty at the most. Her smile was sweet.

'Who was with the lady?' My stomach tightened.

'Her serving man. To take her to her cousin's manor, beyond the mountains.'

Maggie was careful to not look at me. Before I could react, the woman said, 'Old he seemed, for such travel. Spry enough, but old.' She, who never was nor had a servant, shook her head over the ways of ladies, gentlemen and their train.

Old. Who was he? And what 'cousin's manor'? I had never heard of Cecilia having a relative in the Unclaimed Lands, nor that 'cousin' having a manor. Although most of these mountain people had never been more than a few miles from their homes, so that 'beyond the mountains' might be only their words for everyplace different, farther away, unknown to them.

Over the next days, at houses even poorer in mountain dells even higher, I learned more. Cecilia and her servant had stayed one night. The lady looked tired and worn, her servant very old. No, said the next family to give us shelter, he was not her servant; he was her cousin, taking her to his farm. No, said the next, there be no 'manors' in these mountains – was I a fool? Nor were there any 'ladies'. The woman, dressed in a plain wool gown, and her uncle were going home, farther towards the border. As he said this, the man's gaze would not meet my eyes.

'What border?'

But the man turned away and stared into the fire, scowling fiercely.

The last dwelling, the poorest yet, was far along the track from its nearest neighbour. In fact, the track seemed to end here. There was only a rough hut set in a mountain hollow beside a high, thin, cold waterfall. A silent family, parents and four ragged children, crowded into a single draughty room. No one would answer my questions at all. When I repeated them, the man told me to hold my tongue. Maggie and I slept that night in the goat shed.

In the morning a child brought us two small loaves of bread. In the Unclaimed Lands hospitality was practically law, and even unwelcome, too-inquisitive guests must be fed. The bread was hard and sour, the child ragged and barefoot. Some sort of fungus grew on one of his calloused feet, between the toes and over them. It smelled bad. I caught hold of his bony wrist.

'I have something for you.'

'Unhand Jee!'

'Jee, I have something nice for you.' With my free hand I drew from my pocket a carved willow whistle. I had made it one night at a campfire by a small creek, where willows grew. I blew on it softly, and a single sweet note sounded.

Jee stared. It was clear he had never seen such a thing. He wanted it, badly.

I said, 'You can have it if you answer my questions. What is the border?'

For a long moment I thought he wouldn't answer. His little face twisted horribly, he reached down to scratch at the fungus on his foot, but his gaze stayed on the whistle. Greed triumphed over fear. He croaked, 'To the cursed land.'

Soulvine. 'Where is the border?'

'Be due east.'

'How far?'

'A day's walk.'

'And the lady – I mean, woman . . .'

'Hemfree be taking Cecilia home.'

A gasp from the prone figure on the straw. Maggie was awake and had heard. In my astonishment, I let go of Jee's wrist. He snatched the whistle from my hand.

'Hemfree be taking Cecilia home.' The child knew their names, knew who they were. How many others of the householders had also known, and withheld the information from the outlanders, the strangers from The Queendom? Who was Hemfree? And 'home'—

'They maun travel hard,' the boy said. 'Soldiers be coming after them.'

Queen Caroline's soldiers. She had sent men to find Cecilia, who had ruined all of her plans. Was that why Hemfree had brought Cecilia so close to Soulvine Moor – because pursuers were close on their trail? How close?

I seized Jee's arm. 'How do you know that soldiers are after the lady?'

'I see them. From a tree.'

Maggie looked from the boy to me. She said slowly, '"Home". Lady Cecilia is from the Unclaimed Lands. No, she couldn't be. The way she talked, moved . . . she is . . . Is it possible she came from . . .'

'Yes,' I said, 'she did.'

When Cecilia had sent me to Mother Chilton for the milady posset, I had not thought it strange. After all, even Maggie had recognized the name and known the old woman as a healer. But Mother Chilton had done so much more for Cecilia. She had sheltered her when Cecilia fled the queen's wrath. She had sent Cecilia home, with the unknown Hemfree to escort her. And Mother

234

Chilton had said something else on my last anguished visit to her, something about the queen . . .

'*Caroline studied the soul arts but she has no talent. Still, it is why the queen recognized you.*' And I realized with sickness in my belly why the queen had brought Cecilia to court as a child. Caroline hoped that Cecilia would develop the 'talent' that the queen lacked. She had not. But evidently there existed an underground web of these women, a web that spread gossamer threads from The Queendom to Soulvine Moor. Cecilia, Mother Chilton, Queen Caroline. Perhaps that web was why Queen Eleanor had refused to turn The Queendom over to her daughter. She knew that Caroline waded in dangerous waters. And now Cecilia, pursued by Greens, was being driven back to Soulvine Moor.

I don't know how long I sat there on the reeking straw of the goat shed, blind and dumb from my inner terror. Finally Maggie said softly, 'Roger?'

'Yes.' My voice did not sound like my own.

'Is Cecilia on Soulvine Moor?'

'I think so. Yes.'

'Does she . . . Is she . . .'

'I don't know what she is.'

But the moment I said it, I knew it was not true. I knew what Cecilia was. She was exactly as I had always known her: childish, heedless, sweet-natured, lovely, adorable. She was the 'pretty little kitten' that Mother Chilton had called her. No more, but no less. She had no 'talent' – that was why Mother Chilton had hoped that she could 'find some goat herder or scrub farmer to marry her'. That was why this unknown Hemfree had been sent to take care of her. Cecilia needed taking care of. That was why I too was here. To find and take care of Cecilia, my sweet kitten, my love.

Maggie said, 'Who is Hemfree?'

'Some relative or friend of Mother Chilton.' And perhaps of Cecilia as well. Someone who knew the country and the people, and perhaps even knew Soulvine Moor itself. Someone whom Mother Chilton could order about, as the queen ordered Lord Robert. A man who lived in the shadow of female power. Like me.

'Roger, what are you going to do?'

'If Cecilia has gone onto Soulvine Moor, I must go after her.'

'Please do not.' Her voice was reasonable, but reason barely holding back a storm of emotion.

'I must.'

'Why? To find a silly girl who doesn't care three pennies about you?'

'I have to go, Maggie.'

The storm broke. 'WHY?' she yelled. 'To be killed? To have your soul taken? Why?'

'That's a folk tale. No one can take souls from the Dead.'

'You don't know that!'

'Yes,' I said slowly, 'I do.'

'It isn't—'

'Maggie,' I said, taking both her hands in mine, 'I'm going. If you don't want to go, then stay in the Unclaimed Lands. Go back to that farm three days' walk from here – they will take you, you're a hard worker. Here, take this.' I fished out two of my remaining silver coins and held them out to her.

She threw the coins into the straw. 'Keep your filthy money! But you can't go into Soulvine!'

'I can. I will.'

'I won't be—'

I lost all patience. 'No one asked you to be anything! Go back to that last farm! Go back to The Queendom! I don't care!'

She put her head into her hands and wept.

It was a gale of tears such as I had not imagined was in her, a deluge, nothing like the silent tears I had seen her shed for her slain brother. She wailed and sobbed, sensible sharp-tongued Maggie! I didn't put my arms around her. I sat sullen until the storm was over and she had grown quiet, and then I again laid the two silvers on her knee and left the goat shed. I headed east, towards the border, towards Soulvine Moor, and Cecilia.

25

A day's walk, and the land smoothed out. It didn't drop, but the ravines and hollows and mountains flattened to a vast upland plain. Nothing marked the border, but I knew I had crossed it. This was a moor, Soulvine Moor.

Almost treeless, the moor nonetheless had its own beauty. I don't know what I had expected – bare and blasted heath, maybe – but the ground was spongy, covered with moss between clumps of low deep-purple flowers. Occasionally huge outcroppings of rock thrust up from the springy peat. These outcroppings bore green moss, reminding me of the boulder in the village of Stonegreen. But there were no villages here, no cattle grazing on rich grass, no chickens or harvest faires or pretty, doomed girls like Cat Starling.

Something caught my eyes: a bit of cloth snagged on a gorse bush. I seized it. Embroidered green silk. She had been here! I broke into a run.

A shape grew in the far distance. At first I thought it was a trick of the clear high light. But as I drew closer, I saw it was a low hill, far off, and that smoke rose up from it. It could be a town. It could be Hygryll.

But dusk was falling, and the smoke was still far off. A cool wind began to rise. Running had exhausted me, and I could go no farther without rest. I built a small fire, to keep away beasts, in the shelter of an outcropping of stone. The peat burned with its own peculiar smoke, acrid and earthy. There was no moon, and a million stars blazed in a black sky. I had no food, but a little water was left in my waterbag. I drank it, wrapped myself in my fur-lined cloak and fell asleep.

I dreamed of my mother. *She sat in her lavender gown with a child on her lap. I was both the watcher and the child, safe and warm in my mother's arms. She sang to me softly, a tune that I heard at first without words. Then the words became clear, and Roger the watcher's blood froze: 'Die, my baby, die die, my little one, die, die . . .' But Roger the child listened to the monstrous song and nestled closer, a smile on his small face and the pretty tune in his ears. 'Die, my baby, die, die, my little one, die, die . . .'*

Hands jerked me away from her. But they were real hands, neither in the country of dreams nor the country of the Dead, and they were pulling me away from the safe warmth of the campfire. Torches sputtered and flared in the night. Men surrounded me, pulling me with rough hands, turning my face to the flickering light.

Someone gasped.

I thought it was me, so terrible did the men look. And yet there was nothing inhuman about them. They were just men, heavily bearded, dressed in tunics and boots of tanned leather. They carried small knives with handles of carved wood. And the gasp had not come from me. It had come from the man holding my arm as he gazed deep into my eyes.

'Another one!' he said. His accent was like the house-holders in the Unclaimed Lands, like Bat's.

'Let me see,' said another voice. I struggled to be free, but the first man slipped deftly behind me and closed his arm across my neck, while twisting mine up behind me. I could not move.

'Who are you?' I said. 'Do you have Lady Cecilia?'

No one answered. A much older man came forward. Between his white beard and horned hat, only his eyes showed. They were green, the startling green of new leaves. As green as Cecilia's. He studied my face for a long time, and under his gaze strange sensations flowed through me. Not thoughts, not even emotions. It was as if a current moved in a hidden river in my mind, and all at once I remembered something nonsensical: Mrs Humphries, in the country of the Dead, totally absorbed in watching the white stones shift shape under the flowing water of the slow river.

Finally the old man said, 'No. Not another one. He has never been here before.'

'But he is—'

'Yes,' the old man said. 'Oh yes.'

The first man let me go. And then, there in the eerie light on the ground of peat and stone, the men of Soulvine knelt to me, Roger the Fool, and bowed their heads.

The Dead can sit insensible for days, years, centuries. Not so the living. I was aware of every sight, every sound, every prick of sensation on my skin as the men escorted me to Hygryll.

They talked little, and they would not answer my questions about Cecilia. They seemed to know completely who I was (which was more than I knew), so completely that it was a matter beyond discussion, as accepted as air to breathe. I was weak with hunger but afraid to ask for food. If I gave any sign of weakness, would they change from kneeling to me to killing me? Maggie had said they murdered people here to 'take their souls'. The belief might be folklore but the murder would be real, and I had no wish to dwell permanently in the country of the Dead. Not yet. So I walked as swiftly as they, grateful that the pace was not too quick because of the old man. And with each step I felt the peat springy beneath my boots, saw the torches bobbing ahead of me, smelled the sweet night air, experienced all the sensations that meant I was still alive.

Was Cecilia? Was she somewhere just ahead, in that town faint on the horizon?

And so we came to Hygryll. It lay in starlight among a group of hillocks, odd hills that were both wide and low. Then I realized that Hygryll actually *was* the hillocks. Each was a large round building made of, or covered with, earth and peat. A leather flap covered the doorway of the closest one. The old man pushed it aside and we entered.

I stood in a low, windowless, round room of stone. A fire burned in the centre, the smoke going up through a hole in the roof. The men set their torches in holders on the walls, and I saw stone benches heaped with fur blankets ringing the central space. Baskets rested under each bench. The only other furnishing was a large drum. One of my captors took the drum and went back outside. The others tossed fur blankets on the floor beside the fire.

'Sit down, *hisaf*,' the old man said.

I sat. I didn't know what a *hisaf* was, or what they thought I was. I dug the nails of one hand into the palm of the other to steady myself. Outside the drum began to beat, a slow rhythm but not monotonous, a message I could not begin to decode.

One by one, men and women came into the round stone room. None was young, although none seemed as old as the green-eyed leader. I looked eagerly at each, but none was Cecilia. And yet it seemed to me that I could see something of her in this girl's chin, that youth's eyes. Each came to me, knelt and said in their rough accent, 'Welcome, *hisaf*.'

More and more people, until the room was full, warm with the heat of their bodies and heavy with their silence. These were different from the people I had known all my life in The Queendom: the farmers at country faires, the innkeepers and faire folk, the soldiers and courtiers at the palace. They were different from Lord Solek's savage warriors, with their smiling and singing, their ruthless discipline. They were different even from Hartah. These sat somehow heavily, saying nothing, waiting stolidly.

They reminded me of the Dead.

When it seemed the room could hold no more, the drummer came in from outside. He put his drum on a bench and went out again. The old man stood. He spoke slowly, and despite his accent I could understand most of his words.

'Here comes a *hisaf*. There has not been one among us for a very long time. He was not born in Soulvine, and has never been in Soulvine, but Soulvine is his home. He is welcome. Soon he will travel to—'

I didn't catch the word, but of course he meant the country of the Dead. That was, after all, what everyone wanted from me, everywhere.

The old man finished, 'But first we will eat.'

Food! My empty stomach gave a loud growl. Surely food would end my light-headedness. The stuffy room didn't help; I was shifting between a heightened, almost dizzy awareness of every detail and sudden bouts of sleepiness. In the body-packed gloom someone threw a handful of dried leaves onto the fire and it flared. A sweet pungent scent filled the room.

The door flap opened, letting in a brief blast of cold air. Young men and women entered, all about my age, dressed in woven white robes. They carried big bowls of hot meat. All were comely and I looked eagerly for Cecilia. She was not among them, although the girl who held out a bowl to me had the same green eyes and brown hair. Even her smile hinted at Cecilia's. I smiled back and, like the others, took a chunk of meat with my fingers. It tasted greasy and succulent, unlike anything I had eaten before, but delicious.

Again someone threw something on the fire, and it flared with sweet scent.

Drowsiness took me, aided by the good food. Almost I dozed, but then the alert light-headedness was back, and again everything seemed preternaturally sharp and clear. I could have cut myself on the fur hide, the rush torches, the very air. Dimly I realized that there was some drug in whatever had been thrown on the fire. The young men and women left on another blast of cold air.

It was all so strange. And if Cecilia had indeed come from here, how much stranger the court of The Queendom must have seemed to her! I understood a little better now her constant edge of hysteria, that urge always for more excitement, more laughter, more dancing to banish the sense that she would never really belong. I had never really belonged either, not anywhere. It made a bond between us.

Where was she? Surely they would bring her soon ...

The old man rose. 'We are an old race, and we have drawn strength from the souls of others. Now we will go with the *hisaf* to the oldest place.'

Go with me? To the country of the Dead? What did he mean? No one could go there with me, no more than anyone could come back with me. Or did he mean that all these men were going to kill themselves right now?

And me too?

Fear ran over me, banishing all drowsiness. I half-stood. But the old man stood taller than I, and the room was packed with strong men. There was no escape. I had, as always, only my wits. And to my drugged mind it seemed to me that this was a bargain: *Cross over for us, and we will give you what you ask.*

I said, 'What do you wish me to learn for you in ... in the oldest place?'

He looked puzzled, as if my question had no meaning.

243

How could that be? Always those who sent me to the country of the Dead wanted me to bring back information. Hartah, all of Hartah's desperate faire customers, Queen Caroline. But all the old man said was, 'Go.'

I nodded. The men closest to me drew back, as if to give me room to fall. They knew, without being told, what would happen. I drew my knife, jabbed it into my thigh and willed myself to cross over.

Dirt in my mouth—
  Worms in my eyes—
  Earth imprisoning my fleshless arms and legs—
Then I was over. And not alone.

Never, *never* had I felt anything like this! There seemed to be a crowd of others with me, invisible but somehow *there*. They had been with me in that brief moment of death, and they were with me still, pressing like heat all around me. I screamed and ran.

A few steps, and they were gone from around me.

But now I could see them, a faint cloud of grey, like dank fog. The cloud did not move. The men of Soulvine were not present here in body, as I was. A fog could not talk to the Dead, learn from the Dead, instruct the Dead, as I could. But in some sense the men of Soulvine were here. I had not thought such a thing possible.

But now that I was out from the midst of that fog, I could see the country of the Dead, and I saw more things I would not have thought possible.

The land that lay around me was Soulvine Moor. There were no hillock-dwellings, but there was the vast high plain dotted with outcroppings of rock, with forests and mountains in the distance. But the sky overhead flashed with lightning and crackled with thunder. The springy ground beneath my feet lurched, once so hard that I nearly fell over. The boulders *jiggled*, as if with energy that stone never had. And a hard wind blew, a wind that did not dissipate the patch of living fog.

Amidst this chaos the Dead sat serenely, staring at a rock, a withered flower, the roiling sky. There were no drilling dead soldiers here; these men and women did not believe they were in Witchland. I had not told them so, and anyway they believed the hidden creeds of Soulvine.

Here – somewhere – was my mother.

I did not know what the people of Hygryll wanted from me. But I would take the opportunity they had handed me, and I began to search. The countryside was stretched out, as always, and the hordes of Dead scattered among the jiggling boulders. But I had time. No one could call me back to Hygryll until I chose to go. And the Dead did not wander around. I could search methodically, looking into their faces, matching them with my dim memory of my mother in her lavender gown. I began.

For what seemed like hours I walked the plain of Soulvine Moor, struggling to stay upright on the shaking ground, ignoring the churning skies, stooping to study face after face until my knees hurt and my back ached. Still I looked. I saw old men and women, some dressed in weird clothing from long, long ago. A few of the old women looked as if they might talk if I roused them, but I moved on. I saw young men and women, many of the men in armour from different ages. I saw children and babies. I saw the Dead, none of whom bore signs of violence or illness, although they must have died from violence or sickness or accident or childbirth. But not, anywhere, my mother.

And then my heart stopped. I saw Cecilia.

She sat quietly, more quietly than I had ever seen her in life, amid a patch of waist-high purple flowers. Most of the flowers had withered. The wind whipped their stems and brown petals against her skin, but she didn't notice. Cecilia stared calmly at the rumbling ground.

'Cecilia!'

I stumbled over to her. She didn't look up, not even when I grabbed her, pulled her to her feet, and crushed her to me. She didn't seem to notice.

'Cecilia – no! *No!*'

I kissed her lips, as I had longed to do for so many months. I kissed her eyes, her breast, her fragrant hair. Nothing roused her. She stood docilely, unresisting even when, in anguish and despair, I shook her hard enough to make her hair whip around her quiet face. It made no difference. She was dead.

I had failed to find her, to protect her, to keep her safe as I had once promised. Sobbing into her neck, I clutched her as she stood unknowing, all life and joy and playfulness gone. But when I finally led her forward by the hand, she walked after me, looking at nothing, or else looking at whatever the Dead see in their long trance. 'Cecilia, I will find a way to rouse you. I *will!*'

She said nothing.

'I'm going to take you to ... to somewhere else. Maybe once you're away from Soulvine ...'

That made no sense. The Dead of Soulvine were the same as the Dead of everywhere else. But I was beyond sense. The only thing I could think to do was to get Cecilia away from here, back to the Unclaimed Lands, back to The Queendom, where I had known her before. It was a stupid, insane idea, but because it was the only thing I could think of to do, I led Cecilia forward by her limp hand.

We threaded our way among the uncaring Dead, over the quivering ground, against the strong and unearthly wind. Her hair blew loose in wild tendrils. I stumbled, and when I fell, Cecilia fell too. Then I hauled her up and we kept going.

The border was not far; I had walked from it just last night, with the men of Soulvine. Just before I reached it, I tripped over another stone and fell heavily on top of one of the Dead.

'Alghhh! Leave me be!'

It was an old woman. I had roused her with a sharp elbow jab to her chest. She glared at me with indignation and fury.

'I'm sorry—'

She looked closer. 'What be you doing, boy? Oh! You be . . . Oh! A *hisaf*!'

She knew what I was. The next moment she looked around. Her old face, already a mass of deep wrinkles, wrinkled even more. 'I . . . be dead?'

'Yes,' I said. I had scrambled off her and now sat on the ground. Cecilia was standing docilely above us, gazing at nothing.

The old woman said, 'But I cannot die.'

I snapped, 'Everyone dies!'

'No. I drew the strength from other souls. And so . . . so did you!'

All at once she, this dead woman of Soulvine, was everything that had happened to me since I entered both Soulvine Moors, the living and the dead. She was my capture by the men, she was the smoky windowless room covered with earth, as if the feasters were already in a grave. She was whatever drug had been thrown on the fire to alter my mind, sending it between drowsiness and painful sharpness. She was the green-eyed old man who made me cross over, and she was the insane beliefs that had killed Cecilia. I looked at this old woman, and hatred for all of it tore through me, bright and terrible as the lightning flashes splitting

247

the sky. I seized her slight body and shook it like a dog with a rat.

'I drew no "strength" from anything, you evil old woman! There is no strength to be drawn from the Dead, and there is no living for ever! You are dead, dead, dead, just like all the others here! You and all the other murderers in Soulvine killed foreigners for nothing! You killed Cecilia, didn't you? And all for a stupid and pointless ceremony that gained you nothing! Nothing! Nothing! There is no way to gain anything from the souls of the dead!'

She gazed at me without fear. She said simply, 'You be wrong, boy. We can gain the strength. From the souls of the outborn. From the betrayers who left. You did so, last night. You gained that strength in the old and true way, when you ate the meat at the feast.'

She moved her gaze from me to Cecilia.

'From her.'

26

I had thought I knew what horror was. I was wrong.

The girl with the bowl of food, she of the green eyes, and the meat in the bowl, so succulent and greasy, with such a strange taste . . .

I couldn't speak. I couldn't even vomit. But I could kill, and I beat on the old woman with both my fists, kicked her with my hard-toed boots, slammed her head again and again to the ground. She looked at me with bewilderment and then with anger, but without either pain or fear. I couldn't hurt her. She felt alive under my hands, but she was not. Only I was alive, with the monstrous realization of what I had done.

Cecilia . . .

I had . . .

'Leave off, boy!' the old woman finally spat at me, got to her feet and stalked off. A few feet away she sat on a rock and lapsed into the serene trance of the Dead.

'Cecilia,' I said, seizing her hands in mine, 'I didn't know. I'm sorry, I'm so sorry. I didn't *know*—'

She could not hear me.

And then I did vomit, but there was no casting the horror out of my belly. It would live there all my days. In my belly, in my heart, in my bowels. '*They take the souls of the dead*,' Maggie had said to me all those months ago, but she had not said how. And I had not believed her anyway. I was a fool. I was a hundred times a fool, and I had eaten . . .

I had to get out of Soulvine Moor. I could not stay to

search for my mother; I could not stay for anything; I could not stay one more second. The need to leave, *now*, was the only thing that saved me. It was something, at any rate. It was action, motion of legs and lungs and back. I grabbed Cecilia's hand and dragged her forward, both of us stumbling on the quivering ground as the lightning flashed overhead, until I was out of breath. Gasping, panting, I ran on.

But even then I knew I could not outrun Soulvine Moor.

After I could run no longer, I walked. I walked for long, insane hours. I grew bruised from falls, dirty and sweaty and weak. Cecilia stayed unscratched, clean and unresisting, her hair fragrant as rainwater. She would walk as long as I led her, and not know she was doing it.

I kept trying to rouse her, doing everything I could. I kissed her, I shook her, and once in frustration too great to bear I threw her to the ground. She did not respond. Overhead, the storm continued to threaten without ever breaking. The ground shook without ever shattering. The wind blew without ever bringing rain. And Cecilia and I walked north until I recognized the hollow and the high sparse waterfall where Jee's hut stood in the country of the living. The cabin was not there, of course, and the hollow was littered with the usual Dead. But it was across the border. We were out of Soulvine Moor and into the Unclaimed Lands.

Somewhere around here, in the country of the living was Maggie. Unless she had gone back to The Queendom.

I'd had the insane hope that once off Soulvine Moor Cecilia might rouse. She did not. I was so exhausted I could barely see her. 'My lady, I must sleep.'

No answer.

I found us shelter from the wind beneath a stand of pine trees. Cecilia sat where I placed her. I lay on the cold and shaking ground and slept, something I had never done before in the country of the Dead. Almost, as I slipped into darkness, I was afraid that I would not wake. If you slept while here, did you die? Was the little death of sleep a passageway to the final sleep?

Almost I hoped it was. If I died, I would become like the Dead, unremembering of what had happened in Soulvine. I saw then what I had not seen before: that the lack of memory among the Dead might not be a curse, but a blessing.

However, sleep didn't kill me. Eventually I woke, crying out and clutching for Cecilia. She was where I had left her. I was dizzy when I stood up.

I needed more than rest. My body here was a real body, and so was my body there. Days might have passed since I crossed over. Never had I stayed here so long, and I was weak from lack of food. The body I had left in the round windowless room on Soulvine Moor, how long could it last without food or water? What might the men and women of Soulvine do to it if I did not return soon?

I could not rouse Cecilia, but I could talk to her, desperate talk for a desperate situation. 'My lady, I have a plan.'

She stared at the ground, her face expressionless.

'I am going to take you back to The Queendom. We will find a place, somewhere beautiful and far away from here. By the river, maybe, or the sea. Somewhere peaceful and sweet.'

But was there anywhere like that in this changed country of the Dead that I myself had caused to change? So much I had done wrong, so much I had failed at. But there must be some place less damaged than the rest, some peaceful haven somewhere, and I would find it for Cecilia.

'But first,' I told her, 'I must leave you here and cross

back over. I'm getting weak, here and there. After I cross over, I'll be back at ... at ...' I couldn't say it aloud: *Soulvine Moor*. 'Back *there*. But as soon as I can, I will leave, go to where I have left you, and cross back again. And then ...'

And then what? Cecilia would still be dead. But I couldn't think about that, any more than I could think, after my sleep, about what I had done in Hygryll. There are things the mind refuses. I understood now why Maggie and the other servants would not even name Soulvine Moor.

Cecilia stared calmly at the bed of pine needles beneath us.

I couldn't leave her, not yet. So I stayed for hours more in that same mountain hollow by the little waterfall, within sight of Jee's family's Dead. I was too weak to walk. I pulled Cecilia down to me and lay with her in my arms, and I talked to her. I sang to her. I fed the pathetic illusion that she knew I was there. If I hadn't done those things, I don't think I could have gone on at all.

Finally I kissed her unresponsive lips, bit hard on my tongue and found myself in the stone room in Hygryll.

All the men and women remained in the stone hut. For a crazy moment I thought they had all died: they sat in the unresisting trance of the Dead. But as I struggled to sit up, my head spinning, people stirred. I remembered then the grey fog of not-persons that had crossed over with me, and that had remained in that other Hygryll when I had fled. These monstrous flesh-eaters had somehow, in some thin and weird form, crossed over with me. Now they were returning to themselves, even as I was.

I loathed them. If I could have, I would have murdered them all, tortured them as Queen Caroline had once threatened to torture me.

252

The old man said humbly, 'Thank you, *hisaf*.'

It took every ounce of strength I had left, but I staggered to my feet, made my way among the weary bodies, and pushed aside the door flap.

Spring afternoon on the moor. Sunshine washed the air with gold. The small purple flowers bloomed and birds sang and the moss was springy – and not shaking – beneath my feet. I sat, too weak to go further, and ordered myself to not cry. *No tears*.

A girl, the same girl with green eyes and brown hair, brought me a goatskin of water and a loaf of bread. If it had been meat, I think I really might have killed her. But she brought bread, doughy and sweet with honey and berries, and I ate it all. Then I lay face down on the peat and slept.

For the rest of the day and all the next day, plus two nights, I did not move. The girl brought me food and water. At night someone tucked furs around me. No one tried to talk to me. The nights were sharp and cold, and someone built a fire beside me and tended it all night. I slept and I ate, and it was the great mercy of my life – its only mercy, it seemed to me – that I did not dream.

On the third day, at dawn, I sat up, stiff in my limbs. The fire burned brightly. Beside it the old man sat on a rug of fur. He said simply, 'You go now.'

'Yes.' I could barely get out the syllable, so great was my hatred.

'Thank you, *hisaf*.'

I swore an oath I had learned from Lord Solek, in the language I knew that the old man could not understand. Even in that, I was a coward.

He watched as I gathered up the latest offering of bread, took the waterbag, shook out my fur-lined cloak and hung it over my arm.

He said, 'So it is with a *hisaf*. So it was with your father.'

I whirled around so fast my boot heels tore the sod. 'What do you know of my father?'

'Nothing. But he be *hisaf*. Or you could not be.'

My Aunt Jo had never spoken of my father. For this flesh-eating monster to do so was obscene. I raised my arm, but some part of my mind whispered, *If you kill him, they may not let you go. And it looks now as if they will.*

I stalked off, and no one tried to stop me. No one stopped me. I was a *hisaf*, and apparently a law unto myself.

Hah!

I trudged to the border, and over it, and through a day's walk north until in late afternoon I came again to the cabin in the hollow by the waterfall, where Cecilia waited in the country of the Dead.

And Maggie in the country of the living, furious as only Maggie could be.

'You're still here,' I said stupidly.

'Where should I go?' She straightened from her task, digging spring funter roots in a patch of sunshine, and glared at me. Jee's cabin lay beyond, looking deserted except for a thin rope of smoke coiling up against the sky. Maggie looked thinner, dirtier, but somehow less a boy in her trousers and tunic. It was her hair; it had begun to grow back in springy fair curls around her face. That face changed as she looked at me, from fury to something like fear.

'Roger?'

'Did they take you in here, then? Are you well treated?'

'Yes. Roger, what happened?'

I could only shake my head. My legs gave way suddenly and I sat abruptly on the ground. Instantly Maggie knelt beside me. 'Oh, are you hurt? Wounded again? Sick?'

Wounded in my soul, sick at my heart. I could not say

so. Maggie's hand on my forehead was gritty with dirt, cool of skin. She said, 'You have no fever.'

'No.'

A long silence. Then she said, in her kind-Maggie voice, 'Tell me what happened. Did you . . . did you find Cecilia?'

I heard how hard it was for her to ask that, but I had no compassion to spare for Maggie. Nor could I bring myself to tell her what had happened. I said only (and that hard enough to say), 'Cecilia is dead.'

'Oh!'

She was too honest to say she was sorry, and again we sat in prolonged silence. I forced myself to go on. 'She was from . . . from Soulvine Moor originally – or her kin was, or something. She returned there and they killed her.'

Maggie put her arms around me. I let her, but there was no comfort in her embrace. There would be no comfort for me ever again.

She seemed to know that I had said all I would say, or could. She began to talk in a low soothing voice of earthly things, and slowly I felt her matter-of-fact voice pull me back to this world and ground me here. Did she know what she was doing? It didn't matter; the effect was the same.

'The family here took me in, yes, but as a servant rather than a guest. I help gather food, care for the babies, cook, and– I was going to say "clean" but there is no cleaning here. Still, there's more food than you might imagine, since Tob is a good hunter. Yesterday he brought home two rabbits, and today he hunts again, hoping for a deer. Of course in The Queendom it's illegal to shoot deer while they are in fawn, but here the law does not exist. They don't say much, any of them, and they work me much harder than is right, but I can't say they are unkind. Jee is the best of them, a curious little boy, and he will ask me questions if no one else is around. He has learned to play the willow whistle you made him, and wonderfully well. If you are hungry right now, Roger, I can bring you some of the rabbit I made today. It's flavoured with wild onion and there's not much in it except rabbit and funter, but it's hearty. There's no ale, but the water is clean and cold.'

'Thank you. Rabbit would be good.' I didn't want it, didn't want to ever eat meat again. But I would need my strength.

She brought it from the cabin, and Jee came back with her. He squatted on his haunches and stared at me from wary eyes. The willow whistle hung on a strip of cloth around his neck. Some sort of paste covered the fungus on his foot – Maggie's doing, perhaps. I didn't want to see him, and the second I saw the stew, I didn't want that either. My gorge rose.

Meat, succulent and greasy . . .

Just in time I turned my head, retching up long green ropes from my empty stomach.

Jee said, 'Ye went into Soulvine, despite. And saw.'

'Get him away!' I screamed. 'Get him away from me!'

'Jee, go into the house. Now!'

The child obeyed her, although sulkily. All at once I didn't want Maggie talking to him again. I didn't want her learning what Jee meant, didn't want her knowing what had happened to Cecilia. Let her know only that Cecilia was dead. I couldn't bear her knowing the rest.

'We're going, Maggie. Now.'

'Going? Where?'

'Back to The Queendom. Or . . . or somewhere. Come.' I stood, unsteady but determined, and took her hand. She must not talk to Jee, not even a word. Suddenly that seemed the most important thing in the world. In this world.

Maggie said, 'I must get my cloak and the waterbag.'

'Leave it. The weather's warming. You can share my cloak.'

Pleasure flushed her face pink, but Maggie was Maggie. 'No, I should have mine. I'll just be a moment.'

'No! I'll get it!' I stalked off.

The hut was dim and reeking; too many unwashed bodies had dwelt here too long. The woman sat on a rough-hewn chair, her gown open to give a baby the breast. Two smaller children played in a corner with some sticks and pebbles. Jee sat moodily poking the fire; he did not look at me as I snatched Maggie's cloak and our waterbag from a hook on the wall. The cloak too smelled bad, and I doubted that she had been the one sleeping in it. No one spoke. I took the cloak back to Maggie, who stood uncertainly, funter roots in her hand.

'Leave those,' I said. 'I have some coins left.' And Maggie too must have the two silvers I had left her.

But it was not in Maggie's nature to leave behind anything useful, and she tucked the funter roots into her cloak. We started back towards the cabin, and then down the rough track that seemed to be the Unclaimed Land's only road. Under the pine trees by the little waterfall I halted.

'Roger – why, you're trembling!' Maggie said.

Cecilia was here. I couldn't sense her, but she was here, in the country of the Dead that lay invisible all around us. A deep shudder ran through me. This time, however, when I felt Maggie's hand on me, I shook it off.

'I'm all right, Maggie. Just weak. We'll go another few miles and make camp, off the trail. Can you sleep without a fire tonight?'

'Of course,' she said. 'I have my cloak.'

Maggie was never one to let pass a chance to be right.

We walked until dusk, then found a hidden thicket to

257

stay the night. There was nothing to eat; the funter roots could not be eaten raw. Stomachs alive with hunger, we rolled early into our cloaks. When I heard Maggie breathe deep and even, I crept from our thicket and made my way back up the track to the pine grove by the waterfall. There was a waxing moon and the stars shone bright in a clear sky.

In the deep shadows under the pines I cut my arm with my little knife, and crossed over.

Cecilia sat where I had left her, gazing serenely at the same bed of pine needles, oblivious of the ground shaking under her, the lightning flashing above, the stinging wind. I took her in my arms. 'Cecilia, my love.'

She neither resisted nor responded. A faint smile curved her rosy lips, but it was not for me. It was for whatever unknowable thoughts – if they were thoughts at all – lit the minds of the Dead. I sat there, holding my lost love, for too long. Then I stood, pulled her up with me and began to walk.

Wherever I went in the land of the living, Cecilia must be led along the same route in the country of the Dead. That was the only way I could be sure of not losing her. I had to keep her with me, separated from me by only the dirt-and-grave-clogged passageway between my two worlds. I had to do that. I *had* to.

I'm not sure I was quite sane.

We walked for long hours through the hills and around the steep ravines of the country of the Dead, over the shaking ground and under the stormy sky. I left her in a place I would be sure to recognize even in this trackless place where countryside stretched and distorted. It was on a hilltop, beside a swift-running mountain stream. There were other Dead there, men and women dressed in strange clothing, in stranger armour, a whole crowd of motionless Dead. Once, much must have happened in the counterpart of the hilltop, on the other side. All of the Dead sat or stood or lay peacefully, and there would be no difficulty in recognizing them when I returned.

Then I plodded back uphill, short of breath, weak with hunger, and fell asleep beside Maggie just as the sky began to lighten into dawn.

'Roger. *Roger*. We should be going.'

I could not move. 'Sleep,' I muttered. 'More sleep.'

'You can't,' Maggie's voice said. I hated that voice. 'Someone might come after me. Or after you. We have to go.'

'Can't.'

'What's wrong? Are you sick?'

'Tired.'

She said nothing. I opened one eye to her bleak face, and it was that bleakness that gave me strength to sit, to stand. I had brought Maggie into this; I had to get her out.

None of that was true. Maggie had brought herself into this, and I had been willing enough to abandon her to go onto Soulvine Moor, looking for Cecilia. Yet it was also true that now I felt responsible for her. Or was it? I didn't know what was true any more. I stumbled forward.

I don't know how I kept going that morning, on no food and almost no sleep. But there came a moment when I could go no farther. The strength built up in the two days of eating outside the Soulviners' round ceremony chamber, all that strength, was already gone. I sat down on the track, and I could not move.

'Roger?' Maggie said.

'I . . . can't.'

'It's all right. Lean on me. Just a little farther. There you go, just get off the track into these trees . . . See, we're almost there.' Encouraging, cajoling, patting me with her

259

free hand, Maggie got me into a little copse and laid me on the weedy ground. All morning it had been clouding, and now a light drizzle began to fall. I was glad of the rain; it hid my tears. I was at the very end of my strength and wits, the latter never much to start with. Exhausted in body and spirit, I fell asleep.

And when I woke in the evening, the rain had stopped. There was a fire. Food cooked over it. The goatskin bag swelled with water. And there was Jee, blowing softly on the whistle I had made for him.

'He brought the food,' Maggie said before I could say anything, 'and the ropes for snares, to catch small game. He told me it was all right to make a fire because Tob has not yet returned from his long hunt.'

'Jee can't come with us.'

'He says he won't go back.'

'Maggie, consider all the– *No!*'

Jee stared at us both, expressionless, the whistle halfway to his lips. He cupped his other hand protectively over it.

Maggie said, all in a low rush, 'I lied before, Roger. I didn't want you to know. His father beats Jee. He beats Jee's mother too, and he would have beaten me except that he hoped I would lie with him. He stole the two silvers you left me. I was only going to wait for you another day because that's how long I thought I could hold him off, and then I was going to go and take Jee with me. He's too good for that life.' Before I could answer, she raced on. 'He says he won't go back. He says he'll follow us. He says he'll do that even if you beat him too. He says—'

'Can't he say anything for himself?'

Jee blinked and said something. His voice was so thick, from accent or fear, that I couldn't understand the words. But they made no difference anyway.

'Maggie, his father will come after him. Maybe even after you.'

'I told you: he went on a long hunt yesterday, just before you appeared. Jee says it will be at least three more days before he returns. By that time we'll be far away, if we move faster. Here, eat this, and you will feel better.'

If we move faster. The only way we could move faster was if I didn't spend most of the night moving Cecilia to match our daylight travels. But Cecilia was now a night's worth of road ahead of us, and if we travelled for two days before I moved her again . . .

'Eat!' Maggie commanded, and I ate. Roasted rabbit, and delicious. Or so I thought for a moment, until the memory of that other meat returned, greasy and succulent . . .

Maggie said softly, 'What is it? You were eating, and then all at once . . . What is it?'

She was quick, so much quicker than Cecilia, than even the queen. I didn't want her noticing so much. And the taste of rabbit had started all the sweet juices flowing in my mouth, and all the clamour starting in my stomach. I could not forswear meat forever; I would have no strength at all. So I forced down the rabbit, and drank some water, and said, 'What would we *do* with Jee, Maggie? Later?'

'What will we do with ourselves?' she said. To which there was no answer. But Maggie was not the girl for no answers. 'How much money do you have left?'

'Why?' I countered.

'Because we could maybe start a cookshop in some village at the edge of The Queendom, where Solek's soldiers don't go. He hasn't got all that many soldiers, you know, not to post over the whole Queendom. If you have enough money left to rent some poor cottage and buy just a few vegetables to start, I could cook. Jee can hunt the meat, and we could sleep in the cottage at night. Later on, if we save money hard enough, we can add ale. Come on, Roger, *eat*.'

I ate. Her plan could work, maybe. We could survive with a small poor cookshop far on a remote edge of The Queendom. I found I hated the idea. But why?

I didn't know. A year ago, running a cookshop in a quiet village – away from Hartah, away from danger, away from having to cross over – would have seemed the best thing that could ever happen to me. But not now. Things were different. I was different.

Different how? I didn't know the answer to that, either. *'You've grown, lad. You're nearly a man,'* Mother Chilton had said. But it was not that. All boys became men. All boys—

'What is the month and day?' I asked Maggie. She was efficiently stripping the rest of the rabbit meat from the bones and wrapping it in a clean cloth. She didn't even have to ponder in order to answer me.

'Month of Sacter, tenth day.'

A month before the summer solstice. Today was my birthday. I was fifteen.

For two days we walked, camping nights as the moon again waxed towards full. Once, from the crest of a wooded hill, I glimpsed soldiers in the valley below. Looking for Cecilia? They would not find her now. The thought brought no comfort.

Jee said little, but without him we would have needed to buy food at houses or inns, both giving away our presence and depleting my coins. Jee, the child, was the only one of us who could hunt, and the snares he set each night produced a steady stream of rabbits. They were spring rabbits, without much meat on their bones, but Maggie roasted them with wild roots and newly budded herbs that she picked as we walked, and by the third day I had strength enough to go back for Cecilia. When the others slept, I crossed over.

It was a long, weary walk to the windy hilltop where I had left Cecilia. She followed, unresisting, as I led her down the mountains. It was much more difficult here than in the land of the living because the ground shook so. Once it even *shifted*, an abrupt sideways jerk that threw us from our feet into a thicket of thorns. I rose bleeding and bruised. Cecilia rose with her green gown clean as ever, her creamy skin unscratched, her eyes blank. Above us the wind would not stop blowing, and thunder rumbled in streaky clouds.

I could not rouse Cecilia but I had roused the country of the Dead, turned it monstrous and deformed. This too was my fault.

The next night I walked Cecilia past the place where Maggie and Jee lay asleep. Not much farther on, the land abruptly descended. From this point on the track I could see for miles and miles, even under the grey dimness of these thick clouds. On the horizon lay a deeper grey that, I was fairly certain, was the sea.

There was no time to lie with Cecilia in my arms, barely time for a quick embrace. I kissed her cold cheek, sat her down and crossed back over.

Full sunlight struck my eyes, which had become accustomed to the dimness of that other country. Jee's whistle played, stopping abruptly as I rose from my bedding. And Maggie stood looking down at me with accusing eyes.

'So you're back,' she said.

'I was asleep.'

She gave out a single oath, one so filthy that even Hartah had used it only rarely. Maggie said, without looking at him, 'Go find water, Jee. *Now*. Fill the bag.'

The child went, eyes wide with fear.

Maggie said, 'Nothing I did could rouse you. What you … what you …' Her voice dropped to a whisper, and the sudden terror on her face dwarfed Jee's. 'What you told me in the kitchen. It's true. Isn't it.'

I could not see anything to be gained by lying. Not any more. Besides, she would not believe me. When Maggie made up her mind, not all of Solek's army could change it.

'Yes. It's true.'

'You can … you can cross over to the country of the Dead.'

'Yes.'

'You're a witch.'

'No,' I said irritably. 'There is no such thing as a witch. I am a—' I knew only one word for it. '—a *hisaf*'. '*So it was with your father*,' the old man's voice whispered in memory, '*or you could not be*.'

Maggie said, 'What's a *hisaf*?'

'Someone who can cross over. Maggie, I did not choose this. I was born this way. But I am not a witch, and I swear to you on my mother's soul that I am no threat or danger to you. To anyone.'

She considered this, her face still twisted with fear but nonetheless considering. At that moment fair-haired Maggie reminded me oddly of Queen Caroline, at least in expression.

'You go to her at night,' she said. 'You go to Lady Cecilia. That's where you went last night, isn't it? I couldn't wake you this morning but it was not illness, not even exhaustion, it was as if you … weren't here. Because you were not. You were with her.'

'Yes.' Relief washed through me. Maggie understood; she accepted. I could stop hiding and running from her, because now at last there existed one human being who knew what I was but – unlike Hartah, unlike the queen – would not seek to use my gift for their own ends. Relief lightened my mind and, despite everything, I nearly laughed aloud with relief. We were free of lies, Maggie and I, and everything from this point on would be so much simpler.

'I hate you!' Maggie screamed, and threw a roasted rabbit at me. Still warm, it burned my cheek and then fell onto the grass, a wet meaty slab. Maggie put her head in her hands and cried as if she would never stop.

'Maggie, what ... what ...'

'Don't touch me!' she screamed, although I hadn't tried to. 'You don't understand anything! You're the stupidest man I ever met, and the most evil, and the– How can you go to her? She's dead! Dead, dead, dead, and even when she was alive, she was silly and vain and stupid – even stupider than you are! And I followed you and cooked for you and risked everything for you. Don't touch me!'

'I'm not! Maggie—'

'Go! Get away from me! Or stay here with your dead and rotting whore. I don't care! I'm going!' She ran down the uneven track.

Even without much sleep, I caught her easily and pinned her arms to her sides as she tried to hit me. Her face was streaked with dirt and tears, she smelled of days of travel, and she bucked in my arms like a captured boar. Then, all at once, the bucking stopped. She threw her body against mine and kissed me hard.

So at last I knew. The suspicion I had had on the island, the suspicion I had worked so hard to dispel, was true.

'Maggie,' I gasped, when I could tear my mouth free of hers. 'Maggie, no. I—'

She let me go.

We stood there for a long time, not looking at each other, under a warm noon sun. I had no idea what to say, what to do. A few moments ago I had held Cecilia in my arms – Cecilia, cool and unresponsive and unliving. Cecilia, my lady and my love. And yet I stood there on the mountain track, the land sloping away from me towards the distant sea and spring blooming all around, and my body responded to Maggie's nearness. Confusion swaddled me like dense fog.

Maggie did not seem confused. She never hesitated. Keeping her face turned away from me, she started down the track. When I ran to catch up with her, she pushed me away, hard.

I caught up with her a third time, grabbed her hand, and pressed into it three of the six silver coins I had left. Again she pushed me away. When I got back to my feet, she had marched ahead. But the coins were not among the weeds on the track; I looked. She had kept them.

Well, she had earned them.

I watched her until she was out of sight. But I didn't follow her. I couldn't; I was too weary from my night in the country of the Dead. I had to sleep now, to keep my strength up. For Cecilia.

I found a hidden thicket alive with tender green-yellow leaves, crawled into it, and fell asleep in the sweet warm sunshine.

When I woke, at dusk, Jee was not with me, which did not surprise me. It was Maggie whom the child had followed; Maggie who had shown him the only real kindness the poor little rat had ever known; Maggie, who loved me, and whose love I could not return.

Why not? Something whispered inside me. I silenced it. Then, still in my thicket, I crossed over. But this time I had a desperate, hopeful, insane plan.

27

It was the place I had left Cecilia that had started me thinking. She was still there, where the mountainside abruptly descended and the land lay spread to the gaze for miles and miles. I had recognized part of that landscape, far below me and above the sea cliffs. It was the clearing where the old queen's Blues had hung the yellow-haired youth, and the second noose had dangled awaiting me. Below the cliff at the clearing's end was the little beach where Hartah and his cohorts had wrecked the *Frances Ormund*.

I took Cecilia by the hand and led her towards that distant clearing. Each time I could go no further, I left her and returned to my tranced body in some thicket or sheltered ditch. I slept, bought food as I could, and grew so haggard and filthy that farmwives began giving me bread, from pity. The moon again passed full and began to wane. Each time, I stayed in the land of the living only until my strength had returned, strength that I used only to walk forward to where I had left Cecilia, cross over and journey with her again. No moon here, only the grey sky shot with flashes of lightning, the storm that never broke, the rumbling earth. Always Cecilia and I moved lower in the mountains, towards the valley where The Queendom lay.

What can I say of those days of walking with Cecilia in that country that had no days, nor any nights? The ground trembled, the sky rumbled, and she did not really know I was there. Yet that time held a wild sweetness for

267

me. Each time I took Cecilia's hand, put my arm around her slim waist, drew her to lie next to me on the withered ground, feelings surged through me, and none of the feelings fit with any other. I could never have held this woman, a lady, in my arms under any other circumstance. I loved her. And in the round stone house on Soulvine Moor I had—

Whenever that memory assaulted me, I babbled. 'Cecilia, I'm so sorry. I didn't know I didn't *know*. O Cecilia, I'll make it right for you, for us, I promise I *promise*.' And I pressed her to me, and smelled the light flowery scent of her hair, which never changed, and a kind of despairing joy came over me, gone the next moment in a wash of black guilt.

And yet what I remember is the joy.

I don't know how many days passed this way, but eventually we reached, each in our own country, the cliff above that rocky beach.

In the land of the living the cabin still stood, deserted and infested with spiders and mice. The yellow-haired youth's body had disappeared over the winter and spring, probably eaten by crows, but the frayed remains of the noose still swung from the oak tree. I could see the whole horrific scene as if it were not memory but solid reality before me now: Mistress Conyers in her sodden gown, torn between horror and justice. Enfield, the soldier of the Blues, itching to hang me from the same oak tree. And earlier, Hartah on the beach, his arms waving in the driving rain as the *Frances Ormund* struck the rocks and the terrified sailors staggered ashore into the wreckers' knives. My Aunt Jo, shouting to me over the storm, her features blurred by flying water: '*Roger! Go! Go now!*' The one thing I could not see was myself, the snivelling boy who clutched at the hem of Mistress Conyers' gown and begged for his life. That boy would not come clear in my eyes, my mind, my muscles. I was no longer him.

I crossed over.

It was strange to leave a calm spring afternoon in the land of the living and arrive in a storm in the country of the Dead. Always before, it had been the other way around. Now the sky here was as wild, the sea as high, the wind as howling as on the night of the wreck on the other side. The only differences were that no rain fell, and underfoot the ground shook as if it, like the *Frances Ormund*, was about to come apart.

Bat remained where I had left him all those months ago, sitting on a tree stump beside the track from cabin to cliff. He jumped up as soon as he saw me. He looked the same: flat head, big nose, greasy hair, slurred voice. A child in the tattered clothing of a shipwrecked sailor, the knife handle carved like an open-mouthed fish still in his huge hand.

'Sir witch!'

'Yes, Bat.'

'Ye come for Bat!'

'Yes. Are you well?'

The simple question confused him, not unreasonably. What did 'well' mean – either in Witchland or the country of the Dead? Bat said nothing. He eyed me with a mixture of fear, respect and hope. I had no idea what time had meant to him, waiting here on his stump. Nor did I think too deeply about the matter. I was too busy pushing away pity for what I was about to do to him.

It was Bat who had first showed me that the Dead do not always know they are dead. It was Bat who had first showed me that, lacking this essential knowledge, a dead man could will himself to fly up a cliff face. That was what I had later used to save Cat Starling from the Blues intent on burning her. Instead I had sent her flying away through the air, so further convincing the soldiers that

269

they were in Witchland. It was with Bat in mind that I had first devised that stratagem, and it was with Bat that I was now going to test a further idea. I could not risk Cecilia for the experiment; she was too precious. First would have to come Bat.

I said, 'Why do you not kneel to me, Bat? I am, after all, a lord of Witchland!'

Hastily he got down on his knees, muttering apologies I could not understand.

'I am going to release you from Witchland,' I said. 'Come closer.'

On his knees the sailor inched towards me, until I could see the white flakes in his greasy hair. I stepped closer too, and our bodies touched.

'Stay completely still, Bat.'

'Aye, sir.' His voice trembled, but he obeyed.

I put my hands under his armpits and pulled him to me, like a child or a lover. I held him as close as possible. Then I crossed over.

Dirt in my mouth—

Worms in my eyes—

Earth imprisoning my fleshless arms and legs—

But this time it went on and on. I was trapped between, buried in the earth for ever and ever, and the other rotting skeleton buried with me, screaming in my non-existent mind. It went on and on and on . . .

And then I was through, gasping on the fresh spring grass, and Bat sprawled at my feet, howling and terrified and alive.

It took me a long time to recover my breathing, and Bat even longer. Gasping, wheezing, the only thing I could think of was Hygryll. The men and women in the round stone room covered with earth, who had followed me – the *hisaf* – in a grey fog, had existed in the country of the Dead only as wisps, but then they had not actually

270

been dead. Bat, on the other hand, had been fully in the country of the Dead, and he was now fully here.

But was he?

As soon as I had recovered enough breath and wits, I examined Bat. He had jumped up and stood gazing wildly around, panting in great sobs, waving his knife as he looked for something to attack. I said imperiously, 'It's all right, Bat. I have brought you back from Witchland. Kneel!'

He did so, looking glad to have a clear order. Orders were something he could understand. Nothing else was. On his knees he raised his face to mine. 'Bat be saved from Witchland?'

'Yes. *Yes.*'

What convinced me was his smell, so strong that I had to back away. In the country of the Dead odours were not strong. I'd had to hold Cecilia in my arms before I could catch the fragrance of her hair. But now Bat reeked of sweat, of piss, of dirt, of the sea salt dried on his tattered clothes. He was solidly *here*, embodied in the land of the living. He was alive, and he stank to the sky.

All at once my legs gave way and I had to sit on the ground. *Bat was alive*. And I had done this. I, Roger, the *hisaf*.

'*So it is with a* hisaf. *So it was with your father. Or you could not be.*'

Could my father have done this? Perhaps this was what Soulviners meant by living for ever – that the dead could be brought back to life. If my father had not left us before she died, could he have brought back my mother? And if he could have done so, and had chosen not to ...

Hatred exploded in me for this unknown man, and it was the hatred that finished me. Too much, too fast. Maggie, Bat, Cecilia ... I burst into uncontrollable tears. Shamed, I rolled over, hid my face and sobbed like the six-year-old I had been when my mother died. I cried and I could not stop crying.

Bat tended me. Murmuring non-words, he covered me with my own cloak. He found water somewhere and fetched me a few drops in a young leaf. He sat beside me, a huge and stinking man, and patted my shoulder until the paroxysm passed.

'All right, Bat. All right. I am fine.'

'Sir witch,' he slurred. 'Ye fine?'

'I'm fine.'

'Ye fine?'

'I'm *fine*. Thank you, Bat.' Now another problem occurred to me: what was I going to do with him? 'Do you know where you are?'

He gestured towards the beach and said simply, 'Sea.'

Of course. He was a sailor. Wherever the sea was, Bat was at home. He would accompany me to where the coastline flattened, find a ship to sign on to, and resume the life that Hartah had stolen from him – and all without ever realizing that same life had ever been extinguished. If he spoke of Witchland, mumbled of it in his feeble-minded slur, no one would believe him.

Suddenly I wanted him gone. I wanted to be alone, to cross over and bring back Cecilia. Nothing else mattered, nothing else filled my mind.

Why did *hisafs* not always bring back their beloved dead?

The question needled me, and would not go away. One possible answer. *Perhaps they did*. But if so, why had my father not retrieved my mother? That brought me back to my oldest questions: why had he left her in the first place, and what had happened in Hygryll to cause her death? If I had found her in the country of the Dead on Soulvine Moor, I could have asked her these questions. But I had not found her, and I was not returning to

Soulvine Moor just now. I had to bring Cecilia back over.

But first I had to rest. Everything in me had gone weak, used up by my efforts. From my pocket I fished out six pennies and gave them to Bat. 'Here, find a cottage or someplace, and buy bread and cheese. Bring it here.' Almost before the words were out, I was asleep, lying there on the track between the cliff and the clearing where the yellow-haired youth had died kicking the empty air. I must have slept around the clock, because when I woke it was once again afternoon, the sun blazing through the half-unfurled leaves, and Bat was gone.

A loaf of bread, already crawling with ants, lay on the ground beside me. The goatskin waterbag was full. Bat had thought of my needs before running away from Sir Witch, who might at any moment send him back to Witchland. I didn't blame him. I brushed the ants off the bread and ate half, forcing myself to save the rest.

Next I found a stream, bathed, and washed my clothes, longing for the strong soap in Joan Campford's laundry. The stream, racing down from the mountains, was so cold that I yelled when I first ducked into it and the icy water hit my privates. Nonetheless, I scrubbed myself with gravel until my skin was red. I wanted to be clean for Cecilia.

When I and my clothes had been dried by the bright sun, I ran my fingers through my hair to comb it and shaved my face with my little knife, a business that resulted in blood I then had to staunch. When all this was done, I picked a bouquet of spring flowers and a clutch of wild strawberries, made my way back to the cabin in the clearing, and crossed over.

For a long terrible moment, I thought I was back at the wreck of the *Frances Ormund*.

Rain lashed my face, so hard and thick that I could barely see. Rain, in the country of the Dead! The storm

273

blew me sideways, off my feet. I picked myself up and groped my way across the clearing, calling, 'Cecilia! Cecilia!'

A tree crashed to the ground, barely missing me. *I couldn't find her.* The howling wind whipped my cries away as soon as I uttered them, and why was I calling her anyway? She could not hear me, could not respond. Where was she? What if the country had stretched, as it so often did, so that the clearing was not here but miles away, in all this pelting rain ... *Crack!* Lightning hit the ground a league away, deafening me.

But this storm, like those on the other side, waxed and waned. During a lull, when the wind and rain abated a little and the lightning moved off, I could see better. The Dead were still here, sitting or lying on the trembling ground, serene amid the chaos. I stumbled over an old man, who roused enough to snap something at me in an unknown tongue before returning to his eerie calm. *There, ahead!* But no, it was another girl in green, sitting beside a small child.

Then I saw her.

Cecilia sat tranquilly at the very edge of the cliff above the sea. She could not have moved, so the cliff must have. Her green dress was as sodden as Mistress Conyers' had once been, as sodden as if Cecilia herself had been in a shipwreck. Her rich hair whipped in the wind, long tendrils writhing like snakes. I lurched forward and snatched her back from the cliff edge.

The sea below boiled. The rocks were hidden by surf and spray and rain. If there were figures on the beach below – Hartah, Captain James Conyers, my Aunt Jo – I could not see them. I did not want to see them. I clamped my teeth hard enough on my tongue to bring blood, and with Cecilia in my arms, I crossed back over.

Another crossing that seemed to go on and on, with

274

dirt filling my mouth and the sockets of my eyes, so that I could not see the soft body I clung to so ferociously. But it was not soft; it had turned as skeletal and bony as my own. Both of us were trapped here for ever in the grave!

Then I was over, and she was with me.

We lay at the top of the cliff above the beach in a tangle of spring weeds. Cecilia went very still in my arms. Her green eyes blinked: once, twice. A puzzled expression settled on her features like mist on glass. Then she jumped up, looked around and began to scream.

'Cecilia, no! It's all right, it's all right! Cecilia!'

She stopped screaming but backed away from me, clutching her wet skirts, her eyes wide and terrified. 'Roger! Where am I? What have you done?'

And then I saw the moment that memory returned in full. What was she seeing? The round stone house in Hygryll, or had her murder happened somewhere else? How had they killed her? Had she—

Cecilia's eyes rolled back in her head and she crumpled to the ground.

I wasn't in time to catch her. She fell face down, and for a long terrible moment I thought I had lost her again. But she breathed. I rolled her over, laid her head on my lap, and rubbed her cheeks. She opened her eyes.

'Roger?' she said so softly that I barely heard her. And then, 'I died.'

I couldn't bear the look in her eyes. Pain, bewilderment – she was like a small animal whom cruel boys had hurt for sport, a kitten mewling and beseeching, *Make it stop. Oh please make it stop . . .*

I lied to her. 'It was a dream, my lady. You had a bad dream.'

For just a moment some hardness flashed over her face, some glint of a Cecilia I had never seen. Then she seized what I had offered her.

'Yes, of course, a dream! A silly bad dream. Silly me! And we're here because we . . . because we . . .' Frantically she glanced around the clearing. 'A picnic! Yes, of course, I remember now. A picnic. A bad dream. Really, Roger, what are you doing? You must not hold me like that! Bad Roger!' She sprang up and took a few steps away from me, hysteria and flirtation mixed horribly on her face.

'Cecilia—'

'You must remember who you are!' She wagged a finger at me, stopped the gesture halfway. Again panic twisted her face, and again she drove it away. With coquettishness, with silliness, with sheer granite will. 'You must remember who I am! Even on a picnic, it is not fit for you to touch me, you know!'

An enchanting smile, covering terror.

'My lady—'

'I think I want to go on now, Roger. Oh, flowers! Are those for me? Oh, you naughty boy, you shouldn't! But so pretty . . .'

She snatched up the bouquet I had picked for her and held them to the sodden bosom of her gown, smiling at me like a desperate child.

A thought came to me, unbidden and unwelcome: *Maggie would have had the courage to face the truth.*

But Maggie had never died, had never gone to that other country. And if Cecilia was a child, she was still as enchanting as ever. It was easy – so easy! – to slip back into being the humble servant I had been with her at the palace. I knelt and said, 'The flowers are nowhere near as lovely as you, my lady.'

She laughed. 'Oh, you do overstep yourself! What a courtier you are becoming, Roger. I think perhaps I am hungry, after all. What a lovely spot for a picnic, here above that sweet sea!'

I gave her what I had: stale bread and wild strawberries.

I spread my cloak for her on the grass. I passed her the waterbag. She prattled on, covering the strangeness of the situation with silly chatter, the only defence she had. I saw that she would never speak of what had happened to her on Soulvine Moor, nor of the weirdness of finding herself alone in the far reaches of The Queendom with me. Whatever poverty or hardship we endured, she would laugh and prattle and say nothing and rely on me utterly to take care of her, pretending that this was normal because anything else was too terrible to think about.

A child.

When the lovely spring afternoon faded, I led her – without taking her hand, this time – away from the cliff. The sun had dried both our clothes. We slept in the clearing, she wrapped without comment in my cloak, I shivering on the bare ground. The cloak would have held two, but for Cecilia that was not possible. My dreams in that cursed place were terrible, but I didn't mention them. Not then, not ever. Cecilia would not have known how to comfort me even if comfort were possible, for one who had done, seen, been such as I.

28

It is one thing to love a child in a palace, surrounded by comfort. It is another to travel with a child through rough country, trying desperately to think where to go next.

I had three silvers and seventeen pennies left of Mother Chilton's coins. Maggie's scheme of renting a cottage for a cookshop might still be possible if I could earn just a little more money. However, I had trouble visualizing Cecilia as a serving maid. And then I had to spend two silvers on a donkey, because Cecilia could not walk very far or for very long. I had to leave her hidden in a grove of trees to find somewhere to buy this donkey, and the baulky animal cost me more time and money than I had expected. By the time I returned, Cecilia was curled into a quivering ball of terror in my cloak. It took me hours to soothe her.

Not that she complained. She never did that. But she was so weak, so helpless, that I spent most of my last coins on better food, on a few nights' lodgings in an inn, on an enamelled comb for her hair and on a cup so that she would not have to drink from the waterbag. Now there was not enough money left to rent any cottage, anywhere.

We had come to the edge of The Queendom, where the coast began to turn flatter and fishing villages appeared. Perhaps I could find work here? But I knew nothing about fishing, and how would I explain Cecilia? If she would just stay quiet, I might have passed her off as my sister or even my wife. But Cecilia never stayed quiet. A constant, desperate chatter was how she kept memory outside the fortifications of her mind, and her chatter marked her as court-bred.

'My lady,' I said, 'who was Hemfree?'

An expression of complete terror crossed her face, quick as lightning before it vanished. Had I, in fact, seen that expression at all? Her words came too swiftly and too loud. 'I don't remember that name.'

I believed her. Her memory had immediately discarded what she could not bear to remember. I tried something easier.

'When did you first come to the palace?'

'Oh, very young, a little girl! The queen herself sent for me. She knew my mother.' But then something must have threatened to breach her mind, because she threw me a roguish, desperate smile and laughed. 'Why, Roger, are you questioning my age? Don't you know that you must never ask a lady how old she is? Shame on you, naughty fool!'

If she had had a fan, she would have rapped me with it. But I was no longer a fool. I turned away, but then she surprised me.

'I could get work as a lady's maid, I think,' she said.

I jerked my head around to gaze at her. 'A lady's maid? But, my lady, there are no courtiers here!'

'Oh, not here, not in a fishing village!' She laughed. 'Somewhere nicer … Or, at least, I think I could, somewhere there is a need for …' A puzzled expression crossed her face. Memory, or at least realization, was very close. She pushed it away.

'Oh, silly me! Of course I couldn't do that! Really, you shouldn't let me prattle on so, you naughty boy!'

I said quietly, 'I am not a boy, Lady Cecilia.'

And she was not a lady. Not here, in this place. I could not take her anywhere that she could be a lady, because

279

Queen Caroline would have her arrested, tortured, killed – although Lord Solek still held the power at court. I had learned as much from overheard scraps of conversations as I bought Cecilia her comb, her food, her cup, her lodging, her donkey. Probably Cecilia and I shouldn't even stay in these remote fishing villages for very long. Fishing villages brought travellers, both by sea and land, and travellers carried news to and fro. Inevitably, someone would notice the presence of a woman as beautiful and out of place as Cecilia. That traveller would mention it elsewhere, and the news would make its slow way to the queen.

So what was I going to do with my lady, my love? How were we going to live?

If we went inland, but not towards Glory but rather to remote villages where the chance of recognition was less and the old ways were stronger, I could do as Hartah had done. I could sell my services as a visitor to the Dead, bringing false comfort at the summer faires that would soon begin. My flesh writhed at the very idea. However, I could come up with no other. The money was gone, all but a few pennies. We had to eat.

Moodily I walked along the rocky beach, watching the boats set out in the early morning for a day of fishing. I had left Cecilia asleep in the village's only inn, a snug wooden structure with a taproom below and two tiny bedchambers above, both smelling of fish. Cecilia and I shared one of the chambers, she on the bed and I on the floor. The innkeeper's wife, who ran the place while he fished, was much younger than he and frankly curious about Cecilia and me. But she asked nothing and ran her little establishment with a tolerant competence that reminded me of Maggie.

The fishing boats disappeared over the horizon. A dazzling yellow sun broke into view. I skipped a few desultory stones over the calm water, then went back to the inn and paid a precious penny for a mug of ale in the taproom. It was too early for ale, but I needed it. The innkeeper's wife served me and then sat, unbidden, at the trestle table opposite me and rested her rough-skinned elbows on the table.

'Where do ye come from, friend?'

'Many places,' I said wearily. I was in no mood for conversation.

'And where do ye go?'

I didn't answer.

She studied me. Not pretty, she nonetheless had a healthy vitality, like a strong young animal. A lively intelligence glittered in her small brown eyes. 'I ask because we don't be having many visitors here, this early in the year. No, not many visitors.'

'I imagine not.' *Go away*.

'I wonder if ye knew the one here but two days ago.'

'No.'

'That's too bad. I maun return his things to somebody.'

I sipped my ale, looking pointedly away. I had had enough of chattering women.

'Lookee, I show ye.' She jumped up, opened a chest in a corner of the room and pulled out a pile of rags. On top of them lay a knife with a curved blade and a wooden handle carved like an open-mouthed fish.

Bat's knife.

'Ah, I see ye know him, after all,' the woman said.

'Maybe. What ... what happened to him?'

She shrugged. 'No one knows. He took a room upstairs – the room ye be having now – waiting for the fleet to put back in. Out several days, they was that time. And he dint come down. I finally unlocked the door and he be gone, with his clothes on the bed and his knife under the pillow.'

281

'His clothes?'

'Aye. His only clothes, and naught else be stolen. The door was still barred on the inside, but he was just gone. Somebody still owes me his reckoning. But how did he leave all naked, and for where?'

How indeed? All at once the taproom seemed cold, the ale tasteless. My stomach clenched. Bat would not have fitted through the upstairs chamber's one window. The woman had just said the door was barred from the inside. So how . . .

If Bat had somehow gone back to the country of the Dead – or had been, what, snatched back there? – then his clothes and knife would have gone with him. The Dead did not cross over naked.

No, the whole story was a lie, a ruse to get a stranger to pay what Bat owed her. My stomach unknotted and I said, 'I knew the man only in passing. I owe you nothing.' But I stood, my ale unfinished, and climbed the stairs to the bedchamber.

Cecilia still lay asleep. I stared at the tiny window, the thick door. *Two days ago*, the woman had said. Bat would then have been back in the land of the living for . . . how many days? I had lost track of time.

Maggie would have known.

But it didn't really matter. I sat in the chamber's one chair and watched Cecilia. She had washed her hair last night, a laboursome business involving cans of hot water which I had lugged up the stairs, and now her tresses spilled clean and shining over the rough cotton pillow. The lids of her eyes fluttered, translucent, faintly blue. Her strong young throat lay exposed, and the top of one small breast above her shift. I had never touched that breast, never would touch it. Cecilia looked more beautiful than I had ever seen her, and completely desirable. But I felt no desire.

What am I going to do with you?

I watched her for a long time. Then I woke her. I had no money to pay for this chamber for another night; I could barely pay for breakfast. She didn't grumble, but her lovely face was sullen. I went to the stable yard and watered and hitched the donkey, which did grumble. After a silent meagre breakfast, I helped Cecilia mount and we started inland, travelling on a track overgrown with weeds, towards what the innkeeper's wife said was the nearest farm village, several leagues to the north-west. The village was called Ablington. They were having a faire.

'Roger, you're not listening to me!'

I was not. But I was thinking of her, and also of Bat. I believed the innkeeper had been lying, but her story would not leave my mind. I had crossed over with Cecilia the day after I had brought Bat back. Was that significant? What *had* happened to Bat?

'You're not listening!'

'I'm sorry, my lady.'

I plodded on, towards the spring faire. Where I would set Cecilia in some cool grove or on a bench on some village green, and I would try to do what I had vowed to never do again. To be what Hartah had made me: a liar and cheat in two countries, here and there.

But Cecilia and I never reached Ablington. We never reached anywhere at all.

It happened at dusk of the next day, beside a campfire over which I toasted the last of our bread, wishing instead for one of Jee's rabbits. Cecilia sat combing her hair with the comb I had bought her. The hair rippled and shone in the firelight, glinting in a hundred shades of honey, cinnamon, gold, bronze, amber, copper, chestnut. The dusk deepened her green eyes to the colour of emeralds.

283

'Why are you looking at me that way?' A tiny half-smile at the corners of her mouth.

'Because you are the most beautiful thing I have ever seen, Cecilia.'

'You should call me "my lady". Don't be so familiar, Roger!'

She was not teasing. Firelight flickered over the enamelled comb that I could not afford, the bread of which I would give her more than half although my stomach rumbled with hunger, my fur-lined cloak that she sat upon. There rose in me an anger I had not known I felt, had not known I could feel. Not towards her.

I said, my voice low and careful, 'Perhaps the circumstances justify my familiarity.'

'No,' she said with sweet certainty. 'No, that cannot be, Roger. You know that. I am a lady, and you are the queen's fool.'

'Out here there is no queen, and no fool.' *And you are alive only because of me*. Made alive, kept alive.

'But they exist, nonetheless.' She shook her head at me playfully, and her beautiful hair shimmered and danced.

'But things can change.'

'Why should they? Anyway, *that* doesn't change.'

'Why not? Why are differences in rank never to change, when all else has changed in The Queendom, in the world? Why is that one thing the same?'

'It just is.' She smiled at me. The smile of a lady towards a fool. She resumed her combing.

I said, 'No.'

'No what?'

'No, *Cecilia*.'

Her smile disappeared. She said coldly, 'You are impertinent, Roger. Apologize at once.'

I got to my feet. Why? I had no idea. But I stood looking down at her in the firelight: Cecilia, beautiful and dirty, exasperating and desired, enchanting and stupid. I said, 'I will not apologize.'

Her face began to break up. For the briefest part of a moment I thought my words had caused it, thought that her features were merely sliding into anger. Not so.

'Cecilia!'

The skin softened on her face even as her mouth opened in a silent scream. Her nose, mouth, cheeks turned black – *rotting*. Her body slumped sideways as the bones crumbled. A terrible stink rose on the night air. Her eyes melted, staring at me, and then, just like that, nothing remained but a heap of clothing.

'Cecilia! My lady!' I threw myself on the ground, rooting through her cloak and her gown and even her shoes as though I could find some trace of her. There was nothing, not even a strand of the honey-coloured hair. Not even a fingernail. All gone with her – *where*?

I howled like an animal but didn't hesitate. The fire was nearest; I used the fire. Thrusting my left hand into the embers, still crying her name, I crossed over.

She was not there.

The sky snapped and growled and poured rain in the country of the Dead; the ground shook; the Dead sat tranquilly amid the chaos. But I could not find Cecilia. I roused old women and shook them, demanding information. I tripped over rocks and bushes and bodies, searching in the windy storm. I looked in thickets, in groves, behind boulders, in ravines where the rock walls threatened to tumble down and crush me. She was not there.

Not in the land of the living, not in the country of the Dead.

'*He was just gone*,' the innkeeper's wife had said of Bat.

I threw back my head and howled at the stormy sky. I beat my hands on a boulder. To have brought her back,

285

to have come so close to saving her! And now . . .

You could not cheat death. Not for more than a few weeks, which was no time at all. Death always won.

It was morning in The Queendom when I finally crossed back over, a morning fresh with birdsong and golden dawn. The fire was long since out. I sat beside it, too anguished to tend my burned hand, too anguished even to sob.

Cecilia was gone. She no longer existed, not anywhere, in any form. Whatever the serene Dead were waiting for, there in that other country, Cecilia would never find it. This then was why *hisafs* did not cross over with their beloved Dead. By bringing my lady over, I had killed her more completely than the cannibals of Soulvine Moor ever did. I, Roger Kilbourne, *hisaf*.

Roger Kilbourne, the fool to end all fools.

29

I had not known before that there are fates worse than dying, or places worse than the country of the Dead. I knew it now.

It's hard for me to remember what I did that morning of despair, or that afternoon, or that evening. I know I didn't eat because there was no food. I know I didn't tend to my burned hand because my charred fingers blackened and blistered. The blisters burst, spilling pus and blood. Did I sit beside the dead fire, numb for all those long hours? Did I scream or cry? I don't know, and may never know. Those hours are as lost to me as was Cecilia, gone to the same dark place of anguish and utter hopelessness.

I had killed her. I must die for it.

That was the thought that brought me back to life, if life it could be called. I seized on the thought as if it would save me. I could die, and then in the country of the Dead would come oblivion. I would be like the rest of the Dead, serene and mindless and free of pain, sitting tranquilly on the tranquil land.

Except that the country of the Dead was no longer tranquil. And not all the Dead waited in mindless serenity. The soldiers of the Blues. Cat Starling. They had not believed they were dead, and so retained their former selves. And I too knew that death was not final, that it was possible to move and think and live on the far side of the grave. So would I, a *hisaf*, remain aware – perhaps for all eternity?

An eternity of remembering what I had done to Cecilia. Remembering here, or remembering there. No difference.

Death was not a way out. Not for me.

Nonetheless, I think I might have done it, just to do something, *anything*, to bring change to the despair that felt unendurable. My bowels and liver crawled in my body, seeking to get away from me. My eyes burned, hating that they must live in my head. My hands, burned and unburned, clenched into fists and yearned to beat my body into unconsciousness. I could not hold together, could not live with myself, could not endure another moment of this horror.

But the moment existed.

Then another moment.

And another.

'Roger!'

And another.

'Roger! Stop!'

And another. I attacked my enemy, who was myself. I flailed at him, charged him with deadly accuracy.

A kick to my burned hand sent me yowling in pain. My other hand dropped the knife. It was snatched from the ashes of the fire. A smell, another kick, and then a voice, young and high and frightened.

'Roger! Stop! What be ye doing?'

Jee. His skinny form emerged from the evening gloom – how had it become evening again? – at a wary distance. When I went motionless, he crept closer.

'What be ye doing? Stop that!'

'Jee.'

'Aye. I could hear ye a mile off.'

'Jee.'

'Aye! Yer hand . . .'

All at once my burned hand seemed on fire. The pain was unendurable, and I think it was the pain that brought me back to myself. There was no room for anything but the searing pain, and for what Jee said next.

He squatted beside me, peering into my face, his own in the same anguish as mine. I had not known before that the anguish of others can push away our own. Not completely – never that – but enough to survive. Jee was in that kind of anguish. Had he not been, I doubt he could have reached me at all.

'It be Maggie,' he said. 'Soldiers took her.'

'Took her? What soldiers? Took her where?'

'Rough big soldiers,' the child said, and began to cry. 'With green clothes and feathers. They took her.'

The queen's soldiers.

'They be looking for you,' Jee sobbed. 'They asked Maggie about *you*. They took her to the whore queen!'

Me. Maggie had been taken because the queen was looking for Roger Kilbourne, or Lord Solek was, but I guessed it was Her Grace. A desperate Queen Caroline had discovered that I had left the capital with Maggie, and the queen needed me back to use in whatever was her latest desperate bid for power. And once the queen decided she needed something, nothing stopped her from getting it. If Maggie didn't tell the queen where she had last seen me, Queen Caroline would torture it out of her. Even if Maggie did tell, she might be tortured for anything else she might know.

Maggie under those instruments of pain I had heard existed but had never allowed myself to imagine before. I imagined them now. The rack, the nails, the red-hot pincers . . .

Slowly I sat up. Maggie, who had always been a better friend to me than I deserved. I would not fail yet another person. 'Stop crying,' I ordered Jee, more harshly than one should speak to a grieving child. 'Stop it right now. We have to go after Maggie.'

289

The child, raised with a brutal father in the wild Unclaimed Lands, stopped crying at once. His eyes grew huge in his tear-tracked face. 'G-go after Maggie? We uns?'

'Yes,' I said grimly. 'We uns.' Everything that had happened in the last months shifted in my mind, assuming different shapes. Like stones seen under water, shifting with the changing light.

'H-how?'

'Leave that to me.'

Jee would not have been Jee if he had done that. 'Ye have a plan?'

'Yes,' I said, astonished to realize that yes, I did have a plan. And I was willing to bring down two realms to carry it out.

I washed and bandaged my hand. Jee had brought food, and we ate it for strength. We rode Cecilia's donkey, Jee's slight body adding nearly nothing to the weight the beast had to carry. Still, the donkey, being a donkey, protested and refused to move. I beat it with a stick, whacking it across the nose so hard that it started and then trotted forward. I had never beaten an animal before in my life.

We travelled all night. The moon waned but the stars were clear and high. Because I didn't know this countryside, I was forced to backtrack to the fishing village where I had heard about Bat and then take the coastal road towards the mouth of the River Thymar. In this flatter softer countryside the road was well marked. The donkey plodded on, hour after hour. Jee clung to my waist, saying nothing. Perhaps he was asleep. So long as he did not fall off, I looked no closer.

My burned hand sent shards of pain through me. The pain formed its own rhythm, out of time with the clopping of the donkey, and both a dissonance with the images that flashed through my brain, one at a time, with all the power and brilliance and horror of lightning that strikes and chars living flesh.

Cecilia, combing her hair in the firelight just before—

Maggie, kneading bread and smiling at me in the servants' kitchen—

My mother in her lavender gown—

Cecilia—

Maggie—

Slowly, something happened to my pain. My pain, my grief, my guilt. They stopped sending me images and instead shrank inside me, growing hard and sharp, until they settled in my chest like the spiked metal ball at the end of a soldier's mace. I knew that spiked ball would be there for ever. But the shrinking let me go on, and I had a battle to wage.

We travelled by night, hid and slept by day, pushed the poor donkey to its full protesting endurance. On this well-travelled road we didn't dare risk a fire, but nights were warmer now. Without Jee, I could not have done this. There was no time to stop and snare rabbits that we couldn't have cooked anyway, but he knew how to spot buried nuts, spring berries, edible roots. I was always hungry. But finally I was here, in a grove of trees just downriver from the capital. I could see the tower where I had stood with the queen, where I had been left locked out all night after my 'fit'.

'Maggie be there?' Jee said.

'Yes.'

'In that high place?'

'No.' Maggie would be below, in the dungeons I had never seen, the dungeons where advisers and captains loyal to the old queen had been put to death. Or would Queen Caroline keep Maggie with her in her apartments, trying to beguile her into cooperation, as she had once beguiled me? That's what I was hoping: that Maggie was still alive, and whole. That if Queen Caroline had tried wiles and sweet promises instead of torture, Maggie would know enough to play along.

Jee slipped his grimy little hand into mine, a thing he had never done before. He must be terrified to seek such reassurance now. He said, 'Ye look and look ...'

He was right. I had been staring at Glory as if truly ensorcelled. Sunrise, just a few minutes ago, had left long fingers of gold and pink in the eastern sky, curving around the horizon towards the island as if to embrace it. The summer morning was soft-aired, filled with fresh flowers and the trills of birds.

'... and ye look, but we maun *do*.'

'You're right, Jee. We maun do.' I tore my eyes from the tower, knelt and put both hands on his bony shoulders. 'Listen to me. Listen very carefully. I am going to do things that look strange to you, and frightening. All these things will help save Maggie. No matter what I do, you must stay where I put you. You must not run away or scream, or do anything but stay very still. Do you understand?'

'To help save Maggie,' Jee said, seizing on the only words that mattered to him.

'You *must* stay hidden, Jee. And silent.'

'To help save Maggie.'

He trusted me utterly – maybe because he had no other choice. I knew how that felt. I put him in a dense nest of bushes half a mile from the river, where he couldn't be seen. Then I squeezed my burned and bandaged left hand with my right, cried out, and willed myself to cross over.

The storm had, if anything, worsened. Lightning flashed over a river racing with evil-smelling rapids. The ground shook so much that it was hard to stand. Rain pelted my face, soaking through my clothing in just a few moments. I had appeared not far from a captain of the Blues, now on this side of the river. He rushed over and cried, 'The witch's captive! You're back, boy! What news?'

I nodded. It was difficult to hear over the howling wind. Through the rain I saw that the army of dead Blues had swelled to many hundreds. Had Lord Solek killed all those who tried to rebel? It seemed likely, but I had no time to ask.

'The best news,' I shouted, my mouth close to the captain's ear. 'We are going back to The Queendom, to fight and take back our own.'

His face, streaked with rain, lit up. His lips pulled back, baring his teeth, and I almost quailed before the fierce light of hatred in his eyes.

'Aye, and in good time, boy! We have our battle plan at the ready. But something has happened to Witchland.' He waved his arm to indicate the entire landscape: roiling, quaking, stormy, withered, coming apart.

He did not know that what had happened to Witchland was me. I had interfered with the order of life and death. I had convinced large numbers of dead men that they were not really dead, preventing them from lapsing into the serene waiting trance that was their natural next state. Worse, I had brought back Bat and then Cecilia to the land of the living. A *hisaf* could make that journey, but no one else should. Taking away the subjects of the country of the Dead had torn the very fabric of that sacred place.

And now I was going to rend it far more.

'Captain, bring all your men together in—' I grasped at a military term I had heard from the queen. '—in close formation. Here, now. We must act quickly!'

'You have the amulet?'

Amulet? What amulet? Then I remembered: the amulet I had invented to save Cat Starling, the amulets

I had told the soldiers to make. The captain's hung from a string around his neck. Lies upon lies – and all necessary.

'Yes,' I cried over the wind, 'I bring you the amulet, and much more besides! Order your men!'

It took only a few shouts before several hundred men lined up in neat rows on the shaking earth. I said, 'They must hold onto each other around the waists, all together.'

The captain stared at me. Something flared in his eyes, anger mixed with sudden doubt. 'These be soldiers, boy! They can't fight like that!'

'Not to fight. To leave Witchland. Or else they must stay here for ever.'

He stared at me, and for a moment I thought he would not do it. But then he turned and gave the order. His dumbfounded men glanced at each other, scowled, muttered, glared at me – and one by one put their arms around the men closest to them, so that the neat rows became a vast uncomfortable mass. 'You too!' I said to the captain.

'No.'

I shrugged. 'Then stay here.'

He swore and grabbed the man closest to him. I clutched at the captain, bit my tongue so hard that blood spurted into my mouth, and willed myself to cross over, with several hundred men fastened to me like weights, or leeches.

The sky shrieked and split open. Something roared out of the rent, something bright and terrible, just as the ground gave way beneath my feet. I was falling. I was being devoured by the bright monstrosity from the sky . . .

And then I was in the grave, that in-between place of dirt in my mouth and worms in my eyes, of being imprisoned alive in my rotted body. And this time *I could not get free.* The weight of hundreds of men pulled at me, clawing and dragging. We would all stay here for ever, trapped, neither dead nor alive. An eternity of the grave, with worms in my eyes and cold on my bones.

Oh, what had I done?

And still the earth held us, the barrier between the land of the living and the country of the Dead. The grave held my rotting flesh until death – the real thing – would have been welcome. I would just give up, surrender, let myself die.

No. I must save Maggie.

With a last tremendous effort of will, I concentrated upon reaching Maggie again. *Cross over, cross over, cross over for Maggie.*

I tumbled onto the grass beside the placid blue river.

Desperately I gasped for air, the soldiers heaving and moaning beside me. Sensation returned: my arms were flesh, not rotting bones; my eyes brought vision, not maggots; my tongue could move, unchoked by fetid dirt. The weight of men no longer dragged at me. Had there been, it seemed to me now, even one more of them, I could not have made that horrendous crossing. Never again!

When I could stand, I looked for Jee, who was not there. He had stayed hidden as I'd instructed. As soon as he recovered, the captain barked orders and soon the army was in battle formation, swords drawn, shields at the ready. He spared me one glance.

'Thank you, boy. Now go.'

A single look can change worlds. Before the captain's gaze returned to his men, it had gone from gratitude to distaste to dislike. I had brought him out of Witchland, but that meant I was a witch, and witches were to be feared. To be hunted. To be burned. The contradiction was more than the captain wanted to navigate. He wanted me away, so that he would not have to sail those treacherous moral seas.

I faded back into the trees until my back was to the thicket where Jee lay hidden. The Blues began to march towards the river. From below me came a sound. It might have been Jee, breathing 'Roger?' It might have been the rustle of a rabbit or a fox. Or a rat.

All the soldiers would die a second time. Like Bat and Cecilia, their renewed lives were illusory, temporary. In a fortnight – I had finally worked out in my mind the passage of days – they would disappear, burned horribly out of existence like wood that becomes smoke, dissipating on the very air. You could not make smoke become the oak or maple or cherry wood it had once been. And yet if I had not done this monstrous thing, what would have become of these soldiers in the country of the Dead? They did not inhabit it, as the rest of the Dead did, waiting in tranced calmness. Already they were restless, bored, desperate. What would they have become in ten years' time, twenty years, a century? I had seen Dead dressed in garments much more old-fashioned than that. And meanwhile the presence of the restless soldiers, neither dead nor alive, would have gone on destroying that peaceful countryside beyond the grave.

My doing, all my doing. But this was no worse than the rest. As the soldiers marched towards the capital, I followed.

Green archers appeared on the ramparts of the city. Then Lord Solek's warriors, each man with a *gun*. I could see them clearly in the soft summer air, looking like tiny toys carved for children.

'Flank right!' the captain of the advancing Blues called. A detachment of soldiers, shields raised, moved off to the right. They would attack from the east, I guessed. The main army marched forward.

Now I could hear the iron gates to the city being lowered, loud scrapings of metal on metal in the winches. How would this army get into Glory? Not even battering rams would budge those gates. And all the soldiers were doing was marching straight forward. The Blues were locked out and outnumbered, both. And here, unlike in the country of the Dead, they could not just fly through the air.

'Boots off!' the captain called.

Boots off? Each man propped his shield on the ground in front of him and kicked off his boots. The heavy boots, I could see now, had been left unlaced.

The main section of the army broke ranks and ran, following the small section that had veered to the east. All at once I understood the captain's plan. The east side of the city was where the laundry rooms and baths were located. These had been built out over the river to let clean water flow in and out again, carrying soap and dirt downriver towards the sea. This was the first part of the palace I had ever seen, scrubbing myself clean after Kit Beale had brought me here. The attacking soldiers, who were from the palace and knew it as well as they knew their own bodies, would swim under the walls and take the palace from the inside. Solek had positioned his warriors and the queen's Greens on the walls for a more conventional attack. It would take them time to reach the laundry and the baths, with their myriad rooms for each rank of palace dweller, the laundries meanwhile defended only by the unarmed women who served there.

A cry of rage from the castle, and the Green archers let fly their arrows. The warriors fired their *guns*. And a silence fell, a silence of profound astonishment, of frightened disbelief. I stopped in the act of picking up a discarded boot, my body crouched, as silent as everyone else. We had all been struck dumb.

The arrows and the *bullets* from the *guns* had all passed through the bodies of the advancing Blues as if those bodies were so much air.

My mind raced. Cecilia – had I ever seen her fall, seen her injured, seen her so much as stub her toe on an inn table? No, I had not. I had guarded her, hovered over her, kept her safe. Her body had been solid, yes, after I brought her back, but then it had been solid in the country of the Dead too, as she lay unknowing in my arms. The bodies of the dead Blues had been solid, and those of the dead warriors, and I had seen them fight with each other and the weapons pass right through them. But that had been on the other side! Here, the Blues were alive again . . .

No. They were still dead. They were just dead here, in The Queendom of the living.

A great shout went up from the advancing army, part fear and part amazement. Then a din, a babble. I was too far behind to hear the words, but I could see the waving arms, the spreading grins. I did catch a word, then – *witch*. And half the men turned to where I stood.

Some actually knelt – in the middle of battle, with arrows and *bullets* passing through them! '*The amulet and much more,*' I had said to the Blue captain. They thought this was the '*more*'. I had made them invincible.

Then the moment of silence, of obeisance in the midst of the lethal rain of weapons, was over. The Blues continued their dash towards the island. Some threw away their shields. Greens and warriors disappeared from the walls of the palace, presumably rushing down the stone staircases towards the east wall. I picked up a shield and followed slowly. Unlike the Blues, my body was vulnerable. I could be pierced. I could still die. By the time I reached the river, only a few Blues remained by it, as a rearguard. I saw two of them running their swords through each other again and again, in wonderment that each time there was no blood, no pain, no death.

They saw me and fell to their knees. I couldn't bear to look at them. *You will be gone before the full moon.*

There were more soldiers at the river's edge across from the laundries. They too fell on their knees to me. I walked past them, dropped the heavy shield and the boot – Why was I carrying one boot? When had I picked it up? I couldn't remember – and unlaced my own boots. These soldiers, so wrongly on their knees to the boy they wrongly perceived as their saviour, had probably been left as a rearguard because they could not swim. I could swim. I waded into the wide placid river and swam towards the palace.

Near the island I swam through soap, which drifted in slow pools, stinging my eyes. Nearer still, and a thin river of red trickled towards me from under the palace wall. I thought at first it was dye, like the red dye on the face of Lord Solek's singer, or the yellow dye on mine when I had been the queen's fool. Then the trickle of red spread and widened and I saw that it was blood. I thrashed through the viscous oily water, which grew redder and soapier when I swam beneath the wall and into the washroom where once, in another life, I had been a laundress. I swam into the laundry through a pool of soap scum and blood.

Joan Campford was there, standing in a corner, three girls cowering behind her. The girls shrieked as I broke the surface of the water, but Joan recognized me, even through a coating of soapy blood.

'Roger! How . . .'

In six strides I reached her and took her by the shoulders. Around me lay the bodies of Greens and savage warriors, slumped by the washpots and dye vats, floating in the water, sprawled by the fire pits. One man had landed, or been thrown, halfway into a pit, and the smell of burning flesh reeked through the hot air. 'Joan! Where is Maggie?'

It was the only time I ever saw Joan Campford speechless.

'Maggie Hawthorne ! The kitchen maid I left the palace with. I know you know!' *'Everyone always knows everything,'* Maggie had said to me once. The servant gossip spider's web of information.

Joan said in a low voice – as if we might be overheard by the dead! – 'With the queen. The queen keeps her.'

Not in the dungeons. Not tortured. Not yet.

I tore from the room, running through the familiar courtyards. Bodies lay everywhere, none of them Blues. All were Greens or savage warriors, and many more savages than Greens. Had many Greens turned traitor at the last minute, joined the Blues against the queen? It seemed possible. Many of the men on opposite sides were kin to each other, like Maggie and her late brother Richard, and none had any love for Lord Solek.

As I neared the queen's chamber, I came on the last of the fighting. A detachment of warriors stood in the courtyard, blocking the immense carved wooden door to the presence chamber. Among them was Lord Solek.

'For Queen Eleanor!' cried the captain of the Blues. He and his men, six strong to Solek's ten, were covered with drying soap scum. They charged forward with drawn swords. The warriors raised their *guns* and fired. The *bullets* went through the Blues and rang on the stone walls, clear hard sounds like the tolling of a bell. A bullet bounced off the wall and past my ear, and I jumped behind the low wall of an ornamental fountain. Water spouted into the air and down on my head, washing away some of the soapy blood.

The savages fought hard. They fired their guns; their

300

leather shields parried the sword thrusts; in close combat their curved short knives found the bodies of the Blues again and again. Each time the knife sank into flesh and came out again, leaving no wound. The Blues grinned or yelled, and the warriors screamed back in their guttural language. The warriors landed more fatal blows, but 'fatal' no longer had the same meaning. All meaning had been altered, as if the universe were no more than a tunic or gown that hadn't fit properly. One by one the savage warriors fell, pierced by a sword in the belly or eyes or neck. A Blue clubbed a twitching warrior with the butt of the man's own *gun*. Finally only Lord Solek was left alive, and I realized that the Blue captain must have planned it this way, giving his men orders to neither maim nor kill the usurper.

'My lord,' the captain sneered. His six men, all uninjured, stood grouped to one side. From the rest of the palace came shouts as the invincible soldiers cut down the rest of the savage army.

Lord Solek ignored the captain. The chieftain's eyes found me, half hidden by the fountain wall. I stood. I would not cower under that contemptuous gaze.

Solek said something in his own language. Then, shockingly, he laughed. He said, 'Boy ... you win, yes? You win. Boy.' Again that laugh. Quicker than the eye could follow, he raised his short knife and hurled it, without the usual spin or change in stance. The knife flew through the air.

I had raised my right arm – why? To ward off his gaze? To strike him from a distance of twenty feet? There was sense to the action, but my arm was already coming up as he made his quick throw, and the knife found its mark in my right hand. My blood red spurted onto the green tiles of the queen's courtyard.

Dirt in my mouth, worms in my eyes ... *I was crossing*

over. Without will, without planning – that had not happened since my infancy. Was my mind slipping backwards? Was I dying? *No no no no*, some part of my mind shrieked. I did not want to die, not now, it was not time. Maggie! I wanted Maggie. More than anything in my life, I wanted to live long enough to rescue Maggie. That was my only hope for redemption.

I braced myself to land, dying, amid the shaking ground and stormy sky that I had created in the country of the Dead. Instead, I found myself in a landscape as tranquil and calm as the first time I had seen it. No storms, no earthquakes, no sky rent open by a terrible golden light that devoured ... what? Nothing here was devoured; all was serene and unchanging, populated by the serene and unchanging Dead. The poison had been expelled from this place, the wrongness made right when the Blue army had taken away their unbelief, their in-between state of being dead without accepting death. Tranquillity restored when I no longer meddled.

Why? How?

On the grass a little way from me I saw Queen Eleanor, hands folded on her lap, sitting peacefully in the place where her throne room had been. Her blank eyes didn't see me, or anything.

Then I was back in the courtyard of the palace, falling onto the tiles even as I saw Lord Solek's body slashed to bloody ribbons by six swords at once, his blood flowing out towards the queen's door.

The Blues pounded on the door. It did not give, but the intricate green tiles with which it was decorated shattered and fell in shards. Two more Blues entered the courtyard, dragging a man I recognized: the palace steward. His keys hung from his belt.

A sword at his throat, the steward fumbled with his keys. Then his silhouette dissolved; he vanished; and

I stood in the tranquil country of the Dead, but only for a moment. Again I lay in the courtyard, unable to will myself to move.

Unable to will. The savages' knives, Lady Margaret had once said, were tipped with poison. Some poisons affected the mind as well as the body. Was that why I had twice been flung without volition into the country of the Dead? Even as this, my last coherent thought, came to me, my vision wavered again. Cleared, wavered, cleared one last moment.

The steward had found his key. But even before he could insert it into the lock, the door was flung open from within. Queen Caroline walked out of the chamber, her head held high. She wore the Crown of Glory, and in every line of her proud bearing was her refusal to be dragged into captivity but rather to walk towards it. As she stepped over Lord Solek's body, the jewels of her great crown caught the sunlight and blazed.

And from behind her rushed Maggie, unharmed, the last thing I saw before all went dark.

30

I woke in the last place I expected to be. Not in the bloody courtyard, not in the country of the Dead, not in a dungeon, not with Maggie. I woke in a small stone room I had never seen before. I was lying on a bed of straw. I was alone.

After all the killing and screaming, silence.

After dazzling spring sunlight and the bright flash of swords, pale grey light from a single tiny window in the wooden door.

After blood and torn flesh, some of it mine, poultices lay wrapped around my right hand. No pain there, only a soothing coolness. The stone room smelled of medicinal herbs and apples.

I struggled to sit up, but this was a mistake because it sent sharp pain stinging through my arm, worse when I gasped aloud. Slowly I lowered myself back onto the straw, surveying the room with only gentle, cautious turnings of my head.

The chamber was even smaller than I had thought, barely long enough for me to lie full length, and even narrower in width. The stone floor was clean and so was the straw I rested on, although fresh rat droppings lay against the opposite wall. The wall beside me felt cool and faintly damp. I was underground. There were no apples.

'Hello?' I called, but no one answered. I wasn't sure I wanted anyone to answer. Was this a dungeon? I decided not. Dungeons must smell of piss, of blood, of despair. These stone walls bore no stains and no marks scratched by desperate men. So not a dungeon.

I held my left hand, the one I had burned in the campfire, close to my face and studied it. The burn was nearly healed. A patch of new skin grew pinkly amid the rougher skin around it. However, my veins and bones stood out sharply, and my wrist looked thin and weak. I had lain here for quite a while, but then why wasn't I hungry or thirsty? And where was I?

Time passed. Once or twice I called out again, but no one came.

Finally, for something to do, I unwrapped the bandages and poultices from my right hand, to see how much damage had been done by the knife Lord Solek had thrown in the last moments of his life. Poison on the blade had affected my will, I remembered that well enough, but my mind seemed all right now. What of my hand? The last of the bandages pulled free.

My hand was gone.

I stared at the stump of my wrist, where the skin had been wrapped and sewn as if I were not a man but a bolt of cloth. At the seam my flesh puffed red and swollen but without the black-green rot that kills. I had no fingers. No fingers, no fingernails, no palm, nothing to grasp a knife or a cup or a woman's breast, *nothing—*

I screamed, and kept on screaming until the door opened and a voice said severely, 'Hush, Roger. Stop that right now.'

It was Mother Chilton.

She stood filling the doorway, blocking the sudden increase of light, until she knelt beside me. The door remained open. Her young-old face bent above me, her colourless eyes reflecting all light. 'You must stay quiet.'

'My hand . . .'

'I know. I am sorry. If I hadn't cut it off, you would have died.'

'*You* cut it off? But—'

'It was necessary. The black rot had set in. Lord Solek's knife was tipped with poison.'

'But, my *hand*!' It came out a wail, like a six-year-old, and she frowned.

'It was only a hand,' she said severely. 'You have another.'

The callousness and indifference of this shocked me into silence. *Only a hand?*

'Think what else you are, Roger. Now be quiet. I must go.' She rose.

'No, wait! Where am I? What is happening? Maggie—'

Her face softened. 'Good. You can think about someone else. I'll send Maggie to you. But be quiet until then.'

'Wait!'

But she did not. Instead she said something that made no sense: 'You must never seek your mother.' The door closed, and I heard a key turn in the lock.

My mother? What did the witch know of my mother?

Witch. The word had come unbidden to my mind. But yes, of course, Mother Chilton was that thing I had never thought really existed: a witch. She did not have to be a witch to make a milady posset, or perhaps even to cut off my hand and drug me so that I felt no pain, but to know about my mother? And other things she had said to me, half-forgotten but surely they had shown more knowledge than a natural person should possess?

'*Sometimes none of us knows where we are. Or who.*'

'*You've already caused enough disturbance in the country of the Dead.*'

'*You know much, even more than you think, but you don't know what Cecilia truly is . . . a pretty, empty-headed tinder box that will ignite all.*'

And so Cecilia had, and then had died for it. Twice. I stared at the stump of my wrist, and I waited for Maggie, and when she did not come, I went on staring at my maimed arm and silently, as quietly as instructed, I wept.

When Maggie did come, hours later, I had done weeping. Mother Chilton's drugs, whatever they were, had begun to wear off. The stump that was my wrist had begun to throb, not yet a great deal but with promise of real pain to come. I was hungry, and I needed to piss. Carefully I got myself to my feet and used a dark corner of the room, covering the wetness with a little straw. The last of the light faded. I sat in complete darkness, back against the stone wall, cradling my bandaged stump in my good left hand. Finally, a lifetime later, the lock rattled. The door opened.

'Roger?'

Maggie came in with a lantern and a small sack. The lantern threw shadows on the stone wall, on the wooden door, on her. She wore a clean gown of rough blue wool. *Blue*. I had never seen her in anything but green. Her fair hair, short from its cutting when she had pretended to be my brother, curled around her face. A huge bruise, turning all the colours of vegetables, swelled the left side of her face and closed her left eye.

'You're hurt!' I said, the first thing that came to me. 'Were you—'

'Tortured? No. This is nothing.' She set the lantern on the floor and sat beside my straw. The one grey eye that I could see studied me anxiously. 'Does your hand hurt?'

'No,' I said bitterly. 'It can't hurt because it's not there any more.'

'Then does your wrist hurt?'

'Yes.'

'I brought you some more medicine from Mother

Chilton. And some food.' She opened her sack.

I knocked it away, impatient with her stupidity. 'I don't care about food! What happened? That cursed witch cut off my hand—'

'She's not a witch,' Maggie said levelly. 'Only you are.'

That stopped me. Maggie stared at me with all her old disapproving severity, now decorated with fear – for this I had brought back an army from the country of the Dead? To rescue this girl, so that she could call me a witch?

'I'm not a witch; I'm a *hisaf*.'

She didn't know the word, of course. The fear of me was still on her, but she continued. 'Mother Chilton saved your life.'

'Maybe I wish she hadn't.'

'Don't talk like that. Did you . . . Roger, was it you who . . .'

I said simply, 'Yes. To all of it.'

She twisted her hands – her two good hands – together tightly in her lap, and forced herself to go on. 'You brought the Blues back from Witchland? That's what the soldiers are saying. Witchland, where the queen had sent them, when she made it look as if they had died. What we buried – the bodies – they were all false, sorcerous illusion. But not Richard. He was not among the Blues who returned from . . . from there.' Her voice broke. 'The soldiers say the queen is a witch and you are too. But I . . .'

'You what?' I was not going to make this easy for her. She was not making it easy for me.

The hands on her lap tightened until all blood left them. 'I . . . I don't think you brought them back from Witchland. I think you . . . You told me once, in the kitchen, that you can . . . I think you brought them all back from the country of the Dead.'

There. She had said it. I peered at her in the uneven lantern light. Bright light one place, deep shadows a few inches over. The unbruised half of Maggie's face had gone as bloodless as her hands. But she had said it. Disapproval, yes, but also courage. Maggie had always had enough courage for an entire cadre of soldiers.

'Yes,' I said. 'I brought the Blues back from the country of the Dead.'

'And . . . and Cecilia too?'

'No.' I would never tell anyone what had happened to Cecilia. The spiked metal ball twisted in my chest. Those spikes were ones that no Mother Chilton could ever cut out.

Maggie looked away from me. Abruptly she said, 'Jee is safe.'

I had forgotten Jee. *You can think about someone else,* Mother Chilton had said, but I had not thought of Jee.

Maggie continued, 'He's with me in the kitchen. He sleeps under the trestle table where you used to sleep.'

I said, 'It was Jee who told me that the soldiers had taken you. They were looking for me?'

'Yes. The queen wanted you. I don't know why, but if you are . . . that thing that you said, the thing that can travel to the country of the Dead . . .'

'I am, yes. But I am not a witch.'

She nodded, not looking at me. Her hands loosened a little in her lap. I said, 'How did you get that bruise on your face?'

'A Green hit me when I tried to escape. They had orders to bring me back to the palace, if they couldn't find you. The queen knew that we left together. I told her that you had left to find your mother—'

'My mother!'

'You called out for her in your sleep, several times, when we were travelling to the Unclaimed Lands.'

Calling out in troubled sleep – my old problem, the thing that had brought me to Queen Caroline's attention in the first place. But that answered one question: how Mother Chilton had heard of my mother. Maggie must have told her. I wanted to believe that, just as I wanted to believe that Mother Chilton was no more than a skilled healer. I was determined to believe those things.

Maggie continued, 'The queen kept me with her, trying to make me an ally. When she saw that wasn't going to succeed, she threatened me with torture, but she hadn't yet sent me to the dungeon when your Blues arrived. I think she still had hopes of bribing me with silk dresses and green jewels.' Maggie's voice turned scornful.

'Does your face hurt?'

'Not any more. It just looks terrible.' She tried to smile, and failed.

'Where is the queen now?'

'In the dungeon. The Blues hold the castle.' She touched her blue gown. I saw now that it had been hastily and imperfectly dyed. Green streaks showed at the hem and neckline.

I said, 'When I woke here, I thought maybe *I* was in a dungeon.'

She did smile then. 'You're in the dried apple cellar, Roger.'

'I don't see any apples.'

'It's early summer. The apples were all eaten over the winter. That's what you do with dried apples.'

'How did I get here?'

'Joan Campford and I brought you.'

'Joan? The laundress? She was there?'

'She followed you from the laundry. She and I dragged you away. Your hand ... There was so much blood. A Blue captain told us to take you away and hide you. I didn't understand; I still don't. You brought back the

310

Blues, and yet there was such hatred for you on his face!'

I understood. In a soldier fear comes out as hatred, and debt as permission to escape.

Maggie went on. 'You were covered with blood and *soap*. Everything was chaos, with fighting in the palace and killing and shouting . . .' She shuddered. 'Anyway, Joan and I dragged you by your feet, with my petticoat wrapped bloody around your hand, to the kitchens, and then to this apple cellar. I ran for Mother Chilton.'

'And the queen? They will . . .' But I already knew the answer.

'They will burn her as a witch.'

'When?'

'Tomorrow at noon. Roger, is she a witch?'

'I don't know. The queen recognized . . . She could tell . . . Do you think Mother Chilton a witch?'

'No!' Maggie looked shocked. 'She's a healer, is all. And she's a *good* person. Not like the queen!'

The queen was not a good person. She had poisoned her mother, murdered her enemies, threatened helpless servants like Maggie and me with torture. But I also remembered the queen's small and unnecessary kindnesses to me, remembered her desperation to protect The Queendom for little Princess Stephanie, remembered the way her dramatic beauty glowed in candlelight. She would end her life as she lived it, a riddle to all. At noon tomorrow that beauty would blacken in the fire, that creamy flesh roast even as, in Soulvine, Cecilia's flesh had—

Don't think that.

'What is it?' Maggie's frightened voice said. 'For a minute you looked so . . . Does your hand hurt more?'

'No.'

She was silent a long moment. Then she said, 'Your look changed when I mentioned the queen. Did you love her so very much?'

311

'Love the *queen*?'

'Don't be stupid,' Maggie said sharply. 'The queen is a monster. I meant Lady Cecilia. Did you love her so very much?'

'Yes,' I said. 'Once.'

'Once? You don't love her now?'

'She's dead.'

'That isn't what I asked. My mother loved my father long after he died, right up until she went to her own grave. Do you love Cecilia still?'

Maggie was relentless. Moreover, she lacked experience. She didn't know that love could be overwhelmed by guilt, by anger, by childish selfishness on the part of the beloved, and yet still exist, like embers in an ash box. The embers no longer glow, no longer give off warmth. But they still smoulder, and I have known them to eat through the wood of an ash box and set an entire cottage ablaze, destroying it utterly. I had not lied to Maggie. I had loved Cecilia once, and that fire was gone. But neither had I told the entire truth.

Hadn't told it, couldn't tell it. Maggie could not understand. There were only two people in the entire world who might understand. One was Mother Chilton. The other, I suspected but could not know, was my mother.

I tried again. 'Maggie, I didn't bring an army here to retake the palace because of Cecilia.'

Her mouth, pink beneath the huge swollen bruise on her face, frowned slightly. 'You didn't?'

'No.'

'I thought you wanted revenge for ... for her. For Cecilia.'

'No. I came for you. Because Jee told me you'd been taken.'

Maggie went utterly still. For a moment I thought she had ceased to breathe, but then I saw her lashes, downcast, quiver. They cast shadows on the firelit skin of her unbruised cheek. When she opened her eyes, they were blurred under a sheen of tears. She leaned forward and laid her lips on mine.

The kiss was light and sweet, and it stopped time.

But when her lips pressed harder and her hand caressed my hip, I pushed her gently away. 'You don't understand. I have only one hand!'

'So?'

'So,' I said, bitterness rushing back into me, 'I am unmanned.'

Maggie gave a low, throaty chuckle, so surprising that I glared at her in indignation. Didn't she understand what it meant to lose a hand? Was she that insensitive? I was no longer an able-bodied man, no longer *whole*.

'It's not your hand I'm interested in, Roger.' She laid her own hand on me, and instantly my body responded. I was shocked by how instantly, just as shocked as I was by her bawdiness. Maggie!

She wasn't careful about undressing me, or slow. When she pulled her blue gown over her head and undid the strings of her shift, I gasped. She was so beautiful in her nakedness.

The rest of the morning is both a blur and, at the same time, so sharply carved in memory that I can still see every curve of Maggie's body, can still feel every sensation in my own. We manoeuvred around my bandaged stump and her bruised face, tender with each other, full of hesitation and joy. Together we went into that secret dark place of sweetness, and when it was over we fell asleep in each other's arms, on the clean straw, in the tiny stone room that smelled of vanished apples.

I woke first. Maggie slept on, the good side of her face hidden in the good side of my arm. The lantern had gone out, but light came through the small high window. We had slept the entire night, and now it was way past dawn. Bright sunlight beyond the barred window. Maggie had said that the queen would burn at noon.

Staring at the stone ceiling above me, I realized what critical piece of information I did not possess.

'Maggie, wake up!'

She murmured and burrowed deeper into my side. For a moment the movement of her bare breasts against my skin ignited me, but there was no time.

'Maggie! What day is this?'

Her head rose from the straw, eyes bleary, silky curls tousled on her forehead. 'Day?'

'Yes! What day? How long have I been in this apple cellar?'

She looked bewildered, then affronted. 'Why?'

'*How long?*'

'A fortnight. Mother Chilton gave you drugs, and I fed you while you raved. All nonsense syllables but it was terrible to listen to. A horrible song: "Die, die, my baby, die, die, my little one—"'

A fortnight. And I had brought the Blues back over in mid-morning. So now—

'Why was she allowed to live so long?' All those enraged soldiers I had brought back from the dead, eager for Her Grace's blood . . .

Maggie's lip curled. 'The captain held her alive. He tried to force her to bring the old queen back from Witchland. But she would not, or so I was told. And then—'

'Get dressed. Right away. And help me!' I was fumbling at my tunic, my trousers. With every motion, pain throbbed in the stump of my severed wrist. My face must have frightened Maggie.

'Why? Roger, what is it?'

'Something is going to happen. Listen to me. Those

314

Greens who have joined the Blue army, are some of them secretly still loyal to the queen?'

Her lip curled. 'Of course. Not all men are for sale, bend as they will to temporary power.'

'We have to leave the palace. Leave Glory entirely, right now!'

'But ... but why? You aren't strong enough to leave!'

That seemed true. The love-making, on top of the amputation and drugs, had weakened me. It was difficult to even tug on my trousers with my good hand. But I did it.

Maggie said, 'Nobody knows you're here. The fighting is over. Later, when you're stronger and the queen is dead, Joan and I can—'

'The fighting is not over!'

She stared at me, half-dressed and, for Maggie, unusually slow of wits. Perhaps our love-making had affected her too.

'The fighting is not over,' I repeated. 'We have only a few hours to escape. When the Greens take back the throne, they will tear down every stone in the palace looking for me, who led the army that killed their queen.'

'Greens take back the *throne*? Very soon the queen will be dead.'

'But Princess Stephanie will not. The Greens will seek to put her on the throne and rule through her. They—'

'Roger, the Greens left alive are not enough to defeat the Blues you brought back over!'

'I don't have time to explain. Help me, Maggie. Get dressed. We must leave now, while everyone will be watching the queen's death.'

'You're not making sense! The Blue army can't be defeated, can't be ... They're ... if what you told me ...'

I stood, shakily, my good hand braced against the wall. The ceiling of the apple cellar was so low that I had to duck my head, although Maggie, shorter than I, could stand upright. 'Believe me about this, Maggie! Where in the palace are we? Below the kitchens?'

For a long moment she chewed her bottom lip, then gave way. 'We're not below the kitchens. The river comes too close there to dig underground storage rooms. We're farther inside the palace, under the liveried servants' quarters. There's a passage with a door into the couriers' quarters.'

One of the thrilling secret passages I had never found, except that it was not secret, and now I felt not thrills but fear. If we were caught . . .

If we were caught by Greens, torture to a slow death would surely follow. The Blues merely wanted to be rid of me, but the Greens . . . I imagined what could lie ahead for us, and a shudder convulsed my entire body. If it came to that, would I be able to escape the horrible pain by taking Maggie with me to the country of the Dead, as I had taken Cecilia out of it? But the price that Cecilia had paid . . .

We moved out of the apple cellar and along the passage. It was faced with rough-hewn stone, although the smell was of damp earth. The ceiling was even lower than the cellar's, so I had to walk in a half-crouch, and the passage was so narrow we went single file, Maggie in the lead with her lantern. I felt dizzy and my hand ached. Every few yards I leaned briefly against the damp stone to rest. Then I forced myself on.

Other doors, all closed, lined the passage. I smelled grain and wine. Then the tunnel turned, widened, and ended in a low room with a rough wooden staircase going up to a trapdoor. The room was littered with leather boots, riding crops and a girl's soiled shift. Straw, nowhere near as clean as that in my apple cellar, was heaped in one corner.

Maggie said over her shoulder, 'The couriers and kitchen girls sometimes use this room to ... well, you know.'

I didn't ask if she had ever *you-knowed* here. I knew that she had not. I was her first, as she was mine.

'Roger, let me go ahead. To see who is about.'

I nodded. She set down the lantern, climbed the steps, raised the trapdoor, and disappeared.

Alone, I collapsed onto the straw. My breath came heavy and hard. The stump of my wrist began to hurt in earnest, but it was nothing compared to the panic in my mind. How could we get away? And if we escaped the palace, where could we go?

My whole life, it seemed, had consisted of desperate attempts to escape. From Hartah, from the soldiers who had hung the yellow-haired wrecker, from the queen, from Lord Solek's men, from Hygryll. I longed for a place from which I did not have to escape, a place of peace and tranquillity.

But the only place like that was the country of the Dead.

I had just hauled myself to my feet and turned to climb the staircase when the trapdoor opened. Maggie's face loomed above me, her fair hair falling into her bruised eye. The other half of her face was white with shock.

'They are leading the queen to the fire now' she said. 'And Lord Robert rides hard on the horizon with an army!'

31

Lord Robert Hopewell. I had forgotten him – and why not? The last time I had seen him had been months ago, kicking the door of the queen's privy chamber and bellowing, 'Caroline!' And then the queen, barefoot and wearing nothing but a short shift, her dark hair tumbled loose around her bare shoulders, Lord Solek just gone from her bedchamber. Now Lord Robert was riding at the head of an army he had raised somehow, among farmers or outlanders or who-knows-what.

Did he love her still, love the queen's changeable and ruthless and tender beauty, even though she had betrayed him with the savage chieftain? He *must* still love her, to challenge the old queen's Blues for his Caroline's life.

I looked up at Maggie and said urgently, 'Where are they burning the queen?'

'Just beyond the west bridge! So that the villagers can see. The pyre is ready. Come up quickly. There's no one around except the servant who told me, and he's gone. Come up!'

But I was not able to climb the steps. Maggie had to descend and then half-carry me up. She was incredibly strong. We emerged into a room crowded with pallets, saddles, items of blue livery, bridles and the strong odour of horsey men who lived close together. Across the chamber, a doorway opened onto the bright sunshine of a courtyard. I hobbled towards it, Maggie supporting me.

'What's the quickest way out of the palace?'

'Through the kitchens.'

My old route out to the city. After we left the couriers' courtyard, I recognized the route. But we couldn't follow it. All at once people filled the corridors, servants with ashen faces, even a few soldiers shouting orders. Maggie dragged me into a side passage to avoid being seen, and then into another, and all the time we were pushed farther away from the kitchens. Finally we found ourselves in the courtyard outside the throne room. And there stood Mother Chilton.

'Roger,' she said quietly. She looked not at all surprised to see me. 'You should not be up and about.'

'The Blues,' I gasped. 'The battle—'

'Yes. I know. Come with me.'

'I can't . . . I must—'

'You must get away. Yes. But not quite yet.'

She walked to my other side, away from Maggie, who shrank back slightly but did not let go of me. Mother Chilton shifted most of my bulk to herself. She too was much stronger than she looked. Was that true of all women then?

No. Not of Cecilia.

'Drink this,' Mother Chilton said, and I did.

Its effect was immediate. Not only did my pain vanish, but strength surged through me. I stood straight, feeling my knees steady, my head lose its dizziness, my eyesight sharpen.

'It won't last long, and you will pay for it later,' Mother Chilton said. 'One always pays, for everything. But you already know that better than most, Roger Kilbourne, do you not? Come.'

The great throne room doors were unlocked and open, and we walked through them. Something more had happened to my brain. Now it floated just above my head, keen-eyed but somehow unable to formulate a clear thought. I was seeing everything, understanding all, but

319

deciding nothing. Mother Chilton decided, and I was content to obey without question, a plant turning its leaves to follow the sun. The drink ... there had been something in the drink.

Mother Chilton led us through the vast throne room, once filled with Lord Solek's men chanting his glory as he arrived in The Queendom:

> 'Ay-la ay-la mechel ah!
> Ay-la ay-la mechel ah!
> Bee-la kor-so tarel ah!
> Ay-la ay-la mechel ah!'

It seemed as if the savage song still filled my ears, although now the huge room was silent and empty. Mother Chilton stopped at a blank expanse of wall to the left of the dais and moved her fingers quickly over sections of stone: first high, then low, then high again. The stone swung open.

Maggie gasped, but I merely smiled. It was all right. Everything was all right since I drank the potion, and of course there were secret passages in the palace, hadn't I always known so? Silly Maggie, to wonder at that. The queen had needed ... What had the queen needed? There was something I was supposed to remember about the queen, but I could not. All I remembered was her bending over me in the candlelight of her privy chamber, more beautiful than any painting, handing me a goblet of wine. I was just back from a journey – what journey? Where? I couldn't seem to remember, and yet it was there, somewhere in my mind, something about the queen ...

'Come,' Mother Chilton said.

Another staircase. But I climbed this one easily, without strain. And why not? Everything was all right, had always been all right, always would be all right. I smiled at Maggie, who glared at me as I went up the spiral stairs. A tower, we were ascending a tower. Glory had only one tower. Hadn't I climbed it before? I couldn't quite remember.

Another door, and we stood in a tiny room, smaller than even the apple cellar. Two vertical slits in the stone walls let in daylight. Mother Chilton closed the door behind her.

Maggie said fiercely, 'What potion did you give him?'

'That's not for you to question, child,' Mother Chilton said.

'If you knew of this secret room, then why did I have to hide him in the apple cellar, where there was more chance of him being found?'

'This room is not secret while the queen lives.'

The queen. There was something I was supposed to remember about the queen ...

I said lazily, 'I smell smoke.'

Maggie gave a cry and darted to one of the slits in the wall. What could be out there? Smiling at her eagerness, I moved towards the second slit.

'Have a care, Roger,' Mother Chilton said quietly. 'The potion will wear off very soon.'

'Oh,' I said, unconcerned. I put my eye to the slit.

The tiny room looked out over one of the bridges spanning the river from palace to countryside. At first I could not understand what I was seeing. A bonfire – was it Midsummer's Eve then? There were bonfires on Midsummer's Eve, always. But although I couldn't seem to remember the date, wasn't it too early for Midsummer's Eve? Or too late? Anyway bonfires were for night-time. This was full day. People, many people, were running *away* from the bonfire. Villagers and palace servants, all scattering and screaming. What a noise! Other

321

people were trying to get close to the bonfire, and those people seemed to be soldiers, with more soldiers stopping them. None of it made sense.

Why was Maggie crying like that?

Something strange was happening with the soldiers, most of whom were dressed in blue. No, only the closer ones were dressed in blue. There were horsemen too, in green, with one man on a huge black charger. He looked familiar. I could see everything sharply, more sharply than usual even at this distance. The air must be particularly clear.

The air—

The smoke—

The fighting—

'Have a care,' Mother Chilton said.

The *screaming*—

Something lit up in my head, and I understood.

Queen Caroline writhed and screamed, tied to a stake in the centre of the bonfire. The flames had caught her green silk gown. Her black hair, tossing wildly as she flailed, became tipped with fire. Beyond the pyre stood a ring of Blues, the Blues I had brought back from the country of the Dead, and they cut down every man who charged at them. Lord Robert's army vastly outnumbered the few hundred Blues, but the Blues could not be hurt. Swords passed through them, clubs did not crush their skulls. They didn't even bother to carry shields. The attackers, on the other hand, fell to the ground, sometimes two or three deep. Blood spouted from their arms, chests, mouths, and I could see their faces twitch in agony as they died.

The queen went on screaming, a high inhuman shriek, as her flesh began to burn.

Lord Robert's horse plunged through the fighting and somehow reached the pyre. He flung himself off his mount, which had three or four swords sticking from its poor body, just as the beast collapsed on the blood-slimed ground. Lord Robert waded into the pyre, jumped back, went again in. With his sword he slashed at the ropes that bound the burning queen.

A Blue ran up behind him, raised his sword and prepared to pierce Lord Robert's back.

Maggie cried out. But I did not – *could* not. The scene before me wavered, and if it hadn't been for Mother Chilton, I might have fallen. But she held me up, pushing me against the stone wall, and so I saw what happened next. What I had known would happen ever since Maggie had told me in the apple cellar what day it was.

The Blue soldier attacking Lord Robert disappeared. It happened quickly. His flesh melted and ran. I could see the grotesque mask his face became, but only for a moment because it only lasted a moment. His body turned to bones and the bones to dust, and then all that was left was a pile of blue clothing and tarnished armour, the soldier gone.

And so was all the rest of the army I had brought back from the dead.

Lord Robert's army – what was left of it – fell on their knees and covered their eyes. Some cried out, words made unintelligible by fear and distance. The din was terrific. But missing from the shouts and prayers and exclamations was one sound.

The queen no longer screamed.

I sagged in Mother Chilton's arms and she lowered me to the floor. Standing over me, her old face was calm. She said, 'Caroline is dead. But it is not over.'

'Yes,' I managed to say, despite the weakness that suddenly pressed on every part of my body, as if it were covered with heavy stones. 'It . . . is over.'

'Ah, Roger, you don't understand.' And then she said

something more, the last thing I heard her say, and her strangest words. Her voice held despair. 'Ye will seek your mother. Despite anything I would tell ye.'

Sleep pushed at me. I held it off and bit my tongue. With a huge effort of will, I crossed over for the last time.

All was serenity in the country of the Dead. The broad river flowed placidly; the sky shone with its featureless grey light; the Dead sat and stared at nothing. I saw many of Lord Solek's men in their shaggy furs, sitting calmly on the ground, their faces blank and their *guns* stilled. I saw many, many Greens as well. Some had died at the first battle with the dead Blues, the one that began in the laundries and raged through the palace a fortnight ago. Others had switched sides, as some men will always do, and had perished as Blues in the battle at the pyre. Interspersed among them sat the newly slain soldiers of Lord Robert's army, equally tranquil. Up close, I could see how many of them were boys or old men. The desperate Lord Robert had collected what soldiers he could, by force or bribery or – it was possible – from loyalty to Queen Caroline.

None of the Blues I had brought back were among the Dead.

In all that vast peaceful landscape, only one figure moved. She rushed towards me, her beautiful face twisted with fury and grief. 'Roger! Where am I?'

'You're dead, Your Grace.'

Memory took her. 'Yes. I was ... I was burned as a witch.'

'Yes.' And then I said the most futile words of my life, the most futile words of anyone's life, ever, and those words both were and were not true.

'I'm sorry, Your Grace.'

Her fury focused. 'You did this. *You.*'

'Yes.'

'You took my queendom. You *burned* me!'

'No, Your Grace. I did much, but not those things. You did them to yourself.'

Queen Caroline shrieked and launched herself at me. But she was no soldier, and she carried no weapons. I caught her flailing body in my arms. And then, a moment later, I was back in the secret room overlooking the west bridge, sliding into sleep. Mother Chilton had gone. All that remained of my last journey was the feel of Queen Caroline's body against mine, that body calming, going quiet and still.

'Goodbye, Your Grace,' I had whispered to her just before my return, but I don't think she even heard me. She had already been claimed by the eerie tranquillity of the Dead.

32

We were not seen, Maggie and I, as we left the palace. Maggie led the way, following instructions she had been given by Mother Chilton. Secret passageways took us to an inner wall, where an opening led through to Mother Chilton's tent. The tent was completely empty. Gone were the potions, the feathers, the cloth bags of herbs and the poles they had hung upon, the brazier and the single chair. The entrance from palace to tent was so low that Maggie and I had to crawl through on hands and knees. After we did, the stone snapped shut, and nothing we did could open it again.

That must have been how Mother Chilton had helped Cecilia escape from the palace. It must have been too how Mother Chilton had come and gone from the palace whenever the queen summoned her. There had been some tie between them, something I did not understand and did not want to understand. '*Caroline studied the soul arts but she has no talen*t,' Mother Chilton had said to me once. Which was why the queen had sought to use my gift.

Maggie and I stayed in the deserted tent a few days, me resting while she went out to gather food and information. Food was not at first easy to come by. This was not because we had no money; Mother Chilton had once more left me a pile of coins, silvers and one gold piece. I did not understand why Mother Chilton helped me. She was as much a riddle as the queen, and like the queen took her own hidden gambles. But there was no food because there was no one to buy it from. The villagers, along with most of the servants, had fled the capital after the Blue soldiers died a second time. 'Witchcraft!' people cried. 'Sorcery! Run! Run! Save yourselves!'

But there was nothing to save themselves from. No more witchery, no more fighting. The remnants of Lord Robert's ragtag army, plus whatever was left of the queen's Greens, were all the soldiers that remained. They were not witches and they were not fighting. They also needed to eat. One by one, the shopkeepers returned to the city, found it safe, and told others, who also returned.

Lord Robert had the good sense to take away and quietly bury the queen's burned body. Few knew where the 'witch queen' lay. He crowned Princess Stephanie, looking small and frightened in the many-coloured jewels of the Crown of Glory. Lord Robert rules as regent until the princess comes of age.

When I could travel again, Maggie and I left the city. I was disguised as a farmer who had drunk too much, but I was so thin and sick, with such a bristly untrimmed beard that had quite suddenly sprouted in place of my former downy fuzz, that no disguise might even have been necessary. I now looked older than my fifteen years. Besides, no one was looking for me. The rumour was that the witch who had brought the Blue army back from the dead had disappeared into oblivion when they did. It is possible Mother Chilton had something to do with this rumour. It is possible she did not.

The last thing I saw, as I twisted around on the back of our donkey for a final look, was the palace's lone tower rising in the mist. Princess Stephanie's purple banner flew lonely and distant against a foggy grey sky.

We live now in a village called Applebridge. It's far upriver, west of the capital, past where the flat valley has turned to hills, and almost as far as where the hills turn to mountains. Somewhere over those mountains is the realm of Lord Solek's savage people. The River Thymar is swift and shallow here, and barges or ferries cannot navigate the wild waters. But there is an ancient stone bridge connecting the west bank to the east, and so local farmers from all around come to Applebridge. The area grows, besides apples, corn and some other fruits, and the market brings custom to the alehouse Maggie and I bought with Mother Chilton's money.

We pass as brother and sister. After that one sweet afternoon in the cellar of the palace, both of us injured, we have not bedded again. I know Maggie wants to. But she is too proud to ask, and I have not touched her in the months we have lived here. Because of the dreams.

I don't want to think about the dreams.

The alehouse isn't much to look at: a rough taproom, a kitchen, a storeroom where I sleep, and three tiny chambers above, one for Maggie and two to house travellers. Most of our money went to buy the alehouse, which despite its plainness is sound and snug. With the rest of Mother Chilton's coins we bought a good stock of ale, which Maggie serves along with the meals she prepares. She is an excellent cook, a hard-working business partner, a saving manager. When she looks at me with hurt in her eyes I berate myself for a fool for not taking what she offers, for not marrying her. And when these nights of late summer are soft and warm and tiny drops of moisture form on Maggie's full breasts and on her forehead under the springy fair curls, I berate myself for a double, triple, quadruple fool.

But there are the dreams.

I don't want to think about the dreams.

'Peter,' Jee says in his high child's voice, 'Maggie says ye maun come to sup now.'

328

'Tell her I'm coming,' I say, and Jee runs off. I pick up the bucket with my one good hand. I have learned to live with one hand: to keep the house in repair, to pour ale. The village children call me 'Peter One-Hand'. The name I use now, is 'Peter Forest', chosen at random. But it is as Peter One-Hand that I throw the slops to the pig we have recently bought and watch it root eagerly in its wooden pen for something more than what it knows was in the bucket.

Something more than what it knows.

I hear Mother Chilton's despairing voice in my head: *'It is not over.'*

And: *'Ye will seek your mother. Despite anything I would tell ye.'*

And earlier, much earlier, the first time I ever saw her: *'Do you come from Soulvine Moor? Are they ready, then?'*

'Peter! Ye maun come!' Jee again, as insistent as Maggie. And both glad to be here, despite Maggie's unhappiness over me – here, in this snug village where there is peace and enough to eat, and no life-shattering surprises. Everything, in fact, that I once wanted when I lived with Hartah.

Ready on Soulvine Moor for *what*?

I walk towards the taproom, and another of Maggie's excellent soups. After dinner, in the long lingering summer evening, I will walk. Many many miles I will walk, in an attempt to wear myself out so that I will sink into deep sleep and not dream. I already know this will not work.

A flat upland moor, with a round stone house. There is the taste of roasted meat in my mouth, succulent and greasy. Soulvine. In the shadows beyond my torch I sense things unseen. Inhuman things, things I have never met in this land or in that other beyond the grave. Moving among them is a woman's figure, and the voice coming to me from the dark is a woman's voice, and I can see the glint of a jewelled crown: 'Roger. Hisaf.'

'But you're dead,' I say.

'*Nine years dead,' she says, and gives a laugh that shivers my bones.*

Queen Caroline is not nine years dead. She is only three months dead, almost four. The only person I know of who is nine years dead is my mother, and she was not a queen.

Not of any realm I know.

'Peter!' Maggie calls impatiently.

I go in to dinner, knowing I will dream again tonight, knowing that the dream will draw me in, knowing Mother Chilton was right. It is not over.

Turn the page for a sneak preview
of the sequel to *Crossing Over*

Dark Mist Rising
Coming soon from Gollancz

1

It is old women who are most willing to talk to me.

Not all of them, and not only them. Sometimes an old man could be coaxed into talk, especially if I tripped over him. Occasionally a halfwit who did not know where he was. And twice I have talked to queens. But usually, in the Country of the Dead, it was old women who would come out of their eerie trances to prattle of the lives they had lost, some very long ago. But I was not now in the Country of the Dead. I only dreamed that I was, and the dream was even more terrible than the reality had been.

A flat upland moor, with a round stone house. There is the taste of roasted meat in my mouth, succulent and greasy. In the shadows beyond my torch I sense things unseen. Inhuman things, things I have never met in this land or in that other beyond the grave. Moving—

'Peter!'

—among them is a woman's figure, and the voice coming to me from the dark is a woman's voice, and I can see the glint of a jewelled crown. The woman calls my name.

'But—'

'Peter! Wake up!'

'—you're dead,' I say.

'Eleven years dead,' she says, and gives a laugh that shivers my bones. And—

3

'Peter! Now!'

I struck out, blindly, crazed with fear of that monstrous laugh. My fist struck flesh. A cry, and I came fully awake, and Jee lay sprawled against the wall of the sheep shed, his little hand going to the red mark on his cheek.

'Jee! I'm so sorry! Oh, Jee, I didn't mean to . . .'

He stared at me reproachfully, saying nothing. Early-morning light spilled through the door he had opened. The sheep – two ewes and three lambs – stared at me from their bed of straw.

'Jee . . .' But what could I say? I had already apologized, and it changed nothing. The blow could not be undone – like so much else in my life.

'Eleven years dead.'

I took Jee in my arms, and he did not resist. Under the fingers of my left hand his bones felt so small. Should a ten-year-old be so small? I didn't know, having so little experience with children. The village children avoid me, frightened perhaps of the stump where my other hand used to be. 'Peter One-Hand', they called me, not knowing how I lost the other, or that my name is not Peter.

Sometimes I think that even Maggie forgets the past. But I never forget.

Jee freed himself from my clumsy embrace. 'Maggie says ye maun kill a lamb for dinner. The fattest one.'

I blinked. 'Are there travellers?'

'Yes. And their servants. Come!'

Travellers with servants. Our rough inn, perched above the village of Applebridge in the foothills of the Western Mountains, seldom gets travellers, and never travellers with servants. They must have arrived very early in the morning. I had slept in the sheep shed because two days ago a wolf had carried off Samuel Brown's only lamb, killed it right in the enclosure by his cottage. Maggie had

4

insisted that I build a stout shed, and I had chosen to sleep in it. 'There's no need, it's completely enclosed and has no window,' Maggie had said, her lips tightening. I hadn't answered. We both knew why I preferred to sleep out here, and that neither of us could bear to discuss it.

I raised myself from the straw, brushed bits of it off my tunic and leggings, and pulled on my boots.

Maggie and I have run this inn for two years. It is due solely to her that we, two seventeen-year-old fugitives and Jee, have been able to make a living. It was Maggie who bartered the last of our coins for the rent on a falling-down cottage in Applebridge. Maggie who hammered and nailed and scrubbed and drove me relentlessly to do the same, until the cottage had a taproom, usable kitchen, and three tiny bedrooms above. Maggie who cooked stews from wild rabbit and kitchen-garden vegetables, stews so good that local farmers began leaving their own cottages to have dinner and sour ale at the inn, talking through the long winter nights and glad for a gathering place to do it. Maggie who bought the ale, driving such a hard bargain that she won the grudging respect of men three times her age. Maggie who acquired our chickens, sewed our tunics, baked and boiled and roasted. Maggie who, just this spring, bought the two ewes from the Widow Moore with our carefully hoarded money. Maggie who had saved my very life, with Mother Chilton's help. I owed Maggie everything.

But I could not give her the one thing she wanted from me. I could not love her. Cecilia stood between us, just as if she had not died. Twice. Cecilia and Queen Caroline and my talent, which I had not used in over two years but which still festered within me, like a sore that would not heal.

The sheep gazed at me meditatively with their silly

5

faces. Stupid animals, they irritated me constantly. They belched, they farted, they got soremouth and ringworm. They fell on their backs and, when in full wool, couldn't get up without help. They chewed their cud until it was a sloppy wad and then dropped it on my foot. They were afraid of new colours, strange smells and walking in a straight line. They smelled.

Still, I was not looking forward to killing the lamb. One of the ewes lay beside twin lambs, the other nursed a single offspring – which one did Maggie mean by 'fattest'? How many travellers were there, and where did they come from?

I should have been fearful of travellers, but I found I was not. Any change in the small, wearying, unchanging routine of Applebridge was welcome. And there should be nothing to fear: The Queendom had been at peace for two and a half years, ruled by Lord Protector Robert Hopewell for six-year-old Princess Stephanie. No one knew where or who I was. Travellers would be a pleasant break.

'I'm sorry,' I said to the larger and plumper of the twin lambs. It blinked at me and curled closer to its mother.

I left the sheep shed, carefully barring the wooden door, and walked the dirt path to the back of the cottage. The summer morning sparkled fresh and fair. Wild roses bloomed along the lanes, along with daisies and buttercups and bluebells. Birds twittered. The cottage stood on the side of a hill, backed by wooded slopes, and I could see the farms and orchards of Applebridge spread below me, fields and trees all coloured that tender yellow-green that comes but once a year. The river ran swift and blue, spanned by the ancient stone bridge that gave the village its name. Maggie's kitchen garden smelled of mint and lavender.

As I rounded the corner of our cottage to the stable yard, I stopped cold.

'Travellers,' Jee had said, 'and their servants.' But he had not told me of anything like this. Five mules, stronger than donkeys and sturdier than horses, were being groomed and watered by a youth about my own age – although I knew that I, with all that had been done to and by me, looked older than seventeen. The mules were fine animals but looked as if they had been pushed hard to pull the four wagons now drawn off the road. Three of the wagons were farm carts such as everyone used to take crops to market, but they were piled high with polished wooden chests, with expensively carved furniture, with barrels and canvas bags. The fourth was a closed caravan with a double harness, such as faire folk use to take their booths around a more populated countryside than ours. This caravan, however, had gilded wheels and brass fittings and silver trim. Neither wagon nor coach, it was a room on wheels, and probably as rich within as without.

Where had such visitors come from, and what had driven them to travel on a night lit only by the thinnest of crescent moons?

'Good morrow,' I said to the youth. 'I am—'

He snapped something I could not understand through his thick, high-pitched accent.

'What?' I said.

This time I caught enough words. 'Be . . . halfwit? Tell . . . hurry . . . My lady's breakfast!'

Hot words rose to my lips: I was the proprietor of this inn and he but a stable boy! But before I could lambaste him, the cottage door opened and Maggie rushed out.

'Peter! I need that lamb butchered now if I'm to have stew for noon dinner! They leave by mid-afternoon!'

She stood with her hands on her hips, her fair curls drooping from under her cap, kitchen heat filming her forehead with sweat. A white apron covered a trim grey gown of her own making. Maggie will wear grey or red or brown, but never green nor blue, the colours of the two queens for whom she had been a kitchen maid. Her foot in its neat leather boot tapped on the ground. She looked pretty, and determined and very competent: Maggie as master and commander.

As always, this brought out in me a desire to resist, to not be ordered about. All my life I had been ordered about: by my stepfather, by a head laundress, by a queen. In my own cottage I would not be ordered and scolded.

'In good time,' I said testily to Maggie. 'I'm talking to this man here.'

The boy ignored me and went on feeding the mules.

'Peter, we must have—'

'In good time!'

Jee appeared at the door of the cottage. 'Maggie, ye maun come! They want—'

I didn't wait to hear what they wanted. Already my stupid fit of pique had passed. Maggie was working hard for both of us; the travellers were obviously rich and would pay us well; I was a fool to not do as I was told. I started back towards the sheep shed.

But then an old woman emerged from the door in the back of the caravan. She stumbled on the one step and I leaped forward to catch her. Her considerable bulk lurched against me and we both fell to the ground, me underneath. It was like being crushed by a very large, very dense mattress. 'Thank you!' she cried, in that same strange accent.

'Are you hurt, mistress?'

'No, but . . . Catch my breath, lad . . .'

I led her to the wooden bench in front of the cottage. She plopped heavily down. And then she began speaking.

It is old women who are most willing to talk to me. And once again everything in my world changed.

‘F
an
El

‘Po

‘A

‘Thi
few

‘Geo

‘Pele
langu
Capita
munit

‘Once
writing

‘He is,
momen

‘Pelecan   gift of creeping inside the heads of his
characters and making them real’   *Time Out*

George Pelecanos is an independent-film producer, an essayist, the recipient of numerous international writing awards, a producer and an Emmy-nominated writer on the HBO hit series *The Wire*, and the author of a bestselling series of novels set in and around Washington, D.C. He is currently a writer and producer for the acclaimed HBO series *Treme*. He lives in Maryland with his wife and three children.

By George Pelecanos

A Firing Offense
Nick's Trip
Shoedog
Down by the River Where the Dead Men Go
The Big Blowdown
King Suckerman
The Sweet Forever
Shame the Devil
Right as Rain
Hell to Pay
Soul Circus
Hard Revolution
Drama City
The Night Gardener
The Turnaround
The Way Home
The Cut
What it Was
The Double

GEORGE PELECANOS

DOWN BY THE RIVER
WHERE THE DEAD MEN GO

An Orion paperback

First published in the USA in 1995
by St. Martin's Press
This paperback edition published in 2013
by Orion Books,
an imprint of The Orion Publishing Group Ltd,
Orion House, 5 Upper St Martin's Lane,
London WC2H 9EA

An Hachette UK company

1 3 5 7 9 10 8 6 4 2

A CIP catalogue record for this book
is available from the British Library.

ISBN 978-1-4091-2707-9

Printed and bound in Great Britain by Clays Ltd, St Ives plc

The Orion Publishing Group's policy is to use papers that
are natural, renewable and recyclable products and made
from wood grown in sustainable forests. The logging and
manufacturing processes are expected to conform to the
environmental regulations of the country of origin.

www.orionbooks.co.uk

FOR PETER

DOWN BY THE RIVER
WHERE THE DEAD MEN GO

ONE

———

LIKE MOST OF the trouble that's happened in my life or that I've caused to happen, the trouble that happened that night started with a drink. Nobody forced my hand; I poured it myself, two fingers of bourbon into a heavy, beveled shot glass. There were many more after that, more bourbons and more bottles of beer, too many more to count. But it was that first one that led me down to the river that night, where they killed a boy named Calvin Jeter.

This one started at the Spot, on 8th and G in Southeast, where I tended bar three or four shifts a week. It had been a hot day, hazy and soup-hot, like most midsummer days in D.C. The compressor on our ancient air conditioner had gone down after the lunch rush, and though most of our regulars had tried to drink their way through it, the heat had won out. So by ten o'clock it was just me behind the stick, lording over a row of empty bar stools, with Ramon in the cellar and Darnell in the kitchen, cleaning up. I phoned Phil Saylor, the owner of the establishment, and with his okay shut the place down.

Ramon came up the wooden stairs carrying three cases of beer, his head just clearing the top carton. He was smiling stupidly—he had just smoked a joint in the cellar—but the smile was stretched tight, and it looked as if he were about to bust a nut. Ramon in his cowboy boots stood five two and weighed in at 129, so seventy-two beers was pushing it. He dropped the cases at my feet and stood before me, wiping the sweat off his forehead with a red bandanna. I thanked him and tipped him out.

For the next fifteen minutes, I rotated the beer into the cooler, making sure to leave some cold ones on the top, while I listened to Ramon and Darnell cut on each other back in the kitchen. Through the reach-through, I could see Ramon gut-punching the tall and razorish Darnell, Darnell taking it and loving it and laughing the whole time. Then there were loud air kisses from Ramon, and Darnell saying, "Later, amigo," and Ramon motoring out of the kitchen, through the bar area, toward the door.

I finished with the beer and wiped down the bar and rinsed out the green netting and put the ashtrays in the soak sink, leaving one out, and then I washed up and changed into shorts and a T-shirt and high-top sneakers. Darnell shut off the light in the kitchen and came out as I tightened the laces on my Chucks.

"Whas'up, Nick?"

"'Bout done."

"Any business today?"

"Yeah. The catfish went pretty good."

"Used a little Old Bay. Think anybody noticed?"

"Uh-uh."

Darnell pushed his leather kufi back off his sweat-beaded forehead. "You headin' uptown? Thought maybe I'd catch a ride."

"Not yet. I'm gonna call Lyla, see what she's doing."

"All right, then. Let me get on out of here."

On the nights we closed together, this was our routine. Darnell knew I would stick around, usually alone, and have a drink; he'd always try and get me out of there before I did. A stretch in Lorton had straightened him all the way out, though no one mistook his clean lifestyle for the lifestyle of a pushover, least of all me; I had seen what he could do with a knife. Darnell went out the door. I locked it behind him.

Back in the main room, I counterclockwised the rheostat. The lamps dimmed, leaving the room washed in blue neon light from the Schlitz logo centered over the bar. I found WDCU on the house stereo and notched up the volume on the hard bop. I lit a cigarette, hit it, and fitted it in the V of the last remaining ashtray. Then I pulled a nearly full bottle of Old Grand-Dad off the call shelf, poured a shot, and had a taste. I opened a cold bottle of Bud, drank off an inch or two of that, and placed the bottle next to the shot. My shoulders unstiffened, and everything began to soften and flow down.

I looked around the room: a long, railed mahogany bar, mottled and pocked; several conical lamps spaced above, my own smoke swirling in the low-watt light; a rack behind the lamps, where pilsner and rocks and up glasses hung suspended, dripping water on the bar; some bar stools, a few high-backed, the rest not; a couple of vinyl-cushioned booths; a pair of well-used speakers mounted on either side of the wall, minus the grills; and some "artwork," a Redskins poster furnished by the local beer distributor (1989's schedule—we had never bothered to take it down) and a framed print of the Declaration of Independence, the signatures of our forefathers joined in various places by the drunken signatures of several of our regulars. My own signature was scrawled somewhere on there, too.

I finished my bourbon and poured another as I dialed Lyla's number. Next to the phone was a photograph, taped to the yellowed wall, of a uniformed Phil Saylor, circa his brief stint as a cop on the Metropolitan Police force. I looked at his round face while listening to Lyla's answering machine. I hung the receiver in its cradle without leaving a message.

The next round went down smoothly and more quickly than the first. During that one, I tried phoning my old buddy Johnny McGinnes, who had gone from electronics sales to mattresses and now to major appliances, but the chipper guy who answered the call—"Goode's White Goods. My name is Donny. How may I help you?"—told me that McGinnes had left for the evening. I told him to tell McGinnes that his friend Nick had called, and he said, "Sure will," adding, "and if you're ever in need of a major appliance, the name is Donny." I hung up before he could pry his name in again, then dialed Lyla's number. Still no answer.

So I had another round, slopping bourbon off the side of the glass as I poured. Cracking a beer I had buried earlier in the ice bin, I went to the stereo and cranked up the volume: a honking session from some quintet, really wild shit, the Dexedrined drummer all over the map. By the time the set was over, I had finished my shot. Then I decided to leave; the Spot had grown hellishly hot, and I had sweat right into my clothes. Besides, my buzz was too good now, way too good to waste alone. I killed the lights and set the alarm, locked the front door, and stepped out onto 8th with a beer in my hand.

I walked by an athletic-shoe store, closed and protected by a riot gate. I passed an alley fringely lit at the head by a nearby streetlamp. I heard voices in its depths, where an ember flared, then faded. Just past the alley sat Athena's, the last women's club in my part of town. Behind its windowless brick walls came the steady throb of bass. I pushed open the door and stepped inside.

I heard my name called out over a Donna Summer tune and the general noise of the place. I edged myself around a couple of women on the dance floor and stepped up to the bar. Stella, the stocky, black-haired tender, had poured me a shot when she saw me come through the front door. I thanked her and put my hand around the glass and knocked it back all at once. Someone kissed me on the back of my neck and laughed.

I found Mattie, my transplanted Brooklyn friend, by the pool table in a smoky corner of the room. We shot our usual game of eight ball, and I lost a five. Then I bought us a round of beers and played another game, with the same result. Mattie had the whole table mapped out before her first stroke, while I was a power shooter who never played for shape. Some nights I won, anyway—but not that night.

I went back to the bar and settled my tab and left too much for Stella. In the bar mirror, I saw my reflection, bright-eyed and ugly and streaked with sweat. Near the register hung a framed photograph of Jackie Kahn, former Athena's bartender and the mother of my child, a boy named Kent, now nine months old. I said something loudly to Stella then, my voice sounding garbled and harsh. She began to smile but then abruptly stopped, looking in my eyes. I pushed away from the bar and made it out the front door, to the fresh air and the street.

I unlocked the Spot's front door, deactivated the alarm by punching in a four-digit number on a grid, and went back behind the bar. I cracked a cold beer and drank deeply. Then I poured Old Grand-Dad to the lip of a shot glass and bent over, putting my lips directly to the whiskey, drinking off an inch of it without touching the glass. I shook a Camel filter out of my pack and lit it. The phone began to ring. I let it ring, and walked down toward the stereo, stumbling on a rubber mat along the way. I found a tape by Lungfish, a raging guitar-based band out of Baltimore, and slid that in the deck. I hit the play button and gave it some bass.

Black.

I sat on a stool at the bar, tried to strike a match. A cigarette had burned down, dead-cold in the ashtray. I lit a fresh one, tossed the match toward the ashtray, missed. I reached for my shot glass and saw the half-filled bottle of Grand-Dad in the middle of a cluster of empty beer bottles. I tasted whiskey. The tape had ended. There was not a sound in the bar.

Black.

I stepped off the curb outside the Spot. A whooping alarm screamed in the night. Stella walked by me, said, "Nicky, Nicky," went through the open front door of the Spot, reset the alarm. She asked for and took my keys, then locked the front door. A few women had spilled out of Athena's onto the sidewalk. Stella returned, held my keys out, then drew them back as I reached for them.

"Come on, Nicky. Come on and sleep it off in the back."

"I'm all right. Gimme my keys."

"Forget it."

"Gimme my keys. I can sleep in my car. What the fuck, Stella, it's ninety degrees out here. You think I'm gonna freeze? Gimme my fuckin' keys."

Stella tossed me the keys. I tried to catch them, but there was an open beer in one of my hands and the bottle of Grand-Dad in the other. I went to one knee to pick my keys up off the street. I looked up, tried to thank Stella. She had already walked away.

Black.

Driving down Independence Avenue, a Minor Threat tune at maximum volume, blowing through the speakers of my Dodge. I stopped my car in the middle of the street, let the motor run, got out of the car, urinated on the asphalt. To my left, the Mall, the Washington Monument lit up and looming, leaning a little toward the sky. Tourists walked hurriedly by on the sidewalk, fathers watching me from the corner of their eyes, pushing their children along, the singer screaming from the open windows of my car: "What the fuck have *you* done?" Me, laughing.

Black.

I drove down M Street in Southeast, the Navy Yard on my right. My first car, a '64 Plymouth Valiant, bought there at a government auction, accompanied by my grandfather. Must have tried to get back to the Spot, made a wrong turn. Lights everywhere, streetlights and taillights, crossing. I hit my beer, chased it with bourbon. The bourbon spilled off my chin. A blaring horn, an angry voice yelling from the car at my side. The beer bottle tipped over between my legs, foam undulating from the neck. My shorts, soaked; pulled my wallet from my back pocket and tossed it on the bucket seat to my right. Music, loud and distorted in the car.

Black.

The car went slowly down a single-lane asphalt road. Trees on both sides of the road. To the right, through the trees, colored lights reflected off water. No music now in the car. The surge of laughter far away, and trebly slide guitar from a radio. Blurry yellow lights ahead, suspended above the water, shooting straight out into the sky. Had to pee, had to stop the car, had to stop the lights from moving. Heard gravel spit beneath the wheels, felt the car come to rest. Killed the ignition. Opened my door, stumbled out onto the gravel, heard the sound of a bottle hit the ground behind me. Started to fall, then gained my footing, stumbling, running now to the support of a tree. Needed to lie down, but not there. Pushed off the tree, bounced off another, felt something lash across my cheek. Shut my eyes, opened them, began to float into a fall. Nothing beneath me, no legs, a rush of lights and water and trees, spinning. The jolt of contact as I hit the ground, no pain. On my back, looking up at the branches, through the branches the stars, moving, all of it moving. Sick. The night coming up, no energy to turn over, just enough to tilt my head. A surge of warm liquid spilling out of my mouth and running down my neck, the stench of my own flowing puke, the steam of it passing before my eyes.

Black.

A sting on my cheek. Something crawling on my face, my hands dead at my sides. Let it crawl. The branches, the stars, still moving. My stomach convulsed. I turn my head and vomit.

Black.

The slam of a car door. The sound of something dragged through gravel and dirt. A steady, frantic moan.

The voice of a black man: "All right now. You already been a punk, and shit. Least you can do is go out a man."

The moan now a muffled scream. Can't move, can't even raise my head. A dull plopping sound, then a quiet splash.

The black man's voice: "Just leave him?"

Another voice, different inflection: "Kill a coon in this town and it barely makes the papers—no offense, *you* know what I mean. C'mon, let's get outta here. Let's go home."

Black.

I OPENED MY EYES to a gray sky. I ran my hand through dirt and paper and grass, and something plastic and wet. I stayed there for a while, looking at the leafy branches and the sky. My back ached and I felt stiff behind the neck. I could smell the odor of garbage, my own bile and sweat.

I sighed slowly, got up on one elbow. I looked across the water at the sun, large and dirty orange, coming up in the east. I sat up all the way, rubbed a fleck of crust off my chin, ran my fingers through my hair.

I was down by the Anacostia River—in the marina district, where M Street continues unmarked. I recognized it straight away. My grandfather and I had fished here when I was a kid. He had always thrown back the perch and occasional catfish he had reeled in. The river had been virtually dead, even then.

I was sitting in a wooded area, the grass worn down to weeds and dirt, littered with plastic bags and fast-food wrappers, empty beer cans, malt liquor bottles, peach brandy pints, used rubbers, the odd shoe. I turned to the right and saw my car, nearly hidden in the start of the woods, parked neatly and without a scratch between two trees, all dumb luck. Beyond that, I could see the moored runabouts and powerboats of a marina, and past the marina the 11th Street Bridge, leading to Anacostia. Behind me was the road, cracked and potholed, and behind the road a denser block of trees, then railroad tracks, and then more trees. To my left, the woods gave to a clearing, where a rusted houseboat sat half-sunk in the water. After that, another hundred yards down the shoreline, the Sousa Bridge spanned the river, the lights of which I had noticed but not recognized the night before.

The night before. My memory flashed on something very wrong.

I got up on my feet and walked unsteadily through the trees to the clearing, continued on to the waterline. Wooden pilings came up out of the brown river, spaced erratically around the sunken houseboat. Something appeared to be draped around one of the pilings. The sun nearly blinded me, sent a pounding into my head. I shaded my eyes, went to where the scum of the river lapped at the concrete bulkhead, stood there on the edge.

A young black man lay in the water, his head and shoulders submerged, the shirtsleeve of one bound arm caught on a cleat in the piling. Duct tape had been wound around his gray face, covering his mouth. I could see an entry wound, small and purple, rimmed and burned black, below his chin. The bullet had traveled up and blown out the back of his head; brain stew, pink and chunked, had splashed out onto the piling. The gas jolt had bugged his eyes.

I fell to my knees and retched. The dry heave came up empty. I stayed there, caught air, stared at the garbage and debris floating stagnant in the river. I pushed off with my hands, stood and turned, stumbled a few steps, then went into a quick walk toward the trees. I didn't look back.

I picked up the empty bottle of bourbon at the side of my Dodge and opened the door. I dropped the bottle inside and fell into the driver's seat. My keys still hung in the ignition. I looked in the rearview at my eyes, unrecognizable. I checked my watch, rubbed dirt off its face: 6:30 A.M., Wednesday.

My wallet lay flat and open on the shotgun bucket. I picked it up, looked at my own face staring out at me from my District of Columbia license: "Nicholas J. Stefanos, Private Investigator."

So *that's* what I was.

I turned the key in the ignition.

TWO

MY GIRLFRIEND, LYLA McCubbin, stopped by my apartment early that evening. She found me sitting naked on the edge of the bed, just up from a nap, the blinds drawn in the room. I had thrown away my clothes from the night before and taken two showers during the course of the day. But I had begun to sweat again, and the room smelled of booze. Lyla had a seat next to me and rubbed my back, then pulled my face out of my hands.

"I talked to Mai at the Spot. She told me she picked up your shift tonight. You had a rough one, huh?"

"Yeah, pretty rough."

"What's all over your face?"

"Bites. Some kind of roaches, I guess. I woke up—I was layin' in garbage."

"Shit, Nicky."

"Yeah."

"I called you last night," she said.

"I called *you*."

She looked in my eyes. "You been crying or something, Nick?"

"I don't know," I said, looking away.

"You got the depression," she said quietly. "You went and got yourself real good and drunk. You did some stupid things, and then you fell out. The only thing you can do now is apologize to the people you dealt with, maybe try and be more sensible next time. But you shouldn't beat yourself up about it. I mean, it happens, right?"

I didn't answer. Lyla's fingers brushed my hair back off my face. After awhile, she got up off the bed.

"I'm going to make you something to eat," she said.

"Sit back down a minute," I said, taking her hand. She did, and everything poured out.

Later, I sat on my stoop as Lyla grilled burgers on a hibachi she had set up on the brick patio outside my apartment. Lyla's long red hair switched across her back as she drank from a goblet of Chablis and prodded the burgers with a short-handled spatula. My black cat circled her feet, then dashed across the patio and batted at an errant moth. I watched Lyla move against a starry backdrop of fireflies that blinked beyond the light of the patio, and I smelled the deep-summer hibiscus that bloomed in the yard.

After dinner, Lyla drove up to Morris Miller's, the liquor store in my Shepherd Park neighborhood, for more wine. My landlord, who owned the house and lived in its two top floors, came out and sat with me on the stoop. I had my first cigarette of the day while he drank from a can of beer and told me a story of a woman he had met in the choir, who he said sang like an angel in church but had "the devil in her hips outside those walls." He laughed while I dragged on my cigarette, and pointed to my cat, still running in circles, chasing that moth.

"Maybe if that old cat had two eyes, she'd catch that thing."

"She might catch it yet," I said. "Nailed a sparrow and dropped it on my doorstep the other day."

"Whyn't you get you a *real* animal, man? I know this boy, lives down around 14th and Webster? Got some alley cats would fuck up a dog."

"I don't know. I bring a cat around here like your boy's got, might scare away some of your lady friends."

"Wouldn't want that." My landlord hissed a laugh. " 'Cause that woman I got now, that church woman? She's a keeper."

Lyla returned, uncorked her wine, and poured another glass. My landlord gave her a kiss and went back in the house to his easy chair and TV. Lyla sat next to me and dropped her hand on the inside of my thigh, rubbing it there.

"How you feeling?"

"Better."

"You'll be better still tomorrow."

"I guess."

She bent toward me, and I turned my head away. Lyla took my chin in her hand and forced me to meet her gaze. I looked into her pale green eyes. She kissed me then and held the kiss, her breath warm and sour from the wine.

After awhile, we went inside. I dropped a Curtis Mayfield tape into the deck while Lyla lit some votive candles in my room. I undressed her from behind, kissing the pulsing blue vein of her neck. We fell onto my bed, where we made out slowly in the flickering light. Lyla rolled on top of me and put my hands to her breasts. The candlelight reflected off her damp hair, the sweat on her chest like glass.

I shut my eyes and let her work it, let myself go with the sensations, the sounds of her open-mouthed gasps, the rising promise of my own release, the sweet voice of Curtis singing "Do Be Down" in the room. She knew what she was doing, and it worked; for a few minutes, I forgot all about the man I had become. Or maybe I had gone to another place, where I could let myself believe that I was someone else.

* * *

LYLA HAD PLACED MY coffee next to the *Post* on the living room table the following morning. I picked up my mug and sipped from it while I stood over the newspaper and stared blankly at its front page. Lyla walked into the room, tucking a cream-colored blouse into an apple green skirt.

"It made the final edition," she said. "Deep in Metro. The Roundup."

The *Post* grouped the violent deaths of D.C.'s underclass into a subhead called "Around the Region"; local journalists sarcastically dubbed this daily feature "the Roundup." As the managing editor of the city's hard-news alternative weekly, *D.C. This Week*, Lyla was not immune to criticism of local media herself. But her competitive spirit couldn't stop her from taking the occasional shot at the *Washington Post*.

"What'd it say?"

"You know," she said. " 'Unidentified man found in the Anacostia River. Fatal gunshot wounds. Police are withholding the name until notification of relatives, no suspects at this time' — the usual. When you read it, you automatically think, Another drug execution. Retribution kill, whatever. I mean, that's what it was, right?"

I had a seat on the couch and ran my finger along the edge of the table. Lyla kept her eyes on me as she pulled her hair back and tied it off with a black band.

I looked up. "You still got that friend over at the city desk at Metro?"

Lyla moved my way and stood over me. She rested her hands on her hips, spoke tiredly. "Sure, and I've got my own sources in the department. Why?"

"Just, you know. I thought you could see what else they got on this so far."

"So, what, you could get involved?"

"Just curious, that's all. Anyway, it's been awhile. I wouldn't know where to start." I thought of my last case, a year and a half earlier: William Henry and April Goodrich, the house on Gallatin Street—a bloodbath, and way too much loss.

Lyla leaned over and kissed me on the lips. "Get some rest today, Nick. Okay?"

"I'm workin' a shift," I said.

"Good," she said. "That's good."

She gave me one more knowing look and walked from the room. I listened to the slam of the screen door and slowly drank the rest of my coffee. Then I showered and dressed and left the apartment. The newspaper remained on my living room table, untouched, unread.

THE SPOT COOKED DURING the lunch rush that day. Darnell's special, a thick slice of meat loaf with mashed potatoes and gravy, moved quickly, and he was sliding them onto the reach-through with fluid grace. Ramon bused the tables and kept just enough dishes and silverware washed to handle the turns. Our new lunch waitress, Anna Wang, a tough little Chinese-American college student, worked the small dining room adjacent to the bar.

Anna stepped up to the service bar, called, "Ordering!" She pulled a check from her apron, blew a strand of straight black hair out of her eyes while she made some hash marks on the check. I free-poured vodka into a rocks glass and cranberry-juiced it for color. Then I poured a draft and carried the mug and the glass down to Anna, a lit Camel in my mouth. I placed the drinks on her cocktail tray just as she speared a swizzle stick into the vodka.

Anna said, "How about some of that, Nick?"

I took the cigarette out of my mouth and put it between her lips. She drew on it once, let smoke pour from her nostrils, and hit it again as I plucked it out. She nodded and carried off the tray. I watched Ramon go out of his way to brush her leg with his as he passed with a bus tray of dirty dishes. Anna ignored him and kept moving.

"Another martini for me, Nick," said Melvin, the house crooner, whose stool was by the service bar. I poured some rail gin into an up glass and let a drop or two of dry vermouth fall into the glass. I served it neatly on a bev nap, watching Melvin's lips move to the Shirley Horn vocals coming from the Spot's deck, and then I heard Darnell's voice boom from the kitchen over the rattle of china and the gospel music of his own radio: "Food up!"

I snatched it off the reach-through and walked down the bar toward Happy, our resident angry alki, seated alone, always alone. On my trip, I stopped to empty the ashtray of a gray beard named Dave, who was quietly reading a pulp novel and drinking coffee at the bar, his spectacles low-riding his nose, doing his solitary, on-the-wagon thing. Some ashes floated down into Happy's plate, and I blew them off before I placed the plate down in front of him. Happy looked down mournfully at the slab of meat garnished with the anemic sprig of wilted parsley and the gravy pooled in the gluey mashed potatoes. His hand almost but not quite fell away from the glass in his grip.

"This looks like *dog* shit," he muttered.

"You want another drink, Happy?"

"Yeah," he said with a one o'clock slur. "And this time, put a little liquor in it."

I prepared his manhattan (an ounce of rail bourbon with a cherry dropped in it, no vermouth) and placed it on a moldy coaster advertising some sort of black Sambuca we did not stock. Then I heard Anna's tired voice from down the bar: "Ordering!" I moved to the rail and fixed her drinks.

That's the way it went for the rest of the afternoon. Buddy and Bubba, two GS-9 rednecks, came in at the downslope of the rush and split a couple of pitchers. They argued over sports trivia the entire time with a pompadoured dude named Richard, though none of them had picked up a ball of any kind since high school. Before they left, they poked their heads in the kitchen and congratulated Darnell on the "presentation" of the meat loaf. Darnell went about his work, and Buddy sneered in my direction as he and Bubba headed out the door.

After lunch, I put some PJ Harvey in the deck for Anna while she cleaned and reset her station. Phil Saylor had instructed me to keep blues and jazz playing on the stereo during the rush, but Happy, dashing in his dandruff-specked, plum-colored sport jacket, was now the only customer in the bar. Sitting there in a stagnant cloud of his own cigarette smoke, he didn't ever seem to respond to the musical selection either way.

Anna split for the day after bumming a smoke, and Ramon retreated to the kitchen, where he practiced some bullshit karate moves on an amused Darnell while I began to cut limes for Mai's evening shift. I had just finished filling the fruit tray when Dan Boyle walked through the front door.

Boyle parked his wide ass on the stool directly in front of me and ran fingers like pale cigars through his wiry, dirty blond hair.

"Nick."

"Boyle."

His lazy, bleached-out eyes traveled up to the call rack, then settled back down on the bar. I turned and pulled the black-labeled bottle of Jack Daniel's off the call shelf. I poured some sour mash into a shot glass and slid it in front of him.

"A beer with that?"

"Not just yet."

He put the glass to his lips and tilted his head back for a slow taste. The action opened his jacket a bit, the grip of his Python edging out.

On any given night, the Spot could be heavy with guns, as the place had become a favorite watering hole for D.C.'s plain-clothes cops and detectives, the connection going back to Saylor. Guns or no, Boyle had earned a different kind of rep, topped by his much-publicized role in the Gallatin Street shoot-out. I had been there with him, right next to him, in fact, but my participation had remained anonymous. I was reminded of it, though, every time I passed a mirror: a two-inch-long scar, running down my cheek.

"Goddamn it, that's good," Boyle said, wiping his mouth with the back of his hand. "I'll take that beer now."

I tapped him one and set the mug next to the shot. Boyle pulled a Marlboro hard pack from his jacket, drew a cigarette, and tamped it on the pack. He put it to his lips and I gave him a light.

"Thanks." Boyle spit smoke and reached for the mug. I bent over the soak sink and ran a glass over the brush.

"Good day out there?" I said, looking into the dirty gray suds.

"Not bad today, if you really want to know. Picked up the shooter that fired off that Glock on school grounds over at Duval two weeks ago."

"The one where the bullet hit the wrong kid?"

"The wrong kid? If you say so. The kid that got shot, he had a roll of twenties in his pocket, and a gold chain around his neck thicker than my wrist. So maybe he didn't hit the kid he was going for, but he damn sure hit a kid that was in the life. Shit, Nick, you throw a fuckin' rock in the hall of that high school, you're gonna hit someone guilty of something."

"You're a real optimist, Boyle. You know it?"

"Like now I need a lecture. Anyway, you want to talk about sociology and shit from behind that bar, go ahead. In the meantime, I'm out there—"

"In that concrete jungle?"

"What?"

" 'Concrete Jungle,' " I said. "The Specials."

"Gimme another drink," Boyle mumbled, and finished off what was in his glass. He chased it with a swig of beer and wiped his chin dry with the back of his hand.

Happy said something, either to himself or to me, from the

other end of the bar. I ignored him, poured Boyle another shot. I leaned one elbow on the mahogany and put my foot up on the ice chest.

"So, Boyle. How about that kid, the one that got it two nights ago—"

"The one they found in the river?"

"Yeah. I guess that was a drug thing, too."

"Bet it," Boyle said. "But it's not my district. So that's one I don't have to worry about."

"Let me ask you something. You know what the weapons of choice are on the street this month, right? I mean, it changes all the time, but you're pretty much on top of it. Right?"

"So?"

"These enforcers. They in the habit of using silencers these days?"

Boyle thought for a moment, then shook his head. He watched me out the corner of his eye as he butted his cigarette. Happy called again and I went down his way and fixed him a drink. When I came back, Boyle was firing down the remainder of his Jack and draining off the rest of his beer. He left some money on the bar, stashed his cigarettes in his jacket, and slid clumsily off his stool.

"Take it easy, Nick."

"You, too."

I took his bills and rang on the register, dropping what was left into my tip jar. In the bar mirror, I saw Dan Boyle moving toward the front door. He turned once and stared at my back, his mouth open, his eyes blank. Then he turned again and walked heavily from the bar.

I WORKED ANOTHER SHIFT on Friday, and in the evening Lyla and I caught a movie at the Dupont and had some appetizers after the show at Aleko's, the best Greek food in town for my money, on Connecticut, above the Circle. Lyla had a few glasses of retsina at the restaurant and a couple more glasses of white before we went to bed. I didn't drink that night — three days now without a drop, the longest downtime in a long, long while. I had some trouble going to sleep, though, and when I did, my dreams were crowded, filled with confusing detail, unfamiliar places, blue-black starlings rising in the corners of the frame.

On Saturday, Lyla went into the office to put the finishing touches on a cover story, and I rode my ten-speed down to the Mall to catch a free Fugazi show at the Sylvan Theater. A go-go act opened to a polite crowd, and then the band came out and tore it up. I saw Joe Martinson, a friend and contemporary of mine from the old postpunk days, and we hung together in the late-teen crowd that was getting off — clean off — on the music.

That night, Lyla and I stayed at my place and listened to a few records. Lyla drank a gin and tonic and switched over to wine, and around midnight she called me outside, where I found her sitting on a blanket she had spread in the yard. She smirked as I approached her, and as she opened her legs, her skirt rode up her thighs, and I saw what that smile was all about. It was a good night, and another day gone by without a drink. But my dreams were no better than those of the night before.

On Sunday, we drove down to Sandy Point and buried our toes in the hot orange sand, then cooled off in the bay, dodging the few nettles, which were late that year due to the heavy spring rains. In the evening, I drove over to Alice Deal Junior High and worked out with my physician, Rodney White, who ran a karate school in the gym. Though I had resisted "learning" tae kwon do — I had boxed coming up in the Boys Club and was convinced that hand technique was all I needed to know — I had been doing this with Rodney for years now, and he had managed to teach me some street moves as well as the first four forms of his art. I finished the last of those forms, and Rodney and I got into some one-step sparring.

"All right, man," Rodney said.

We bowed in, and then I threw a punch. Rodney moved

simultaneously to the side and down into a horse stance, where he sprang up and whipped a straight, open hand to within an inch of my throat. I heard the snap of his black gi and the yell from deep in his chest.

"What the hell was that?"

"Ridge hand," Rodney said. "Keep the first joints of your fingers bent. You'll be striking with the whole side of your hand. And the kicker's in the snap of the wrist, right before the strike. Step aside, and use the momentum coming up to drive it right into the Adam's apple. You do it right, man, you'll ruin somebody's day."

I tried it, then tried it again. "Like that?"

Rodney gave a quick nod. "Something like that. More snap, though, at the end. Like everything else, it'll come."

"What now?"

"Get your gloves, man," Rodney said. "Let's go a few."

After we sparred, I drove back to my place and grabbed a beer out of the refrigerator and took it with me into the shower. I didn't think about it one way or the other, as this was something I did every time I returned from Rodney White's dojo. No bells went off and I felt no guilt. The beer was cold and good.

I stood in the spray of the shower, leaned against the tiles, and drank. I thought about what had happened at the river, and what I had heard: the inflection of the voices, the words themselves, the animal fear of the boy. The memory had resonance, like a cold finger on my shoulder. Everyone else had this wrapped up and tied off as a drug kill, another black kid born in a bad place, gone down a bad road. But I had been there that night. And the more I went back to it, the more I suspected that they were wrong.

I got out of the shower and wrapped a towel around my middle, then got myself another beer. I cracked the beer and went to the living room, where I phoned Dan Boyle.

"Yeah," he said, over the screams and laughter of several children.

"Boyle, it's Nick Stefanos. What's goin' on?"

"These fuckin' kids," he said, letting out a long, tired breath into the phone. "What can I do for you?"

I told him, and then we went back and forth on it for the next half hour. In the end, against his better judgment, he agreed to do what I asked, maybe because he knew that we both wanted the same thing. I set a time and thanked him, then hung the receiver in its cradle. Then I tilted my head back and killed the rest of my beer.

I could have called Boyle back and ended it right then. If I had just called him back, things might not have gone the way they did between Lyla and me, and I never would have met Jack LaDuke. But the thirst for knowledge is like a piece of ass you know you shouldn't chase; in the end, you chase it just the same.

THREE

A FTER MY MONDAY shift, I walked out of the Spot and headed for my car, with Anna Wang at my side, a colorful day pack strung across her back. She wore black bike shorts and a white T-shirt that fell off one muscled shoulder, leaving exposed the lacy black strap of a bra. I let her into the passenger side and then went around and got myself behind the wheel.

"Boss car," Anna said as she had a seat in the shotgun bucket of my latest ride.

"I like it," I said with deliberate understatement. Actually, I thought it was one of the coolest cars in D.C.: a '66 Dodge Coronet 500, white, with a red interior, full chrome center console, and a 318 under the hood. After my Dart blew a head gasket a year earlier, I had gone into the Shenandoah Valley and paid cash—two grand, roughly—to the car's owner in Winchester, and I hadn't regretted it one day since.

Anna snagged a cigarette from the pack wedged in my visor

and pushed in the dash lighter. I hit the ignition, and the dual exhaust rumbled in the air. Anna glanced over as she lit her smoke.

"What are you, some kind of gearhead, Nick?"

"Not really. I just like these old Chrysler products. My first car was a Valiant with a push-button trans on the dash. After that, I had a '67 Polara, white on red, the extralong model, a motel on wheels. My buddy Johnny McGinnes called it my 'Puerto Rican Cadillac.' It had the cat-eye taillights, too. A real beauty. Then I had a '67 Belvedere, clean lines, man, and the best-handling car I ever owned. I guess because of the posi rear. Then my old Dart, and now this. I'll tell you something, these Mopar engines were the strongest this country ever produced. As long as there's no body cancer, I'll keep buying them."

Anna took a drag off her cigarette and smirked. " 'Posi rear'? Nick, you *are* a gearhead, man."

"Yeah, well, I guess you got me nailed." I looked her over and caught her eye. "Speaking of which, there's this tractor pull, next Saturday night? I was wonderin'…if you're not doing anything, I'd be right proud if you'd care to accompany me—"

"Very funny. Anyway, you can just take your girlfriend to that tractor pull, buster."

At the top of 8th, we passed an old haunt of mine, a club where you used to be able to catch a good local band and where you could always cop something from the bartender, something to smoke or snort or swallow in the bathroom or on the patio out back. I had met my ex-wife Karen there for the first time one night. The original club had closed years ago, shut down at about the same time as my marriage.

Anna looked out the window. "You ever go in that place?"

"Not anymore."

"I thought 'cause, you know, they cater to that thirty-plus crowd."

"Thanks a lot." I could have backhanded her one, but she was so damn cute. "Where you headed, anyway?"

"Drop me at the Eastern Market Metro, okay?"

I did it and then got on my way.

I DROVE DOWN M Street, past the Navy Yard and the projects and the gay nightclubs and the warehouses, and kept straight on past the 11th Street Bridge ramp as M continued unmarked, past Steuart Petroleum, down through the trees toward the water, past a couple of marinas and the Water Street turnoff, to the wooded area where the rusted houseboat sat submerged in the river amid the wooden pilings. I pulled off in the clearing and parked my car next to Boyle's.

An old man with closely cropped salt-and-pepper hair sat in a metal folding chair, holding a cheap Zebco rod, a red plastic bucket and green tackle box by his side, a sixteen-ounce can of beer between his feet. Two young men leaned against a brilliantly waxed late-model Legend parked beneath the trees and looked out toward the carpet green of Anacostia Park across the river. Boyle stood on the edge of the concrete bulkhead, his shirtsleeves rolled above his elbows, his beefy hands at his side, a manila envelope wedged under one arm, a hot cigarette drooping lazily from his mouth. I walked across the gravel and joined him.

"You're a little late," Boyle said, glancing at his watch.

"Had to wait for Anna to clean her station. Gave her a lift to the subway."

"What're you, sniffin' after that Chinee heinie now?"

"Just gave her a ride, Boyle."

"Like to have me some of that. Never did have a Chinese broad when I was single. Any suggestions on how to get one?"

"You might start by not calling them 'broads.' Women don't seem to like that very much these days. They haven't for, like, forty years."

"Thanks for the tip. I'll work it into my next sensitivity discussion. The department's very big on that now, since those uniforms handcuffed that drunk broad—I mean, *inebriated woman*—to that mailbox last winter. Maybe I could get you to come down and lecture."

I looked at the envelope under Boyle's arm. "So what you got?"

"Not yet," Boyle said. He transferred the envelope to his hand and dragged deeply on his cigarette. A large drop of sweat ran down his neck and disappeared below his collar. "Where were you that night?"

I pointed to a dirt area of paper and cans and garbage just inside the tree line, behind the fisherman. "Right about in there." One of the young men leaning on the Legend gave a brief, tough glance my way, and the other stared straight ahead.

"If they were parked where we are—"

"I don't know where they were parked. I didn't see anything. I couldn't even lift my head."

"Well, the freshest tire prints we got were there. We were lucky to get those—someone called in an anonymous on the murder pretty soon after it happened. That was you, right?"

"Yeah."

Boyle moved his head in the direction of our cars. "So if that's where they were parked, and they took the kid straight down to the water and did him, then went right back to their vehicle, it's possible they didn't see you layin' back there in the trees."

"What, you don't believe me?"

"Sure, I believe you all right." Boyle took a last hit off his smoke and ground it under his shoe. "Just tryin' to figure things out. C'mon, let's take a walk, get away from those two entrepreneurs."

"Those guys dealers?"

Boyle shrugged. "That's a thirty-thousand-dollar car, and they ain't real estate developers. Anyway, I'm Homicide, not Narcotics, so I couldn't give a rat's ass. But it's a bet that they aren't holdin' right now. This road dead-ends up ahead, past the bridge at the last marina. The locals know not to do business down here—no place to run to. Those guys are probably just relaxing before going to work later tonight. But I don't need any witnesses to what I'm about to do. Come on."

We went back to the road and walked north toward the Sousa Bridge. A mosquito caught me on the neck. I stopped and slapped at it, looked at the smudge of blood on my fingers. Boyle kept walking. I quickened my step and caught up with him.

Boyle said, "That thing you pulled with the silencer. That was pretty cute. It didn't hit me until I got off my bar stool. 'Course I phoned the detective in charge of the case soon as I left the Spot. Ballistics report had come in earlier that day."

"And?"

"You were right. A silenced twenty-two. A Colt Woodsman, I'd guess, if it was some kind of hit."

"A twenty-two. That proves it wasn't a gang thing, right?"

"It doesn't prove anything. A kid on the street can get his hands on any piece he wants, same as a pro, and for all I know, a twenty-two is the latest prestige weapon. Don't get ahead of yourself, Nick."

We went beneath the bridge and moved to the last set of legs before the river. A gull glided by and veered off toward the water. The metallic rush of cars above us echoed in the air.

Boyle leaned against a block of concrete, one of many that sat piled near the legs. "Tell me why else you think this isn't a drug kill."

"Let me ask you something, Boyle. You ever know whites and blacks to crew together in this town?"

"'Course not. Not in this town or any other town I ever heard of."

"It was a white man and a black man killed that kid. I heard their voices. And I'll tell you something else. You might want to check up in Baltimore, see if some similar shit has gone down. The white guy, he talked about going 'home,' used that extra long *o* the way they do up in South Baltimore. The guy was definitely out of BA."

"You got it all figured out. A pro hit, out-of-town talent. Come on, Nick, you're puttin' an awful lot together with nothin'."

"I'm telling you what I heard."

Boyle looked down at the manila envelope in his hand, then back at me. "I give you what we got, what are you gonna do with it?"

"I know what's going to happen to this if the shooters aren't found in a few more days. Not that it's the fault of you guys. They got you working two, maybe three homicides at a time, and I know it doesn't stop." I shrugged. "I'm just going to get out there, ask around like I always do. I find anything you can use, I'll head it in the direction of the guy who's assigned to the case."

"Through me."

"Whatever. Who's on it?"

"Guy named Johnson's got it. He doesn't come in the Spot, so you don't know him. He's a competent cop, a little on the quiet side. But he is straight up."

"If I find out anything, it'll come to you." I pointed my chin at the envelope.

Boyle breathed out slowly. "Well, we got nothing, really. Nothing yet. The kid's name was Calvin Jeter. Seventeen years of age. Dropout at sixteen, high truancy rate before that, no record except for a couple of f.i.'s, not even misdemeanors. Johnson interviewed the mother, nothing there. Said he was a good boy, no drugs. It's like a broken fuckin' record. Jeter didn't run with a crowd, but he hung real tight, all his life, with a kid named Roland Lewis. Haven't been able to locate Lewis yet."

"Lewis is missing?"

"Not officially, no."

"What about forensics, the crime scene?"

"The slug was fired at close range. You saw the burn marks yourself. A twenty-two'll do the job when the barrel's pressed right up there against the chin." Boyle's eyes moved to the river.

"The tire tracks indicate the doers drove some kind of off-road vehicle. Similar tracks were found in a turnaround area at the end of the road, past the last marina. Which tells me that when they left, they headed right for the dead end, had to backtrack — so maybe they weren't local guys after all." Boyle looked at me briefly, then away. "Like you said."

"What else?"

"One important thing, maybe the only real lead we got. There's a potential witness, someone who actually might have seen something. A worker down at the boatyard says there's this guy, some crazy boothead, sits under this bridge" — Boyle patted the concrete — "sits right on these blocks, wearing a winter coat, every morning just before dawn, reading books, singing songs, shit like that. And the estimated time of death was just around dawn."

"That's about right," I said.

"And if your friends drove under the bridge, then turned around and drove back, and if this mental deficient was here, there's a very good chance he got a good look at the car. Maybe he noticed the license plates. Maybe he can ID the shooters themselves."

"So who's the guy?"

"The guys at the boatyard, they don't know him. They never introduced themselves, on account of the guy was stone-crazy."

"Anybody interview him since?"

Boyle flicked a speck of tobacco off his chin. "He hasn't been *back* since. We don't even know if he was here that particular morning. Johnson's checked it out a couple of times, and we've got a couple of uniforms sitting down here at dawn for as long as we can spare 'em. But so far, nothing."

"All this stuff in the reports?"

"Yeah." Boyle pushed the envelope my way but did not hand it over.

"What's the problem?"

"I know what's going with you, that's all. You think because you got polluted and happened to fall down near where a kid got shot, that makes you responsible in some way for his death. But you ought to be smart enough to know that you had nothin' to do with it—that kid woulda died whether you had been laying there or not. And consider your being drunk some kind of blessing, brother. If you coulda got up off your ass, most likely they woulda killed you, too."

"I know all that."

"But you're still gonna go out and ask around."

"Yes."

Boyle sighed. "You got no idea what kind of trouble I could get into." He pointed one thick finger at my face. "Anything you find, you come to me, hear?"

"I will."

Boyle tossed me the envelope. "Don't fuck me, Nick."

He walked away and left me standing under the bridge.

FOUR

THAT EVENING, I categorized and studied the Xeroxed police file on the Jeter case, and in the morning I sat at the desk of the small office area in my apartment and studied it all over again. I showered and dressed, grabbed some of the pertinent material, and took a few legitimate business cards and some phony ones and slid them in my wallet. Then I took a dish of dry cat food and a bowl of water, placed them out on the stoop, and got into my Dodge and headed downtown.

I stopped for some breakfast at Sherrill's, the Capitol Hill bakery and restaurant that is the last remnant of old Southeast D.C., and had a seat at the chrome-edged lunch counter. My regular waitress, Alva, poured me an unsolicited coffee as I settled on my stool, and though the day was already hot, I drank the coffee, because you have to drink coffee when you're sitting at the counter at Sherrill's. Alva took my order, watching me over the rims of her eyeglasses as she wrote, and five minutes later I was sweating over a plate of eggs easy with a side of hash browns and sausage and toast. After the food, I had a second cup of coffee and a cigarette while I listened to a nearby conversation — the uninitiated might have called it an argument — between the owner, Lola, and her daughter, Dorothy. I kept my eyes on the Abbott's ice cream sign hung behind the counter and grinned with fondness at the sound of their voices.

Out on the street, I fed the meter and walked the four blocks down to the Spot. Darnell was in the kitchen prepping lunch and Mai sat at the bar, drinking coffee and reading the *Post*. The sandaled feet at the end of Mai's stout wheels barely reached the rail of the stool, and her blond hair was twisted and bound onto her head in some sort of pretzelized configuration. Phil stood at the register, his back to me, his lips moving — I could see them in the bar mirror — as he counted out from the night before.

"What's going on, Mai?" I said, walking toward the phone.

"Jerome," she said happily. Jerome had to be her latest Marine from the nearby barracks, but I didn't ask.

I placed the list of numbers and addresses in front of me on the service bar and picked up the phone. I began to dial Calvin Jeter's mother, then lost my nerve. Instead, I dialed the number for the Roland Lewis residence. Ramon walked from the kitchen, smiled a foolish gold-toothed grin, and sucker punched me in the gut as he passed. I was coughing it out when a girl's voice came on the other end.

"Yeah."

"Is Roland there?"

"Uh-uh."

"How about Mrs. Lewis? Is she in?"

"Nope." Some giggling by two other females in the background over some recorded go-go. I listened to that and watched Mai send Ramon down to the basement for some liquor.

"You expect her in?"

"She's workin', fool." A loud explosion of laughter. "Bah."

I heard the click of the receiver on the other end. I hung up the phone and checked the list for Mrs. Lewis's work number, saw that I had it, and decided, Not yet. Phil walked by me without a glance or a word, took his keys off the bar, and split.

I went into the kitchen. Darnell stood over a butcher block, chopping white onions, a piece of bread wedged inside his cheek to staunch the tears.

"Goin' on, Nick?"

"Just stopped in to make a couple of calls."

"You see Phil?"

"Yeah. He's still punishing me over last Tuesday night."

"You got all liquored up, left his place wide open, and walked out into the street. You can't really blame the man, can you?"

"I know."

"Yeah," Darnell said. "You know. But do you *really* know?"

"Thanks, Father. Light a candle for me the next time you're in church."

"Go on, man, if you're gonna be actin' funny." Darnell cocked his head but did not look up. He said quietly, "I got work to do."

I left the kitchen and walked through the bar. Ramon came up from the cellar, both hands under a bus tray filled with liquor bottles and cans of juice. I slapped him sharply on the cheek as he passed. He called me a *maricón* and we both kept walking. He was cackling as I went out the door.

THE LEWIS RESIDENCE, A nondescript brick row house with a corrugated green aluminum awning extended out past its front porch, was on an H-lettered street off Division Avenue in the Lincoln Heights area of Northeast. I had taken East Capitol around the stadium, over the river, past countless liquor stores, fried-chicken houses, and burger pits, and into the residential district of a largely unheralded section of town, where mostly hardworking middle-class people lived day to day among some of the highest drug and crime activity of the city.

I parked my Dodge on Division, locked it, and walked west on the nearest cross street. I passed a huge, sad-eyed guy — a bondsman, from the looks of him — retrieving a crowbar and flashlight from the trunk of his car. Three more addresses down the block and I took the steps up the steeply pitched front lawn of the Lewis house to its concrete porch, where I knocked on the front door. No one responded and no sounds emanated from the house. The girl who had answered the phone earlier and her friends were obviously gone. I stood there, listening to a window-unit air conditioner work hard in the midday heat.

I waited a few minutes, looked over my shoulder. The bondsman had gone off somewhere, leaving an empty street. I went to the bay window, stepped around a rocker sofa mounted on rails and springs, and looked through an opening in the venetian blinds: an orderly living room, tastefully but not extravagantly furnished, with African-influenced art hung on whitewashed walls.

I dropped my card through the mail slot in the door and walked back down to the street.

DIVISION LIQUORS STOOD ON a corner a couple of blocks south of the Lewis house, between an empty lot and the charred shell of something once called the Strand Supper Club. Two other businesses on the block had burned or been burned out as well, leaving only the liquor store and a Laundromat open on the commercial strip. I parked in front of the Laundromat and walked towards Division Liquors.

Several groups of oldish men stood in front of the store, gesturing broadly with their hands and arguing dispassionately, while a young man stood next to his idling Supra and talked into a pay phone mounted on the side of the building that faced the lot. The young man wore a beeper clipped to his shorts — some sort of statement, most likely meaning nothing—and swore repeatedly into the phone, punctuating each tirade with the words *my money*. I passed a double amputee sitting in a wheelchair outside the front door. His chair had been decorated with stickers from various veteran's groups and a small American flag had been taped to one of its arms. The man sitting in it had matted dreadlocks tucked under a knit cap, with sweat beaded on the ends of the dreads.

"Say, man," he said.

"I'll get you on the way out," I said, and entered the store.

I grabbed two cans of beer and a pack of Camels, paid a white man through an opening at the bottom of a Plexiglas shield, and left the store. Out on the sidewalk, I slipped a couple of ones and some coin into Knit Cap's cup, checked to see if the young man was still using the phone, saw that he was, and walked back to my car. Sometime later, as I finished off my first can of beer, the young man dropped into the bucket of his Supra and drove off. I got out of my car and walked to the pay phone, where I sunk a quarter in the slot and punched in a number that was written on the notepad in my hand.

"Mrs. Jeter, please."

A bored young female said, "Hold on." A television set blared in the background, competing against the sounds of young children yelling and playing in the room. A woman's voice screamed out, silencing the children. She breathed heavily into the phone.

"Yes?"

"Mrs. Jeter?"

"Y-y-yes?"

"My name is Nick Stefanos. I'm working with the Metropolitan Police on your son Calvin's murder," I said, breaking some kind of law with the lie.

"I've done talked to the p-p-police three times."

"I know. But I'd like to see you if possible. I'm in your neighborhood right now." I gave her the name of the liquor store.

"You're in the neighborhood all right. Fact, you're just

around the corner." I listened to the TV set and the kids, who had started up again, as she thought things over. She told me how to get to her place.

"Thanks very much. I'll be right there." After I shotgun another beer, I thought, hanging the phone in its cradle.

THE JETER APARTMENT WAS in a squat square structure housing five other units, oddly situated on a slight rise in the middle of a block of duplex homes. I parked in a six-car lot to the right of the building, beside a green Dumpster filled to overflowing with garbage. Bees swarmed around a tub-sized cup of cola abandoned on top of the Dumpster, and two boys stood nearby on brown grass and swung sticks at each other in the direct sun. I finished my beer, popped a stick of gum in my mouth, locked my car, and walked across the grass. One of the boys, no older than eight, lunged at me with his stick. I stepped away from it and smiled. He didn't smile back. I walked around to the front of the apartment.

A woman sat in a folding chair outside the entrance, her huge legs spread, the inside of each wrinkled thigh touching the other, fanning herself with a magazine. Some kids stood out on the street, grouped around an expensive black coupe, the name MERCEDES scripted along the driver's side rocker panel. Bass boosted and volumed to distortion thumped from the sound system, burying the rap. A kid looked my way and spread his fingers across his middle, and one of his friends smiled. I approached the woman and asked her the number of the Jeter apartment. A wave of the magazine directed me to a dark opening centered in the front of the building.

The Jeter apartment was one of two situated down the stairs. The stairwell smelled of urine and nicotine, but in the depth and insulation of the cinder block, things were cooler and there was less noise. I wiped sweat off my face and knocked on a door marked 01.

The door opened, and a woman who could have been forty or sixty-five stood in the frame. She wore turquoise stretch pants and a T-shirt commemorating the reunion of a family name I did not recognize. Her breasts hung to her belly and stretched out on the fabric of the T-shirt. Her face was round as a dinner plate and her hair was doing different things all at once on different parts of her head. By anyone's standard, she was an unattractive woman.

"Mrs. Jeter? Nick Stefanos." I put out my hand.

She took it and said, "C-c-come on in."

I walked into a living room crowded with a plastic-covered sectional sofa and two nonmatching reclining chairs. Over the sofa, on a pale yellow wall, hung a black blanket embroidered with a fluorescent wild pony. A rather ornate sideboard of cheap material stood against the next wall, with just about a foot of space between it and the sofa. Except for one dusty teacup, the shelves of the sideboard were empty. A big-screen television sat flush on a stand against the next wall, with wires extending from the Sega beneath it, the wires leading to the hands of a young man sitting on the sofa next to a young woman. Around them both, and on the table where the young man's feet rested, were scattered junk-food wrappers and plastic cups. The young man played the game with intensity, his features twitching with each explosion and laser simulation from the set. As I entered, he glanced up briefly in my direction with a look that managed to combine aloofness with contempt. The young woman, who I guessed had answered the phone when I called, did not acknowledge me at all.

I followed Mrs. Jeter toward the kitchen, looking once into a deep unlit hallway where a little boy and a toddler of indeterminate sex jostled over a rideable plastic fire engine. In the shadows, I saw another young man move from one room to the next.

The kitchen, lit with one circular fluorescent light and a bit of natural light from a small rectangular window, was through an open doorway to the right of the television. Mrs. Jeter leaned against an efficiency-size refrigerator and folded her arms.

"Can I get you somethin', Mr. Stefanos?"

The heat, oppressive in the living room, was stifling in the kitchen; I rolled my sleeves up over damp forearms to the elbow. "Water. A little water would be great, thanks."

"H-h-have a seat."

She gestured to one of four chairs set tightly around a small folding table with a marbleized red Formica top. I sat in one, under a clock whose face featured a Last Supper depiction of white disciples grouped around a white Jesus. Mrs. Jeter turned her back to me, withdrew a glass from a sinkful of dirty dishes, rinsed the glass out, and filled it from the spigot. She placed the glass in front of me and took a seat in a chair on the other side of the table.

Mrs. Jeter watched my face as I looked at the grayish water in the glass, the lip of which was caked yellow. I turned the glass inconspicuously in my hand and had a sip from the cleanest side. The water was piss-warm and tasted faintly of bleach. I put the glass down on the table.

"Mrs. Jeter—"

"Call me Vonda, if you don't mind. I ain't all t-t-that much older than you."

I nodded. "My sympathies on your son's death, Vonda."

"Your sympathies," she said quietly and without malice. "Your sympathies gon' bring my baby back?"

"No," I said. "It's just that...I'd like to help, if I can." I rotated the glass in the ring of water that had formed beneath it and listened to the sounds of the toddler crying in the hallway and the explosions coming from the game on the television set in the other room.

"You say you're with the p-p-police?" She closed her eyes tightly on the stutter, as if she could concentrate her way through it.

"Unofficially, yes. I'm working with them on this," I said,

repeating my lie. "I know what you've told them already. I need to know if there's anything else."

"Like?"

"Things the police may not have asked. Like where Calvin usually went when he went out. What he did for money. That sort of thing."

"You mean, was he druggin'? Ain't t-t-that what you mean to say?" Her eyes flared momentarily, then relaxed. "Calvin wasn't in the life. He was just a boy. Just a boy."

I looked away from her. The crying from the toddler in the hallway intensified. I wondered, Why doesn't someone pick that goddamned baby *up?*

"Those your children out there?" I said, hoping to loosen what had fallen between us.

"The girl is my oldest. The babies, m-m-my grandchildren, are hers. That boy out there, on the couch? That's Barry. He's the father to the youngest child. His little brother, the one back in the bedrooms, he's stayin' with us awhile. Got put out, up his way."

"Mind if I talk to your daughter?"

"She don't know nothin' more than what I told you. What I already told the police."

The television set clicked off and the sound from it died. The front door opened and shut, and soon after that the toddler stopped crying. The older child came into the kitchen then and stood by his grandmother's side, patting his hand against her thigh. She picked him up and sat him in her lap, rubbed her palm over his bald head.

"Have the police been back in touch with you?"

"'Posed to be," she said, brushing some crumbs off the child's lips.

"They're trying to find Calvin's friend Roland," I said. "Know if they had any luck?"

"Roland? If they did, n-n-nobody said nothin' to me."

I rubbed a finger down the scar on my cheek. "Mind if I have a look in Calvin's room?"

"You can look," she said, with a shrug and a grunt as she picked up her grandson and rose from the chair. "Come on, Mr. Stefanos."

We walked out and through the living room, where the girl sat on the sectional couch, giving the toddler a short bottle of juice. I followed Vonda Jeter into the hallway, past a bathroom and then four bedrooms, which were really two rooms divided by particle-board in one and a shower curtain hung on laundry cord in the other. Three of the rooms contained single beds and scuffed dressers and small television sets on nightstands or chairs. In one of the rooms, the younger brother of the toddler's father slept on his back, bare-chested in his shorts, with one forearm draped over his eyes. Vonda Jeter directed me into the last room, which she said was Calvin's. She pulled on a string that hung from the ceiling and switched on a light.

The room was windowless, paneled in mock birch, separated from its other half by a chair-supported board running floor to ceiling. An unfinished dresser stood flush against the paneling, and next to that an army-issue footlocker. Some change lay on the top of the dresser, along with a set of house keys on a rabbit's foot chain and a knit cap with the word TIMBERLAND stitched in gold across the front.

"The detective, that Mr. Johnson? He went through C-C-Calvin's stuff."

I looked back at Vonda Jeter. Her eyes, yellow and lifeless before, had moistened now and pinkened at the rims.

"Do you have a photograph of Calvin that I could borrow? In the meantime, I'd just like to have a quick look around. I won't disturb anything."

"Go on ahead," she said, and walked from the room without another word.

I went through the dresser drawers, found nothing to study or keep. As a teenager, I had always kept a shoe box in my dresser filled with those things most important to me, and in fact, I still had it; Calvin's drawers were filled with clothing, nothing more, almost obsessively arranged, as if he had no personal connection to his own life.

In the footlocker, a basketball sat in the corner on a folded, yellowed copy of *D.C. This Week*. Several shirts hung on wire, along with a couple of pairs of neatly pressed trousers. I ran the back of my hand along the print rayon shirts, my knuckle tapping something in one of the breast pockets. I reached into the pocket and withdrew a pack of matches: the Fire House, a bar on 22nd and P in Northwest. Across town, and in more ways than one a long distance from home. I slipped the matchbook into my shirt pocket, switched off the light, and left the room.

Vonda Jeter stood in the living room, by the door. I stepped around the couch and met her there. She handed me a photograph of a tough, unsmiling Calvin wearing a suit jacket and tie. He looked nothing like the boy I had seen lying in the river.

"Thank you," I said. "I'll be in touch."

"Whatever you can do," she said, looking away.

She opened the door. I stepped out, quickly took the concrete steps up the stairwell, and walked out into the white sunlight. I heard her door close behind me as I moved across the grass.

I went to my car, unlocked it, and rolled the windows down. The father of the toddler, the game player from the couch, stood looking under the hood of a burnt orange 240Z parked beside my Dodge. He wore shorts that fell below his knees and a black T-shirt showing Marley hitting a blunt. Like most of the young men I had seen that day, he was narrow-waisted, thin, and muscled, with hair shaved to the scalp, broken by a short part. I put him somewhere at the tail end of his teens.

"Is it burnin' a lot of oil?" I said, walking up beside him.

He pulled the dipstick, read it, wiped it off with a cranberry red rag, and pushed it back down into the crankcase.

"Nick Stefanos," I said, extending my hand. "It's Barry, isn't it?" He ignored the question and my gesture. "These old Zs, they're trouble. But they do have style. The two-forties have those headlights—"

"Somethin' I can do for you? 'Cause if not, whyn't you just go on about your business." He closed the hood, wiped his hands off on the rag.

I placed my card on top of the hood. He read it from where he stood without picking it up.

"I'm looking for Roland Lewis," I said. "Thought maybe he could tell me something about Calvin's death."

"That punk," he muttered heavily, staring at the asphalt. He went around to the driver's side and began to fold himself into the bucket. I could see some sort of garishly colored uniform thrown on the floor behind the seat.

"Let me ask you something, Barry," I said, stopping him. "What do *you* think happened to Calvin? At least you can tell me that."

He stopped, chuckled cynically, and looked me in the eyes for the first time. "What do *I* think happened? Whyn't you just take a look around you, chief, check out what we got goin' on down here." Barry made a sweeping gesture with his hand and lowered his voice. "Calvin *died*, man. He died."

He got into his car, started it, and backed out of the lot. My card blew off the hood, fluttered to the asphalt. It landed next to a fast-food wrapper dark with grease. I left it there, climbed into my Dodge, and steered it back onto the street.

I STOPPED FOR ANOTHER can of beer at Division Liquors and went back to my car, where I found some dope in the glove box and rolled a joint. I smoked half the number driving across town, slid an English Beat into the deck. By the time I hit my part of the world, upper 14th around Hamilton, "Monkey Murders" poured out of the rear-deck speakers of my Dodge, and I was tapping out the rhythms on my steering wheel, and singing, too, and many of the things I had seen that day seemed washed away.

I stopped at Slim's, near Colorado Avenue, for a beer, drank it while I listened to some recorded jazz, then hit the Good

Times Lunch on Georgia for an early dinner. Kim, my Korean friend who owned the place, put a can of beer on the counter when I walked in, then went off to fix me a platter of fried cod and greens and potatoes. I took the beer to a pay phone near the front register, stood beneath a malt-liquor poster featuring a washed-up black actor embracing a light-skinned woman with Caucasian features, and dialed the number once again to the Lewis residence.

This time, the mother of Roland Lewis answered the phone. She had just gotten in from work and had found my card in the pile of mail inside her door. Her tone was cool, even, and clear. I explained to her that I needed to speak with her son, adding for the third time that day that I was "with" the police on the Calvin Jeter case. I listened to my own voice, caught the slur in it from the alcohol and the pot, wished then that I had waited to straighten up before I called. But after a moment or two, she agreed to meet me, and I set something up for the next day at her place of business, on M Street in the West End.

I returned to my stool at the counter and ate my food. A man came into the restaurant and ordered a beer, talked to himself as he drank it. I pushed the empty plate of food away and smoked a cigarette while I watched rush hour dissipate through the plate-glass window of the Good Times Lunch. I butted the smoke and went to the register to get my check from Kim.

"Any trouble down this way lately?" I asked as he ripped a green sheet of paper off a pad. There had been two gun deaths, merchant robberies on the strip, in the last six months.

Kim produced a snub-nosed .38 from somewhere under the counter. He waved it briefly, then replaced it as quickly as he had drawn it. Kim blinked, wiped a forearm hard as pine across his brow.

"Take care," I said. I went back down to my spot, left ten on seven, and walked out under the damp veil of dusk.

When I got back to my apartment, I fed the cat and phoned Lyla. Her recorded message told me that she had gone out for happy hour with a friend and that she'd check the machine later that night. I left my own message, asking her to come by, adding, "I could use some company."

But Lyla did not call back or drop in on me. I ended the night sitting on a bench in the back of my yard, another beer in my hand, listening to the crickets sounding out against the flat whir of air conditioners from the windows of the neighboring houses. My cat slinked out from the darkness and brushed against my ankles. I scratched behind her ears. After awhile, I walked back inside and fell to alcohol sleep.

FIVE

THE POLICE REPORT had the only potential witness to the
Jeter murder as a black male, mid-forties, average height and
build, with no distinguishing characteristics, a typically blank
cross-racial description. It wasn't much to go on, not anything at
all, in fact, but the boatyard worker had mentioned that the man
wore a brilliant blue winter coat year round. Everyone concerned had accepted the worker's opinion that the man who sat
singing under the bridge every morning at dawn was crazy.
Crazy, maybe, but not necessarily stupid. If he knew that he had
witnessed a killing and understood the implications, then he
had probably disposed of the coat by now, or, at the very least,
quit wearing it. I was reminded of the time when, as kids, my
friends and I had stood on a hill and thrown hard-packed snow-
balls at cars driving south on 16th Street. One of my buddies
had winged a smoker that shattered the side window of a green
Rambler Ambassador, bloodying the driver's lip. We all scat-

tered and ran; the cops nailed me at the end of a nearby alley, identified me by my neon orange knit cap, which I had neglected to remove from my head. The hat had been the only thing the driver had remembered from his brief look at us on the hill. I figured that nobody, even a straitjacket candidate, is as mindless as a kid who is running from the cops for the first time. But I hoped that I was wrong.

So the next morning, I woke up in the dark and headed downtown and into Southeast, down M Street to the waterline, in search of the man in the brilliant blue coat. By the time I got there, the sky had lightened and a line of orange had broken the green plane of Anacostia Park across the river. A blue-and-white sat parked beneath the Sousa Bridge, with two uniforms in the front seat. They noted me without incident as I went by. I turned the car around at the end of the road and passed them again on my way back out. No man sat singing or reading on the concrete pilings beneath the bridge, blue coat or otherwise. I moved on.

I drove all the way across town, bought a go-cup of coffee at a market on Wisconsin and P in Georgetown, then went up to R and parked near Dumbarton Oaks. I walked through open grounds, down into the woods of Rock Creek Park, and found my seat on a large gray rock at the crest of a winding bridle trail overlooking the creek and Beach Drive. I watched the cars and their occupants, making their morning rush to wherever it is that people who wear ties and business suits go, and I listened to the serpentine creek running to the Georgetown Channel and the songbirds in the trees above. Everyone has their own spot in their hometown, and this was mine.

Afterward, I walked to the iron fence surrounding Oak Hill, wrapped my hands around the rungs, and admired the most beautiful cemetery grounds in D.C. Privileged people lead privileged lives, and even find privileged places to rest. I wondered idly about the final whereabouts of Calvin Jeter's body. Then for a while I thought of nothing earthbound at all. I noticed an old man in a physical-plant uniform sitting atop a small tractor in the cemetery, and for a moment our eyes met. Then he looked away, and we both went back to what we had been doing for the last half hour: trying to find a kernel of spirituality before returning to the cold reality of our day.

I spent that morning reading local history in the Washingtoniana room of the Martin Luther King Memorial Library, then walked into Chinatown and met Lyla for lunch at a nondescript restaurant packed with locals at the corner of 7th and H. I crossed the dining room with a bag in my hand and had a seat next to Lyla.

"Hey," I said, kissing her mouth.

"Hey, you." She looked me over. "Why so sporty?"

I wore an open-necked denim, sleeves up, and a pair of khakis, with monk-straps on my feet. "You think this is sporty?"

"Well, you ran an iron over the shirt."

"Just for you, baby. And, I'm meeting a woman this afternoon."

"What, I'm not a woman?"

"Sweetheart, you're all woman. But I'm talking about a business appointment. Over at Ardwick, Morris and Baker, in the West End."

"That's the firm that defended those S and L boys."

"I don't know anything about that. I'm meeting one of their secretaries."

"Uh-huh." She smiled maternally. "You're poking around on the Jeter murder, aren't you? I can see it on you, Nick. The only time you get wired during the daylight like this is when you're juiced on some kind of case. Am I right?"

"I'm asking around, that's all. Maybe I'll kick something up."

"Yeah," she said.

Our waitress, an angular woman with coal black hair and bad teeth, arrived at the table. I ordered steamed dumplings with a main of squid sautéed in garlic, and Lyla ordered the special, asking only if it contained chicken. We avoided anything in the way of chicken here, as several of them hung plucked in the midday heat of the window. Lyla asked for white wine, and I took ice water.

"What do you suppose is in the special?" Lyla said.

"I'm not sure," I said. "But it's probably better you didn't ask."

The waitress came back momentarily with our drinks.

Lyla lifted her wineglass. "Takes the edge off," she said, and had a sip. "Yeah, that'll do it."

"I thought you looked a little thick today," I said. And I had noticed her hand shaking as she picked up her glass.

She shrugged apologetically. "Happy hour stretched to last call. Sorry I didn't make it over last night."

"That's okay."

She flicked the brown paper on the table. "So, what's in the bag?"

"Some stuff I picked up at the Chinese store on H. Something for you."

I withdrew a small ceramic incense burner, hand-painted lilacs on a black background, and put it in front of her.

"Love it." She smiled, turned the burner in her hand. "What else?"

"Something for me." I took a videotape from the bag and waved it in front of her. "A Ringo Lam flick, for the collection."

"Okay. What else?"

"Something for us." I pulled out a tub of cream, labeled completely in Mandarin characters. "The lady at the counter said it was 'very special lotion for lovers.'"

"What's so special about it?"

"I don't know. But we've got a date, tomorrow night, right?"

"Yeah?"

"So I was thinkin'—"

"Oh boy," she said.

"That, at the end of the night, maybe you'd care to dip your fingers in this jar and give me a back rub. And maybe after that, I could return the favor and give you a front rub."

"Here it comes."

"And then we could rub it all over us and get some kind of friction going."

"You could get a burn like that."

"And maybe we'd get so much friction going, that, I don't know, the two of us could just explode."

"At the same time?"

"Well, we could try."

"Nick, why are you such a dog?"

"Speaking of dog," I said, "here comes your food."

Lyla and I spent a couple of hours in the restaurant, enjoying the food and talking and having a few more laughs. There was a sign over the kitchen door that read MANAGEMENT NOT RESPONSIBLE, and Lyla commented dryly on that. I stuck with water and she had another wine. Lyla paid the check and I left the tip, and we kissed outside on the street. I stood there and watched her walk in the direction of the subway stop, moving in that clipped, confident way of hers in her short peasant dress, her red hair brilliant in the sun and long on her back. You're a lucky bastard, I thought, and then I added, Nick, just try not to fuck this up.

THE OFFICES OF ARDWICK, Morris and Baker occupied the top floors of an Oliver Carr building on M Street at 24th. I have to laugh now when I hear any law firm's name; a guy by the name of Rick Bender comes in the Spot for a vodka gimlet once a week—I don't know what Bender does, but he's a profoundly silly guy, and I know he's not an attorney—and always leaves a business card on the bar with his tab: "Rick Bender, Esquire." Printed below his name is the name of his "firm": "Bender, Over, and Doer."

I passed through the marble-floored lobby and made an elevator where a couple of secretaries stood huddled in the back. I was of the tieless variety, and after a quick appraisal, the two of them went right on complaining about their respective attorneys. A few floors up, a paralegal joined us, a guy in his twenties who was struggling mightily in his attire and haircut to look fifteen years older. Then on the next floor, we picked up a real attorney, wearing a real charcoal suit with chalk stripes and a really powerful tie. I said hello to him and he looked both confused and scared to death. Finally, we made it to the top floor of the building, where I put my back to the door to let the ladies out first, which seemed to perplex everyone further. My grandfather taught me to do that, and it isn't done much in D.C. anymore. I'm almost never thanked for it, but that doesn't mean that I'm going to stop.

I announced myself to the receptionist, had a seat in a very comfortable chair, and leafed through a *Regardie's* magazine set on a round glass table. I wasn't far into it when Mrs. Lewis walked into the lobby on two nice cocoa-colored legs and stood over my chair. I got up and shook her hand.

She wore a tan business suit and a brown blouse with an apricot scarf tied loosely around her neck. Her face was long and faintly elastic, with large brown eyes and a large mouth lipsticked apricot like the scarf. She was younger than the voice on the phone, and I bet she had a good smile, but she wasn't using those muscles just yet. I looked at the fingernails on the spidery fingers that rested in my hand; the polish on the nails was apricot, too. Neat.

"Nick Stefanos. Thanks for seeing me."

"Shareen Lewis. We can use one of the conference rooms. Follow me."

I did it, walked behind her, passing open-doored offices where men stood reading briefs or sat talking on telephones. They wore British-cut suits with suspenders beneath the jackets and orderly geometric-patterned ties. I thought, Why the suspenders? Did these guys collectively buy their pants in the wrong size?

Shareen Lewis directed me into a conference room whose

center held a long, shiny table with gray high-backed swivel chairs grouped around it. The shades had been drawn, and when she closed the door the room became cool and quiet as a tomb. We sat next to each other by the windows. She turned her chair in my direction, folded her hands on the table in front of her, and faced me.

"Are we being recorded?" I said, kidding only by half, trying to break things down.

"Should we be? You look a little uncomfortable."

"Well, I'm playing an away game here. This isn't my usual arena."

"That much I can see." Her enunciation was careful, slightly forced.

"So I'll be brief. I've got to get to work myself."

"What do you do, Mr. Stefanos? Besides...this."

"I work in a bar, a place called the Spot. Over on 8th in Southeast."

"I don't know it."

"You wouldn't," I said, intending it as a compliment. But she didn't know what I meant by the remark, and the muscles of her jaw ratcheted up a notch.

"What can I do for you?" she said.

"Like I told you on the phone, I'd like to have the opportunity to speak with your son, Roland. Everything I've been able to uncover tells me that he was the closest friend that Calvin Jeter had. I'm assisting the police on the Jeter murder."

"I don't believe that I can help you."

"Maybe Roland might like to help."

"I don't think so."

"Could you tell me where to contact him?"

"No."

"Is that because you don't know where he is?"

"Roland is seventeen years old. Almost a man. He comes and goes as he pleases."

"So he's not missing."

"No."

"But he didn't attend Calvin's funeral, did he?"

"How do you know that?"

"The police haven't talked with Roland since the murder. Don't you think it's odd that Roland didn't attend Calvin's funeral, seeing that the two of them were best friends?"

She spoke quietly, but for the first time her voice registered emotion. "I would hardly say, Mr. Stefanos, that Roland and Calvin were best friends. Roland might have felt sorry for that boy, but nothing in the way of real friendship. After all, the Jeter boy lived in a welfare setup, down in those…apartments."

So she was about that. I didn't like it, and stupidly, I've never been one to hide it. I leaned forward. "I've been to your house, remember? And those apartments are just a few blocks away from you. The people who live in them are your neighbors. And I've got to tell you, Calvin's mother—that welfare mother you're talking about—treated me with more dignity and grace than you're showing me here." I relaxed in my chair, then tried to throw some water on the fire. "I'm only trying to help."

But it didn't move her. If anything, she sat up straighter, eyeing me coldly. She tapped her fingernail on the lacquered table—the only sound in the room.

"All right," she said. "Let me tell you why I agreed to see you today. It's not to talk about my son, I can assure you of that. You just told me that you were 'assisting' the police on the Jeter case. It's the second time you've told me that. And not only is what you're telling me a straight-up lie; it happens to be a criminal offense. I work in a law firm, Mr. Stefanos. I'm not an attorney, but I'm not just a message-taker, either, and I've had this checked out. I could turn your ass in to*day*, my friend, bust you right out of your license. I don't know what your business is with this, but I'm telling you, I don't want to know. I don't ever want to see you or hear from you or have you around my house or near my children again. Understood?"

"Yes."

"This conversation is over." She stood from her chair and left the room.

I waited a couple of minutes to let the heat dissipate. I found my way out.

I FIRST NOTICED THE white sedan as I drove east on Constitution toward the Spot. The driver had tried to catch up by running a red, and the horns from the cars starting through the cross street caught my attention. It wasn't until I got stuck in a bus lane and saw the white sedan deliberately pull into that same stalled lane that I knew I was being tailed. I made a couple of false turn signals after that, saw the tail make the amateur's mistake and do the same. I hit the gas at the next intersection and hooked a wild right into the 9th Street tunnel. I lost him in the Southwest traffic and went on my way.

The Spot was empty of customers when I arrived. Mai untied her change apron as I entered and tossed it behind the cooler. She wore her angry face, splotched pink, and she left without a word. An argument with Jeremy, most likely—or had she said Jerome? Anna Wang had hung out past her shift and now stood in the kitchen, talking with Darnell, showing him some crystals she had bought in Georgetown. The week my son was born, when I flew out to San Francisco to visit Jackie and her lover, Sherron, Anna had given me four crystals wrapped and tied in a square of yellow cloth, crystals specifically selected to protect me on my journey. The crystals hung now in their cloth sack from the rearview of my Dodge, along with a string of worry beads given to me by my uncle Costa, the two elements forming some hoodoo version, I suppose, of a St. Christopher's medal.

I changed into shorts and a T-shirt, poured myself a mug of coffee, put some music on the deck, and began to slice fruit for the tray. After that, I washed the dirty glasses from lunch, soaked the ashtrays, and wiped down the bar. Mai should have prepped all that, but I didn't mind. The dead time between lunch and happy hour, standing idly in front of the sexy, backlit pyramid of liquor with nothing much to do, was just plain dangerous for a guy like me.

Mel came through the door as I finished the prep. He found his stool, ordered a gin martini, and requested "a little Black Moses." I managed to find our sole Isaac Hayes tape buried in a pile of seventies disco and funk and slipped it into the stereo. Mel closed his eyes soulfully, began to sing off-key: "You're my joy; you're everything to me-ee-eee." Happy entered at about that time, sat at the other end of the bar, complained about the speed of my service as I placed his manhattan down in front of him, stopped complaining as he hurriedly tipped the up glass to his lips. Then it was Buddy and Bubba taking up the middle of the place, two pitchers deep, and later a gentleman I'd never seen before, who started off fine but degenerated spectacularly after his first drink, and an obnoxious judge named Len Dorfman, who spouted off to a dead-eared audience, and Dave, reading a paperback Harry Whittington, and a couple of plainclothes detectives talking bitterly about the criminal-justice system, cross-eyed drunk and armed to the teeth. Finally, after all of them had gone or been asked to leave, it was just Darnell and I, closing up.

"You about ready?" Darnell said, leaning one long arm on the service bar.

"Yeah, but—"

"I know. You're gonna have yourself a drink."

"Just one tonight. If you want to stick around, I'll give you a lift uptown."

"That's all right." Darnell tipped two fingers to his forehead. "Do me good to catch some air, anyhow. See you tomorrow, hear?"

"Right, Darnell. You take care."

He went through the door and I locked up behind him. I dimmed the lights and had a shot and a beer in the solitary coolness of the bar. I smoked a cigarette to the filter, butted it, and removed my shirt. I washed up in the basin in Darnell's kitchen, changing back to my clothes from the afternoon. Then I set the alarm and walked out onto 8th.

Parked out front beneath the streetlamp was a white sedan, a big old piece-of-shit Ford. I recognized the grille as belonging to the car that had tailed me earlier in the day. No one sat inside the car. I looked around and saw nothing and began to walk. A voice from the mouth of the nearby alley stopped me.

"Stevonus?"

"Yes?"

I turned around and faced him. He walked from the shadows and moved into the light of the streetlamp. He had a revolver in his hand and the revolver was pointed at my chest.

"Who are you?" I said.

"Jack LaDuke," he said. He jerked the gun in the direction of the Ford. "Get in."

SIX

I STOOD THERE staring at him. He had a boyishly handsome face, clean-shaven and straight-featured, almost delicate, with a long, lanky body beneath it. His light brown hair was full and wavy on top, shaved short in the back and on the sides, a *High Sierra* cut. His manner was tough, but his wide brown eyes were curiously flat; I couldn't tell what, if anything, lived behind them. He tightened his grip on the short-barreled .357.

"Why aren't you moving?" he said.

"I don't think I have to," I said. "You're not going to mug me, or you'd already have me in that alley. And you're not going to shoot me—not with your finger on the outside of that trigger guard. Anyway, you're not throwing off that kind of energy."

"That a fact."

"I think so, yeah."

He shifted his feet, tensed his jaw, and tilted his head toward his car. "I'm not going to ask you again, Stevonus."

"All right." I moved to the passenger side and put my hand to the door.

"Uh-uh," he said, and tossed me his keys. "You drive."

I walked around to the front of the car and got into the driver's seat. LaDuke settled into the shotgun side of the bench. I fitted his key in the ignition and turned the engine over.

"Where to?"

"It doesn't matter," he said, the gun still pointed at my middle. He wore a long-sleeved white shirt and a plain black tie tightly knotted to the neck. His slacks were no-nonsense, plain front, and he wore a pair of thick-soled oxfords on his feet. A line of sweat had snaked down his cheek and darkened the collar of the shirt. "Drive around."

I pulled the boat out of the space and swung a U in the middle of 8th. I headed toward Pennsylvania Avenue, and when I got there, I took a right and kept the car in traffic.

"You gonna tell me what this is about?"

"I'll tell you when I'm ready to tell you."

"That's a good line," I said. "But you're in the wrong movie. Let me help you out here. This is the part where you're supposed to say, 'I'm asking the questions here, Stevonus.'"

"Shut up."

"You're making a mistake," I said, speeding up next to a Mustang ahead of me and in the lane to my left. "You've been making mistakes all day. Your shadow job was a joke. Stevie Wonder could have made your tail."

"I said, shut up."

"Then you sit out front of where I work for I don't know how long. How many people you figure walked down 8th in that time happened to see you? Those are all people that could ID you later on."

"Just keep pushing it," he said.

"And now this. 'You drive'—that's some real stupid shit, pal. You let me drive, and who do you think's got the power? Yeah, you're holding the gun, but I've got both our lives in my hands. I can drive this shitwagon into a wall, or into a cop car, or I can drive it right into the fucking river if I want to. Or I can do this."

I stuck my head out the window and yelled something at the driver of the Mustang. The man turned his head, startled. I yelled again and flipped him the bird. The driver was alone, but he was a Southeast local, and he wasn't going to take it. He screamed something back at me and swerved into my lane.

"Now he'll remember us," I said, talking calmly over the man's angry shouts. "And he'll remember the car. In case you got any ideas of doing me and dumping me out somewhere. I guess I better make sure he's got our plate numbers, too."

I accelerated and cut in front of the Mustang, then jammed on the brakes. The Mustang missed us, but not by much. I floored it, leaving some rubber on the street.

LaDuke's fingers dug into the armrest on the door. "What the fuck are you doing, man!"

"Put that gun away," I said, and cut across two lanes of traffic. The oncoming headlights passed across LaDuke's stretched-back face. I jetted into a gas station without braking. The underside of the Ford scraped asphalt, and as the shocks gave it up, the top of LaDuke's head hit the roof. I continued straight out of the station lot, tires screaming as I hit the side street.

"Put it away!" I said.

"Fuck," he muttered, shaking his head. He opened the glove box in front of him, dropped the revolver inside, and shut it. I pulled the car over in front of some row houses and cut the engine.

LaDuke wiped his face dry with his shirtsleeve and looked across the seat. "Fuck," he said again, more pissed off at himself than at me.

"Just sit there and cool down."

"You know," he said, "she told me she had the feeling you were some kind of headcase."

"Who told you?"

He turned his head and stared out the window. "Shareen Lewis."

"What is she to you?"

He withdrew his wallet from the seat of his pants and slid out a business card. I took it and read it: "Jack LaDuke, Private Investigations." His logo—I'm not kidding—was one large eye. I stifled a grin and slipped the card into my shirt pocket.

"You know," I said, "you didn't need to pull that gun."

"Just wanted to see how you'd handle it."

"Am I auditioning for something?"

"You might be," he said, giving the mysterious routine one last try.

I shrugged and fished a smoke out of my pack and pushed in the dash lighter. "Cigarette?"

"I don't smoke."

"Okay." I lit the Camel and drew some tobacco into my lungs. I noticed that my hand was shaking, and I put it by my side. On the corner up ahead, a neighborhood market stood open for business, moths swarming in the spotlight mounted above the door. Young people walked in and out carrying small packages and forties in brown paper bags wrapped to the neck. An older man leaned against the store's plate glass and listlessly begged for change, barely raising his head. I sat there calmly and smoked my cigarette and waited for Jack LaDuke to regain his composure and enough of his pride to the point where he could talk. After awhile, he did.

"Shareen Lewis hired me to find her son," he said.

"So she *is* worried about him."

"Yes."

"Why'd she call you?"

"She didn't," he said, "at first. She called a bondsman she knew named William Blackmon."

"I've heard of him."

"Yeah, they tell me he's been around forever. But he farms out a lot of his work now. First thing I did when I came to town,

I went to all the skip tracers and bondsmen, went to see if I couldn't work something out."

"Blackmon recommended you to Shareen Lewis."

"They go to the same church. Blackmon took me for a flat referral fee."

"And when I dropped my card in the Lewis's door, she wanted to know what was going on." LaDuke nodded. "She agreed to meet with me just so you could set up the tail, check me out."

"That's right," LaDuke said. "Now I've been straight with you. What *is* going on, Stevonus?"

"I'm working on the Calvin Jeter murder," I said, "just like I told her. Roland Lewis seems to be the key."

"Working for who? And don't kid me with that 'police assistant' crap, okay?"

I considered how much I wanted him to know. "I was the first one to find Jeter's body. I came on it by accident. I called it in anonymously to the cops. The cops have gone as far as they're going to go on it. I'm doing some digging on my own."

"For who?" he repeated.

"Jeter's mother. And me."

LaDuke eyed me suspiciously. "There's more to it than what you're telling me. But I guess that's good enough for now, Stevonus."

"The name's *Stefanos*. What have you got, a speech impediment or something?"

"I've got trouble with names," he said with a touch of embarrassment. "That's all."

"Call me Nick, then. You can remember that, can't you?"

"Sure."

I flicked my cigarette out the window and watched its trail. LaDuke shifted nervously in his seat, tapped his fingers on the vent window.

"So what are we going to do now?" I said.

"Well," LaDuke said, "I could use a little help on my end."

"I bet you could." I looked him over. "How long you been in D.C.?"

"Does it show?"

"A little."

"I don't know. Six, maybe seven months."

"Six months. Shit, LaDuke, you don't even know your way around yet. You're never gonna find that kid."

"It's beginning to look like that." He rubbed the top of his head. "How much have you got on the Jeter case?"

"A few things," I said.

"I was thinking...maybe you and me, we ought to work together on this. You know, feed each other information. I mean, you're not getting paid right now, isn't that right? We could cut it straight down the middle."

"Cut what? After Blackmon's piece, that doesn't leave enough for two."

"I've got a couple of other cases I'm working on," he said. "I'm after a deadbeat husband, for one. Maybe you could help me out there, too."

"I don't think so," I said.

"Sleep on it," he said. "Because, the thing is, if you're set on talking to Roland Lewis about Jeter, you're going to have to go through me. Shareen Lewis isn't going to let you near her house, that's for sure. I don't think she cares too much for you."

"She must prefer them on the clean-cut side," I said, scanning his shirt-and-tie arrangement, damp and limp now in the evening heat.

"Yeah, well, this is a business. If you're going to make it, you've got to treat it like a business, act in a businesslike manner, and be presentable."

"And brush your teeth after every meal."

"What's that?"

"Forget it. We about done?"

"Yeah," he said, "let's go. But move over, will you? This time, I'm gonna drive."

* * *

HE PARKED THE FORD in front of the Spot and let it idle. I got out, went around to the driver's side, and leaned my arms on the lip of the open window.

"Think about my proposition," he said.

I nodded and said, "I will."

He looked at me curiously. "Something else?"

"There's one thing I wanted to tell you."

"What's that?"

"Don't ever pull a gun on a man unless you intend to use it. And even then, don't pull it. Do you understand?"

"I know all about guns," he said. "I grew up in the country. I've known how to shoot since I was a kid."

"Congratulations. But it's not the same thing. An animal's not a man."

"No shit," he said with a cocky grin.

I pushed off from the car and stood straight. "Well, I guess you already know everything there is to know. So you might as well get on home."

"Right. I'll call you tomorrow."

"Take care, hear?"

I walked across the street to my car. LaDuke drove away.

SEVEN

I WOKE UP early the next morning, fed my cat, went outside and picked my *Post* up off the stoop, then went back in and read it over a couple of cups of coffee. After a week, there had still been no follow-up on Calvin Jeter's murder. Nothing in the *Post* or in the *Washington Times*, and nothing on the TV news.

I phoned Boyle, and when he phoned me back he confirmed it: "This one's already cold, Nick."

He asked me what I had. I said, "I've got nothing." It wasn't exactly the truth, but it was close enough. Boyle told me to keep in touch before he cut the line.

I paced around some after that, did a few sets of sit-ups and push-ups in my room, showered, dressed for work, and paced around some more. I found Jack LaDuke's business card on my dresser and rubbed my finger across its face. I put it down and walked into another room. A little while later, I returned to my bedroom and picked the business card up off the dresser once again. I went to the phone and dialed LaDuke's answering service. He phoned me back right away.

"Glad you called," he said.

"Just wanted to make sure you were all right after last night."

"I've got a hell of a stiff neck. All that bouncing around and shit. Where'd you get your license, anyway? Sears?"

"You were holding a gun on me, remember?"

"Yeah, well..."

"Listen, last night's over, as far as I'm concerned. You say you can get me into the Lewis house."

"Sure I can."

"Well, let's do it. Today."

"It'll have to wait until after Shareen gets off work."

"That's fine. I've got a day shift at the Spot. I can swing by afterward, pick you up. Where's your crib?"

"Never mind that," he said. "I'll pick you up at the bar. You tellin' me we got a deal?"

"Not so fast. Let's take this a little bit at a time, okay?"

"Just don't want to give everything away and get nothing back."

"I don't blame you. But let's see if we can work together first. And LaDuke?"

"Yeah?"

"Don't forget your tie."

He didn't forget it. He was wearing it, a solid blue number on a white shirt, knotted tightly despite the heat, when he walked into the Spot at half past four that afternoon. LaDuke had a seat next to Mel, who had stretched a lunch hour into three and was working on his fifth martini of the day. Anna stood by the service bar, counting the sequence of her checks. She glanced at LaDuke when he entered, then gave him a second look as he settled onto his bar stool.

"Nice place," LaDuke said. "Really uptown." He wiped his hands off on a bev nap and left the crumpled napkin on the bar.

"Thanks," I said. "Get you something?"

"I'll just have a Coke, please."

"So you don't drink, either."

"Not really, no."

"Okay, Boy Scout. One Coke, coming up." I shot a glassful from the soda gun and placed it in front of him. "Want a cherry in it?"

"No. But do you have a place mat I can color on?"

I heard Anna laugh from the service end of the bar. Ramon walked behind her on his way to the kitchen and patted her ass. She slapped his hand away. Mel continued to croon along to the Staple Singers coming from the system, doing a Mavis thing with his pursed-out mouth. Happy sat in the shadows, his hand curled listlessly around a manhattan.

"I'll be ready to go," I said, "soon as my replacement shows up."

"I'll just sit here and soak up the atmosphere," said LaDuke.

"Cash in!" Anna yelled.

I went to her and took her tip change, all lined up in neat little rows, and turned it into bills. I handed it over to her and she put her hand into my breast pocket and withdrew a smoke. I lit it for her and she blew the exhale away from my face.

"Who's the guy?" she said.

"Name's Jack LaDuke."

"I like it," she said.

"The name?"

"The whole package."

"You go for the puppy-dog type?"

"Not usually," she said. "But he's cute as shit, man. What's he do?"

I winked broadly. "Private dick."

"Why's he keeping it private?"

"I don't know. Why don't you ask him?"

She did, but it didn't work out. She started by getting herself a beer and having a seat next to LaDuke and initiating some conversation. LaDuke was polite, but clearly uncomfortable. Anna took his manner for disinterest; she downed her beer quickly and drifted away. Darnell came out of the kitchen and introduced himself, and soon after that Mai arrived in a chipper mood and relieved me of my position behind the stick. I changed into something presentable and told LaDuke that it was time to go.

We headed into Northeast in LaDuke's Ford. He stared ahead as he drove, his hands tight on the wheel, ten and two o'clock, right out of driver's ed. I tried to get a station on his radio, but he reached across the bench and switched it off. I wondered, What does this guy do to get off?

"Anna thought you were interesting," I said.

"You know that little guy? The busboy, the guy with the gold tooth?"

"You mean Ramon?"

"Yeah," LaDuke said. "Him. Does he like her or something?"

I laughed. "Ramon likes anything that has to sit down to take a piss. But no, they got nothin' going on."

"Well, she's really cute."

"That's what she said about you. So why'd you blow her off?"

LaDuke blinked nervously. "I didn't mean to, exactly. I'm not very good with women, to tell you the truth."

"I'm not very good with them, either. But when I find one I like and I think she likes me back, I give it a better shot than you did. Anyhow, a pretty motherfucker like you shouldn't have any problems."

"I'm not pretty," he said, a touch of anger entering his voice.

"Relax, man, I'm only kidding around."

"Look," he said, "just forget it, okay?"

"Sure."

We drove for a couple of miles in silence. LaDuke looked out the window.

"Maybe I'll give her a call," he said.

*   *   *

SHAREEN LEWIS WAS SITTING on the rocker sofa on her porch when we reached the top of the steps leading to her house. She stood and took LaDuke's hand, then briefly shook mine without looking in my eyes. She wore linen shorts and a short-sleeved blouse, with a masklike brooch pinned beneath the collar. As on the day before, the makeup somehow managed to match the clothes. She was a handsome woman, nicely built; she might have been lovely had she simply smiled.

We followed Shareen through the front door and found seats in her comfortably appointed living room. For my benefit, LaDuke repeated to Shareen what they had obviously discussed earlier over the phone: that I would team up with him in trying to locate her son, and that the teaming could only double our chances of finding him. Her eyes told me that she doubted his reasoning, but she nodded shortly in agreement. I asked her for a recent photograph of Roland. Shareen Lewis nodded with the same degree of enthusiasm. I asked her if she had heard from her son either directly or by message and she said, "No." I asked her if she had any idea at all as to his whereabouts. To that one, she also said, "No." We sat around and listened to the clock tick away on her mantelpiece. After some of that, I asked to see Roland's room.

We took the carpeted stairs to the second floor—three small bedrooms and a bath. We passed the largest room, which I guessed to be Shareen's. Its absolute cleanliness and frilly decor told me that, under this roof at least, Shareen Lewis slept alone. The next room belonged to the teenaged daughter, Roland's sister, who had blown me off two days earlier on the phone. She was in there, sitting at a desk, listening to music through a set of headphones. She was already heavier than her mother, and she had chunkier features, or it could have been that she was at an awkward age. We made eye contact, and for some reason, I dumbed up my face. She laughed a little and closed her eyes and went back to her groove. Then we were in Roland's room at the end of the hall.

Shareen pulled the blinds open and let some light into the space. LaDuke leaned against a wall and folded his arms while I took it in: another clean room, too clean, I thought, for a boy his age. Maybe Shareen had tidied it up. But even so, there was something off about it, from the rather feminine color scheme to the schmaltzy souvenir trinkets on the dresser. A large dollar sign had been cut out and tacked to the wall. On an opposite wall, a poster of the group PM Dawn. No pictures of fat-bottomed women, no basketball stars, no hard rappers, no gun-culture or drug-culture symbolism, nothing representative of the mindless, raging testosterone of a seventeen-year-old city boy trying to push his manhood in the 1990s. Nothing like my own bedroom at seventeen, for that matter, or the bedrooms of any of my friends.

"Mind if I look in the closet?" I said.

"Go ahead," Shareen said.

I went to it, opened it. I scanned a neat row of clothing, shirts of various designs and several pairs of slacks, the slacks pressed and hung upside down from wooden clamps. I put my hand on the shelf above the closet rod, ran it along the dustless surface. I found a back issue of *D.C. This Week* and took it down. I looked at it with deliberate disinterest, folded it, and put it under my arm.

"Anything?" LaDuke said, nodding at the newspaper.

"No," I said, and forced a smile at Shareen. "You don't mind if I take this, do you?"

"I don't mind," she said, looking very small, hugging herself with her arms as if she was chilled.

"Thanks. By the way, did you clean this room recently?"

"I haven't touched a thing. Roland always kept it this way."

"Have you noticed anything missing? Did he take any clothes with him, pack anything before…the last time you saw him?"

"I don't think so," she said, a catch in her voice.

"You keep a nice house," I said, trying to keep things light.

"Thank you. It's not easy with these kids, believe me."

"I can imagine," I said, but it was too much.

"You can?"

"Well, no. Actually, not really."

"Then don't patronize me." The resentment crept back in her tone. "Let me tell you how it is. When I inherited this house from my mother, I also inherited the balance of the mortgage. That, and everything else it takes to be a single working mother—car, clothing, new stuff for the kids all the time. You come into this part of town, see what it is over here, and maybe you make a judgment about where I prioritize my family in the scheme of my life. What you don't know is, I'd like to get my children out of this neighborhood, too, understand? But the way it is out here, in this economy, me and everyone I know, we're all one paycheck away from the street. So, no, it's not easy. But I've done pretty good for them, I think. Anyway, I've tried."

I didn't ask for all that, but I allowed it. LaDuke cleared his throat and pushed off from the wall.

"I'll take that photograph of Roland now," I said, "if you don't mind. Then we'll be on our way."

She left the room. I walked out with LaDuke and told him to meet me at the front door. After some hesitation, he followed Shareen downstairs. I went to the daughter's room, knocked on her open door. She pulled one earphone away from her head and looked up.

"Yeah."

"I'm Nick Stefanos."

"So?"

"What's your name?"

"Danitra."

"So how's it going?"

"It's goin' all right."

"Listen, Danitra, I'm here because your mom hired me and my friend to find your brother, Roland."

"So?"

"Just wanted to introduce myself, that's all. What are you listening to?"

"Little bit of this and that. Nothin' you'd know."

"Yeah, you're probably right. But I recognized that Trouble Funk you and your friends had on the other day when I called."

"That was you?"

"Yep."

For a second, she looked like she might apologize for her attitude that day, but she didn't. Instead, she shrugged and began to replace the earphone over her ear.

"Hold on a second," I said.

"What?"

"You got any idea where your brother went off to?"

"Uh-uh."

"You think he's okay?"

"That fool's all right," she said.

"Why are you so sure?"

"'Cause if he wasn't, he would've called. Listen, most likely he's off on one of his money things. That boy just wants to be large, know what I'm sayin'? Always wantin' to be like some movie star, ride around in a limousine. When he finds out it ain't like that, he's gonna come home."

"You think so, huh?"

I stood there and waited for a reply. But she turned away from me then and went back into herself. I left her alone and headed back down the stairs.

"MRS. LEWIS REALLY DIGS you, man," LaDuke said with a laugh as he negotiated the Ford around RFK, then got it on to East Capitol. "Every time you open your mouth, she'd like to bite your head off."

"Yeah, thanks for all your support back there."

"Kinda liked watchin' you bury yourself."

I fired a smoke off the dash lighter. "Well, the funny thing is, in some ways I agree with what she's saying. She's out there working for a big firm, and she probably knows just about as much law now as the people she's working for. You know how that goes, Xeroxing and taking messages for people who really have no more intelligence than you. I mean, lawyers, they've got the degree, and they worked for it, but that doesn't necessarily make them geniuses, right? But I'm sure that doesn't stop them from condescending to her all day long. Then she's trying to raise those kids in a bad environment, with no way to get out.... I don't know...I guess I can see why she's so angry. 'Course, that doesn't explain why she's so angry at me."

"Maybe you remind her of the type of guy that left her with those kids," he said.

"Yeah, maybe." The thought of my failed marriage crossed my mind. The thought must have transferred to my face.

"Hey look, Nick, I didn't mean anything."

"Forget it."

LaDuke punched the gas and passed a Chevy that was crawling up ahead. He drove for a couple of miles, then said, "You get anything from the sister?"

"Uh-uh. Typical teenager with no time for me, and nothing good to say about her brother. She thinks he's just out there being an entrepreneur, trying to make some kind of score."

"You saw the dollar sign plastered on his bedroom wall. Maybe that *is* all he's into. Maybe he's running some kind of game."

"What else you see in that room?"

"I saw what you saw," he said.

"No, I mean the details."

LaDuke rubbed the top of his head, something I had seen him do over the last couple of days when he was trying to think. "Well, it's kind of a funny room for a seventeen-year-old boy. It looked like it could have been his sister's room."

"Right. How about that PM Dawn poster?"

"PM Dawn? What the hell is that?"

"It's a rap group—but soft, man, all the way soft. Not what anyone down here would call 'street authentic.' Like what U2 is to rock and roll."

"U2?"

"Yeah. The Eagles, in black leather."

"What?"

"Never mind. It's just not the kind of music a kid in that neighborhood would want to advertise that he was into. That and the room, you know, if it got around, it's something that could get your ass kicked for you."

LaDuke breathed out through his mouth. "You sayin' that maybe him and the Jeter kid were boyfriends?"

"No, not exactly."

But I thought of Barry calling Roland a "punk." And the killer had called Calvin one, too. And then there was the Fire House matchbook from Calvin's room. I dragged on my cigarette, blew the exhale out the open window.

"What, then?"

"It's just that this Lewis kid is different, that's all, at an age when being different from your peers is the last thing you want to be. It might not mean anything. I don't know if it does, not yet."

I picked up Roland Lewis's photograph: unsmiling, like Calvin's, but with a certain vulnerability. Unlike the sister, Roland looked very much like his mother. I slipped the photograph in the folded-up newspaper. LaDuke watched me do it.

"What's with the paper, anyway?" he said.

"Nothing."

"Bullshit. Don't hold out on me, Nick."

I hot-boxed my cigarette and pitched it out the window. "I'm not."

"Yes you are," he said. "But you won't keep holdin' out, not for long. 'Cause we're gonna do this thing, you and me. You hear me?" He was pumped, his face lit and animated. A horn blew out as he lost his attention and swerved into another lane.

"Okay," I said. "We'll find the kid, LaDuke. But do me a favor."

"What?"

"Keep your eyes on the road."

He dropped me in front of the Spot. I thanked him for the lift, picked up the newspaper, and started to get out.

"What are we, done already?"

"I am. I've got a date tonight." He looked a little deflated. "Listen, man, we'll get on this again, first thing tomorrow. Hear?"

"Sure, Nick. I'll see you later."

He pulled away from the curb and drove down 8th. I went to my Dodge and fumbled with my keys. When LaDuke was out of sight, I walked into the Spot, phoned Lyla, and told her I'd be a little late. Then I returned to my car, ignitioned it, and headed back into Northeast.

EIGHT

THE HEAVY WOMAN with the elephantine thighs sat out front of the Jeter apartment, her folding chair in the same position as it had been two days before. I turned into the lot and parked beside Barry's Z, walked across the worn brown grass, into the cool concrete stairwell, and down the steps to the Jeters' door. I knocked on it, listening to the noises behind it, television and laughter and the cry of a baby, until the peephole darkened and the door swung open. Calvin's sister stood in the frame, her baby resting on her hip.

"Yes?"

"Nick Stefanos. I was here the day before yesterday, talking to your mom."

"I remember."

"Is she in?"

The girl looked behind her. Barry's younger brother and another shirtless young man about his age sat on the couch, describing a movie they had both seen, talking loudly over the minstrel-like characters acting broadly on the television.

"Uh-uh," the girl said. "She's at the store."

"Can I talk to Barry for a minute?"

She thought about it while I listened to the shirtless young man talking about the movie: "Carlito" did this and "Carlito" did that, and "Carlito, he was badder than a motherfucker, boy." Then the young man was on his feet, his hand figured in the shape of a pistol, and he was jabbing the hand back and forth, going, "Carlito said, bap-bap-bap-bap-bap."

"Come on in," the girl said, her lips barely moving.

I followed her into the room and back through the hall. The young men stopped talking as I passed, and when my back was to them, they broke into raucous laughter. I supposed that they were laughing at me. Calvin's sister gestured me toward a bedroom. I stepped aside to let her pass back through the hall.

I went to the bedroom and knocked on the frame. Barry stood next to an unmade double bed in a room as unadorned as the rest. He read from a book, one long finger on the page. He looked up at my knock, gave me an eye sweep, and returned his gaze to the book.

"Wha'sup?"

"I need to get something out of Calvin's room. It's nothing personal of his. Would that be all right?"

Barry closed the book and sighed. "Come on."

He walked with me to Calvin's bedroom. Barry folded his arms, watched me go to the footlocker and get the folded copy of *D.C. This Week* that sat beneath the basketball. When I turned around, he was looking at the paper. I thought I saw some kind of light come into his eyes.

"What am I, getting warm or something?"

Barry said, "You're really into this shit, aren't you?"

"I'm going to find out who killed Calvin, if that's what you mean."

"And if you do? What's that, gon' bring Calvin up from the dead?"

"No. But maybe his mother might rest a little easier if she knew what happened to her son. You ever think about that?"

Barry breathed out heavily through his nose. "Moms ain't worried about no justice. She thinks Calvin's up there, sittin' by the right hand of Jesus and shit, right now. Anyhow, who *asked* you to get on this?"

"That doesn't matter. The point is, I'm being paid now, and that makes it work. And when someone pays you to do something, you do it. Once you accept that, you don't think about why, and you finish whatever it is you started."

"I wouldn't understand about all that."

"The thing is, I think you do understand. See, I noticed that uniform in the back of your car. You got that fast-food job of yours—what do you make, five and a quarter an hour, maybe five-fifty?"

Barry's eyes narrowed. "So?"

"So, you could be like all those other knuckleheads out there, making ten times that a week on the street. But instead, you're being a man, trying to be right for your family."

"Listen, man, I ain't got time for all this bullshit, understand? Matter of fact, I got to get into work, right now."

I withdrew my wallet, slipped out a card, and handed it to Barry.

"Here," I said. "You dropped this the first time around."

"I got to go to work," he said softly, slipping the card into his shorts. "Come on, I'll let you out."

We walked back into the living room. Barry stopped by the TV set and I headed for the front door.

The shirtless young man said, "Hey, Barry, who's your boy?"

"Man's a private detective," Barry said mockingly. "He *finds* things."

Barry's younger brother said, "Maybe he could find Roger

some onion, know what I'm sayin'? 'Cause Roger ain't *had* none in a long time."

"Go on, man," Roger said. "I forgot about more pussy than you ever had, boy." Barry's brother and Roger touched hands and began to laugh.

I looked at Barry. He wasn't laughing, and neither was I. I tucked the newspaper under my arm and left the room.

ON THE WAY TO my place, I stopped at Athena's and had a seat at the bar. I lit a cigarette, drew on it, and laid it in the ashtray. It was early yet for any kind of crowd, but I recognized a couple of regulars in quiet conversation, along with an Ultimate solo drinker who was as beautiful as a model and an intense woman I knew who was running the pool table on a youngish woman I had never met. Stella came over and wiped the area in front of me with a damp rag. She cocked her head and raised her eyebrows. I nodded my head one time. She reached into the cooler and pulled a bottle of beer. She popped the cap and set it down on a dry coaster. I thanked her and had a swig.

"So you're back to it," she said.

"Never had any intention of getting off it. I've never kidded myself about what I am. I've just got to try and not be so stupid about it, that's all. Like I was that night."

Stella adjusted her eyeglasses, put her fist on her hip. "That some kind of back-door apology?"

"Yeah, and a thank-you at the same time. I was probably rude about you stepping in—you know how I get. I know you were just trying to look out for me."

"Don't worry about it," she said. "You'd do the same for me, right?"

"You bet."

"Anyway, nobody got hurt."

I left that alone and reached across the bar and shook her hand.

"So what're you up to tonight, Nick?"

"Date with Lyla. But I wanted to ask you something."

"Go ahead."

"You still play in that gay and lesbian bartenders' softball league?"

"Every Monday night."

"You know anybody from over at the Fire House, on P?"

Stella rubbed a finger under her nose. "There was this guy, Paul Ritchie, played for a long time on our team. Knees went out on him a couple of years back. Good guy. Good ballplayer, too. Ritchie, he could really hit."

"You ever in touch with him anymore?"

"He still comes to the games. It's more a chance to see old friends now than it is a competition. So, yeah, he stays up with us."

"He still tends at the Fire House?"

"He's been there, like, a hundred years. Where's he gonna go?"

I drank off some of my beer. "I need to talk with him, if I can. I'm working on something that might involve that place."

"Something that could get him into trouble?"

"Not unless he's directly involved. The truth is, I don't know yet. But I'll do my best to keep him out of it. Could you hook me up?"

Stella took her hand off her hip, pointed a stubby finger at my face. "I thought you came in here to apologize, Nick."

"I did, Stella."

"Uh-huh. Well, I'll give Paul a call, see what he says."

"Tomorrow would be good for me," I said.

"Don't push it," Stella said sternly. "I'll call him."

I told her to leave a message about it on my machine. She nodded and went to fix a cocktail for a customer. I drank the rest of my beer and put my cigarette between my teeth. Stella winked and gave me a little wave. I left ten on three and went out the front door. I walked to my car in the gathering darkness.

* * *

THE TWO COPIES OF *D.C. This Week* were identical, the last ones printed before Calvin Jeter's murder. That the issues were the same couldn't have been a coincidence, but as I looked through them, sitting at the desk of my makeshift office in my apartment, I saw no connection to either Calvin's death or Roland's disappearance. I skimmed every article, weekly feature, arts review, and column and came up empty. So I showered, changed into slacks and a blue cotton shirt, and went to pick up Lyla.

"Wow," I said as she opened her door.

She wore a gauzy green-and-rust sundress cut high above her knees. Her hair was pulled back, with some of it left to fall around her lovely face, the light catching threads of silver in the red.

"You're late, Nick."

"I know. I'm sorry, I just got hung up in what I've been working on."

"That's okay." She held up her goblet of wine. "But I got started without you."

"I'll catch up," I said. "Let's go."

We drove across town in my Coronet 500, all four windows down, some Massive Attack pumping from the deck. Lyla was moving her head, digging on the music and the night, and I reached across the buckets and put my hand in her hair. At the next stoplight, we kissed and held it until the green. The air felt clean, with a crispness running through it, a rarity for that time of year; it was a fine summer night in D.C.

We ate at a Thai place on Massachusetts Avenue, in a row of restaurants east of Union Station. We talked about our respective days over satay and spring rolls and a barbecued beef salad; Lyla stayed with white wine while I worked on a couple of Singhas. By the time the waitress served our main course, a whole crispy fish with hot chili and garlic, the subject turned to Lyla's newspaper and what I had found that day.

"Any thoughts?" I said.

"If you think something criminal is going on in relation to the newspaper, a good bet would be the personals."

"What do you mean?"

"There's all sort of things happening in there—messages for meeting places that are really drop locations, model searches looking for porno candidates, stuff like that. Nick, you wouldn't believe how many of the entries are just ads for prostitution, or for some other scam that's even worse."

"And you guys know about it?"

"We don't knowingly take any ads or personals that are criminal. But we're running a business. The *Post* and *City Paper* are doing it and making good money at it, and we have to do it, too. With the personals—it's a nine hundred number—we get ninety-five cents a minute. There're a couple hundred of those in each issue. When you annualize the revenue—well, you figure it out."

"Yeah, I see what you're saying. I'll go back to it, check it out." I cut a piece of fish off and dished it onto Lyla's plate. "Here."

"Thanks." Lyla had a bite and signaled the waitress for another wine.

"You're hittin' it pretty good tonight," I said.

"It's all this hot stuff," she said. "This fish is making me thirsty."

"It's making me thirsty, too. Next time that waitress goes by, get me a beer, as well."

After dinner, we walked across Mass to a nice quiet bar in a fancy restaurant run by friends of Lyla's. We ordered a couple of drinks—a bourbon rocks for me and a vodka tonic for Lyla—and had them slowly, listening to the recorded jazz that was a particular trademark of the house. A local politician whom Lyla had once interviewed and buried in print stopped on his way to the men's room and talked with her for a while, leaning in close to her ear, a toothy smile on his blandly handsome face. I sat on my stool and drank quietly and allowed myself to grow jealous. On the way out of the place, Lyla tripped on the steps and fell and scraped her knee on the concrete. We got into my car and I leaned forward and kissed the scrape, tasting her blood with my tongue. From that fortuitous position, I tried to work my head up under her dress. She laughed generously and pushed me away.

"Patience," she said. I mumbled something and put the car in gear.

We stopped once more that night, to have a drink on the roof of the Hotel Washington at 15th and F, a corny thing to do, for sure, but lovely nonetheless, when the city is lit up at night and the view is as on time as anything ever gets. We managed to snag a deuce by the railing, and I ordered a five-dollar beer and a wine for Lyla. We caught a breeze there, and our table looked out over rooftops to the monuments and the Mall. A television personality—a smirky young man who played on a sitcom called *My Two Dads* (a show that Johnny McGinnes called *My Doo-Dads*)—and his entourage took a large table near ours, and on their way out, Lyla winged a peanut at the back of the actor's head. The missile missed its target, but we got a round of applause from some people at the other tables who had obviously been subjected to the show. I could have easily had a few more beers when I was done with the first, could have sat in that chair for the rest of the night, but Lyla's eyes began to look a little filmy and unfocused, and her ears had turned a brilliant shade of red. We decided to go.

We drove to Lyla's apartment off Calvert Street, near the park, and made out like teenagers in her elevator on the way up to her floor. At her place, I goosed her while she tried to fit her keys to the lock and then we did an intense tongue dance and dry-humped for a while against her door, until a neighbor came out into the hall to see what the noise was all about. Inside, she pulled a bottle of white from the refrigerator, and we went directly to the bedroom. Lyla turned on her bedside lamp and pulled her dress up over her head while I removed my shirt. The sight of her—her freckled breasts, the curve of her hips, her full red bush—shortened my breath; it never failed to. She draped the dress over the lamp shade, kicked her shoes off, and walked naked across the room, the bottle in her hand. She took a long pull from the neck.

"We don't need that," I said.

Lyla pushed me onto my back on the bed and spit a mouthful of wine onto my chest. She straddled me, bent over, and began to slowly lick the wine off my nipples.

"You sure about that?" she said.

I could only grunt, and close my eyes.

LYLA'S HEAVY BREATHING WOKE me in the darkness. I looked at the LED readout on her clock, laid there for a half hour with my eyes open, then got out of bed, ate a couple of aspirins, and took a shower. I dressed in my clothes from the night before, made coffee, and smoked a cigarette out on her balcony.

I came back into the apartment, checked on Lyla. In the first light of dawn, her face looked drawn and gray. Her mouth was frozen open, the way she always slept off a drunk, and there was a faint wheeze in her exhale. I kissed her on the cheek and then on her lips. Her breath was stale from the wine. I brushed some hair off her forehead and left the place, locking the door behind me.

I drove straight down to the river, passed under the Sousa Bridge, turned the car around, and parked it in the clearing. No sign of a crazy black man in a brilliant blue coat. No cops, either; I guessed that, by now, the uniforms had been pulled off that particular detail.

I got out of my car, sat on its hood, and lit a cigarette. A pleasure boat pulled out of its slip and ran toward the Potomac, leaving little wake. Some gulls crossed the sky, turned black against the rising sun. I took one last drag off my cigarette and pitched it into the river.

Back in Shepherd Park, my cat waited for me on my stoop. I sat next to her and rubbed the hard scar tissue of her one empty eye socket and scratched behind her ears.

"Miss me?" I said. She rolled onto her back.

I entered my apartment and saw the blinking red light of my answering machine. I hit the bar, listened to the message. I stripped naked, got into bed, and set the alarm for one o'clock. Stella had come through; I had an appointment with Paul Ritchie for 2:30 that afternoon at the Fire House on P.

NINE

THE FIRE HOUSE had changed hands several times in my life-time, but as long as I could remember, it had been a bar that catered primarily to homosexuals, in a neighborhood that had always been off center in every interesting way. This particular corner unofficially marked the end of Dupont Circle, where the P Street Bridge spanned the park and led to the edge of George-town. There were many hangouts down here, restaurants and a smattering of bars — the Brickskeller for beerheads, Badlands for the discophiles — but the Fire House had become some-thing of a landmark for residents and commuters alike. For many years, gas logs burned day and night behind a glass window that fronted P at 22nd, the logs being the establishment's only signage. The building's facade had been redone now in red brick, and the window and the logs had been removed. But the fire imagery remained in the bar's name, a small nod to tradition.

I had taken the Metro down to Dupont, then walked down P.

By afternoon, the day had become blazing-hot, with quartz reflecting off the sidewalk and an urban mirage of shimmering refraction steaming up off the asphalt of the street. My thrift-shop sport jacket was damp beneath the arms and on my back as I reached the entrance to the Fire House. I pushed on the door, removed my shades, and entered the cool darkness of the main room.

Several couples and a few solo drinkers sat in booths and at tables partitioned off from the empty bar. I went to the stick and slid onto a stool, dropping the manila folder I had been carrying on the seat to my right. The heat had sickened me a bit, that and my activities from the night before. I peeled a bev nap from a stack of them and wiped my face.

A thin young waiter stepped up to the service area and said in a whiny, very bored voice, "Ooordering." The bartender ignored him for the time being, walked down my way, and dropped a coaster in front of me on the bar.

"How's it going?" he said. He was large-boned, with some gut to go with it. His brown hair had streaks of red running through it, and there was a rogue patch of red splotched in the chin area of his beard.

"Hot."

"Not in here, it isn't. Thank God for work, when it's air-conditioned. What can I get you?"

"A cold beer."

"Any flavor?"

"A bottle of Bud. And a side of ice water, thanks. By the way, where's the head?"

"Top of the stairs. You'll see it."

I took the stairs, passed an unlit room where a piano sat in the middle of a group of tables. The men's room was at the end of the hall. I went in and took a leak at one of two urinals. A mirror had been hung and angled down, centered above the urinals. I understood its purpose but didn't understand the attraction. Years ago, I had a date with a woman who at the end of the night asked me to come into her bathroom and watch her while she took a piss. I did it out of curiosity but found it to be entirely uninteresting. I never phoned her again.

I zipped up my fly, bought a pack of smokes outside the bathroom door, and went back down to the bar. The bartender had served my beer and was placing the ice water next to it.

"Nick Stefanos," I said, extending my hand.

"Paul Ritchie." He shook my hand and said, "How do you know Stella?"

"I tend at the Spot. A couple times a week, I go into Athena's, shoot a little pool."

"You that guy that used to hang out with Jackie Kahn?"

"You knew Jackie?"

"Sure. I heard she had a kid."

"Yeah."

"Heard she had some straight guy impregnate her."

"I heard that, too."

"You know, I think I met you, in fact, one night when I was in Athena's with a friend." His eyes moved to the beer in my hand, then back to me. "I guess you don't remember."

"Must have been one of those nights," I said. "You probably know how that is."

"Not anymore," he said.

"Ooordering, Paul!" said the prematurely world-weary voice from down the bar.

Paul Ritchie said, "Give me a minute," and went to the rail to fix the waiter a drink. I gulped down the ice water and lit a cigarette. By the time Ritchie returned, I had finished half my beer; my stomach had neutralized, the quiver had gone out of my hand, and my head had become more clear.

"Thanks for seeing me."

"No problem. What can I do for you?"

I put the manila folder on the bar, opened it, and slipped out the photographs of Calvin Jeter and Roland Lewis. I turned them around so that Ritchie could have a look.

"You recognize either of these guys?"

Ritchie studied the photos. "Uh-uh. I don't think so."

I searched his face for the hint of a lie, saw nothing irregular. I tapped my finger on Calvin's photo. "This one here, I found a book of Fire House matches in one of his shirts."

"What'd he do?"

"He got himself murdered."

Ritchie breathed out slowly. "I don't work every shift, obviously, so I can't say he's never come in here. But I know he's not a regular. And these two look like minors on top of that, and we make a pretty good effort not to serve minors. They *are* minors, right?"

"Yeah. What else?"

"To tell you the truth, neither of these kids look like my type of clientele."

"You mean they don't look gay."

"Look schmook, Stefanos. I don't have much of an idea what a gay person 'looks' like anymore. Do you?"

"I guess not. But what *did* you mean? They're not your clientele—what, because they're black?"

"No," he said tiredly, "not because they're black. Turn your head and take a look around this place."

I did. I saw some men getting on into their thirties and forties, some wearing ties, most of them with expensive haircuts and fine watches. The racial mix seemed to be about 80 percent white to 20 black; on the social and economic side, though, the group was homogenous. I turned back to Ritchie.

"So you run a nice place."

"Exactly. These men that come in here, they're not just well-adjusted; they're well-connected. That guy's suit over there—no offense, Stefanos—it's probably worth more than your whole wardrobe. I know it's worth more than mine."

"What about these kids?"

"Straight or gay," Ritchie said, "it's irrelevant. These two are street. This isn't their kind of place."

"So how do you think this kid came to get a hold of your matchbook?"

Ritchie shrugged. "Who knows? Maybe they were working the corner outside, working with all those other hustlers. The ones I'm talking about, they come in here, snag matches, bum smokes, sometimes try to hit on my customers. I'm telling you, my clientele's not interested. I know a couple of these hustlers, and some of them are all right. Most of them are country kids. You look at 'em, weight lifters, gym rats, with the sideburns and the pompadours, they all look like young Elvises. But usually, if they're not drinking—and most of the time they're not—I ask them to leave. There've been a couple incidents, and I just don't want those guys in here."

"What kind of incidents?"

"Where some people got hurt. See, the way it typically goes down, the way I understand it, these hustlers make the arrangement with the customer, usually some closeted business-man who works up around the Circle, and then they go down to the woods around P Street Beach. The money changes hands, and after that they do whatever it is they do—giving, receiving, whatever. But what happened last month, a couple of kids were leading those businessmen down there to the woods, then taking them for everything they had."

I dragged on my cigarette. "You know who these guys were?"

"No. 'Course, it never got reported to the cops. But it got around down here fast. What I heard, the other guys out on the street, they took care of the problem themselves. The whole thing was bad for their business."

"Ooordering," came the voice from down the bar.

Ritchie rolled his eyes. "Be back in a minute," he said.

I stood up and finished my beer, slid the photographs back in the folder. I took out my wallet and left money on the bar for the beer, and an extra twenty for Ritchie, with my business card on top of the twenty. Ritchie came back, wiping his hands with a damp rag.

"Thanks for your help," I said.

"Wish I could have done more."

"You did plenty. Any chance you could hook me up with one of those hustlers you were talking about? There's money in it for them — I'd pay for their time."

"I could give it a try, yeah. I don't see why not, if you're talking about money. I don't know what an hour of their time is worth, though. I'm out of that scene, way out. Not that I didn't have my day in the sun. But I've had the same boyfriend for the last five years. When I'm not in here. I'm sitting at home on the couch, watching sports on the tube, like the old fart that I am."

"Stella said you used to be pretty good with a bat."

"Yeah," he said. "I blew out my fucking knees. Now about the only thing I can do is water sports."

"Water sports, huh."

"Don't be a wise guy, Stefanos. I'm talking about swimming laps, down at the Y."

"Sorry." I ran my hand down the lapel of my sport jacket. "So you don't think too much of my threads, huh?"

A light came on in Ritchie's eyes. "Hey, look, don't feel bad. I used to have a jacket just like that."

"Yeah?"

"Yeah," Ritchie said. "Then my father got a job."

"Lucky me. I get to talk to an ex-jock bartender who doesn't drink. And I get a comedian in the bargain."

"I'm crackin' myself up here."

"Take it easy, Ritchie."

"Yeah, you, too. I'll let you know if I can set that thing up."

"Gimme a call," I said. "The number's on the card."

TEN

I HEARD FROM Paul Ritchie, and some others, early on Saturday morning at my apartment. Boyle called first, and he asked about my progress on the case. I told him that up to that point, my few leads had led only to blind alleys. I kept on that tack, and when I was done, I had managed to dig a big hole and fill it to the top with lies. I asked Boyle if the cops had anything new. He told me that an informant in a Southeast project had claimed that Jeter and Lewis were mules for a supplier down that way. I asked them if his people had any details on it and he said, "Nothing yet." We agreed to keep up with each other if something shook out on either end. I didn't like lying to him, and I wasn't exactly sure why I was doing it, but I had the vague feeling that I could see the beginning of some kind of light off in the distance. And it just wasn't in me to give anything away.

Paul Ritchie called next. I thanked him and promised to buy him a beer the next time he was in my part of town. He reminded me that he didn't drink, and I suggested that instead I'd buy myself one and dedicate it to him. Ritchie laughed, but he couldn't help mentioning how good it felt each morning to wake up with a clean head and be able to remember all the details from the night before. I told him I appreciated the testimonial, thanked him once again, and said good-bye.

Later in the morning, the phone rang for the third time that day. I thought it might be Lyla, but instead I heard the excited voice of Jack LaDuke.

"Nick!" he said.

"LaDuke!"

"What do we got?"

"I don't know. Maybe something, maybe not."

"I called you yesterday, Nick. Why you didn't call me back?"

"I was out during the day. And then I had a night shift, got home late."

"Out doing what? Working on the case?"

"Well, yeah. LaDuke, you got to understand, I've got to ease into this, man. I'm used to working alone." He didn't respond. I crushed the cigarette I had been working on in the ashtray. "Listen, LaDuke, I've got an interview with this guy, later today. You want to come along?"

"Damn right I do."

"Okay. I'll pick you up in an hour."

"Uh-uh. I'll pick *you* up."

"What's the big secret? You don't want me to know where you live?"

"I'll swing by in an hour, Stevonus."

"It's Ste*fa*nos, you asshole."

"One hour," LaDuke said, and hung up the phone.

PAUL RITCHIE HAD SET me up with one of the hustlers who worked the corner outside the Fire House, a guy who called himself Eddie Colorado. The name was a phony, but it sung, a canny cross of urban hood and westerner. Over the years, I had seen some of the men who stood around and worked that part of the street, and out of all the butch gimmicks that had passed through town—soldier of fortune, construction worker, lumber-jack, and others—the cowboy thing seemed to have more stay-ing power than the rest.

"What have you got goin' on this weekend?" LaDuke said. We were sitting in my Dodge, alongside a small park near the P Street Bridge.

"Dinner with Lyla's folks tomorrow, at their house. What about you?"

"I've got a date with Anna Wang tonight." LaDuke grinned, proud of himself. "I called her up."

"Congratulations," I said, then pointed through the wind-shield to the bridge. "Here comes our boy."

Eddie waited for the green at 23rd, crossed the street, and headed for my car. Ritchie had told me to look for an unnatural blond, a "skinny rockabilly type with bad skin," and Eddie fit the bill. His orangish moussed hair contrasted starkly with his red T-shirt, the sleeves of which had been turned up, the veins popping on his thin biceps. His jeans were pressed and tight, and he walked with an exaggerated swagger, a cigarette lodged above his ear, a cocky smile spread across his face.

"Look at this guy," LaDuke said with naked disgust.

"Relax," I said, "and get in the backseat. Okay?"

LaDuke got out of the shotgun bucket, left the door open for Eddie, and climbed into the back. Eddie stepped up to the door, took a look around like he owned a piece of the park, pulled a wad of gum from his mouth, and chucked it onto the grass. He leaned a forearm on the frame and cocked his hip.

"You Stefanos?" he said.

"Yeah. Get in."

"Sure thing," Eddie said with a slow accent that had just crawled down off the Smokies. He dropped into the bucket and pulled the door closed.

I looked across the console at Eddie. "Paul Ritchie said twenty-five would buy some of your time."

"A little of it."

"Here." I passed him a folded twenty along with a five. Eddie Colorado pushed his pelvis out and jammed the bills into the pocket of his jeans. He hit my dash lighter, slid the cigarette off the top of his ear, and put the filtered end in his mouth.

"No," LaDuke said from the backseat, "we don't mind if you smoke."

Eddie turned his head, gave LaDuke a quick appraisal, smiled, followed the smile with a tight giggle. "Who's your friend?"

"His name's Jack."

Eddie smiled again, raised his eyebrows, touched the hot end of the lighter to his smoke. He held the cigarette out the window, settled down in his seat, the sun coming directly in on his face. The acne on his cheek looked red as fire in the light.

Eddie stared straight ahead. "Paul told me you wanted me to look at some pictures."

I opened the chrome cover on the center console, took out the photographs of Calvin and Roland, gave them to Eddie. He dragged on his cigarette and blew smoke down at the images in his hand.

"You know them?" I said.

Eddie's mouth twitched a little. He nodded and said, "Yes."

"Were they workin' this area?"

"For a little while, yeah."

"And you and your buddies kicked them out."

"Right."

"What'd they do to make you do that?" I said.

Eddie grinned. "You're getting into somethin' here that might come back to me. It's gonna cost you another twenty-five."

"Bullshit," LaDuke said. "This guy didn't kick anybody out of anywhere, Nick. Look at him."

"Your friend thinks I'm weak," Eddie said. "But I've been

dealing with rednecks all my life, calling me this and that, beatin' me up on the way to and from school. Let me tell you somethin', it ain't no different here in Washington D.C. than in the country. First day I got into town, I went into this burger joint off New York Avenue. This guy says to me, 'Hey, you fuckin' queer.' You wanna know what I did about it? I broke his fuckin' jaw."

I watched a man with matted hair carry a backpack past my car. "So, what, you kicked these two off your turf because they called you a name?"

Eddie shook his head and said, "The twenty-five."

I said, "Give it to him, Jack."

LaDuke pulled his wallet, withdrew the money. He crumpled the bills and dropped them over Eddie's shoulder, into his lap. Eddie smoothed the bills out carefully, folded them, and slipped them into his pocket.

"You say you knew these two," I said. "What were their names?"

"I don't know. Ain't nobody uses his real name down here, anyhow."

"They were doing prostitution down in those woods?"

"'Doing prostitution'?" Eddie laughed. "If you want to call it that. They were *workin'*, Stefanos, that's what they was doin'."

"Down in those woods?"

"On the edge of the beach," Eddie said. "At first, it didn't bother anybody, 'cause, you got to realize, there's a certain kind of man only goes for boys got dark meat."

"Jesus Christ," LaDuke muttered.

"So," Eddie said, "it wasn't no competition for the rest of us. But then this one here — Eddie put one dirty finger on the face of Roland Lewis — "he took some man's money. I mean all his money. Took more than they agreed to. Just took it."

I said, "You sure he wasn't provoked? Maybe one of these johns threatened him or something, tried to hurt him."

Brown lines of tobacco stain ran between the gaps of

Eddie's toothy grin. "The *johns*, man, they don't hurt us. Most of the time, if there's anything like that to be done, they want us to do it to *them*. Just last week, I had this old man down in the woods, this lawyer works for some fancy firm, down around 19th? He had me slide this rod with little barbs on it right up into his dick. And right before he came, he had me rip it out. Man, you should have seen the blood in his jizz. With all his screamin' and shit, it was hard to tell the pleasure from the pain."

"Goddamn it," LaDuke said, "stick to what we're talking about here."

"Stick to it, Eddie," I said. "We don't need all the extra details."

"All right." Eddie looked in the rearview at LaDuke, back at me. "So anyway, we find out from some of our regulars that this thing has been happening again and again. That these boys are rolling our businessmen on a regular basis, takin' the short road to big money. But there is no short road, see? This is work, like anything else. You don't treat your customers right, they're gonna go somewheres else. So we went and had a meeting with your boys one night, down in the woods."

"You told them to get lost?" LaDuke said.

"It wasn't all that dramatic," Eddie said. "The one who started all the shit said that they were off to something better, that they didn't need this anymore."

"Off to what?"

Eddie stabbed a finger at Roland's picture once more. "He said they were going to get themselves into the movies. Said they met a man who was going to make them a whole lot of money. Big money, man, extralarge."

LaDuke said, "Porno?"

"What do *you* think?" Eddie said.

"This kid you keep pointing to," I said. "Did he seem to be the leader of the two?"

"Appeared to be."

I took a cigarette from the pack on the dash, rolled it unlit between my fingers. "Eddie, did these guys seem like they were into what they were doing?"

"They were into making money," Eddie said. "But what you really mean is, Were they faggots? If I had to make some kind of guess, I'd say the other kid was kinda, I don't know, not sure about anything he was doing. The leader, though, he was definitely into it."

"Into it how?"

"His eyes." Eddie looked in the rearview at LaDuke, held his gaze. "Me and my friends, when things are slow out here, we play this game: Gay, Not Gay. We check out these suit-and-tie boys walking down the street and we make the call. Me, I look at their eyes. And when it comes to knowing what it really is that they're about, I believe I'm usually right." Eddie smirked a little at LaDuke.

"Fuck this," LaDuke said. "I've had enough."

"A couple more questions," I said. "You know anybody in this movie business you were talking about?"

"Uh-uh," Eddie said. "Not my thing. I like the fresh air, Stefanos. Can't stand being cooped up in a small space, under some hot light. I ain't got no ambition to be that kind of star."

"Some of your friends might know something about it."

"Maybe," Eddie said. "I'll ask around. I find out anything, I'll give you a call."

I gave him my card. "There's money in it for you if you come up with something."

"That's the case," Eddie said, "you *know* I'll call."

"We about done?" said LaDuke.

"Your friend needs to relax," Eddie said. "It's not good for him to be so angry."

"See you later, Eddie," I said.

Eddie turned to LaDuke. "Take care of yourself, Stretch."

He got out of the car, and shut the door behind him. I watched him strut across the street and disappear over the hill at the start of the bridge. He lived for money, but he was stupid and he was sloppy, and he had a short attention span. He'd lose my card, or forget my name; I knew I'd never hear from him again.

"*God*damn it," LaDuke said softly from the backseat.

I lit the cigarette that I had been playing with for the last five minutes, took some smoke into my lungs. "Listen, Jack. These kids out here, man, they're going to get into some shit. You didn't think Roland was totally innocent, did you? If you're going to do this kind of work, you've got to stop setting yourself up for disappointment."

"It makes me sick, that's all. To think that Roland comes from a home where his mother raised him with love, and then he ends up down in some woods, having some middle-aged man suck his dick, maybe go butt-up in some porno movie. A kid is confused enough, Nick; he doesn't know shit yet about what he is. To have all these adults doing these things to him...I swear to God, it just makes me sick."

"We're not done yet," I said. "And what we found out here, it could be nothing compared to what we're going to find. Earlier today, I talked to this cop I know. He told me that they've got some information—I don't know how reliable it is—that Calvin and Roland were moving drugs."

"Who were the cops talking to?"

"An informant of theirs, out of Southeast."

"Well, let's find this guy, talk to him ourselves!"

"There's things we can't do, LaDuke. The cops can go into those projects, ask around, because they're cops. We go in there, a couple of white-boy private cops, nobody's gonna talk to us. And it's a good way to get ourselves capped."

"What now, then?"

"We keep doing what we're doing, work with what we know. Here's the thing: Calvin was killed because of something wrong he and his friend got themselves into—there's no doubt about that now. You're going to have deal with it, Jack—Roland might be dead, too."

"*God*damn it," LaDuke said again, and shook his head.

We didn't say much after that. I sat there and smoked my cigarette and checked out the flow of traffic while the bike messengers and the homeless and the hustlers moved about in the park. LaDuke mumbled to himself occasionally, and once he slapped the back of my seat with his palm. Then he picked up a couple of empty beer cans that were at his feet and told me he was going to throw them away.

I watched him walk around the front of the car, moving heavily, shifting his shoulders awkwardly, a tall, gawky guy not entirely comfortable in his own skin, like an adolescent who has grown too fast. There was something else, too, something a little off center and soiled beneath Jack LaDuke's fresh-scrubbed looks. I couldn't put my finger on it that day, and when I did, it was way too late. Eventually, the snakes that were crawling around inside his head found their way out. By then, there was nothing I could do but stand beside him, and watch them strike.

ELEVEN

LYLA MCCUBBIN HAD grown up in a boxy brick house on a street named Bangor Drive, in an unremarkable but pleasant development called Garrett Park Estates in the Maryland suburb of Kensington. Her parents had raised three children there, and they had remained long after Lyla, the last child, had graduated from college and gone out on her own. Lyla said that the neighborhood had changed very little since her childhood: a mixture of starter homes and rentals, none too ostentatious, a comfortable kind of place, where you came to recognize the bark of every dog through the open window of your bedroom as you drifted off to sleep on summer nights.

Lyla's mother, Linda, had practically raised the children herself, as the father, Daniel McCubbin, was usually off at some meeting, organizing the unions or planning the demonstration for his latest cause. The first day I met Lyla, in her office at *D.C. This Week*, I had noticed the photograph of her as a child, standing between her bearded father and straight-haired mother, at a Dupont Circle rally circa 1969. Lyla said that the family never had a dime, but there was some pride in her voice as she said it, never regret. Her father, a fine trial lawyer by all accounts, had managed to resist the advances of the corporate firms in town throughout his career, preferring to use his talents to advance the causes of those individuals whom he considered to be on the side of "right." He wasn't your typical pompous windbag, though. I liked him and I admired him, despite the obvious fact that he was not awfully crazy about me.

We were greeted at the door by Linda McCubbin, who kissed Lyla and then me on the cheek. Linda was Lyla with thirty years added to the odometer, with more silver in the hair than red now and an organic heaviness around the waist and in the hips. Men were always told to look at the mothers, as if that was some kind of test; it never had been for me, but if it had been, then Lyla would have passed.

"Here, Ma," Lyla said, handing Linda a bag containing two liter bottles of white wine. Lyla had insisted we stop for it, though both of us had once again consumed a little too much the night before.

Linda took it, said, "Come on in."

Daniel sat under an overextended air conditioner in the simply furnished living room, in a La-Z-Boy chair, the arms of which had been shredded by the McCubbin cat, a mean tom that someone had ironically named Peace. Lyla bent to her father and kissed him, and then he shook my hand without rising from the chair.

"Don't get up," I said.

"Didn't plan to," he said. "Hot day like this, I'm going to expend as little energy as possible. How's it going, Nick?"

"Good. Good."

Daniel smiled, studied me, and kept the smile until it looked nothing like a smile at all. Maybe I had overdone the aftershave, or maybe it was the unironed khakis or the color of my shirt. Or maybe he liked me just fine, and it was just that I was dating his baby daughter.

"Linda," Daniel said, watching my eyes. "Get Nick here a drink. What'll it be, Nick?"

"Nothing just yet. Too early for me," I said, rocking on my heels.

"Is it?" Daniel said, scratching beneath the white of his beard.

"Well," Lyla said, "*I'll* have one. C'mon, Mom, let's go in the kitchen. I'll help you get ready."

Lyla winked, left me there with her dad. I gave her a brittle smile as she walked away. I had a seat on the sofa, crossed one leg over the other, nervously missed it on the first go-round.

"Where's the rest of the family?" I said.

"They'll be along," Daniel said. "How's the bar business going?"

"Good. Real good."

"You know, I used to go into that place, in the old days, when I was working on the Hill."

"Really."

"Yes, it was called something else back then. You've been there awhile, haven't you? Thought you might own a piece of it by now."

"No, not me. Tough business, that." Real tough.

"And your investigative work?"

"Coming along," I said as I watched my free foot wiggle in the air. "How about you...how's retirement?"

Daniel raised his substantial eyebrows. "Linda says I don't know how to spell the word *retirement*. I guess the difference is, now I don't get paid for what it is I do. Right now, I'm setting up group homes for Haitian refugees. Our church owns these properties, so...I'm helping fix them up."

"Why fix them up?" I said, my foot pinwheeling now, out of control. "You could make more profit by, you know, leaving them the way they are. Crowd a bunch of people in the rooms, I mean—where they come from, they're used to it. Jack up the rents, too, while you're at it."

A smile came into Daniel's eyes. "Of course," he said, "you're ribbing me, aren't you?"

"Just a little."

"You know, you don't always have to work so hard at being cynical around me, Nick. I know that, in your own way, you have a fairly clear idea of what's right and what's wrong. Not all the good that gets done in this world gets done in a church or a meeting hall, I realize that."

"Yeah, well, we make do with what we have, and work with it, you know?"

"Yes, I do."

He stopped giving me the business and picked up the Outlook section of the *Post* that was lying by his chair. I noticed a makeshift bar that had been set up on a mobile cart near a mirrored armoire in the corner of the room. There were bottles of gin and vodka, tonic and ginger ale, an ice bucket, and a sealed bottle of Old Grand-Dad. Apparently, that had been purchased just for me; I had never seen the old man take a drink, and Lyla's mother drank wine, and only with dinner. Something pushed out at the base of the curtains at the bay window and moved along behind them with a deliberate slink: That would be Peace, stalking me as he always did when I came to the McCubbin house for dinner.

I was watching the curtains, thinking of my possible defense against an attack from that lousy cat, when the front door opened and four people stepped inside: Lyla's brother, Mike, his wife, Donna, Lyla's older sister, Kimmy, and Kimmy's husband, Leo. This time, Daniel stood up from his chair, and we all did our back-slapping moves around the living room. A half hour later, we were seated at a cramped table in the dining room, with Daniel McCubbin leading a prayer. During the prayer, our hands were all joined underneath the table, a McCubbin tradition, and my index finger was wiggling around on the inside of Lyla's thigh. Lyla, seated to my right, dug a fingernail into my own thigh, leaving a crescent mark that I discovered an hour later in the bathroom.

"Amen," everybody said, and then Leo, as usual, reached across the table for the first shot at the main course, and started pushing thick slices of roast beef onto his plate.

"Leave some for the rest of the family, Leo," Kim said, only kidding by half.

"Sure, honey," he said, then issued his trademark high cackle, a sound that was always surprising coming from a man as fat as Leo. "You know I can't help it. The Irish love their liquor, and us Greeks love to eat. Right, Nick?"

Daniel McCubbin's eyes flashed on Leo. I nodded weakly, not wanting to appear too anxious to admit to being a member of Leo Charles's ethnic tribe. Leo *was* a Greek—the Charles had been Charalambides before his grandfather stepped off the boat—but he was not a kid my friends or I had known growing up. Leo Charles was also a bigot, and like all bigots, black and white, he was a loser, and he directed his shortcomings and utter lack of self-confidence outwardly and onto the backs of others. Lyla said Kimmy had zero self-esteem and that was why she had married him. And all the time, I'd thought it was his 280-pound frame, all five foot eight inches of it.

"How about those Orioles?" Mike said in the too-gentle way of his that unfortunately suggested a weaker version of his father. Mike ran a volunteer soup kitchen operation out of Le Droit Park. He plopped a mound of mashed potatoes onto his plate and passed the platter to his wife, Donna, a shame-about-the-face public defender with just a killer body. All these do-goodniks at the table, and me. Well, there was Leo, too.

"Yeah, how about 'em, Nick?" Leo said. "Think the bull-pen's gonna take 'em through to the Series?" Leo loved to talk sports but couldn't do a push-up.

"Lookin' good," I said, feeling not so good. I really could

have used a drink. "I'm going up to Camden Yards tomorrow with a buddy of mine, a guy named Johnny McGinnes."

"An Irishman," Leo said, spitting a little ball of mashed potato across the table in the process.

"They love their liquor," Daniel said, but it went over Leo's head, missed him by a mile. He kept right on chewing, breaking down the load that was in his mouth. Lyla's mother laughed a little, and she and Mike exchanged fond looks.

"You didn't tell me you were going to the game," Lyla said.

"Yeah, Johnny won some tickets, sold a million refrigerators last month in some promotion, something like that."

"*That* ought to be interesting," Lyla said, killing the remainder of the wine in her glass. She picked up the bottle off the table and poured herself some more, clumsily trying to fill the glass to the top, spilling some in the process. Daniel looked at her and then at me. Lyla's ears were a little red, her cheeks flushed.

"Anybody want a little more cool in here?" Lyla's mother said. "We could turn up that air conditioner."

"Let me handle this," I said with a wink. "I used to be in electronics—I know how to operate the unit."

I got out of my chair and walked to the window where the air conditioner had been set. As I got to it, I saw something black seem to rise out of nowhere from behind the curtains near my feet, and I heard a woman's voice cry out behind me just as the wail of an animal pierced the air. I felt a slash of pain, pulled my hand back as the crazy tomcat cartwheeled in the air, landed on his feet on the carpet, and took off back across the room, scurrying for his hiding place behind the drapes.

"Fuck!" I shouted, waving my hand, the blood already coming to the surface of the cut. That quieted the rest of them down.

Mike got up and found the cat, carried him back into the room. Lyla tossed me a napkin and went to get a Band-Aid. She returned with it, but by now the cut had stopped bleeding. I put the Band-Aid on anyway, a sympathy play to make my obscenity seem more justified.

"Peace, man," Mike whined, stroking the cat.

"Peace, man," I said, and made a V with my fingers, smiling stupidly at the McCubbin family. Nobody laughed.

"I guess that cat doesn't like you so good," Leo said. "Right, Nick?"

"Leo," Kimmy said, "you've got a piece of lettuce on your cheek."

I sat back down. Lyla patted my thigh under the table. We finished our Sunday dinner.

A COUPLE OF HOURS later, when Lyla's siblings and their spouses had gone and Lyla went to the kitchen with her mother to wash and dry the dishes, I took a beer to the concrete patio out back and had a seat in one of four wrought-iron chairs grouped around a glass-topped table. I lit a cigarette and watched a young father play catch with his son in an adjacent yard. The man rubbed the top of his son's head when they were done, and the boy skipped off toward their house. Then the back door of the McCubbin house opened and Daniel came out and stepped down to the patio.

"Mind if I join you?"

"Of course not," I said. "Have a seat."

He grunted as he settled into a chair across the table. I dropped my lit butt into the top of the beer can and heard it hiss as it hit the backwash. I put the can at my feet.

"How was it?" Daniel said.

"Cold beer on a Sunday in the summer, it's always pretty good."

"Yes, I remember. Watching you today, it took me back to when I was first dating Linda, the times we'd go to her parents' house for dinner. I could have used a drink on those occasions, wanted one desperately, as a matter of fact. It really would have relaxed me, taken the edge off. There's nothing more humbling than dealing with the potential in-laws, no matter how much confidence you have. It's like, all of the sudden, you're a little boy again."

"You guys aren't so bad," I said, and a smile passed between us. "Besides, it's Lyla, so it's worth it."

"You love her, don't you?"

"Yes, sir. I believe I do."

"How much do you love her? Do you love her enough to do what's right for her, even if it means losing her?"

"I don't follow you."

Daniel sat back in his chair, looked into the depths of his own yard. "I told you earlier today that I used to frequent that place you bartend in, when I was on the Hill. I don't know if Lyla's ever told you the...degree to which I frequented those types of establishments."

"No," I said, "she hasn't."

"Well, I was quite a regular in those days, in that place and plenty of others. I wish that I could give you the details, but I don't remember all that much of those years. If it wasn't for photographs, it would be difficult to recall even the faces of my children as they were growing up. All that wasted time. But I can't get it back now, so..." Daniel pulled at the errant edges of his beard. "Anyway, things turned out all right, I think. I got myself into a program, managed to see my children become wonderful adults, with most of the credit for that going to Linda, of course, and I ended up doing a bit of good along the way. So I think you'll understand it when I say, maybe because of the fact that I wasn't always there for them, that I'm rather fiercely protective of my children to this day."

"I understand."

Daniel breathed out slowly, folded his hands on the table, bumped one thumb against the other. "Lyla, she's always taken on my traits, even as a child. I know you think she looks like her mother, and certainly she does. But I'm talking about resemblances in less obvious ways."

I didn't respond.

Daniel kept on: "When Lyla was a teenager, when she used to come home late at night, I could always tell what she had been up to. Her own body, it betrayed her. When she drinks, you know, even now, her ears turn this blazing shade of red. That same thing used to happen to me—in fact, they used to call me 'Red' in some of the bars where they knew me pretty well." Daniel looked me in the eyes. "She's got a problem with it, you know. It's hereditary, I suppose, in a gene I gave her. The researchers, they've been claiming that for quite some time now. She's got the same problem that I had when I was her age. And I see it…I see it only getting worse."

Again, I didn't answer him or respond in any way. A drop of sweat moved slowly down my back. Daniel leaned in, rested his forearms on the table.

"You're an alcoholic, Nick," he said. "You would never admit to it, but that's what you are. You've probably done some binge drinking in your day, but I would say that in general you're what they call a controlled drinker. The worst kind, because it allows you to convince yourself that you don't have a problem, and now you've managed to bury the thought of doing something about it entirely. I've been around enough people like you; I just don't think you're ever going to give it up."

"I know what I'm about."

"Yes, I think you do. But I'm not responsible for you, so that's not good enough. Lyla needs someone strong to tell her what she is and to stand next to her and help her through it. You're just not that person."

I pushed away from the table and stood slowly from my chair. "It's getting late. I better be going."

I began to walk past him, but he wrapped a hand around my forearm. I looked down on him, saw that his eyes had softened.

"I like you, Nick. I want you to know that. I think that you're a good man. You're just not good for *her*."

"Thanks for dinner."

I walked across the patio in the dying light.

"WHAT WERE YOU AND Dad doing out back?" Lyla said. We were driving south on Connecticut, to Lyla's apartment. "What was he, asking about your intentions?"

"Something like that."

"Dad's always been tough on my boyfriends."

"He's only looking out for you," I said.

"I know," Lyla said, and touched the Band-Aid on my finger. "Tough day, huh, Stefanos?"

"Tough day."

I stopped at Lyla's apartment building off Calvert, let the engine idle.

"What, you're not coming up?"

"I better not," I said. "Got something going on early tomorrow on this Jeter thing."

"I should chill out, too. My editor left a message on my machine yesterday. That story I've been working on, the one I finished and turned in after we had lunch the other day, in Chinatown? He wants to meet with me about it in the morning. Sounds ominous."

"You've always been able to control him. You'll do fine."

Lyla leaned across the seat, put her hand behind my head, and kissed me on the mouth. "Love you, Nick."

"I love you too, baby. Take care."

TWELVE

N D.C., IT'S tough to find a good clean place to catch an art film anymore, and next to impossible to find consistency in repertory. The near-legendary Circle Theater on Pennsylvania Avenue, where many Washingtonians got their film education, is long gone, its "ten tickets for ten dollars" deal a permanent fixture now in the local nostalgia file. Georgetown boasts the Key and Biograph theaters, but Georgetown has devolved into a slum-out for suburban teens, drunks, and tourists—a guy I know calls it a "shopping mall without a roof"—and a lot of in-towners just don't care to bother. Out-of-town bookers place the rest of the films in their corporately designated "art theaters," their unfamiliarity with our city demographics resulting in sometimes laughably illogical bills. It's true that you can catch some cool stuff at the Hirshhorn or at other galleries or museums, but you have to know where to find the listings, and by the time you've gotten around to checking out the art calendars in *City Paper* and *D.C. This Week*, it's often too late.

I have a friend named Gerry Abromowitz, whom I've known since the club days in the early years of the New Wave—music, not film. Gerry owned his own club for a while, a place called the Crawlspace, a venue for harDCore bands and slammers. Off and on, Gerry went by the name of Gerry Louis, Jr., and even looked into having the legal change. But he stopped short of doing it about the time that the Crawlspace closed down after one steaming-hot summer. A personal-injury suit put a lock on the front door, but in truth, the place was a loser from the word go. Now, Gerry Louis, Jr., was back to Gerry Abromowitz and settling into the beginnings of middle age, working as the owner/operator of a movie theater called the Very Ritzy down on 9th.

The Very Ritzy had just been the Ritz, of course, in its original incarnation, but as usual, Gerry couldn't resist fucking around with the name. It started out as a burlesque house, and then it was the last of the burlesque houses, and then it was the last of the porno houses, and when Gerry took it out of mothballs on a short-term lease, his intention was to make it an art house. But he soon found out that it was difficult to outbid the more powerful competition for the bookings, and when he could get a decent film, nobody seemed to be interested in traveling to that part of town after working hours. So he quietly took it back to porno for the matinees and made it straight repertory at night, taking in the spillage and the last-call crowd from the Snake Pit and other clubs in the surrounding area. He seemed to make a living from this novel arrangement, though that was probably due to the fact that his skin-flick matinees were all profit; over the years, Gerry Abromowitz had amassed one of the most extensive privately owned sixteen-millimeter porno collections south of Jersey.

"Ge-roo," I said, shaking his hand. He had agreed to meet me Monday noon at the theater. We stood in the red-carpeted lobby.

"Nick the Stick," Gerry said. "Lookin' good. How about me... I gain much weight?"

About forty, I thought. But I said, "Nah."

"C'mon up. I'm runnin' the projector. My kid's up there; I don't want to leave him alone."

A man in a business suit walked into the lobby, his eyes straight ahead. An usher—long hair, wearing a black T-shirt and ripped black jeans—took the man's ticket, tore it in half, then returned to the paperback he was reading without moving from his stool. The business suit scurried quickly through the lobby to the darkness of the theater. I followed Gerry up a carpeted set of stairs.

We hit a landing and then an office area, where a boy just past toddler played with an action figure that looked to me like the Astro Boy of my youth. All four walls of this room had film cans racked and labeled on wooden shelves, with a large slotted area set aside for one-sheets and stills.

"Gerry junior," Gerry said, tipping his head proudly at the boy.

"Gerry Louis, Jr.?" I said.

"Nick, Nick, Nick," Gerry said.

I turned to his kid. "What's that guy's name?" I said, nodding at his toy.

"Jason the Power Ranger!" the kid said, puffing out his chest and his cheeks. When he did that, the little fats looked a lot like his dad.

"Aw, man," I said, "I wish *I* had one of those." That got Gerry junior excited, and he started running around the room, holding up Jason the Power Ranger in the go-fly position. Gerry senior motioned me up another short set of stairs.

We took seats outside the shut door of the projection booth, close enough to hear if something mechanical went wrong. The air was stagnant and warm, but I was in shorts and a T-shirt, and Gerry was dressed approximately the same way. Gerry's kinky hair had plenty of gray in it, and he had one of those faces that always seemed to be smiling, even when it was not.

"So what's on the bill today?" I said. *"The Sorrow and the Pity?"*

"Not quite. *Crotchless in Seattle.* It's a big title for me this summer."

"I'll bet. So the porno's keeping this place afloat."

"So far. The associations, the exodus of the law firms moving east into the city, that's helped. These guys pay their seven bucks, come in for the first show, fifteen minutes, wack-adoo, wack-adoo"—Gerry contorted his face, made a fist, pumped out a two-stroke jack-off mime—"they're in and out. It's cheaper than a prostie, Nick. And with the plague out there, it's damn sure safer. Everyone thought, with videotape rental, the theatrical was gonna go the way of quadrophonic sound. And that was true to some degree, especially with the pervs. But these married guys, for whatever reason—maybe they're not gettin' enough at home, whatever—they can't pop in a porno tape in their own house. What are they gonna tell junior? 'Keep it down. Daddy's tryin' to watch Stormy Weathers give Ralph Rimrod some head'? Excuse me." Gerry pulled balled Kleenex from his pocket, blew his nose loudly into the tissue. "I'm telling you, this porno thing is a growth market, if you got the right location."

"Yeah, but who cleans up the theater?"

Gerry smirked. "That kid you saw in the lobby, he came to me, said he wanted to learn the exhibition business. I gave him a bucket and mop, said, 'Here, go to school.' Between shows, he does the honors. But it's not as bad as you think, Nick. These business types are very fastidious—they bring their own socks, *Wall Street Journal*s, shit like that. They're better behaved than my nighttime repertory crowd, I'll tell you. But even that's beginning to pick up. Kids are smoking pot again, you know it?"

"Sure," I said, thinking of the stash in my glove box.

"That helps. Helps the 'appreciation of cinema.' Helps

music, and fucking, and everything else, too, right? Anyway, I'm gonna start adding psychotronic midnights on the weekends—"

"Listen, Ger—"

"I know, you don't have all day. You called because you needed some information."

"That's right. I'm looking for a kid, got himself into some local porn action."

"How old?"

"Seventeen."

"What genre?"

"Man on boy, what I can make out. Maybe interracial, if that narrows it down. The kid is black."

Gary scratched behind his ear. "I wouldn't know, directly. Everything I got here is classic, on celluloid, from the archives. The video business is wide open, man; anybody can do it. Let's say you want to make a movie with a school theme. All's you need is a camera, a couple of lights if you want it real clean, some props—a piece of chalk, maybe a blackboard—and you got yourself a real intricate story about a teacher disciplining his student."

"Isn't there any risk? I mean, it's got to be illegal, right?"

"Yes and no. The situation you're describing, if the kid's a minor, yeah, that's illegal, but lookswise he's probably right on the cusp, so who's gonna check? Basically, as long as there're no penetration shots, you're in the clear."

"The business is that scattered."

"Sure. It's done all over the city. Like I say, I wouldn't have any idea where to tell you to start. I'm not in that business."

"Somebody's got to distribute the stuff, though."

Gerry shifted in his seat. "In the man-boy arena? All the homo stuff, and the different varieties of it, everything comes out of this little warehouse around 2nd on K. This guy owns a storefront porno operation. I think it's called the Hot Plate."

"What's his name?"

"Bernard Tobias. Bernie."

"Think he'll talk to me?"

"Not *just* to you, no. Bernie, he's a weird bird. Well, maybe not so weird if you're an amateur psychiatrist. He's a little guy who always needs to be the big magilla. I've met him a few times; he's always bragging about how he only does business with 'executive officers,' never meets with anybody's assistant, like we're talking about Wharton graduates in the skin trade here. I think if you go in with a couple of guys, wear ties, do the dog and pony show, you'll be all right."

"Thanks, Gerry. Appreciate the help."

"Hey, Nick—how'd you end up in this, anyway? I ran into one of my old bartenders from the Crawlspace a few months ago—"

"Joe Martinson."

"Joe, right. He told me what you were doing. The way I remember you, you were this music-crazy guy used to stand in the corner watching the bands, a beer in each hand. Fact, I used to call you 'Nick Two-Beers,' remember?"

"You said it was my Indian name. 'Course, I remember when you insisted everyone call you Gerry Louis, Jr. Things happen to people—you never know where they're going to end up."

"You got that right. That guy in that band Big Black, Durango's his name, remember? He's a corporate lawyer now. I saw his picture in a magazine, little bald guy in a hot-shit suit like every guy you see walking out of Arnold and Porter. So yeah, you never know." Gerry got out of his chair. "Speaking of Jerry Lewis, I'm doing a retrospective next month, kicking it off with *The Nutty Professor*. I can get you a pass."

"I don't think so."

"It's an American classic!"

"So are you, Ger." I shook his hand. "Listen, thanks again, man. Thanks a million."

I USED GERRY'S DIRECTORY before I left, then found a pay phone out on 9th and called Bernie Tobias. I identified myself as Ron

Roget—an appropriately lizardly name I had just seen in the directory—and bullshitted him about my production company out of Philadelphia, which I said did the "man/boy discipline thing" better than anyone "on the East Coast." He said he couldn't meet with me that week, but when I told him that "my associates" and I would be in D.C. tomorrow, and only for one day, he agreed. As Gerry had predicted, the "associates" tag hit Bernie's hot button. We agreed on a time the next day.

I made it to the Spot after the lunch rush had subsided. Mai was behind the bar, bent into the soak sink with a glass load, and Phil Saylor stood at the register counting checks. Anna was by the service bar, arranging her tip change in dollar stacks on the green netting. I spoke to Mai briefly, thanked her for what we had arranged over the phone the day before.

"Hey, Phil," I said, speaking to his back. "I'm taking some time off. Mai and I set it up. That okay by you?"

"I need the shifts, Phil," Mai interjected.

"She told me already," Phil said without raising his head. He didn't add anything, so I went down to the service end of the bar and rubbed the top of Anna Wang's head.

"Hey, Nick."

"Hey, what's up?"

"Got a cigarette?"

"Sure."

I gave her one, lit it for her. She leaned her back against the wall, dragged sharply on the smoke, exhaled just as sharply. "Some woman called you," she said. "Said your uncle wants to see you."

"Costa," I said. "The woman would be his nurse."

"He sick?"

"Cancer," I said. Anna looked at the cigarette in her hand, thought about it, took another drag.

"That's rough."

I nodded. "How'd your date go with LaDuke?"

"Okay, I guess."

I reached out and Anna passed me the cigarette. I took a puff, handed it back. "Just okay?"

"It was fun." Her eyes smiled. "He took me to the Jefferson Memorial last night. We sat on the steps, split a bottle of wine. Or rather, I drank most of it. No guy's ever tried anything so obvious with me. I know it's a corny move, but I got the feeling he didn't think it was, if you know what I mean."

"He's strictly from L-Seven, but genuine."

"Exactly. Most of the guys I meet still in their twenties, they're so ironic, so cynical, you know, I just get tired of it sometimes. Jack's cute, and he's funny, and all those good things, but he's also really square. In some weird way, that's refreshing."

"So why was the night 'just okay'?"

"It always comes down to the big finish, doesn't it?" Anna butted the smoke in an ashtray, looked up. "Well, at the end of the night, I wanted to kiss him, you know? And I'm pretty sure he wanted to kiss me, too. So I took the initiative." Anna grinned. "I gave it to him pretty good, I think. But he was shaking, Nick. I mean, shaking real deep. It's like, I don't know, he was scared to death. And then he just pulled away, and it was like something just seemed to go out of him."

"Maybe it's been awhile for him."

"I guess."

"You gonna see him again?"

"Maybe. I don't know. The guy's carrying something serious around on his back. I'm not sure if I need that right now."

I touched her arm. "Listen, I've got to go."

"Take it easy," she said.

I poked my head into the kitchen, hooked Darnell up as the driver for my appointment the next day. Then I phoned LaDuke from the bar, got him in on it, too. On the way out the door, Phil Saylor grabbed my arm.

"What's your hurry?" he said.

"I'm off to the ball game with a friend of mine. Got to pick him up where he works."

"Don't stay away too long, hear? Mai, she's okay, but after she works a few days straight, she starts jumping all into the customers' shit."

"I thought you were mad at me, Phil."

"You made a mistake. You're allowed one or two."

I moved to shake his hand, but he turned away. The two of us were square again, I guess.

WHEN I WALKED INTO Goode's White Goods in Beltsville, the first thing I saw was Johnny McGinnes, bent into an open refrigerator, blowing pot smoke into the box. During working hours, McGinnes's pants pocket always contained a film canister and a one-hit pipe, which he lit at regular intervals right on the sales floor. After the exhale, he would tap the ashes out against his open palm and drop the pipe back into his pocket in one quick movement. I had worked with him for many years, and to my knowledge, no one, customer or management type, had ever caught him in the act of getting high.

McGinnes saw my entrance, pulled a six of Colt 45 tall boys from the fridge, held them up, winked, and put them back inside. He shut the door and goose-stepped down the aisle back to his customer, a middle-aged woman looking at a dishwasher. As usual, McGinnes was done up synthetic-crisp: navy blue slacks, poly/cotton oxford, and a plain red tie with a knot as pretty as a fist. His thinning black hair slashed down across his high forehead, with only his silver sideburns betraying his age. McGinnes managed to throw me a mental patient's grin as he spoke to the woman; even across the showroom, I could see that he was half-cooked.

Goode's White Goods, one of the few major appliance independents left in the D.C. area since brand-name retailing came to Sears, had managed to carve out a niche for itself as a full-service operation. *White goods* was the industry term for big-ticket appliances, and the company's owner, Nolan Goode — it was inevitable that McGinnes would dub him "No Damn Good" — mistakenly overcalculated the public's comprehension of the wordplay in the store's name. Confusion notwithstanding, Goode's White Goods had managed to survive. And after McGinnes had joined the team, it had actually begun to thrive.

In contrast to the noise common on an electronics' floor, No Damn Good's appliance shop seemed quiet as a museum, orderly rows of silent, shiny, inanimate porcelain aligned beneath wall-to-wall banners. In the center aisle, a young man used an unwieldy buffer to wax the floor, solemnly repeating the phrase "Slippery, slippery," though there were no customers anywhere near him. A man I pegged as the manager — prematurely bald, prematurely overweight — stood behind the counter, hiking his pants up sharply, as if that was the most aggressive act he would attempt all day. On the other side of the counter stood a young, square-jawed guy, smiling broadly, arranging point-of-purchase promotional materials. He had the too-handsome, dim-bulb look of a factory rep, *Triumph of the Will* in a navy blue suit. Out of the corner of my eye, I saw a little guy shoot out of the stockroom and head in my direction, his hand extended all the way out, his hip-on-the-cheap clothing drooping everywhere on his skinny frame.

"And how are we doin' today?" he said as he reached me, his hand still out.

I shook it and said, "Waiting on McGinnes."

"Anything I can do for you while you're waiting?"

"No thanks."

"Well, if you have any questions about a major appliance —"

"The name is Donny," I said.

Donny smiled a little strangely and I smiled back. He scratched his ratty 'fro and walked back down the aisle, slinking behind the counter. I checked McGinnes: He had removed the dishwasher's wash tower — it looked exactly like a vibrator — and was making little jabbing movements with it behind the customer's back, pitching the merits of the machine to her all the while. This was for my benefit, I supposed, or maybe he was just bored. Then a young couple came through the door with buy signs practically tattooed on their foreheads—any salesman worth his salt can tell—and McGinnes excused himself to greet them.

Donny yelled across the sales floor, "Hey, Johnny, you got a call on line one. Guy wants to give you an order," and he pointed to a wall-mounted phone where a yellow light blinked clear as a beacon. McGinnes hesitated, went to take the call. Donny racewalked toward his new customers. Even before I saw McGinnes pick up the phone and make a bitter face, I knew what Donny Boy had done: gotten a dial tone and put it on hold, then used the phony bait to draw McGinnes away from the live ones coming through the door. Johnny should have known; in fact, it was one of the very first tricks he had played on me years ago.

McGinnes closed his deal, though, and Donny did not. Afterward, when I had been introduced to the boys and stood with them around the counter, there seemed to be no residual animosity coming off Johnny. Just another way to grab an up, the memory to be filed away by McGinnes under "payback," to be retrieved the next time a *yom* came walking through the door.

"So, Tim," a very serious Donny said to the factory rep. "You read about Maytag in the paper today?"

"No," Tim said, breathing through his mouth. "What about Maytag?"

"Kelvinator!" Donny said. "Get it? Kelvin…he ate 'er!" Donny cackled, slapped his own knee.

"Ha, ha, ha." Tim's laughter and the brittle smile that went with it failed to mask his contempt.

"'Course," Donny continued, "that ain't nothin', compared with what the general did."

"What general?" Tim said, and I saw it coming.

"General Electric!" Donny said. "He was Tappan Amana, dig? Put his Hotpoint right on her Coldspot. Know what I'm sayin'?"

Tim began to turn red. McGinnes walked up to the group, a brown paper bag in his hand. He looked at me and smiled.

"You ready, Jim?" he said.

"I'm ready."

"Hold on a second," the manager said.

"What?" McGinnes said.

"I got a belch a few minutes ago," the manager said. "That's what. Customer called, said you stepped him off an advertised single-speed washer to what you claimed was a two speed—an LA three-five-nine-five."

"So?"

"An LA three-five-nine-five is a single-speed washer, too, McGinnes. You told him it had two speeds!"

"It does have two speeds," McGinnes said. "On...and off."

"Off's not a speed, McGinnes!" the manager yelled, but Johnny had already pulled me away, and the two of us were headed for the front door.

McGinnes drew a malt liquor out of the bag and popped the top. He handed the open one to me, found one for himself.

"Off is not a speed!..." The manager's voice trailed off as we pushed through the store's double glass doors.

Out in the lot, McGinnes tensed up his face. "All these complaints. I'm gonna get a sick stomach."

"Had a lot lately?"

McGinnes nodded. "This guy called this morning, all bent out of shape. Says when I sold him his refrigerator, I guaranteed him it was a nice box. And the thing's had three service calls in the last month."

"So? Did you guarantee it?"

"Hell no! I never said it was a nice box. I said it was *an ice-box!* The guy just misunderstood me."

"I can't imagine how that happened, Johnny."

"The guy was a putz," McGinnes said. "You know it?"

THIRTEEN

MY FIRST DAY as a stock boy at Nutty Nathan's on Connecticut Avenue, back in 1974, I checked out this pale, speeded-out looking Irishman named Johnny McGinnes and I thought, Who *is* this guy? It didn't take too long to find out. Shortly after meeting him, I watched him volunteer to microwave the frozen dinner of a visiting district manager, and I pegged him as a brownnose. That notion was dispelled a few minutes later when I walked around the display rack and caught him hawking a wad of spit into the DM's food, his chest heaving in suppressed laughter as he carefully mixed it in. By the end of the day, I had witnessed him hit his pipe repeatedly, knock down a steady succession of beers, and swallow two suspicious-looking pills, all the time maintaining his mastery of the floor. Then, at closing time, he laid "Willie the Pimp" on the store's most expensive system, and eighty watts of Zappa were suddenly blowing through a pair of Bose 901s, and Johnny stood atop a vacuum cleaner display, playing air guitar, his bleeding red eyes closed as if in prayer. Even a sixteen-year-old stoner like me could see that Johnny McGinnes was one man who would never grow up.

"You're drinking too slow," McGinnes said, as my Dodge pushed up 95.

"*You're* not," I said. We were nearing Baltimore and the six of tall boys was almost done.

McGinnes gave the radio some volume. "Hey," he shouted, "how you like being a parent?"

I turned the volume down a notch. "I'm not a parent. A kid's parents are who raises them, and I've got nothing to do with that."

"Yeah, but"—McGinnes wiggled his eyebrows foolishly—"you gave her your seed, didn't you?"

"Yes, Johnny, I gave her my seed."

"So, what did Jackie name the boy?"

"Kent," I said, and waited for his comment.

"She named him after a cigarette?"

"It's British or something."

"Her last name's Kahn, isn't it? I thought Kahn was a Jewish name—"

"Shit, Johnny, I don't know. She liked the name, that's all."

I swigged my malt liquor. Some of it ran down my chin. I went to wipe it off and swerved a bit into another lane. Someone reprimanded me with a polite beep and I got the car back between the lines.

McGinnes said, "I don't like it."

"What?"

"The name."

"Why not?"

He raised a finger in the air, like he imagined an academic might do. "You know how kids are. I mean, the other boys, on the playground, they're gonna give him shit about it, twist it all around."

"I don't follow."

McGinnes sighed, exasperated. "You say his name's Kent, right? Nick, the other kids—well, they're gonna call him 'Cunt'!"

"Aw, come on, man…"

"Hey, look!" McGinnes said, pointing through the window excitedly. "Baltimore!"

We stopped in a bar near the stadium, split a pitcher, and watched the first two innings from there. We would have made it for the third, but we got waylaid by the kick-ass food at the concession stands inside the Yards. McGinnes and I both had half smokes smothered in kraut and mustard and two more beers before we got to our seats. By then it was the fourth and the Birds were down by two to the White Sox.

Our seats were in section 330, to the right and way up from home plate. A deaf kid sat alone in front of us, and next to him sat a solid Korean man and his two sons. The Korean ate peanuts the entire game, a mountain of shells at his feet. Behind us a red-bearded, potbellied man loudly heckled the players, with most of his choice obscenities reserved for Sid Fernandez, who that night was truly getting rocked. Near him, a couple of D.C. attorneys in polo shirts talked about how "quaint" the Bromo-Seltzer Tower looked against the open B-A skyline and how D.C. had nothing "like that." It was the kind of boneheaded conversation you heard from transient Washingtonians every time they went to Camden Yards, as if one old building set against a rather ordinary backdrop had any significance at all. Not that I had anything against this city—Baltimore was a fine town, with top-notch food and bars and good people. But Baltimore wasn't mine.

"Hey," McGinnes said, pointing to a vendor. "Let's get a pretzel, man."

"I'd love to," I said. "The trouble is, you gotta put mustard on a pretzel, and I had too much mustard on my half smoke. I feel like it and I don't feel like it, you know what I mean?"

"A couple more beers, then." McGinnes whistled at a guy coming up the steps with a tray of them.

We drank those, and another round, and then it was the sixth. The Sox were taking off behind their suddenly hot bats and the awesome heat coming from Jack McDowell on the mound. McDowell's goateed photograph was up on the tele-screen, and McGinnes gestured to it with his head.

"What's with the goatee action?" McGinnes said, loud and a little drunk. "McDowell looks like a Chink! Like he ought to be servin' us dinner and shit."

The Korean looked at McGinnes out of the corner of his eyes and cracked a peanut shell between two thick fingers.

"Johnny, keep it down."

"What," McGinnes said, nodding to the deaf kid, "am I bothering him or somethin'?"

"Listen," I said, changing the subject. "I've got something going on tomorrow, an acting job, for you and a buddy, if you're interested."

"Oh yeah? What's it about?"

After I briefed him, I said, "How about your boy Donny? Think he can handle it?"

"That guy *is* an actor. Sure, it gets on my nerves, I got to listen to him run his cocksucker all day long. But he's all right. Good salesman, too."

"Set it up, then," I said.

McGinnes nodded, then stared sadly at the hot-pretzel man, who was moving our way once again.

"If you want one," I said, "just get one."

"No, that's okay."

"Then what's the problem?"

McGinnes said, "I put too much mustard on my half smoke, too."

McDowell retired the side, three up, three down. We left in the eighth, when the stadium stopped selling booze.

At a liquor store outside the Yards, we stopped for another six, then drank it on the drive back to D.C. McGinnes talked about his girlfriend, Carmelita, and about his "spot" of TB and how the doctors had treated it with INH, which he had taken every morning for a year. Then McGinnes told a very funny joke about an Indian named Two Dogs Fucking, and about that time we killed our last beer and crossed over into PG County. I dropped him at his car in Beltsville, then drove to my apartment, where I fed the cat and paced around listening to records, too drunk to have the sense to go to bed but not drunk enough to pass out. I called Lyla, but she wasn't in, so I left a message on her machine. I thought of Joe Martinson, rang him up.

"Hello."

"Hey, Joe—'Where you goin' with that gun in your hand?'"

"Nick!"

"Thought you might be up for some music."

"I might."

"Snake Pit?"

"Sounds good."

"Meet you in there in a half hour or so."

"Who's playing?"

"What difference does it make, right?"

The Mekons were playing, and the place was jammed. The band had been around forever, but it had still managed to retain its indie status, so the crowd was a mixture of young introductees and veterans like Joe and I. I grabbed two Buds at the door bar and pushed my way back to the right corner of the stage, my usual spot. Joe found me in midset, guitars flailing against the saw of a fiddle, the band just pushing it all the way out, and that's where we stayed until the end of the first show. The Snake Pit can be a drag with its put-on attitude, but on hot summer nights, when the acts are really cooking and the place is drowned in music and sweat, there's still nothing better in D.C.

Out on F, I stumbled into the alley a few doors down from the club to urinate, Martinson filing in behind me, laughing. A lighted office building rose out of the darkness ahead, cutting the symmetry of the brick walls running at my side. I looked into the alley, where rats moved about in the shadows of several green Dumpsters. The picture was odd but strangely beautiful. A smile of relief spread across my face as I stood there, peeing on the stones, and I thought, You know, I really do love this fucking town.

JOE AND I GOT into my Dodge and headed west. Joe found some pot in my glove box and dropped a bud onto the hot end of the lighter from my dash. We took turns snorting the smoke. I pushed a Stereolab tape into the deck and boosted the bass, and we tripped on that as we made our way across town, drinking a couple of beers we had smuggled out of the club. I found a place to park on U at 16th—had to piss again. Did it right on the street.

"Hey, ladies," Joe screamed at some women passing by. "This here is my friend, Nick Stefanos."

Black.

I sat at the full bar at Rio Loco's, Joe Martinson on the stool to my right. There was a bottle of beer in front of me, a shot of bourbon next to that, and a cigarette burning in the ashtray. I sampled all three. A floor waitress I knew, on the heavy side, real sweet, with missile tits and a plain-Elaine face, came by and smiled, and we exchanged a few smart sentences. She drifted, and Joe tapped his bottle against mine.

"I thinks she digs you, man," Joe said.

"Yeah, sure."

"I know she does. What's her name?"

"I think it's Lynn," I said. Or was it Linda?

Joe swigged from his beer. "One thing about you, Stefanos. I wanna get fucked up, I can hook up with you anytime. I know you're never gonna disappoint me, man. With you, it's like it's still 1980. One thing's for sure, I couldn't run with you all the time."

"Yep."

"Okay, so…" Martinson leaned in. "Best tracks, 1990s."

"Best tracks, huh?" I tried to concentrate against the bar noise and the zydeco jump coming from the juke.

"I'll start," Martinson said. "'Get Me'—Dinosaur Jr."

I hit my cigarette. "Dinosaur Jr.? Who does he think he is, Frank Marino or somethin'? You smoke too much weed, Joe."

"Listen to it some time—the kid Mascis can really fuckin' play."

"Okay," I said. "'Summer Babe.' Pavement."

Joe smiled. "'Chapel Hill.' Sonic Youth."

"'Instrument,'" I said. "Fugazi." On that one, Martinson slapped me five.

"Desert island LP," said Joe. "If you had to pick one, what would it be?"

"'Let It Be,'" I said without hesitation.

"The Beatles?" he said, screwing up his face.

"Fuck the Beatles!" I said. "I'm talkin' 'bout the Replacements!"

Joe laughed. I reached for my drink. A lot of time passed, or maybe it did not. I looked to my right, and Martinson was gone. A couple of white boys wearing baseball caps were sitting a few stools down. One of them was looking at me and laughing.

Black.

I sat at a deuce under the harsh lights of last call. Lynn or was it Linda? sat in the chair across the table. She raised her shot glass, tapped it against mine, and smiled. I closed my eyes and drank my goddamned whiskey.

Black.

The sound of an engine turning over, streetlights and laughter and double white lines.

Black.

I was standing in an unfamiliar apartment.

"Where are we?" I said.

"My place," said Lynn or was it Linda? "Adams Morgan."

"What about my car?"

"Out on Belmont," she said with a laugh. "And by the way, you drove great."

I stood in a living room, where a long-haired girl and a long-haired guy were sitting on a couch, cleaning pot in the lid of a shoe box. A singer wailed over some very druggy guitar.

"So what are we listenin' to?" I said to the guy.

"Smashin' Pumpkins," the guy said.

"I want to listen to this kinda shit, I'll dig out some old Sabbath albums. 'Masters of Reality' maybe."

"Yeah?" the guy said. "Well, you had your day, didn't you? Anyhow, your girlfriend's waitin' for you, ace." He and the long-haired girl laughed.

I found my girlfriend in the bedroom, lying on a floor mattress, nude above the waist, her hands locked behind her head. The room was lit by candles, and a stick of incense burned by the bed. I climbed out of my shorts clumsily and pulled my T-shirt over my head.

"I didn't bring anything," I said.

"That's not what I had in mind," she said, pushing her huge breasts together until there was a tight tunnel formed between them. "Come here, Nick."

I straddled her chest and gave her the pearl necklace she was looking for. Our shadows slashed across the wall in the dancing light.

Black.

THE ROOM WAS DARK. Through the slots in the curtains, I could see that the sky had not yet begun to turn. I rose and sat naked on the edge of the bed, listened to the steady snore of the woman next to me, waited for my eyes to adjust to the absence of light. I made my way to the bathroom, put my mouth under the faucet, and drank water until I thought I would be sick. I took a shower, scrubbing my genitals and fingers until I was certain that her smell was gone, then dried off and found my clothes lying in a heap by the bed. I dressed in the light of the bathroom and left the room.

Out on the stoop of her apartment building, I looked down the slope of Belmont, saw my car parked at the bottom of the street. My stomach flipped and I took a seat on a step. I leaned my head against a black iron railing and closed my eyes. A woman and a man argued violently in Spanish not very far away.

Black.

I woke up behind the wheel of my car. My keys were in my hand. The windows were rolled up and the heat was hideous, my hair and clothing wet with the smell of alcohol and nicotine. I turned the ignition and drove northeast into Shepherd Park.

I entered my apartment and looked into my room. Lyla slept in my bed. I fed my cat, took another cold shower, and got under the covers, turning onto my side. Lyla moved herself against me and draped a forearm over my shoulder, brushing her fingers across my chest.

"You okay?" she said drowsily.

"I'm fine."

"I was worried about you."

"I'm here now, baby. Relax."

She drifted off, holding me. I fell to sleep knowing we were done.

FOURTEEN

SLEPT UNTIL noon and woke with a head full of dust and a stomach full of rocks. Lyla had gone, left some chocolate kisses on top of a note in the kitchen. The note said that she'd call me later and that she loved me.

I ate the chocolate out on my stoop, where I drank the day's first cup of coffee and sat with the worn copy of *D.C. This Week* spread open between my feet. My cat rolled on the grass in the high sun. The phone rang inside my apartment. I went back into the living room and picked it up.

"Nick!"

"LaDuke."

"You sound like you just woke up."

"I'm just sitting here, going through the classifieds in the newspaper. One of the two we found at Calvin's and Roland's."

"Anything?"

"Uh-uh. A few ads, escort services specializing in young

black males, that kind of thing. They could be solicitations for prostitution, but, I don't know, there's more than a few of them, and to me they look too organized, too legit."

"Maybe you're looking in the wrong place," LaDuke said.

"Say what?"

"You're assuming that Calvin and Roland were using the personals to sell themselves, maybe set up prospective johns for some sort of roll. Right?"

"That's what I was looking for, yeah."

"Well, I've been thinking about it—maybe our boys were the buyers, not the sellers. Maybe they read an ad in there, got themselves hooked up as actors in this porno thing."

I pushed my coffee cup around on the table. "You know, Jack, you might not be as dim as you look."

"If that's some kind of compliment, then I guess I better take it."

"You pick me up at my place?"

"In an hour," he said. "Look presentable, okay?"

"Sure thing, Boy Scout. See you then."

After several forced sets of push-ups and sit-ups, I took a long, cold shower. I didn't feel much better, but I felt human. LaDuke swung by right on the button, and I went out to meet him with one of the newspaper copies in my hand. I got into the passenger side of the big Ford and dropped the tabloid on the seat between us. LaDuke wore a starched white shirt with a solid black tie. He had shined his thick black oxfords, the only shoes I had ever seen on his feet. I nodded at the newspaper on the seat.

"Good call," I said. "I was looking in 'Adult Services,' when I should have been looking under 'Wanted.' I found a couple of items in there...could be something. One's a photographer looking for healthy young black males to pose nude. The other one's got a local filmmaker looking for young African-American males for his next production."

"Might be a winner," LaDuke said.

"We'll check it out later," I said. "Let's go."

LaDuke looked me over. "You look like hell, you know it?"

"Thanks for the observation."

"You ought to slow it down a little, Nick."

"Just turn this piece of shit over," I said. "We gotta go pick up Darnell."

At the Spot, Darnell was finishing his load of lunch dishes, so LaDuke and I had a seat at the bar. Boyle sat alone, a beer and a Jack in front of him, two stools away from Mel, who softly sang along to the Stylistics coming from the deck. I ordered a quick beer from Mai, just to steady my hands. It worked. Mai put an ice water on the bar, and I chased the beer with that. LaDuke got up and went to talk to Anna, who was cleaning her tables in the other room. Boyle looked down the bar in my direction.

"Who's your friend?" he said.

"Guy's name is LaDuke," I said.

"I knew that," Boyle said. "Johnson's been talking to Shareen Lewis. She told him all about him—and you."

"So why'd you ask?"

"Just wanted to see how deep you'd go in your lies, Nick. You keep playing me, tellin' me you've got nothing on the case. But you and Boy Detective over there are working on some kind of angle, am I right?"

"I said I'd square it with you when I had something concrete."

"Sure you will."

"How about you? Johnson get any more evidence that Roland and Calvin were moving drugs?"

"I'm done feeding you information," Boyle said. "You're on your own."

"Okay," I said. "Okay."

Darnell came out of the kitchen, rubbing his hands dry on a rag. I left a few bucks for Mai and got LaDuke's attention. He said good-bye to Anna and tossed Darnell the keys to the Ford. The three of us went out the door.

*   *   *

DARNELL PARKED NEAR THE entrance to Goode's White Goods, and soon afterward McGinnes came goose-stepping out into the lot. He got into the back with LaDuke, introduced himself, said hello to Darnell. Darnell, his hands on the wheel, gave McGinnes an amused smile.

"Where's Donny?" I said.

"He'll be along," McGinnes said, and just as he got the words out, Donny came through the double glass doors. He was wearing some sort of green double-knit slacks and two-inch heeled shoes, with a green shirt and green tie combo to complete the hookup.

"I remember this movie," Darnell said, "when I was a kid. Had Sammy Davis, Jr., in it, playing some cavalry guy, like Sammy was supposed to be Gunga Din and shit."

"*Sergeants Three,*" I said.

"With all this green this cat's wearin'," Darnell said, "kind of reminds me of Sammy, tryin' to be Robin Hood."

"Donny's all right," McGinnes said.

Darnell said, "Must be one of those Baltimore brothers, with those threads and shit."

"Here," McGinnes said, passing a few spansules over the front seat, pressing them into my hand. "Eat one of these, man. It'll do you right."

"What is it?"

"Make you go, Jim," McGinnes said.

"Maybe later." I stashed the speed in my pocket.

Donny got in the car, next to McGinnes in the backseat. He shook hands with everyone, gave Darnell a different shake than he gave everyone else. Darnell rolled his eyes and put the Ford in gear.

On the way to the Hot Plate, I gave everyone some background and general instructions. I wasn't worried about McGinnes—I knew he would pick up on the rhythms once we got started. LaDuke sat quietly next to the open window while McGinnes and Donny bantered verbally over who would play what roles when the time came.

"Listen," I said, "we're all supposed to be equal, management-wise—that's the whole point of this thing. This Bernie guy, he likes to feel like he's being courted by a bunch of execs, get it?"

"I get it," Donny said. "But I ain't never run down this kind of game before. Understand what I'm sayin'?"

"Hey, Donny, if you're not comfortable—"

"I'll be all right. It's just that, you know, I don't want anybody thinkin' I'm some kind of *punk*. See what I'm sayin'?"

"We're just businessmen selling this stuff," I said. "So relax."

"'Cause I ain't no punk," Donny said, unable to give it up. "I ain't never had nothin' back there didn't belong back there. Fact is, I'm so tight, it hurts me to fart."

"Shit," Darnell mumbled.

"Now, women?" Donny continued, moving forward and leaning his arms on the front seat. "I *get* me some women. Had me this girl last night, this freak from Dundalk?"

"Told you he was from Baltimore," Darnell said.

"Anyway," Donny said, "in the beginning, this freak didn't want to come over to my place, on account of I'm on the...slight side. Maybe she thought that meant I was light in other ways, too. See what I'm sayin'? But when I unspooled that motherfucker"—and here Donny imitated the sound of a line being cast—"the freak says, 'Goddamn, Donny, where'd a little man like you get so much dick?'"

"Step on it," LaDuke said, "will you, Darnell?" Darnell gave the Ford some gas.

THE ONLY SIGN OUTSIDE the Hot Plate said NEWSPAPERS, MAGAZINES, BOOKS. The address, however, jibed with the one given to me by Gerry Abromowitz, so Darnell parked the car on K. We left him sitting behind the wheel, reading a paperback on the teachings of Islam, and went inside the shop.

The first section of the store featured racks of daily

newspapers and magazines, weeklies and monthlies, all of the legitimate variety. The clerk behind the counter did not so much as look up when we entered. We went through another open door, into a considerably livelier and more populated section where the real business was being conducted.

A couple of employees—one skinny, one fat, there never seemed to be middle physical ground in places like these—were ringing up sales and keeping an eye on the display floor. Donny immediately went to a rack containing shrink-wrapped magazines whose covers almost exclusively featured women with extralarge lungs. McGinnes seemed more interested in the business aspect of things, wondering aloud how the "profit pieces" were merchandised. LaDuke stood with his hands in his pockets, clearly disgusted at the sight of middle-aged men eye-searching the mags that specialized in man-boy action. Most of the activity seemed to be in that area of the store. I waited for one of the clerks to get free, the pock-faced, skinny one, and announced myself. The kid punched an in-house extension, spoke to someone on the other end, pointed to another open door, and told me we could "go on." I got everyone together and we went through to the back.

We entered a large warehouse arrangement where three men sat in an office area in front of computers, taking orders over the phone. I guessed that the mail-order end of things was Tobias's biggest number, the on-line factor a big element in the company's growth, a way for pedophiles and other pervs to home-shop and network coast to coast without fear of exposure. Progress.

Bernard Tobias stepped out from a row of shelves. He was short and dumpy, but clean, the kind of man who has a wife and kids and a house in Kemp Mill or Hillandale, complete with ashtrays stolen from Atlantic City hotels and clown prints hung on the bathroom walls. He would have told you that he was providing a service, a form of release for those "poor slobs" who "have a problem" with kids, and that maybe, just maybe, it was safer to sell a magazine to a guy who could take it home and jerk off on some boy's photograph, rather than have him out prowling the local video arcade, trying to hand quarters out to someone's son. I hadn't come here to judge him, though, only to get some information: I smiled warmly and shook his hand.

"Ron Roget," I said.

"Bernie Tobias," he said, and looked expectantly at the rest of my group.

"My associates," I said, presenting them with an elaborate swing of my hand. "Mr. Franco, Mr. Magid, and Mr. Jefferson."

The names were characters from the film *The Dirty Dozen*. After a pointless argument on the drive over—McGinnes wanted to be Jefferson, but Donny, of course, wouldn't let him—we had agreed on the aliases.

"I've heard of you guys," Bernie said, scratching his head.

"Of course you have," Donny said. "We're large."

"Follow me," Bernie said, and we all walked through the warehouse aisles to an open area that looked like a small-timer's idea of a meeting room. We took seats around a shiny oval table, with Tobias in the sole chair with arms. There was a desk near the table. Plaques of some sort hung on cinder block. A wooden shelf over the desk contained a row of trophies.

"Thank you for seeing us," I said. "I can see you're very busy."

"Business is good," Bernie said, his fingers locked and resting on his ample belly. "You say you guys are out of Philly?"

"South and Main," Donny said.

"I'd give you a card," I said, "but the truth is, we didn't come prepared for this. We're on a kind of vacation here."

"A retreat," McGinnes said.

"Down south," I said.

"Miami," LaDuke said, probably just wanting to hear his own voice.

"*South* Miami," Donny said, as if he had ever been out of the Baltimore-Washington corridor. "South Beach."

"We got a boat down there," McGinnes said.

"A yacht," said Donny.

"So," I said, "we were passing through town, heading south, and I thought I'd look you up, make an introduction."

Bernie Tobias looked at Donny and McGinnes, back at me. "What exactly is it that you and your associates do, Mr. Roget?"

"Ron," I said.

"What do you do, Ron?"

"Like I told you on the phone, we cater to the NAMBLA crowd—man-boy discipline, that sort of thing."

"In what capacity?" Bernie said.

"We're producers," I said. "We specialize in the type of product you specialize in, on the distribution end."

"And how do you know of me?"

"The network," I said mysteriously, and with a wink.

"But we ain't no punks, now," Donny said.

"It hurts him to fart," McGinnes said, giving a quick head jerk toward Donny.

Bernie Tobias looked oddly at Donny, and then the phone rang on his desk. He excused himself, got up to answer it. LaDuke and I simultaneously shot killer looks at Donny and McGinnes. Tobias raised his voice into the phone, hung it up, and returned to his seat.

"I'm sorry," he said. "I really don't have much time today. There's a lot going on."

"We won't keep you," I said. "But I just wanted to let you in on what we're doing. As far as production values go, we're doing the highest-quality videos for the broadest customer base of anyone else on this coast."

"But I'm very satisfied with what I have," Bernie said. "I deal with only a couple of suppliers. They're local, so there's never any problem in getting merchandise quickly. And they know just what I want—this discipline thing is really taking off for me right now, I'm telling you. It's legal, too—no penetration shots, no actors who are obviously underage."

"Not obviously underage," LaDuke said.

"Well, you have to know how to straddle that line, don't you?"

"Of course," LaDuke said, struggling to form a smile.

"Your suppliers," I said, "they wouldn't be the Brontman Brothers, out of Northwest, would they?" I had seen a sign for Brontman Bakers on a storefront on the way downtown.

"No," Bernie said, distracted by Donny, who had gotten out of his chair and picked up one of Tobias's trophies off the shelf. "I don't even know them. Look, Mr.—"

"Jefferson," Donny said.

"Mr. Jefferson, please put that down, it's my son's—"

"Mr. Tobias," McGinnes said, warming to it now, "you sure you're not getting your product from the Brontmans? Because I know—I *know*—that our product has ten times the value—"

"Sir," Bernie said, "I'm getting most of my product out of Southeast right now, the Buzzard Point area. Some of my stuff comes out of an apartment house in Silver Spring. I mean, I know where my product's coming from."

"We wouldn't suggest otherwise," LaDuke said. "But aside from the fact that we offer the best value for the money, we also offer a steady supply of product. New titles every two weeks."

"I've even got you there," Bernie said. "My suppliers, they shoot one night a week, deliver me new product each Saturday. I couldn't be happier with the situation I've got."

"They shoot on what night?" I said, and saw from the exasperated look on Tobias's face that I had pushed it too far.

He breathed out slowly, let his composure creep back in. "Gentlemen, I know what you're trying to do here. You're trying to pump me for information, gain some kind of competitive advantage so you can come back to me with a program. But that's not the way I do business." Tobias smiled genially. "Listen, the next time you're in town, bring some samples of your product. We'll have a look, sit down, work on some pricing. If I like what I see, who knows, maybe we'll make a deal. In the meantime, I've really got to get back to work."

"Fair enough," I said, and pushed myself up from my chair. My associates followed suit. I shook Tobias's hand.

"Thanks for your time, Mr. Tobias," I said. "We'll be in touch."

"I'm sure you will," Bernie said. "You fellows have an unusual style, by the way."

"We try," I said. "Thanks again."

LaDuke went to shake Tobias's hand. I heard a bone crack, and Tobias jerked his hand back.

"You've got a hell of a grip," Bernie said with a nervous chuckle. "That's my golf hand, you know."

"Sorry," LaDuke said. "I'm stronger than I look, I guess." He smiled, his teeth bared like a dog's. We walked from the room, leaving Tobias staring at his hand.

DARNELL DROVE US BACK to the lot of Goode's White Goods. Donny and McGinnes got out of the car, and I got out with them. The heat rose off the black asphalt of the lot. I put fire to a smoke.

"How'd I do?" Donny said. He looked shrunken in his clothes, his mouth screwed up to one side.

"You did good," I said. "When I get paid on this one, I'll send you and Johnny a little piece of it."

"At your service." Donny looked at Darnell through the open window of the Ford and said, "My brother." Darnell smiled, and Donny stepped across the parking lot, toward the double glass doors.

McGinnes said, "Told you he was all right."

"Thanks, man. Thanks for everything."

"Hey, you and me…" McGinnes shuffled his feet. "Nothing to it." He rubbed at the bridge of his nose. "By the way, No Damn Good's got an opening on the floor. Any interest? You can't keep doing this sideline thing of yours forever."

"It's not a sideline," I said. "It's what I do."

"Right," McGinnes said, unconvinced. "Just thought I'd ask."

"You wouldn't want me to take the food out of your mouth, would you?"

"Wouldn't want that."

"Take it easy, Johnny."

"You too, Jim." McGinnes grinned. "Better get my ass back inside. The little bastard's probably in there stealing all my ups."

He put his hands in his pockets and walked away, whistling through his teeth. I hit my cigarette, dropped it, and ground it under my shoe.

We dropped Darnell back at the Spot, and afterward LaDuke took me back to my place. We sat out front, the Ford idling at the curb.

"Wish we could have gotten more out of Tobias," LaDuke said.

"We got everything we could," I said. "And anyway, I think we got plenty."

"Like?"

"Just a feeling. This thing's getting ready to bust."

"You think?"

"Yeah." I put my hand on the door latch and lightly tapped his arm. "You did all right back there, you know it?"

"I'm catching on."

"I'll call you in the morning," I said. "We'll put it in gear."

"Why not tonight?"

"'Cause I got to go see somebody right now."

"On the case?"

"No."

"What, then?"

"Look, LaDuke, you don't have to worry. I'm not gonna leave you behind. We're partners, right?"

LaDuke smiled, sat a little straighter behind the wheel. I got out of the car, rapped the roof with my knuckles, and walked toward my apartment as he pulled out from the curb. Some electric guitar and a screaming vocal cut the quiet of the early-evening air. If I hadn't known better, I would have sworn LaDuke had turned his car radio on, and was playing it loud as he drove away.

FIFTEEN

M Y UNCLE COSTA is not my uncle. He is not my father's brother, or my grandfather's, or a distant cousin, and I'm fairly certain that there is none of his blood running through my veins. But to Greeks, this is a minor detail. Costa is as much a part of my family as any man can be.

Ten years younger than my grandfather, Big Nick Stefanos, Costa came to this country from a village outside Sparta. Though I've not confirmed it, it's been said that Costa killed his sister's groom over a dowry dispute the night after their wedding and then left Greece the following day. He worked for many years as a grille man in my grandfather's coffee shop downtown and lived above it in a small apartment with his wife, Toula. In the forties, my grandfather hit the number in a big way and staked Costa in his own store, a lunch counter on 8th and K.

Children tend to force assimilation in their immigrant parents, and as Costa and Toula were childless, Costa never fully embraced the American culture. But he loved his adopted country as much as any native-born, and he was especially enamored of the opportunities available for men who had the desire to work. Fiercely loyal to my grandfather, he remained friends with him until Big Nick's death. I saw Costa on holidays after that and spoke to him on the phone several times a year. The last time he phoned, it was to tell me that he had cancer and had only a short time to live.

The beer in my hand wouldn't help Costa, but it would make it easier for me to look at him. I sat in my car on Randolph Street, off 13th, in front of Costa's brick row house. When I had taken the last swig, I crushed the can and tossed it over my shoulder behind the seat. I locked my car and took the steps up to his concrete porch, where I rang the bell. The door opened, and a handsome, heavy-hipped woman stood in the frame.

"Nick Stefanos. I'm here to see my uncle."

"Come on in."

I entered the small foyer at the base of the stairs. The air was still, as it always was in Costa's house, but added to the stillness now was the distinct stench of human excrement. The nurse closed the door behind me and caught the look on my face.

"He's nearly incontinent," she said. "He has been for some time."

"That smell."

"I do the best I can."

I could hear Costa's voice, calling from his bedroom up the stairs. He was speaking in Greek, saying that his stomach was upset, asking for some ginger ale to settle it.

"He wants some soda," I said.

"I can't understand him," she said, "when he's talkin' Greek."

"I'll get it for him," I said, and moved around her.

I went to the kitchen, dark except for some gray light bleeding in from the screens of the back porch. Two cats scattered when I walked in, then one returned and rubbed against my shin as I found the ginger ale and poured it into a glass. There were probably a dozen cats around the house, on the porch or in the dining room or down in the basement. Generations of them had lived here and out in the alley; Costa collected them like children.

The nurse sat in a chair in the foyer as I walked out of the kitchen. She fumbled in her pack for a cigarette. I struck a match and gave her a light.

"Thanks."

"I'll just go on up," I said.

"There's a metal cup by the bed. He probably needs to urinate. You might want to help him out. He won't wear those panties from the hospital. You know I tried—"

"I'll take care of it."

I went up the stairs, made an abrupt turn on the narrow landing, and entered his room. Several icons hung on florid, yellowed wallpaper and a candle burned in a red glass holder next to the door. A window-unit air conditioner set on low produced the only sound in the room. Costa was in his bed, underneath the sheets. Even though he was covered, I could see that he had atrophied to the size of a boy.

"Niko," he said.

"Theo Costa."

I pulled a chair up next to the bed and had a seat. With my help, he managed to sit up, leaning on one knotty elbow. I put the glass to his lips and tilted it. His Adam's apple bobbed as he closed his eyes and drank.

"Ah," he said, his head falling back to the pillow, two bulged yellow eyes staring at the ceiling.

"You gotta take a leak now?"

"Okay."

I found the metal cup on the nightstand, pulled back the covers on the bed. He couldn't have weighed more than a hundred pounds. Pustulated bedsores ringed the sides of his legs and the sagging flesh of his buttocks. Freshly scrubbed patches of brown, the remnants of his own waste, stained the bed. I took his uncircumcised penis in my hand and laid the head of it inside the lip of the cup. Costa relaxed his muscles and filled the cup.

"Goddamn," he said. "That's good."

I put the cup back on the nightstand and pulled the covers over his chest. He left his arms out and took my hand. The American flag tattoo on his painfully thin forearm had faded to little more than a bruise.

"Does it hurt much?" I said.

Costa blinked. "It hurts pretty good."

"That nurse taking care of you?"

"She's all right. Now, the one before, the other one?" He made a small sweep of his hand, as if the hand had kicked her ass out the door. "But this one, she's okay. Has two kids; she's raising them by herself. She's a hard worker. This one, she's okay." Costa licked his blistered lips.

"You want some more ginger ale?"

"I'd like a real goddamn drink, that's what. But I can't. It hurts, after."

"I'll get you one if you want."

"So you can have one, too, eh?"

"What do you mean?"

"You been drinkin' already. I can smell it on you."

"I had a beer on the way over. Can't get anything by that nose of yours."

"You got a nose on you, too, goddamn right."

He laughed, then coughed behind the laugh. I waited for him to settle down.

"You know what?" he said. "I think I had a pretty good life, Niko."

"I know you did."

"I had a good woman, worked hard, stayed here in this house, even after everyone else got scared and moved away. You know, I'm the last white man on this block."

"I know."

"I did a few bad things, Niko, but not too many."

"You talking about your brother-in-law, in Greece?"

"Ah. I don't give a damn nothing about him. No, I mean here, in the old days, with your *papou*, before you were born. We got into some trouble, had a gunfight with some guys. Lou DiGeordano and a Greek named Peter Karras, they were with us. I was thinking of it this morning. Trying to think of the bad things I did. Trying to remember."

"What happened?"

"It doesn't matter. Your *papou*, he stopped that kind of business when you came to him. I stopped, too." Costa turned his head in my direction. "You're going to come into some money, Niko, when I go. You know it?"

"What are you talking about?"

"Your *papou*—everything he had, the money from the businesses, what he made from the real estate, everything, it's going to come to you. I've been taking care of it, just like he had it in his will. I swear on his grave, I haven't touched a goddamn penny."

"I thought it all went to his son in Greece—my father."

"*You* are your *papou's* son. He felt it, told me so many times. He always said that the best Greeks were the ones who got on the boats and came to America. It was the lazy ones that stayed behind. He thought his own son was not ready to inherit his money." Costa grimaced. "He was waiting for you to grow up a little bit before he gave it to you, that's all."

"I don't want his money," I said as a cold wave of shame washed through me.

"Sure you don't," he said. "But money makes life easier. Anyway, when the lawyers get through with it, and Uncle Sam, there's not going to be much left, believe me. So take it. It's what he wanted."

Costa sucked air in sharply and arched his back. I squeezed his hand. He breathed out slowly, then relaxed.

"You better get some rest," I said.

"I got plenty time to rest," he said.

"Go to sleep, Theo Costa."

"Niko?"

"Sir?"

"Enjoy yourself, boy. I can remember the day I stepped off the boat onto Ellis Island. I can still smell it, like I stepped off that boat this morning. It's like I blinked my eyes and now I'm old. It goes, Niko. It goes too goddamn fast."

He closed his eyes. Slowly, his breathing became more regular. Some time later, his hand relaxed in mine and he fell to sleep. Sitting there, I found myself hoping that he would die, just then. But he wasn't ready. For whatever reason, he held on until the fall.

When the light outside the window turned from gray to black, I left the room and walked back down the stairs. I went to the dining room and found the liquor cabinet, near an ornate wall mirror covered with a blanket. Costa's nurse sat at the dining room table, smoking a cigarette. I took a bottle of five-star Metaxa and couple of glasses and had a seat across from her. I poured her a brandy, then one for me. We drank together without a word, beneath the dim light of a chandelier laced with cobwebs and already shrouded in dust.

WHEN I RETURNED TO my apartment, I saw that Lyla had left a message on my machine. I phoned her and she asked if I wanted some company. I told her that it might not be a good idea.

"What, have you got something else happening?"

"No," I said. "I'm just a little tired, that's all."

"Maybe tomorrow night, huh?"

"Tomorrow's looking kind of busy for me."

"Nick, what's going on?"

"Nothing," I said, and shifted gears. "Hey, how'd it go with your editor yesterday?"

"It went all right," she said, and then there was a fat chunk of silence.

"What happened?"

"It was about that day, after we had lunch. In Chinatown?"

"Sure."

"Well, I had a few wines that day, if you remember, and then I went back to the office and finished off this story I was working on. Usually, I wait, go back to it, check it for style and all that. But I was on a deadline, so I turned it in right after I finished it."

"And?"

"It was all fucked up, Nick. Jack gave me an earful about it, and he was right. It was really bad."

"So what's the mystery? You shouldn't be drinkin' when you're writing copy, you know that."

"That's some advice," Lyla said, "coming from a guy who stumbled in this morning after sunup and couldn't even get out of his own pants."

"That's me, baby. It doesn't have to be you."

"Anyway, Jack hit me right between the eyes with it. Said I drink too much, that maybe I've got a problem. What do you think?"

"You said yourself, I'm not the one to ask. All's I know, you wanted to be a journalist since you were a kid. I guess you've got to figure out what you want more. I mean, fun's fun, but the days of wine and roses have to come to an end."

"'The Days of Wine and Roses'?" she said. "The Dream Syndicate."

"That's my line," I said.

Lyla said, "Yeah, I beat you to it. I knew you were going to say it."

"It only shows, maybe you been with me too long."

"I don't think so, Nick."

"Lyla, I've really got to go."

"You sure there's nothing wrong?"

"Nothing wrong," I said. "Bye."

I had a couple of beers and went to bed. My sleep was troubled, and I woke before dawn with wide-open eyes. I dressed and drove down to the river, looking for a crazy black man in a brilliant blue coat. Nothing. I watched the sun rise, then drove back to Shepherd Park.

After I made coffee, I phoned Jack LaDuke.

"LaDuke!"

"Nick!"

"Get over here, man. Early start today."

"Half hour," he said, and hung up the phone.

I found my Browning Hi-Power, wrapped in cloth in the bottom of my dresser. I cleaned and oiled it, loaded two magazines, and replaced the gun in the drawer. Just as I closed the drawer, LaDuke knocked on my front door.

SIXTEEN

"NOTHIN'!" LADUKE SAID as he hung up the phone in my apartment.

We had just called the first prospect from the classified section of *D.C. This Week*. LaDuke had done the talking, and he had put too much into it in my opinion, his idea of some swish actor.

"What'd he say?"

"Guy turned out to be legit. Some professor at Howard, doing a theatrical feature on street violence in D.C., trying to show the 'other side,' whatever that means. He was looking for young blacks males to play high school athletes sidetracked by drugs."

"All right, don't get discouraged; we've got another one here."

LaDuke put his hand on the phone. "What's the number?"

"Uh-uh," I said. "I'm doin' this one."

I checked the number in the ad—this was the photographer, in search of healthy young black males—and pulled the phone over my way. My cat jumped up onto my lap as I punched the number into the grid.

"Yes?" said an oldish man with a faintly musical lilt in his voice.

"Hi," I said. "I'm calling about an ad I saw in *D.C. This Week*, about some photography you were doing?"

"That's a pretty old ad."

"I was at a friend's place; he had a back issue lying around. I was browsing through it—"

"And you don't sound like a young black male."

"I'm not. But I *am* healthy. And I've done some modeling, and a little acting. I was wondering if you were exclusive with this black thing."

The man didn't answer. Another voice, stronger, asked him a question in the background, and he put his hand over the receiver. Then he came back on the line.

"Listen," he said. "We're not doing still photography here, not really. I mean, you got any idea of what I'm looking for?"

"Yes," I said. "I think I know what you're doing."

"How. *How* do you know?"

"Well, I just assumed from the ad—"

"An assumption won't get you in. And like I said, that's an old ad. You have a reference?"

"I'd rather not say."

"If you know what's going on, then someone referred you. No reference, no audition." I didn't respond. The man said, "If you've got no reference, this conversation's over."

I took a shot. "Eddie Colorado," I said, then waited.

"Okay," the man said. "You come by tonight, we'll have a look at you."

"I don't think I can make it tonight."

"Then forget it, for now. We're shooting tonight, and we only shoot once a week."

"I'll be there," I said. "I'll make it somehow. You're down in Southeast, right?"

"That's right. A warehouse, on the corner of Potomac and Half. The gate looks locked, but it's not. What's your name?"

"Bobby," I said, picking one blindly. "What time?"

"No time. We'll be here all night." The phone clicked dead.

I looked somberly at LaDuke. Then I broke into a smile and slapped his open palm.

"You got something?" he said, standing up abruptly from his chair.

"Yeah. Get your shit, LaDuke. We're going for a ride."

"WHY'D YOU HAVE THE smarts to mention Eddie Colorado?" LaDuke said. We were driving east on M in my Dodge, the morning sun blasting through the windshield. The wind was pushing LaDuke's wavy hair around on top of his square head.

"No other option," I said. "He asked for a reference, and that's the only name that fits with Roland and Calvin. It was a lucky call. Apparently, Eddie's referring potential movie stars to this guy, whoever he is. Eddie's been siphoning it off from both ends."

"Eddie. That mother*fucker*. I'd like to go back there and fuck him up, too."

"Relax, LaDuke. Guys like Eddie dry up and blow away. We've got to concentrate on Roland now."

"You think this is it?"

"Too many other things are falling into place. Bernie Tobias talked about the Southeast location and the-one-night-a-week shoot. This guy I just talked to on the phone, he confirmed it."

"Where we going?"

"Check the place out."

"We goin' in right now?"

"No. Chances are, even if this is the place, Roland's not there yet. I want to see it, then we're gonna find out who owns the warehouse, see if he's got any information on his tenants."

I put a cigarette to my lips, hit the lighter. LaDuke, nervous as a cat, nodded at the pack on the dash.

"Give me one of those things," he said.

"You really want one?"

"Nah," he said. "I guess not."

Past the projects, we cut a right off M and went back into the warehouse district that sits on a flat piece of dusty land between Fort McNair and the Navy Yard. It was midmorning. Trucks worked gravel pits, drivers pulled their rigs up to loading docks, and government types drove their motor-pool sedans back toward Buzzard Point. In the daytime, this area of town was as populated and busy as any other; at night, there was no part of the city more deathly quiet or dark.

"That's it," LaDuke said, and I parked along a high chain-link fence where Potomac Avenue cut diagonally across Half.

The warehouse was squat, brick, and windowless, as undistinguishable from any of the others I had seen on the way in. A double row of barbed wire was strung around the perimeter, continuing at a sliding gate. One car, a Buick Le Sabre, sat parked inside the gate. Across the street was an almost identical building, similarly fenced and wired, with windows only at two fire escapes set on opposing faces. In front of that one, two white vans were parked, advertising LIGHTING AND EQUIPMENT. Next to this warehouse stood a lot containing a conical structure, some sort of urban silo, and an idling dump truck.

"What do you think?" LaDuke said, pointing his chin toward the warehouse where the Buick sat parked.

"That's it," I said. "We know where it is now, and it's not going anywhere. We'll come back tonight."

"Lot of activity around here."

"Not at night. Used to be a couple of nightclubs, ten, fifteen years back, that jumped pretty good. But nothing now." I pushed the trans into drive.

"Where now?" LaDuke said.

"Office of Deeds," I said. "We find out who collects the rent."

*   *   *

THE OFFICE OF THE Recorder of Deeds sat around 5th and D, near Judiciary Square, the area of town that contained the city's courts and administrative facilities. The building has a funny old elevator that doesn't quite make it to the top floors; to get to where the records are kept, you have to get off the lift and take the stairs the rest of the way. LaDuke and I did it.

There was one disinterested woman working a long line, but I was lucky to see a bar customer of mine, a real estate attorney by the name of Durkin, sitting in a wooden chair, waiting for his number to be called. He also had a copy of the *Lusk's Directory*, a crisscross land reference guide, in his lap. I borrowed it from him and promised him a free warm Guinness Stout—his drink—the next time he was by the Spot. Durkin tipped the fedora that he wore even indoors and gave me the book. By the time my microfiche had been retrieved from the files, I knew enough with the help of the *Lusk's* to have the name of the landlord who owned the warehouse at Potomac and Half. The name was Richard Samuels.

From there, it wasn't a stretch to get an address and phone. If Samuels was like every minimogul/land baron I've met, he could not have resisted putting his name on his own company. He would have told you the ID made good business sense, but it was as much ego as anything else. And his name *was* on the company—Samuels Properties was listed in the first phone book we hunted down, right outside the District Building; the address matched that printed on the deed. LaDuke flipped me a quarter and I rang him up.

"Samuels Properties," said the old lady's voice on the other end.

"Metropolitan Police," I said, "calling for Richard Samuels." LaDuke shook his head and rolled his eyes.

"Let me see if he's on the line." She put me on hold, came

back quickly. "If this is about the fund-raising drive, Mr. Samuels has already sent the check—"

"Tell him it's about his property at Potomac and Half."

"Hold on." More waiting, then: "I'll put you through."

Another voice, deep and rich, came on the line. "Yes, how may I help you?"

"My name is Nick Stefanos—"

"Officer Stefanos?"

"No."

"You're not a cop?"

"Private."

"Well, then, you've misrepresented yourself. I guess we have nothing to talk about."

"I think we do. You might be interested in some activity going on in your property on Half Street in Southeast. And if you're not interested, maybe Vice—"

"Vice?" His tone lost its edge. "Listen, Mr. Stefanos, I'm certainly not aware of any illegal activities, not on Half Street or on any of my properties. But I am interested, and I'm willing to listen to what you've got to say."

"My partner and I would like to see you this morning. The conversation would be confidential, of course."

"That would be fine," Samuels said. He confirmed the address.

"We'll be right over," I said, and hung up the phone.

LaDuke scrunched up his face. "You identified yourself as a cop, Nick. This guy Emmanual—"

"It's *Samuels*."

"He could turn us in."

"Come on, LaDuke. We're standing at the door. Let's go see what the man's got to say."

THE OFFICE OF SAMUELS Properties was on a street of commercially zoned row houses just north of Washington Circle, in the

West End. We parked the Dodge in a lot owned by Blackie Auger, one of D.C.'s most visible Greeks, and walked to the house. Samuels's office was on the second floor, up a curving line of block steps.

We had expected the geriatric receptionist, but it was Samuels himself who answered the door. He looked to be reasonably fit, a thin, silver-haired man at the very end of his middle years, with prosperity—or the illusion of it—apparent in every thread of his clothes. He wore a nonvented Italian-cut suit over a powder blue shirt with a white spread collar, and a maroon tie featuring subtle geometrics, gray parallelograms shaded in blue to pick up the blue off the suit. His face was long, sharply featured, and angular, except for his lips, which were thick and damp and oddly red, reminding me somehow of a thinly sliced strawberry.

"Mr. Stefanos?" he said in that fine brandy baritone.

"Yes. My partner, Jack LaDuke." The two of them shook hands.

"Please, come in."

We followed him through the reception area, low-lit and deeply carpeted, with stained wood trim framing Williamsburg blue walls. Next was his office, the same cozy deal, but with a bigger desk, walls painted a leafy green, and a window view that gave onto the street. LaDuke and I sat in two armchairs he had arranged in front of his desk. Samuels had a seat in his cushioned broad-backed chair and wrapped his hand around a thick Mont Blanc pen.

"You're all alone," I said.

"Yes," he said. "My receptionist is taking lunch. For one hour each day, I field my own calls."

"It's just the two of you here?"

"It hasn't always been this way. I had a staff of six at one time, including my own in-house real estate attorney. But that was the eighties. And the eighties are over, Mr. Stefanos. The banks went through some tremendous changes near the end of the decade, as you know. When the flow of money stopped, everything stopped—all the growth. But this is a cyclical business that, by definition, adjusts itself. There are signs that the residential is coming back, and the commercial will naturally follow."

"Of course," I said, though I didn't have a clue. LaDuke had tented his hands, his elbows on the arms of his chair, and he was tapping both sets of fingers together at the tips.

"So how can I help you?" Samuels said.

"I'm working on a murder investigation," I said. "As I mentioned to you on the phone, I've been privately retained. Through a series of interviews—I won't bore you with the details—I've come to believe that there might be some criminal activity going on in your warehouse property at Potomac and Half."

"You mentioned that it might be related to Vice."

"For starters. I suspect pornography involving male minors. That kind of business is usually tied to something else."

Samuels frowned. "Let me say first that I'm not cognizant of any such activity in any of my properties. If what you're claiming is a reality, however, it disturbs me. It disturbs me a great deal. You can never anticipate this kind of thing, not totally. All my potential tenants are interviewed, but as long as the rent checks arrive in a reasonably timely manner and there are no major physical problems with the property, you lose touch. Often a tenant will sublet without my knowledge and—"

"We'd like to get in," LaDuke said sharply.

Samuels kept his dignity and his eyes on me. "I pulled the file after you called, Mr. Stefanos." He fingered the edges of some papers on his desk. "The tenants on the lease are using the area both as a silk-screen production house for T-shirts and as a storage facility."

"Would it be possible to get in there and talk to them?"

"Mr. Stefanos, in my business, in any business, in fact, control is very important. If I could both own these properties and run my own profit centers out of them—in other words, if I could control every aspect in the chain, all the way down the line—believe me, I'd do it. But unfortunately, I can't. So essentially I'm in a partnership arrangement with my tenants, for better or worse. And I have to honor that partnership. So you can see why I just can't let you in there, willy-nilly, on the basis of some unsubstantiated accusation."

"But you also wouldn't want the inconvenience, and publicity, of an official police intervention."

Samuels said, "And neither would you. You say you're privately retained—if the cops, in effect, solve whatever it is you're working on, wouldn't that essentially make you unemployed?"

"We're talking about boys," LaDuke said with obvious impatience. "They're being forced against their will—"

"Hold on a second," Samuels said, his voice rising. He turned a framed photograph around on his desk so that it faced LaDuke. In the frame was a family picture—the businessman's favorite prop—of Samuels, his wife, and two children, a teenaged boy and girl. Samuels regained his composure. "You see this? I'm a father, young man. Now, I didn't say I wouldn't help you. I'm only saying that we have to do this properly. Do you understand?"

LaDuke didn't answer. I said, "What did you have in mind?"

"I'm going to speak to my attorney this afternoon. We'll see how we can work this out. I'm thinking maybe by tomorrow, we'll be able to get you in there, or at least get you some kind of answers. How can I reach you, Mr. Stefanos?"

"I'll call *you*, first thing in the morning. And thanks. I appreciate the cooperation."

We all stood then, as there was nothing else to say. Samuels showed us to the door. Out on 22nd, we walked to the Dodge.

"How'd I do?" LaDuke said.

"You gotta learn when to use the muscle and when not to. Samuels, he's not going to respond to that. He doesn't have to.

He's a developer—he probably has a relationship with every member of the city council. He could erase us, man, if we push it too hard."

"You sayin' I almost blew it?"

"You could use a little seasoning, that's all."

"You think he's gonna help us?"

"He'll help us," I said. "He's a smart man. The way I put it to him, he's got no other choice."

I drove to my apartment and cut the engine. LaDuke said that he had something to do, and I let him go. I watched his brooding face as he walked to his Ford, then I watched him drive away. Then I went inside and sorted through my mail, my cat figure-eighting my feet. The red light was blinking on my answering machine. I hit the bar.

A voice that I recognized came through the speaker: "Stefanos, this is Barry. I met you at Calvin Jeter's apartment, at his mom's? I'm the father to his sister's baby.... Anyway, I was headin' over to Theodore Roosevelt Island this afternoon. Up behind the statue, there's a trail, to the left? Down there to the end, where it comes to a T. You go straight in, on a smaller trail, down to the water, facing Georgetown. That's where I'll be. I just thought, man... I just thought you might want to talk. Like I say... *I* don't know. That's where I'll be."

I walked quickly from the apartment, the sound of the machine rewinding at my back.

SEVENTEEN

T HEODORE ROOSEVELT ISLAND is a nature preserve, eighty-eight acres of swamp, forest, and marsh in the middle of the Potomac River, between Virginia and D.C. I took the GW Parkway to the main lot and parked beside Barry's Z. A couple of immigrant fisherman sat with their rods on the banks of the Little River, and a Rollerblader traversed the lot, but typical of a midweek day in midsummer, the park looked empty.

I took the footbridge over the river, then hit a trail up a grade and into the woods, to the monument terrace. I crossed the square, walking around the seventeen-foot-high bronze statue of a waving Teddy Roosevelt that sat on a high granite base, and walked over another footbridge spanning a dry moat. Then I cut left onto a wide dirt path that wound through a forest of elm, tulip, and oak and took the path down to where it met the swamp trail that perimetered the island. I stayed straight on in, toward the water. Barry was there, wearing a white T-shirt and shorts, sitting on a fallen tree, beneath a maple that had rooted at the eroded bank.

"Hey, Barry."

"Hey, man."

I sat on the log, my back against the trunk of the maple. Barry watched me as I shook a cigarette out of my deck and struck a match. I rustled the pack in his direction. He closed his eyes slowly and I put the pack away.

Across the channel, the Georgetown waterfront sprawled out, with K street running below the Whitehurst Freeway. Behind it were buildings of varying size, with the smokestack tower of the Power House rising above the skyline. To the right was the Kennedy Center; to the left, Key Bridge; and on the hill beyond, the halls of Georgetown University. Barry stared at the crew-graffitied bulkhead on the D.C. side, transfixed by it, or maybe not thinking of it at all.

"You come down here a lot?"

"Yeah," he said. "This here's my spot. Know what I'm sayin'?"

"Sure." I thought of my own place, the bridle trail off Oak Hill.

"Use to be, I'd ride my bicycle across town, come down here, when I was in junior high and shit, just look up at Georgetown U. Patrick was playin' then, and Michael Graham. I used to dream about going to Georgetown some day, playin' for Coach Thompson. 'Course, I never even thought you had to get the grades, the scores on the tests. Didn't know that shit was all decided for you, even before the first day of elementary school. Just some kind of accident, where you get born, I guess." Barry chuckled cynically to himself. "And you know what, man? I never could play no ball, anyway."

"What about now?"

"Now? I come down here just to get away. You still see some of the city on this island—the drug deal once in a while, and sometimes those sad-eyed old motherfuckers, walking around the trail, lookin' to make contact with some boy. But mostly, over here, it's clean. It makes me feel good, for a little while, anyway. And jealous, too, at the same time. I look across this river, I see the people on the freeway in their cars, and sometimes a plane goes over my head, takin' off from National—everybody but me, *goin'* somewhere."

I blew some smoke down toward the water. A breeze came off the river and picked it up. "You're not doin' so bad, Barry. You've got a steady job, and you're sticking with your family. It means something, man."

"My job. You know how I feel sometimes, workin' there, with these young drug boys comin' in, parkin' their forty-thousand-dollar shit right outside the door, makin' fun of me, of my uniform?"

"I know it can't be easy."

"Then I read the *Post*, these white liberals—so-called—talkin' about this brother, wrote this book, talkin' about how he went into some *Mac*Donald's with a gun, stuck up who he called the 'Uncle Tom' behind the counter, then went to prison, got reformed and shit, became a newspaper writer himself."

"I read about it."

"That man behind the counter, he was no Uncle Tom. He was probably some young brother like me, just tryin' to do a job, maybe pay the bills for his family or have a few dollars in his pocket to take his girl out on Saturday night. And that punk calls *him* an Uncle Tom? And those white boys at the *Post*, print that magazine they got, they be glorifyin' that shit. Makes *him* wanna holler? Man, that shit makes *me* wanna holler!"

"What you're doing," I said again, "it means something."

Barry looked in my eyes. "You really believe that tired shit, don't you?"

"I do."

"I know you do. That's why I called you up. You got this one way of lookin' at things, like it's right or it's not, and nothing in between. I guess, in my own way, that's the way I got to look at things, too. I mean, somebody's got to, right?"

I hit my cigarette hard and ground it under my shoe. "What did you want to tell me, Barry?"

Barry picked up a twig lying at his feet and snapped it in his hands. "About Calvin."

"Yeah?"

"He was mulin' powder."

I felt something twist in my stomach. "For who?"

"I don't know. But I do know this: The powder's for the white man, and the rock is for the niggas. You know it, too. Even got separate laws for that shit."

"Muling it where?"

"Into the projects, man, straight to the cookin' house."

"You got names?"

"Uh-uh," Barry said. "You?"

"No. But I found out he was involved in some other things, too. Prostitution, and pornography."

"That was Roland," Barry said hatefully. "That punk."

"Roland got him into it?"

Barry nodded, spoke quietly against the sound of the current lapping at the bank. "The man in charge, the man with the drugs—whoever he is—he favored boys. Told Roland that if he and Calvin got into this...*movie* shit, they could mule the powder for him, too. Calvin came to me—he wanted the money, man, he wanted to get out of his situation in a big way, like we all do, where we live. He didn't know about that other shit, though. Calvin wasn't no punk. Roland could do it, man, without a thought, 'cause inside he always *was* a bitch. He told Calvin, 'Just do it, man—it's only lips.' I got no thing against a man who *is* that way—understand what I'm sayin'? Matter of fact, I got this cousin like that, over in Northwest, and the man is cool. But Calvin wasn't about that. I told him, 'Don't be lettin' no man suck your dick, not for money or for nothin', not if you don't want to.'"

"Calvin went ahead with it, though, didn't he?"

"The last time I saw him, he was scared."

"When was that?"

"The night he died. He told me they only did this shit once a week, and he had to make his mind up right then, or the mule job, and the money, was out. I told him not to go with Roland that night. He did, though. I got to believe he changed his mind, but too late. I think he tried to get out of the whole thing. And they doomed his ass because of it. They put a gun in his mouth and blew the *fuck* out of that boy."

I said, "And you don't know any more than that."

Barry said, "No."

I lit another cigarette and took my time smoking it, staring across the river. When I was done, I got up off the log and stood over Barry.

"I'm going back," I said.

"You go on," he said.

"Don't you have to work this afternoon?"

"I got a four o'clock shift."

I glanced at my watch. "You better come with me, then."

"Yeah," Barry said, smiling weakly. "Don't want to be late for work."

I put out my hand and helped him up. We took the trail back into the upland forest and walked across the island under a canopy of trees.

I BOUGHT A CAN of beer at the nearest liquor store and drank it on the way home. In my room, I drew the blinds, undressed, and lay down on my bed. I was sick-hot and tired, and my head was black with bad thoughts. I closed my eyes and tried to make things straight.

I woke up in a sweat, lying naked on top of my sheets. The fading light of dusk lined the spaces in my blinds. I took a shower, made a sandwich and ate it standing up, and changed into jeans and a loose-fitting short-sleeved shirt. I listened to my messages: Lyla and Jack LaDuke had phoned while I was asleep. I left a message with LaDuke's answering service, and ten minutes later he called me back.

"Nick!"

"LaDuke. Where you been?"

"I went looking for Eddie Colorado."

"And?"

"I found him."

I had a sip of water and placed the glass down on the table, within the lines of its own ring. "What'd you do to him, Jack?"

"We talked, that's all. I put an edge on it, though. I don't think Eddie's gonna be hanging around town too much longer."

"What'd you find out?"

"Roland Lewis is still alive, and still with them. Calvin tried to get out—that's what got him killed. They're filming tonight."

"I know it. I found out a few things, too. The porno's just a sideshow compared with their drug operation. Calvin and Roland were delivery boys. The cops have been following that angle. I'm not sure if they know anything about the warehouse on Half Street, not yet. We're one step ahead of them there, but it's a short step. They've got informants, and I imagine they're working them pretty good. So we don't have much time."

"Say it, man."

"I know we told Samuels we'd wait till tomorrow. But you and me, we've got to go in there...tonight. We've got to get Roland away from that place before the cops dig deep and bust that operation, put that kid into a system he'll never get out of. We'll get Roland out, get him back home, straighten his shit out then. You with me?"

"You know it."

"You got a gun?"

"The one I held on you that night. And more."

"Bring whatever you got."

"I'll be right over," he said.

"We're gonna need a driver," I said. "I'll call Darnell."

LaDuke said, "Right."

I phoned Darnell at the Spot. I gave him the Roland Lewis story and described the kind of trouble the kid was in.

"You interested?"

"First I got to get to these dishes, man."

"We'll pick you up around ten."

"Bring your boy's Ford," Darnell said. "I'll be standin' right out front."

I went into my room and got my Browning Hi-Power and the two loaded magazines from the bottom of my dresser. McGinnes's benny spansules were on my nightstand, next to my bed; I swept them off the top and dropped them in my pocket. The phone rang. I took the gun and ammunition back out to the living room. I picked up the receiver and heard Lyla's voice.

"Nick."

"Hey, Lyla."

"I've been calling you —"

"I know. Listen, Lyla, I've been busy. Matter of fact, I'm heading out the door right now."

"What's going on with you, Nick?"

"Nothing. I've got to go."

"You can't talk to me, not for a minute?"

"No."

"Don't do this to me, Nick. You're going to fuck up something really good."

"I've got to go."

"Bye, Nick."

"Good-bye."

I hung up the phone, closed my eyes tightly, said something out loud that even I didn't understand. When I opened my eyes, the red of LaDuke's taillights glowed through my screen door as the Ford pulled up along the curb. The clock on the wall read 9:40. I slapped a magazine into the butt of the nine, safe-tied the gun, and holstered it behind my back. LaDuke gave his horn a short blast. I killed the living room light and walked out to the street.

EIGHTEEN

LADUKE HAD PARKED the Ford under a dead streetlight and was standing with his backside against the car. I went to him, reached into my pocket, and pulled two of the three spansules out. I popped one into my mouth, dry-dumped it, and handed him the other.

"What's this?"

"Something to notch you up. It came from McGinnes, so it's got to be good. Eat it."

"I don't need it. I'm already wired."

"I don't need it, either. But this'll shoot us all the way through to the other end. Eat it, man."

The truth was, I did need it. And I wanted LaDuke right there with me. He looked at me curiously but swallowed the spansule.

LaDuke pushed away from the car, went to the trunk, opened it. The light inside the lid beamed across his chest. I walked over and stood next to him and looked inside. An Ithaca twelve-gauge lay on a white blanket, the edge of the blanket folded over the stock. The shotgun had been recently polished and oiled, but I could see it had been well-used; the blueing on the barrel had been rubbed down where the shooter's hand had slid along with the action of the pump.

"This ain't no turkey shoot, LaDuke."

"I know it."

"Why the Ithaca?"

"Bottom ejection. I don't need shells flyin' up in front of my eyes when I'm tryin' to make a shot."

"What, you think you got to aim that thing? For Chrissakes, just point it."

"I got something else if I want to aim."

"Put everything in the trunk and cover it. We get stopped, we're fucked."

LaDuke dropped to one knee, pulled his snub-nosed revolver from an ankle holster. In the light, I could read the words KING COBRA etched into the barrel—a .357 Colt. He dropped it on the blanket, next to the shotgun. I drew my Browning, whipped the barrel of it against the trunk light, shattered the light. We stood in darkness.

"What the hell did you do that for?" LaDuke said.

"I'll buy you a new bulb. That light was like wearing a billboard. When we get down to Southeast, it's gonna be stone-dark. We don't need the attention."

I put the Browning and the extra clip on the blanket, covered the guns, and shut the lid of the trunk.

"You coulda just unscrewed the bulb," LaDuke said.

"I wanted to break something. Come on."

WE PICKED UP DARNELL outside the Spot. He got behind the wheel, and LaDuke slid across the bench to the passenger side. I got out and climbed into the back. Darnell looked at me in the rearview and adjusted the leather kufi that sat snugly on his head.

"Where to?"

"Half Street at Potomac," I said.

"Back in there by the Navy Yard?"

"Right." I caught a silvery reflection in my side vision, a flash, or a trail. Fingers danced through my hair and something tickled behind my eyes—the familiar kick-in of the speed. Darnell pulled out from the curb.

"This Ford's got a little juice," Darnell said. "I noticed it the other day."

"A little," LaDuke said, tight-jawed now from the drug.

I lit a cigarette and drew on it deeply. "We're gonna go in like we're knocking the place over. You got that, Jack?"

"Why?"

"I'm thinking we're going to make like we're taking the kid hostage, so they think he's got nothing to do with us. They'll probably come after us. But I want to make sure they leave the kid alone."

"How're we going to get in?"

"I'm Bobby, remember? The aspiring actor. I called earlier in the day, spoke to the man in charge...like that. Assuming I get that far, you step around the corner, show your shotgun to whoever it is we're talking to, let him know what it means. After that, we'll improvise."

"Improvise?"

"You'll get into it. And...LaDuke?"

"What?"

"We get in there, don't call me by my name."

Darnell pushed the Ford down M, made a right onto Half. Off the thoroughfare, the street darkened almost immediately.

"I'm thirsty," LaDuke said quickly. "I need something to drink."

"We'll have a drink," I said. "Let's just get this done now. Then we'll drink."

"Up around there?" Darnell said.

"That's the place," I said. "Drive slow by it, then drive around the block."

The perimeter was lighted by floods. Three cars, including the Le Sabre, were parked in the surrounding lot. A heavy chain connected the gate to the main fence. As we passed, I could see a padlock dangling open on one end.

Darnell drove slowly around the block and stopped the Ford along the fence of the warehouse across the street, where the white LIGHTING AND EQUIPMENT vans were parked. I took the last spansule from my pocket and broke it open. I leaned over the front seat.

"Make a fist, LaDuke, and turn it."

He did it, his eyes pinballing in their sockets. I poured half the spansule out on the crook of his hand, then poured the other half, a tiny mound of shiny crystal, on mine. I snorted the powder off my hand and up into my nose, feeling the burn and then the drip back in my throat. LaDuke did the same. His eyes teared up right away.

"Goddamn," LaDuke said.

"Let's go," I said.

Darnell gave me one last look, and then we were out of the car. LaDuke popped the trunk, reached inside, pulled back the blanket. He holstered the revolver on his ankle, picked up the shotgun, cradled it, dropped extra shells in his pocket. I found the Browning, switched off the safety, and put one in the chamber. I slid the gun, barrel down, behind the waistband of my jeans, covered it with the tail of my shirt. We crossed the street.

The gate was a slider. I pulled the chain through the links. LaDuke pushed the gate along a couple of feet and the two of us slipped inside.

We moved quickly across the lot, over to the side of the building, where there was a steel door behind a flatbed trailer. Above the door, a floodlight blew a triangle of white light onto a two-step concrete stoop. LaDuke and I flattened ourselves against the brick side of the building, outside the area of the light. LaDuke rested the butt of the Ithaca on his knee.

"I'm all right," he said, though I hadn't asked him.

"Good," I said. "I'm going to go up on that stoop now, ring the bell."

"I wanna *move*, man."

"That's good, too. LaDuke?"

"Yeah."

"This goes off right, you won't have to use that shotgun. Hear?"

"Let's do this thing," he said.

I stepped up onto the stoop, rang a flat yellow buzzer mounted to the right of the door. I rang it once, then again, and waited. Moths fluttered around my head. My bottom teeth were welded to my top and it felt as if someone were peeling back the top of my head. A lock turned from behind the door and then the door opened.

A wiry white man stood before me, his long brown hair tied back, knife-in-skull tattoos on thin forearms, the veins throbbing on the arms like live blue rope. He had a slight mustache and a billy-goat beard, and almond-shaped, vaguely inbred eyes.

He looked me over and said, "What?"

"Hi," I said. "I'm Bobby."

And then LaDuke, wild-eyed and chalk white, jumped into the light, a frightening howl emanating from his mouth. I stepped aside and the man stepped back, reaching beneath the tail of his shirt. The almond eyes opened wide and he made a small choking sound; he knew it was too late. LaDuke swung the shotgun like he was aiming for the left-field bleachers. He hit it solid, the stock connecting high on the wiry man's cheek. The man went down on his side, all deadweight hitting the floor, no echo, no movement. When he found his breath, he began to moan.

LaDuke pumped the shotgun, pointed it one inch from the man's face.

"Don't talk unless I tell you to talk," LaDuke said. The man closed his eyes slowly, then opened them. He stared blankly ahead.

We were in a long hall that had thin metal shelving running along either side. Paints and hardware sat on the shelves. I found a rag and dampened it with turpentine. Then I went to an area where there appeared to be several varieties of rope and cord. I took a spool of the strongest-looking rope and walked back to LaDuke, picking up a cutting tool—a retractable straight-edged razor used by stock boys and artists—along the way.

"What now?" LaDuke said. He was sweating and his knuckles were white on the pump.

"Go ahead and ask the man some questions." The man's face had swelled quickly; I wondered if LaDuke had caved his cheekbone.

"What's your name?" LaDuke said.

"Sweet," the man said.

"Okay, Mr. Sweet," LaDuke said, "this is a robbery. We know about the business you're running here. We'd like all the cash money you have on hand. First we want to talk to your associates. Where are they?"

The man closed his eyes. "Straight down the hall"—he winced at the movement in his own jaw—"Straight down the hall, then right. To the end, last door on the right. Metal door."

"How many in the room?"

"Four."

"How many guns?"

"One."

I cut a long length of rope, then a shorter one. I tied Sweet's hands to his feet, behind his back. Then I stuffed the rag into his mouth and wrapped the short length of rope around his face. I tied it off behind his head and slipped the razor in the seat pocket of my jeans.

LaDuke sniffed the air. "What's that, paint thinner?"

"It won't kill him," I said. "It'll make him too dizzy to move much, though. Come on."

LaDuke took the barrel away from the man's face, rested it across his own forearm. I pulled my Browning, picked up the spool of rope, and gave LaDuke's shirt a tug.

We walked quickly down the hall, our steps quiet on the concrete floor. At the end, we made a right and went down a hall no different from the first. I had to jog a few steps to keep pace with LaDuke.

"I could run right through a fucking wall," he said.

"You're doing fine," I said. Just as I said it, we reached the last metal door on the right.

We stood there, listening to male voices behind the door; under the voices, the buzz of a caged lightbulb suspended above our heads. I looked at LaDuke and placed the spool of rope at my feet. LaDuke managed a tight smile.

I stood straight, knocked two times on the door.

Footsteps. Then: "Yes?"

"Sweet," I said with an edge.

The knob turned. When the door opened a crack, I put my instep to it and screamed. Something popped, and the man behind the door went down. LaDuke and I stepped inside.

"This is a robbery," LaDuke said.

I made a quick coverage. The man on the floor: heavy, bald, and soft, holding his mouth, blood seeping through his fingers, repeating, "Oh, oh, oh…" A black man, mid-thirties, sat on a worktable set against a cinder-block wall. He watched us with amusement and made no movement at all. Two shirtless actors stood in front of a tripoded camera, in the center of a triangular light arrangement, a spot and a couple of fills. The first actor, who wore a tool belt around his bare waist, could have been the star of any soap, some housewife's idea of a stud, all show muscles, his plump mouth open wide. The second actor, the only one of them with the nerve or the stupidity to scowl, was a young black man, thin and long-featured — Roland Lewis, no question.

LaDuke motioned the barrel of the shotgun at the pretty

actor. "First, you get down, lie flat, facedown. Don't hurt your-self, now."

"Better do it, Pretty Man," the black man said.

"This isn't what you think," Pretty Man said. "This is just a job. You think I'm some kind of faggot? I have a girlfriend...."

The black man laughed. I kept my gun dead on him.

"Get down," LaDuke said, "and put your face right on the concrete." Pretty Man got down.

"You have a gun," I said to the black man. "Pull it slow, by the barrel, and slide it to the end of the table."

"Now what makes you think that I have a gun?" the black man said.

"I talked to your friend Sweet. He talked back."

"Sweet?" The black man smiled. "I thought you were Sweet. You said you were Sweet, just before you came in."

"No," I said. "I'm not Sweet."

"Then where's Sweet?" said the black man.

"We put him to sleep," said LaDuke.

"He ain't gonna like that, when he wakes up."

"Pull it," LaDuke said. He had his shotgun on the black man now, too. I had an eye on Roland, who had not yet spoken but who stared at us hatefully.

"You know," the black man said to LaDuke, "you kinda pretty, too. Maybe you and Pretty Man here ought to get together and—"

"You shut your mouth," said LaDuke.

"Relax," I said, looking at the black man but speaking to LaDuke.

"You boys are higher than a motherfucker," the black man said, studying us with a hard glint in his eye. "You ought to cool out some. Maybe we can talk."

"Pull it!" LaDuke screamed.

"You're the man," the black man said, "for now." He put one hand up and reached the other behind his back. For a moment, I thought Roland might make a move—he was balling and unballing his fists, and he was leaning forward, like he was in the blocks—but then the black man's hand came around, dangling an automatic by the barrel. He tossed it on the work-table and it slid neatly to the end. I went and picked it up, slipped it behind my back.

"All right now," LaDuke said. "The money."

"You've broken my crown," the plump man whined, still on the floor, his hand and face smeared with blood. "You've broken it! Are you satisfied?"

The black man laughed.

Pretty Man raised his head from the floor, tears on his face. He looked at LaDuke.

"Put your head down," LaDuke said.

"Please don't make me put me head down," Pretty Man said, his fat lip quivering like a piece of raw liver. "Please."

LaDuke pushed the muzzle of the shotgun against Pretty Man's cheek, forced his head to the floor. Pretty Man's back shook as he sobbed, and soon after that, the stench of his voided bowels permeated the room.

"Whew," the black man said.

"Don't be givin' up no cash money, Coley," Roland said to the black man.

"Shut up," LaDuke said.

"Yeah," Coley said, "you really ought to shut your mouth, Youngblood. 'Specially when a couple of crazy white boys are holdin' the guns. You ought to just shut the fuck up and shit. Understand what I'm sayin'?"

But Roland did not appear to agree. He went on staring at LaDuke and I as if we were stealing his future. Then Coley got off the table, went to a metal desk that adjoined it, and opened a drawer. He withdrew a cash box, the type used in restaurants and bars, placed it on top of the desk, and opened it.

"It's not all that much," he said with a flourish and a wave of his hand. "Take it and go."

I wrist-jerked the Browning in the direction of the table,

and Coley went back to it and took his seat. He was tall and lean, and he moved with an athletic confidence. He would have been handsome, if not for his pitted complexion and his left ear, which had been removed to the drum. I grabbed the money from the cash box—three banded stacks of hundreds and fifties—and stuffed it into my jeans.

I said to LaDuke, "I'm gonna get the rope."

The spool was right outside the door. I came back in with it, tied Pretty Man's hands to his feet, tried not to gag at his smell.

"Yeah," Coley said, "Pretty Man done shit his drawers. Kinda funny, tough man like him, needin' diapers and shit. See, in the movie we're makin', he's supposed to be some kind of carpenter. Guess you can tell by that tool belt he's wearin'. And Youngblood here, he's like the apprentice, come in for his lesson. The way the story line goes—what we call the *screen treatment*—the carpenter's gonna teach the apprentice a thing or two about showin' up late for his lesson—"

"Oh no," the plump man said. Blood and saliva pooled on the concrete where it had splashed from his mouth.

"This here's our director." Coley gestured to the plump man with a contemptuous limp wrist and a flick of his fingers. "Maybe I ought to let him tell you about tonight's film."

"My crown," the plump man said.

"Everybody," LaDuke said, "keep your mouths shut."

I tied the plump man up, then pointed my chin at Coley. "Put the shotgun on him," I said.

I told Coley to roll over onto his stomach and lie facedown on the table. He did it without protest, and I bound him in the same manner, but more tightly than the others. I cut the excess with the razor and slipped the razor back in my jeans.

I looked at Roland. "All right. You, come here. You're next."

"No," LaDuke said. "We're taking him with us."

"Why?" I said.

"Insurance," LaDuke said.

"*Fuck* no," Roland said. "I ain't goin' nowhere with you motherfuckers—"

"You're coming with us *now*, Roland!" LaDuke said, and then he looked at Coley, who had rested his cheek on the work-table. "If you try and follow us, we'll kill him. You understand?"

"I understand everything just fine," Coley said, a thread of a smile appearing on his face. His eyes moved to mine. "That gonna do it for you boys?"

"No," LaDuke said. "I don't think so."

LaDuke walked over to the spotlight. He raked the barrel of the shotgun sharply across the bulb. The bulb exploded, glass chiming, showering the plump man's head. LaDuke went to the fills and did the same. The stands fell to the floor, sparking on contact. The color of the light changed in the room.

"That about how you did the one in my trunk?" LaDuke said, his eyes wide and fully amphetamized.

"Something like that," I said, knowing he wasn't done.

LaDuke said, "Watch this."

He turned, pointed the shotgun at the video camera. Roland hit the floor and Coley closed his eyes.

"Hey," I said.

LaDuke squeezed the trigger. There was a deafening roar, and then the camera was just gone, disintegrated off its base.

"Oh no," the plump man moaned, against Pretty Man's steadily rising sob. "Oh no."

My ears stopped ringing. I checked the rest of them—no one appeared to have been hit.

LaDuke pumped the Ithaca, smiled crazily, walked through the smoke that hovered in the room. "All right," he said. "All right."

He picked up a T-shirt that was draped over a chair and dropped it on Roland's bare back. Roland got to his knees shak-ily and put the T-shirt on. LaDuke grabbed him by the arm, pulled him up. He hustled him toward the door and the two of them left the room. I walked backward, the Browning at my side.

"You made a mistake tonight," Coley said in a very easy way. "Now you're fixin' to make the biggest one of your life."

"That right," I said, the speed riding in on the blood that was pumping through my head.

"Yeah. You're gonna walk out of here and let us live. When really, what you ought to do—if you really think about it—is kill us all." His eyes were dead as stone. "I mean, that's what *I* would do."

"I'm not you," I said.

I backed away and left him there, moved into the hall. LaDuke and Roland had already turned the corner. I followed them, caught them at the end of the next hall, near the outside door. Sweet was lying there, unconscious and bound, his face ballooned out and black. We stepped around him and walked out to the lot.

LaDuke pushed Roland toward the gate. Darnell kept the headlights off and pulled the Ford along the fence. We slipped out, then put Roland in the backseat. I gave LaDuke my Browning and the extra clip, along with Coley's automatic. He dumped them and his own hardware into the dark trunk. He went around and got into the front seat and I climbed into the back with Roland. Roland looked at the back of Darnell's head, then at me.

"I don't wanna die," Roland said, looking suddenly like the teenaged kid he was.

"Boy?" Darnell said. "These two just saved your dumb life."

I reached over the front seat and found a cigarette in the visor. LaDuke grinned and clapped my arm. I sat back, struck a match, and took in a lungful of smoke. Darnell pulled out into the street and headed north. He switched on the lights and gave the Ford some gas.

"Where we goin'?" Roland said, the toughness back in his voice.

"We're takin' you home," I said.

None of us said anything for some time after that.

* * *

DARNELL GOT US OUT of the warehouse district and kept the Ford in the area of the Hill, driving down the business strip on Pennsylvania and then into the surrounding neighborhoods. It was near midnight, and most of the shops were closed, but people still moved in and out of the doorways of bars, and on the residential streets the atmosphere was thick and still.

"Pull over," LaDuke said, pointing to a pay phone standing free in the lot of a service station. Darnell drove the Ford into the lot.

"What we gonna do now?" Roland said.

"Call your mom," said LaDuke.

"Shit," Roland said.

LaDuke left the car and made the call, gesturing broadly with his hands, smiling at the end of the conversation. He returned and settled back in the front seat.

"Let's go," LaDuke said to Darnell. "His mother's place is in Northeast, off Division."

"I ain't goin' home," Roland said. "Anyway, we got some business to discuss."

"What kind of business?" I said.

"That money you took, it must have been ten, maybe more. I can turn that ten into twenty."

"Forget about the money."

"I only want what's mine. I worked for it. On the real side, man, that shit is mine."

"Forget about it," I said.

LaDuke pointed to the shifter on the steering column. "Put it in gear," he said.

"I told you," Roland said, "I ain't goin' nowhere."

I shifted in my seat, turned to Roland. "Maybe you'd like just to sit here and talk."

"About what?"

"We could start with what happened to Calvin."

Roland licked his lips and exhaled slowly. "Man, *I* don't know. Calvin just left—see what I'm sayin'? He didn't want to come along. The next thing I knew, I was readin' about that shit my own self, in the papers."

"You must have been real broken up about it," I said. "You didn't even go to his funeral."

"Look, Calvin was my boy. But I had my *own* thing to take care of."

"Get going," LaDuke said to Darnell.

Roland said, "I ain't goin' nowhere, not till we settle up on my cash money."

Darnell's eyes met mine in the rearview. "You thirsty, man? You look kinda thirsty."

"Yes," I said. "I'm thirsty."

"Why don't I just drop you off, maybe the two of you could have a beer. I'll swing back, pick you up."

"What're you going to do in the meantime?"

"Me and Roland here," Darnell said, "we're gonna drive around some. Have ourselves a little talk."

DARNELL PUT US OUT on Pennsylvania. LaDuke and I went into the Tune Inn, noisy and packed, even at that hour, with Hill interns and neighborhood regulars. We ordered a couple of drafts from one of their antique bartenders and drank the beers standing up, our backs against a paneled wall. LaDuke and I didn't say a word to each other or anyone else the entire time. At one point, he began to laugh, and I joined him, then that ended as abruptly as it had begun. I was killing my second beer when the Ford pulled up on the street outside the bar window.

We drove across town and over the river, deep into Northeast. Roland sat staring out the window, the streetlights playing on his resigned face, his features very much like his mother's in repose. I didn't ask him any more questions; I was done with him for now.

We pulled up in front of the Lewis home, Darnell letting the engine run on the street. On the high ground, where the house sat atop its steep grade, I saw Shareen in silhouette, sitting in the rocker sofa on her lighted porch. She got up and walked to the edge of the steps. Roland stepped out of the car, moving away from us without a word of thanks. We watched him take the steps, slowly at first, then more quickly as he neared his home. As he reached his mother, she embraced him tightly, and even over the idle of the Ford, I could hear her crying, talking to her son. Roland did not hug her back, but it was more than good enough.

"Let's get out of here," I said.

"Sure," Darnell said.

LaDuke did not comment. He smiled and rubbed the top of his head.

We dropped Darnell at his efficiency near Cardoza High, in the Shaw area of Northwest. I thanked him and peeled off a couple of hundreds from the stack. He protested mildly, but I pressed it into his hand. He shrugged, pocketed the cash, and walked across the street.

"I could use a drink," I said.

"Yeah," LaDuke said, surprising me. "I could use one, too."

NINETEEN

STEVE MAROULIS SHOUTED. "*Ella*, Niko!" as LaDuke and I entered his bar.

Maroulis was the tender at May's, below Tenleytown on Wisconsin, a liquorized pizza parlor and hangout for many of the town's midlevel bookies. Though quantities of cocaine had moved through the place for a brief time in the eighties, gambling remained the main order of business here, a place where men in cheap sport jackets could talk with equal enthusiasm about Sinatra's latest tour or the over/under on the game of the night. LaDuke and I had a couple of seats at the bar.

Maroulis lumbered our way, put a smile on the melon that was his face. "Way past last call, Nick. Drinks got to be off the tables in a few minutes."

"Put four Buds on the bar, will you, Steve? We'll leave when you say."

"Right."

He served them up. I grabbed mine by the neck and tapped LaDuke's bottle, then both of us drank. Tony Bennett moved into Sam and Dave on the house system, a typical May's mix of fifties pop and sixties frat. I shook a cigarette out of my pack, struck a match, and put the flame to the tobacco.

"How'd you think it went tonight?" LaDuke said.

"We got Roland out of there."

"You didn't push it too hard with him."

"I'll talk to him again."

LaDuke motioned to my pack of smokes. "Give me one of those things."

"You really want one?"

"I guess not. No."

I dragged on mine, flicked ash off into the tray.

LaDuke said, "Those guys at the warehouse — Sweet and Coley. You think they had anything to do with Calvin's death?"

"I'm not sure yet. But I'd bet it."

"Why didn't you press Coley?"

"Calvin's dead. Gettin' another kid killed isn't going to even anything up. The object was to get Roland the fuck out of there. We did that. It's only over for tonight. That doesn't mean it's done."

"Why you figure it was Sweet and Coley?"

"It was a black man and a white man killed Calvin."

"How do you know that?"

I hit my cigarette, watched myself do it in the barroom mirror. "Because I was there."

LaDuke whistled through his teeth. "That's not what you told me."

"I know what I told you. I wasn't hired by Calvin's mother. I stumbled right up on that murder, man. I got drunk, real drunk that night, and I ended up down by the river, flat on my back and layin' in garbage. I heard the voices of a black man and a white man; they were dragging someone to the waterline. I heard them kill him, man, but I couldn't even raise my head. I was just fucked up, all the way fucked up, understand?" I rubbed at my eyes, then killed the first bottle of beer. I pushed that one away with the back of my hand. "That's the way this thing started—with me on a drunk."

I picked up the fresh beer, drank some of it off. LaDuke looked at the bottle in my hand.

"You better be careful with that stuff," he said. "You fall in love with it too much, there's no room for anyone else."

"I know it," I said, closing my eyes as I thought of Lyla.

"How is she, anyway?" LaDuke said.

"Who?"

"You know who. You haven't mentioned her much these last few days."

"It's over," I said, hearing the words out loud for the first time. "I've just got to work out the details. I'm doing it for her, man. She's going nowhere fast, hanging out with me."

"Self-pity, Nick. Another curse of the drinking man."

"Thanks for the tip, Boy Scout."

"I'm only talking about it because I know. My mother left us when I was a kid. She liked the bottle better than she liked raising a family."

"Your father raised you?"

"Me and my brother, yeah."

"Where you from, anyway?"

"Frederick County, not far over the Montgomery line. Place about forty minutes outside of D.C."

"Your father still alive?"

"Yeah," LaDuke said, and a shadow seemed to cross his face.

"What's he do?"

"Country veterinarian. Horse doctor, mostly." LaDuke swigged at his beer, put it back on the bar. "What are you, writin' my life story?"

I shook my head. "It would take way too long. You're a work in progress, LaDuke." I got off my bar stool, grabbed my beer. "Be right back. I gotta make a call."

I went back to the pay phone outside the rest rooms. A couple of kitchen guys were working a video game nearby, and someone was puking behind the men's room door. I sunk a quarter in the slot, dialed Boyle's number at the station, and left a taped message directing his Vice boys to the warehouse on Potomac and Half.

LaDuke was finishing his beer when I returned to the bar. Maroulis had brought the white lights up, and he had put on "Mustang Sally," the traditional "clear out" song for May's. Most of the regulars had beat it. I ordered a six to go, and Steve arranged them in a cardboard carrier. I left thirty on eighteen, and LaDuke and I headed out the door.

We drove southeast, all four windows down and the radio off. The streets were empty, the air damp and nearly cool. I lit a cigarette, dangled the hand that held it out the window, drank off some of my beer. The speed had given me wide eyes and a big, bottomless thirst; I could have gone all night.

I had LaDuke stop at an after-hours club downtown, but even that had closed down. We sat on the steps of it, drank a round. Then we got back into the Ford and headed over to the Spot. LaDuke urinated in the alley two doors down while I negotiated the lock and got past the alarm. He joined me inside and I locked the door behind him. The neon Schlitz logo burned solo and blue. I notched up the rheostat, the conicals throwing dim columns of light onto the bar. My watch read half past three.

LaDuke had a seat at the bar and I went behind it. I iced a half dozen bottles of beer and put two on the mahogany, along with the bottle of Grand-Dad from the second row of call. I placed a couple of shot glasses next to that, an ashtray, and my deck of smokes.

"You with me?" I said, my hand around the bottle of bourbon.

"Maybe one," said LaDuke.

I poured a couple, lifted my first whiskey of the night. It was hot to the taste and bit going down. My buzz went to velvet, as it always did with the first sip. I moved down to the deck and put on some Specials. Then I came back and LaDuke and I had our drinks. We chased them with beer and listened to the tape for its duration without saying much of consequence. I stayed in the ska groove and dropped a Fishbone mix into the deck. Walking back, I noticed that my watch read 4:15. I poured LaDuke another shot, then one for me. LaDuke sipped at it, followed it with beer.

I took the stickup money from my pockets, dumped it all on the bar. LaDuke didn't comment, and neither did I. I lit a cigarette, gave it a hard drag, looked at the long night melting into LaDuke's face.

"You're hangin' pretty good for a rookie," I said.

"I'm no rookie," LaDuke said. "I just haven't done anything like this for a while, that's all."

"You gave it all up, huh?"

"Something like that. The funny thing is, after all that time off it, I don't even feel that fucked up. I could drink whatever you put on this bar tonight, I swear to God. And I could keep drinking it."

"The speed," I said. "You'll feel it in the morning, though, boy. You can believe that shit."

"I guess that's what got me going back there, too."

"You blew the fuck out of that camera, LaDuke. I could have done without that."

"I wanted to break something."

"I know."

"Anyway, it's not like I don't know how to handle this stuff. You rib me all the time, Stevonus, 'Boy Scout' this and 'Boy Scout' that. Shit, I was like any teenager growing up when I did—I tried everything, man. The difference between you and me is, I grew out of it, that's all."

"So when'd you stop?"

LaDuke said, "When my brother got killed." He pointed his chin at the pack of smokes on the bar. "Give me one of those, will ya?"

"Sure."

I rustled the deck, shook one out. LaDuke took it and I gave him a light. He dragged on it, held the smoke in, kept it there without a cough. He knew how to do that, too.

I put one foot up on the ice chest, leaned forward. "What happened?"

"My brother and I, we were both up at Frostburg State. I was in my senior year and he was a sophomore. It was Halloween night; there were a lot of parties goin' on and shit, everybody dressed up in costume. I was at this one party; all of us had eaten mushrooms, and the psilocybin was really kicking in. Just about then, a couple of cops came to the door, and of course everybody there thought they had come to bust the shit up. But they had come to get *me*, man. To tell me that my brother had been killed. He had been at this grain party, up over the Pennsylvania line. Driving back, he lost it on a curve, hit a fuckin' tree. Broke his neck."

I hit my cigarette, looked away. The tape had stopped a few minutes earlier. I wished it hadn't stopped.

"So anyway," LaDuke said, "they took me to identify the body. So I was in the waiting room, and there was this big mirror on one wall. And I looked in the mirror, and there I was: I had dressed up like some kind of bum that night, for the party, like. I had bought all this stupid-lookin' shit down at the Salvation Army store, man. None of it matched, and goddamn if I didn't look like some kind of failed clown. I looked at myself, thinkin' about my brother lying on a slab in the other room, and all I could do was laugh. And trippin' like I was, I couldn't stop laughing. Eventually, they came and put me in another room. This room had quilted blankets on the walls — the kind moving guys use to cover furniture — and a table with a pack of Marlboro Lights in the middle of it, next to an ashtray. And no mirrors. So that was the night, you know? The night I decided, It's time to stop being some kind of clown."

I stabbed my cigarette out in the ashtray, lit another right behind it.

"That's rough, Jack," I said, because I could think of nothing else to say.

"Sure," he said. "It was rough." He rubbed at the tight curls on top of his head, looking down all the while. I drew two beers from the ice, put them on the bar.

"How'd your father handle it?" I said.

"My father," LaDuke muttered, savagely twisting the cap off the neck of the bottle.

I watched him tilt his head back and drink.

"What's wrong with you, man?" I said.

LaDuke tried to focus his eyes on mine. I could see how drunk he was then, and I knew that he was going to tell it.

"My father was sick," LaDuke said. "*Is* sick, I guess. I haven't seen him for a long time. Not since my brother's funeral."

"Sick with what?"

"His problem."

"Which is?"

LaDuke breathed out slowly. "He likes little boys."

"Shit, Jack."

"Yeah."

"You tellin' me you were abused?"

LaDuke drank some more beer, put the bottle softly on the bar. "I was young...but yeah. When I finally figured it out—when I figured out that what he was doing, when he was coming into my room at night, handling me that way—when I figured out that it was wrong, I asked him about it. Not a confrontation, just a question. And it stopped. We never even talked about it again. I spent the rest of my childhood, and then my teenage years, making sure the old man stayed away from my little brother. When my brother died, man, my life was finished there. I got through college and then I booked."

"Booked where?"

"I went south. I never liked the cold. Still don't. Lived in Atlanta for a while, Miami after that. I had a degree in criminology, so I picked up work for some of the security agencies. But, you know, you tend just to come back. I've been looking for answers, and I thought I might find out more about myself the closer I got to home."

"You've talked to your father?"

"No." LaDuke took in some smoke, crushed the cherry in the ashtray. "I guess you think I ought to hate him. But the truth is, I only hate what he did. He's still my old man. And he did raise me and my brother, and it couldn't have been easy. So, no, I don't hate him. The thing is now, how do I fix my own self?"

"What do you mean?"

"I don't believe in this victimized-society crap. All these people pointing fingers, never pointing at themselves. So people get abused as kids, then spend the rest of their lives blaming their own deficient personalities on something that happened in their childhoods. It's bullshit, you know it? I mean, everybody's carrying some kind of baggage, right? I know I was scarred, and maybe I was scarred real deep. But knowing that doesn't straighten anything out for me." LaDuke looked away. "Sometimes, Nick, I don't even know if I'm good for a woman."

"Oh, for Chrissakes, Jack."

"I mean it. I don't know what the fuck I am. What happened to me, I guess it made me doubt my own sexuality. I look at a man, and I don't have any desire there, and I look at a woman, and sometimes, sexually, I don't know if it's a woman I want, either. I'm tellin' you, I don't know *what* I want."

"Come on."

"Look here," LaDuke said. "Let me tell you just how bad it is with me. I go to the movies, man. I'm sitting there watching the man and the woman makin' love. If it's really hot, you know, I'll find myself getting a bone. And then I start thinking, Am I getting hard because I wish I was him, or am I getting hard because I wish I was her?"

"Are you serious, man?"

"I'm not joking."

"Because if you're serious, LaDuke, then you are one fucked-up motherfucker."

"That's what I'm trying to tell you!" he said. "I am one seriously fucked-up motherfucker."

Both of us had to laugh a little then, because we needed to, and because we were drunk. LaDuke's eyes clouded over, though, and the laughter didn't last. I didn't know what to do for him, or what to say; there was too much twisting around inside him, twisting slowly and way too tight. I poured him another shot of bourbon, and one for myself, and I shook him out another smoke. We sat there drinking, with our own thoughts arranging themselves inside our heads, and the time passed like that. I looked through the transom above the front door and saw the sky had turned to gray.

"You know, Jack," I said, "you were right about everybody having some kind of baggage. I never knew my mother or father; they sent me over from Greece when I was an infant. I got raised by my grandfather. He was a good man—hell, he *was* my father—and then he died, and my marriage fell apart, and I thought I was always gonna be alone. And now I'm fixing to blow the best thing that's ever come my way. But, you know, I've got my work, and I've got this place and the people in it, and I know I can always come here. There's always someplace you can go. There's a whole lotta ways to make a family."

"So, what, you're sayin' this place is like your home?"

"I guess so, yeah."

"But it's a shithole, Nick."

I looked around the bar. "You know somethin'? It *is* a shithole." I smiled. "Thanks for pointing that out to me."

LaDuke smiled back. "Yeah, you gave it a good try."

We had some more to drink, and after awhile his eyes made their way over to the money heaped on the bar. I watched him think things over.

"It's a lot of cash," I said, "you know it?"

"Uh-huh. What are we gonna do with it?"

"I don't know. You want it?"

"No." LaDuke shook his head. "It's dirty."

"It's only dirty if you know it's dirty."

"What's your point?"

"I was thinkin'... why not just take this money, put it in an envelope, and mail it off to Calvin's mother. I've been to her place, man, and she sure could use it. There's a couple of babies there—"

"What, just put it in the mail?"

"I've got an envelope around here somewhere."

LaDuke shrugged. "All right."

I found a large manila envelope in Darnell's kitchen. There was a roll of stamps back there, too, in a file cabinet next to Phil Saylor's logbook. I ripped off a line of stamps and took them and the envelope back to the bar. Then I grabbed a D.C. directory that was wedged between the cooler and the wall and put that on the bar, as well. I looked through the Jeter listings while LaDuke stuffed the money into the envelope.

"There's a shitload of Jeters," I said.

"You know the street?"

"I think so."

"You think so? We're gonna mail out ten grand on an 'I think so'?"

"Here it is," I said. "Gimme the envelope."

I used a black Magic Marker to address it, then applied the stamps and gave it a seal. LaDuke had a look at my handiwork and laughed.

"It looks like a kid did this," he said. "Like it's first grade, and you just learned how to write and shit."

"What, you could do better?"

"Man, I can barely see it."

"Come on," I said. "Let's go."

I set the alarm, locked the place up. The two of us walked out the door. Dawn had come, the sun was breaking over the buildings, and the bread men and the icemen were out on the streets.

"Shit," I said, shaking my head as we moved down the sidewalk.

"What?" LaDuke said.

"I was just thinking of you sittin' in a movie theater, not knowing if it's the man or the woman givin' you a hard-on. I mean, it's really hard to believe."

"I guess I shouldn't have told such a sensitive guy like you. I know you're never gonna let me forget it. But believe it or not, you're the first person I ever unloaded this on. And I gotta tell you, just letting it out, I do feel a little better."

"You'll get through it, LaDuke."

"You think so, huh."

"It'll pass. Everything does."

I dropped the envelope in the mailbox on the corner. LaDuke slipped, stepping off the curb. I grabbed him by the elbow and held him up. We crossed the street and headed for the Ford, parked in a patch of clean morning light.

TWENTY

I **WOKE UP** a little after noon. I was spread out on top of the sheets, soaked with sweat, still dressed right down to my shoes. My cat was lying sphinx-style on my chest, kneading her claws through my shirt, her face tight against mine. Starved for food or attention, it didn't matter which. I got up and opened a can of salmon and spooned it into her dish. The smell of the salmon tossed my stomach and I dry-heaved in the kitchen sink. I stripped, climbed into the shower, stood in the cold spray, going in and out of sleep against the tiles. When I stepped out, the phone was ringing, so I went into the living room and picked up the receiver. Boyle was on the line, thanking me for the previous night's tip.

"You get anything?"

"Nothing human," Boyle said. "All the warm bodies were long gone by the time Vice secured the warrant. They found a whole bunch of tools, some lighting and equipment, a camera that had been blown to shit. Looked like someone had quite a party in there, from what I understand. I guess they were in a hurry clearing out."

"I guess."

"You sound a little tired," Boyle said.

"It's hot in here, that's all."

"Heat wave moved in this morning. Say it's gonna be up around a hundred the next few days."

"I'm working a shift this afternoon, so I'll be out of it."

"Uh-huh." Boyle cleared his throat. "The porno operation in that warehouse — that have anything to do with the Jeter murder?"

"No. I thought it did, but it didn't. I got in there, saw what was going on, and got out. Then I called you."

"Right," Boyle said after a meaningful pause. "Well, I guess that's it. Take it easy, Nick."

"You, too."

I hung up the phone, got myself into shorts and a T-shirt, and headed down to the Spot.

Mai was behind the stick when I walked in. She gave me a wave, untied her apron, and walked out the front door. I stepped behind the bar. Happy, Buddy, Bubba, and Mel were all in place, snuggled into their stools, drinking quietly under the buzz of the air conditioner and the Sonny Boy Williamson coming from the deck. Buddy asked for another pitcher, his lip curled in a snarl. I drew it for him, placed the pitcher between him and Bubba. Happy mumbled something in my direction, so I fixed him a manhattan. I placed the drink on a bev nap in front of him, and he burped. The smell of Darnell's lunch special drifted my way. I replaced the blues on the deck with an Impressions compilation, and the intro to "I've Been Trying" filled the room. Mel closed his eyes and began to sing. Looking through the reach-through to the kitchen, I could see Ramon doing some kind of bull-jive flying sidekick toward Darnell, Darnell stepping away from it with grace, the two of them framed beneath the grease-stained Rudy Ray Moore poster thumbtacked to the wall. I knew I was home.

Anna Wang came in from the dining area, leaned on the service bar, and dumped out her change. She began to count it, arranging it in sticks. I poured a cup of coffee for myself, added some whiskey to the cup, and took it over to Anna. She reached into the pocket of my T and found a cigarette. I gave her a light. She exhaled and shook a bunch of black hair out of her face.

"Welcome back."

"Thanks."

She grinned. "How you feelin', Nick?"

"Better now," I said, holding up the cup. And I did, too.

"Phil came in first thing this morning. Said there were enough Camels in the ashtray to service the Egyptian army."

"Yeah, that was me. And LaDuke. Was Phil pissed?"

"Not really. At least you set the alarm this time."

Anna pushed the stacks of change across the bar. I went to the register, turned the coin into bills, took the bills back and handed them to Anna. She folded her take and stuffed the money in the pocket of her jeans.

She said, "So how's Jack?"

"He's fine."

"Tell him I said hey, will you?"

"Sure, Anna, I'll tell him."

Happy hour was on the slow side, but I had plenty to do, restocking the liquor and arranging the bottles on the call shelf to where they had been before I left. Evening came and my regulars drifted out like pickled ghosts, and then it was just me and Darnell. I locked the front door and drove him back to his place through the warm, sticky night. He didn't mention the warehouse affair, and neither did I.

Back at my place, Lyla had phoned, so I phoned her back. She wanted to come over and talk. I said that it was probably not a good idea, and she asked why. I said it was because I didn't want to see her. She raised her voice and I raised mine back;

things just went to hell after that. The conversation ended very badly, and when it was done, I switched off the light and sat at the living room table and rubbed my face. That didn't amount to much, so I went to the bedroom and lay down in the dark and listened to the purr of my cat somewhere off in the apartment. It seemed like a long time before I fell asleep.

Jack LaDuke phoned early the next morning. Roland Lewis had been found dead beneath the John Philip Sousa Bridge: one bullet to the head.

TWENTY-ONE

THE AUTOPSY DELAYED the funeral, so it wasn't until Monday that Shareen Lewis put her son in the ground. Roland made the Roundup in Saturday's *Post*, with a corresponding death notice in the obits giving out the funeral home's location and burial particulars. There had been a dozen gun kills that weekend, so column-inch space was at a premium, and even for a young black male, Roland's death received very little ink. He had spent his whole life wanting to be large, but in the end his public memorial was two generic sentences buried deep in Metro; he was simply erased.

I retrieved my one suit, a charcoal three-buttoned affair, from out of the cedar closet on Monday and made it over to the service at a Baptist church off East Capitol Street. The attendees were racially mixed — the whites representing fellow employees from Shareen's law firm; the blacks representing family and friends. This was not a gang-death funeral, so there was not the traditional garb worn by crew members to honor their fallen comrade. In fact, there were very few young people in attendance at all. LaDuke, in his black suit and black tie arrangement, stood near the front, at the end of a pew. I watched him from the back of the church, his hands tightly clasped in front of him, as the beautiful voices of the choir resonated in the room.

They buried Roland in a cemetery off Benning Road in Marshall Heights. I brought up the rear of the procession and watched the ceremony from a distance, leaning against my Dodge, smoking a cigarette in the shade of an elm. An unmarked car pulled up behind mine and Boyle stepped out of the passenger side. He came and stood next to me, his face hard and grim.

"Nick," he said.

"Boyle."

"Thought you might be here."

"You were right on the money, then. I always said you were a good cop."

"Turn around," Boyle said, "and look at the car I just got out of."

I did it, looked through the tinted windshield, saw no one identifiable, just the featureless outline of a suit-and-tie black man behind the wheel.

"That good enough?" I said.

Boyle nodded. "That's Detective Johnson, assigned to the case. I told you about him. He just wanted to get a good look at you in case he gets proof that you been holding out on us with this one. If that's true, he's gonna want to talk to you again."

"Fair enough," I said.

"The ME's report came in. The shooter used a silenced twenty-two on Roland Lewis. Same markings as on the Jeter murder. Same gun. But I guess you knew that."

I dragged on my cigarette, dropped it under my shoe. "I don't know anything."

"You pulled the Lewis kid out of the warehouse on Potomac and Half, I'm pretty certain of that. His prints were all over the place. If you had turned him in to us, he'd be alive right now. He would have talked, too, and we'd probably have this whole thing wrapped up by now." Boyle put his face close to mine. I could smell the nicotine on his breath and the previous night's alcohol in his sweat. "You got this kid killed. Think about that, hotshot."

"Take it easy, Boyle."

"Yeah," he said. "Yeah, sure."

I listened to his footsteps as he walked away, and to the sound of the door shutting and Johnson putting the car in gear. I stared straight ahead, at the black pool of mourners huddled against the rolling green grounds. Low-slung sheets of flannel-colored clouds were moving in from the northeast. I reached into my jacket for another cigarette and fumbled through my pockets for a light.

THE BAPTIST'S VERSION OF a wake was held at Shareen Lewis's house off Division, directly following the burial. I dropped by, then stood around uncomfortably and wondered why I had. Shareen attended to the food table, a mix of fried chicken and cold cuts and some sort of dry punch, in a fragile but efficient manner, and Roland's sister helped her, passing me several times without acknowledgment, trays and bowls balanced in her hands. LaDuke stood across the room talking to Blackmon, the bondsman who had turned him on to the case. LaDuke met my eyes only once, giving me an abbreviated nod with his chin, his own eyes drawn and red. I jiggled the change that was in my pocket and smiled when someone smiled at me, and after a while I left the house and walked outside to have a smoke.

I went to the edge of the porch and looked down to the cars, shiny and wet, lined along the curb below. The rain had come in steady, quiet waves, clicking against the leaves, drumming on the aluminum awning of the porch. The rain brought steam up off the street, and woke the green and living smells of summer. I lit a cigarette, flipped the spent match off the porch, toward the grass.

"You have an extra one of those?" said a woman's voice behind me.

I turned around. The voice belonged to Shareen Lewis. She was sitting on the rocker sofa in front of the bay window.

"Sure," I said. I went to her and shook out a cigarette, struck a match and gave her a light. She wore a simple black dress, black stockings, and black pumps. An apricot brooch closed the dress at the chest. Her nails were painted apricot, with her lips the color of the nails.

She took some smoke into her chest, kept it there, closed her eyes as she let it out. "Sit down with me. Please."

"All right."

The springs creaked as I took a seat, and the sofa moved back and forth on its track. It settled to a stop, and then there was just the clicking on the leaves and the drumming on the awning. Shareen flicked some ash to the concrete of the porch and I did the same.

"Thank you," she said.

"It's okay," I said.

"Thank you for bringing my son back to me."

"It's okay."

Shareen put her lips to the cigarette, dragged on it, blew a stream of exhale. The smoke jetted out, then slowed and roiled in the stagnant, heavy air.

"You know," Shareen said, "I only had him for that one night. He left the next day."

I flicked a speck of lint from my trousers.

"Before he left," she said, "I made him his favorite lunch: a grilled cheese sandwich on white bread, with tomato right out of my garden, and a little mustard. Mustard on the bottom *and* the top slice of bread. The way he liked it, from when he was a little boy. He'd come in after the playground, come runnin' through that screen door there—don't you know he'd always slam that screen door—and he'd say, 'What's for lunch, Mom?' And I'd say, 'Grilled cheese, honey.' And he'd say, 'All right!'" Shareen flipped her hand in an excited, childish gesture, the way her son might have done.

I hit my cigarette and looked down at my shoes. One foot was moving metronomically, left to right and back again.

"After he had lunch on Thursday," Shareen said, "he said he had to go out, and out he went. He slammed that screen door, too. You know that, Mr. Stefanos?"

"Mrs. Lewis—"

"Then they called me on Friday and asked me to come down to the morgue. And I went in there to identify him; they pulled back the sheet, and there he was. And for a moment there, you know, I just didn't believe it was him. I mean, intellectually, I knew it was my son. But it just wasn't *him*. You understand? This was just a dead thing lying on a piece of cement. Not my son. Just something dead."

Shareen took in some more smoke, then dropped the cigarette and crushed it with the toe of her pump. She stared off into her front yard and flattened her hands in her lap.

"When he was first starting out school, he hated it, you know. As many times as I'd call upstairs to him in the morning, try to get him to wake up, he'd never answer. He'd just keep pretending that he was asleep, 'cause he didn't want to go to school. So I had this thing: I'd go into his bedroom and shake him and shake him and shake him. And finally, I'd put my index finger up into his armpit, just touch it, you know. And Roland, ticklish as he was, he'd still have his eyes closed, but he couldn't help but crack a smile. We did that every morning, Mr. Stefanos, when he was a boy. That was our routine. It was the only way I could get him up to go to school."

"Mrs. Lewis, maybe we better go on inside."

"Down in the morgue on Friday, I put my finger there, underneath his arm. Don't you know, that boy didn't even crack a smile!" Shareen grinned, the grin horrible and artificial. "I could have put my mouth right up to his ear and screamed to

God in heaven. It wouldn't have made any difference. And that's when I knew—I *knew*—that the boy in there on that slab, that boy was not my Roland. 'Cause Roland, when I touched him there? My Roland would have smiled."

"Mrs. Lewis," I said.

Her grin slowly went away. I put my hand on top of hers. The hand was cool and thin, wormed with veins across its back. She looked at me, then through me, her eyes hollow and all the way gone. We sat there and listened to the rain. After a while, she rose abruptly and walked back into her house. I got up off the rocker, crossed the porch, and took the steps down to my car.

I HAD ANOTHER EVENING shift at the Spot, and I worked it without saying much of anything to anyone, not even Anna or Darnell. The regulars made comments on my attire between calling for their drinks, and I let them, and when the bar fell silent for long periods of time, they reminded me to change the music on the deck. I started drinking in the middle of happy hour, one beer after another, buried in the ice chest to the neck. By the time I closed the place down, I had a beer buzz waiting on a shot of liquor to keep it company, so I poured two ounces of call bourbon into a glass.

Darnell shut off the light in the kitchen, stopped to get a good look at me, and walked out the front door. He didn't even bother asking for a lift uptown. I had a couple more rounds and somewhere around eleven I heard a knock on the front door. I turned the lock and LaDuke stepped inside.

"Hey," I said, clapping him a little too roughly on the shoulder.

"Nick."

He was still in his suit and tie, jacket on in the heat, the tie's Windsor knot centered and tight.

"Come on in, Jack, have a drink with me."

"I don't think so," he said.

"Suit yourself."

I went back behind the bar. LaDuke stayed where he was, at the top of the two-step landing, leaning against the entrance-way's green wall. I had a sip of bourbon and put fire to a smoke.

LaDuke said, "You're wasting time with that shit. We've got work to do."

"Maybe tomorrow," I said. "Tonight I'm gonna drink."

"Tonight and the next," he said, "and the one after that. You're no good that way."

"Thanks for the lecture, Boy Scout."

"We've got to finish what we started."

"I am finished," I said. "I don't want to see any more death. They kill and we kill and it doesn't stop and nobody wins. I'm tellin' you, man, I'm through with it."

"Well, I'm not through," he said, his voice cracking. "Roland's dead because of me. I've got to fix it now."

"Roland offed himself. He went back to them because of greed, flat out. They killed him, Jack, not you."

"No, Nick. It was me. That night in the warehouse, I called him by his name. You remember? I said, 'You're coming with us, Roland!' The one named Coley, he must have picked up on it. It made it look like Roland was in on the robbery, in on it with us. You understand, Nick? It was *me*."

"Roland was headed that way all along. You had nothing to do with it, hear?"

LaDuke pushed off from the wall. "I'm not done. Come along or don't come along—it makes no difference to me."

"Come on." I smiled and raised my bottle of beer. "Come on over here, Jack, and sit down with me. Sit down with me and have a drink."

He looked me over slowly, his eyes black with contempt.

"The hell with you," he said.

LaDuke walked from the room. I listened to the door close, then the silence. My shot glass sat empty on the bar. I reached for the bottle and poured myself a drink.

TWENTY-TWO

CASES BREAK, AND major changes get put in motion, in seemingly innocuous ways.

My ex-wife and I met in a bar, on a night when I decided to go out for a late beer at the incessant goading of an acquaintance whose name I don't remember. Similarly, I got my start in the sales business when, as a teenager, I happened to be hitching down Connecticut Avenue and found myself standing in front of the Nutty Nathan's plate-glass window, staring at a HELP WANTED sign. And then there was my friend Dimitri, a Greek boy out of Highlandtown, who got into a car he didn't know was stolen, then died after a high-speed chase at the age of seventeen. I often wonder how my life would have turned out had I not gone out for that beer, or had I been picked up hitchhiking farther north on the avenue that day. And I think about Dimitri, an innocent smile on his face as he climbed into that car, and I think of all the things my friend has missed.

The Jeter case was like that, too. The Jeter case might have ended with me and LaDuke parting company on a hot summer night. It might have ended, but it did not. The very next morning, I took a different route to work than I normally take, and everything got heated up again and boiled over in a big way.

My normal path out of Shepherd Park is 13th Street south, straight into downtown. From Hamilton Street on down, there was some road repair that morning, forcing a merge into one lane. I got into the lane and inched along for a while, but my hangover was scraping away at my patience. So I cut right on Arkansas, with the intention of hitting Rock Creek east of 16th.

I wasn't the only one with that plan, however, and the traffic on Arkansas was as backed up as it had been on 13th. After Buchanan Street, the flow ebbed considerably, and just before Allison, things came to a complete stop. I was idling there, looking around absently and trying to clear my head, when I noticed the brick building of the Beverley ice company on my right. Some employees were walking out of the rear door of the icehouse, on the way to their trucks. The temperature that morning had already climbed to ninety-plus degrees, the sun blazing in a cloudless sky. Sitting in my car, I could feel the sweat soaking into my T-shirt; the men walking out of the icehouse wore winter coats.

I landed on my horn. The guy ahead of me moved up a couple of feet, enough for me to put two wheels on the sidewalk and get the car onto Allison. I punched the gas and got it on up to 14th, parking in front of a corner market. There was a pay phone outside the market, with a directory, miraculously intact, beneath the phone. I opened the book, flipped to the *I*'s. I found plenty of wholesale ice merchants, most of them located in Northeast. There was only one located in Southeast: a place called Polar Boys, northwest of M, not too far from the Anacostia River—not too far from the river and only a short walk from the John Philip Sousa Bridge.

I dropped a quarter in the slot, woke Mai at home, and asked if she could work my shift.

"I'll do it," she said after the obligatory mild protest. "But I still want my whole two shifts tomorrow. And you owe me now, Nicky."

"I'll cover for you, Mai, anytime. Thanks a million, hear?"

She said good-bye. I ran down the sidewalk to my car.

MOST DETECTIVE WORK CONSISTS of watching and waiting. The job requires patience and the ability to deal with boredom, two character traits I do not possess. It's one of the reasons I don't take tail gigs anymore, following errant wives and hard-dick husbands to motel parking lots, waiting for them to walk out the door of room 12 so I can snap their pictures. The tip jar from the Spot not only keeps me solvent, it also allows me the luxury of selectivity.

I was thinking of the waiting game as I sat across the street from Polar Boys off M. I had parked near a store called Garden Liquors, though there appeared to be no garden or greenery of any kind in the general vicinity. The projects were located one block over, and some vampire was doing landmark business out of the store, selling forties and pints and lottery tickets at 11:30 in the morning. I sat behind the wheel of my Dodge, alcohol sweat beaded on my forearms, my ravaged stomach and my own smell making me sick. I could have used a beer myself, and another one after that.

A half hour later, some men began to filter out of the steel door of Polar Boys, removing their jackets in the sun as they walked across the broiling brown grass, some toward the liquor store, others toward a roach coach parked by the loading dock. Soon another man walked out alone, a bearded man approaching middle age, with a pleasant face framing quiet, serene eyes. He wore khaki pants, thick-soled boots, and a brilliant blue coat. I felt my pulse quicken as I stepped out of my car, then a chemical energy as I crossed the street.

"How's it going?" I said, blocking the man's path on the sidewalk.

"Very well," he said, "thank you." He went to move around me. "Excuse me, please."

I stepped in front of him, keeping a friendly smile on my face. "Kind of hot to be wearin' that coat, isn't it?"

"Hot? Yes, I suppose it is." He tried again. "Excuse me."

I withdrew my wallet from my back pocket, flipped it open. "My name is Nick Stefanos. I'm a private investigator." He glanced at my license despite himself.

"Yes?"

"There was a murder down by the river a couple of weeks ago. A young man was shot in the mouth."

He waited, spoke carefully. "I read about it in the papers, I think. Yes, I seem to recall it."

"I'm working on that case. I'm going to be blunt with you, because I don't have much time. I believe you witnessed the murder."

"You're mistaken," he said. "Or misinformed. Now if you'll excuse me, I only have one hour for lunch."

"I'll just talk to your employer, then. And maybe after that I'll go over to that pay phone, give the police a call. Since this is just a misunderstanding, you won't mind clearing things up with them, right? Upstanding citizen like you—"

"Now wait a minute," he said, his shoulders relaxing. "What is it that you want?"

"An hour of your time, an answer or two. And then I'll go away."

He looked back at the icehouse, then at me. "You have a car?"

I jerked my chin toward the Dodge. Something came into his eyes, passed just as quickly. The two of us crossed the street. I opened the passenger door, looked at him as he began to climb inside.

"You know?" I said. "You don't look too crazy to me."

"Crazy?" he said, glancing up at me as he settled into his seat. "Why, Mr. Stefanos, of course I'm crazy. As crazy as Ahab, or Lady Macbeth, or the quiet man who trims your neighbor's lawn. We're all a little bit crazy, in our own way. Don't you agree?"

I GOT BACK ON M and took the 11th Street Bridge over the river, heading toward Anacostia. On the bridge, I caught him glancing over the rail, at the marinas and the clearing and the sunken houseboat below.

"What's your name, anyway?" I said.

"William Cooper."

I pushed in the dash lighter and put a cigarette to my lips. "I read a short story collection last year that I really liked. The stories were all set in D.C., written by a local guy. Guy's name was William C. Cooper."

"William C. Cooper," he said, "is me."

Cooper directed me to a short street off the east side of the bridge. We parked in front of his place, a clapboard row house fronted by a shaky wood porch, and went inside. I sat in a dark, comfortable living room while Cooper went off and built a couple of sandwiches and made a pitcher of iced tea. Books lined the shelves along the wall and were stacked on tables and beneath chairs throughout the room. I stood in the icy cool of the air conditioning and read the titles of the books, and after awhile Cooper, still wearing his coat, reentered the living room with lunch on a tray.

"You ever take that coat off?" I said between bites of a sandwich of sliced chicken on French bread with creole mayonnaise.

"I wear it from the time I leave every morning to the time I return from work."

"It's cold enough in the icehouse, and it's definitely cold enough in here. But why outside, in this heat?"

Cooper shrugged. "I've worked in that icehouse for many years and my body has just adjusted. I found that I was getting ill very often in the beginning, taking my coat off outdoors, putting it on again when I went back inside. My body temperature is kept constant this way, I suppose. These days, I rarely get sick. I guess you could say that this old coat has contributed quite nicely to my continued good health."

"You talk kinda funny, you know it?"

Cooper smiled tolerantly. "You mean, for a black man, don't you?"

"Partly," I admitted, "yeah. But to tell you the truth, I don't know many white folks who talk like you, either. And zero Greeks."

"It's not the world you travel in, that's all. I'm hardly a blue blood. I was raised in Shaw, but my higher education was extensive, and strictly Ivy League. It's not an affectation, I can assure you of that. It's simply where I spent my adult life."

"So a guy like you... why an icehouse?"

Cooper had a long drink of his tea. "I wore the white collar and the rep tie and the Harris tweed and found that the life of an academic bored me. The politics, and the people, all of it was utterly bloodless, and ultimately quite damaging to my work. I took the job in the icehouse so that I could once again have the freedom to think. It might appear to the outsider that I'm doing menial labor, but what I'm really doing, all day, is composing—writing, in effect, in my head. And the amount of material I soak up in that place, it's tremendous. Of course, I need the money, as well."

"What about your morning routine, under the bridge. The boatyard workers, they all pegged you as a headcase."

Cooper smiled. "And I did nothing to dispel their suspicions. That was always my time to be alone, and I preferred to keep it that way. I'd wake up in the morning, walk across the bridge, take my book and my cup of coffee, and have a seat under the Sousa. Sometimes I'd read, and oftentimes I'd sing. I'm in the choir at my church, you know, and the acoustics beneath that bridge are outstanding."

"Were you there the morning that boy was killed?"

"Yes," Cooper said with a nod. "And so were you. Your car was parked in the wooded area, to the right of the clearing. I recognized it as soon as you pointed it out to me."

"I didn't see anything, though. What did *you* see?"

"Not much. I heard a muted gunshot. Then a car drove by me, turned around at the dead end, and drove by once again."

"You see the driver or the passenger?"

"No."

"You read the plates?"

"No."

"What kind of car?"

"One of those off-road vehicles—I don't recall the model or make. A white one."

"Anything else to identify it?"

Cooper looked in my eyes. "A business name was printed on the side. 'Lighting and Equipment,' it said. Does that help you?"

I sat back in my chair. "Yes."

We finished our lunch in silence. He picked up the dishes and took them back into the kitchen. When he returned, I got up from the table.

"That do it?"

"One more question," I said. "Why didn't you go to the police?"

"I'm no one's hero, Mr. Stefanos. And I had no wish to become involved. My anonymity and my solitude are my most prized possessions. I don't expect you to understand. I'm sorry if you don't."

"I'm the last guy qualified to judge you."

"Then I guess we're through."

"Yes. I never met you and you never met me."

"Agreed," he said. "Though don't be surprised if you end up in one of my stories."

"Make me handsome," I said. "Will you?"

Cooper laughed and looked at his watch. "I'd better get going. Will you drop me back at work?"

"Yeah. I've gotta get to work, too."

I HIT THE FIRST pay phone past Polar Boys and called LaDuke. I got his machine, and left a message: "Jack, it's Nick. It's Tuesday, about one-thirty in the afternoon. I found the witness to the Jeter murder. The shooters drove a white van, said 'Lighting and Equipment' on the side — the van came from the lot of the warehouse on Potomac and Half, across the street from the warehouse we knocked over last week. The killers didn't leave town, Jack, they moved across the fucking street. Anyway, I'm headed home. Call me there when you get in; we'll figure out what to do next. Call me, hear?"

BUT LADUKE DIDN'T CALL. I waited, did some push-ups, worked my abs, and then took a shower. I dried off and put some Hüsker Du on the platter, then a Nation of Ulysses, and turned the volume way up. When the music stopped, I left a second message for LaDuke and sat around for another hour. Then I got my ten-speed out and rode it a hard eight miles, came back to the apartment, and took another shower. I dropped a frozen dinner in the oven, ate half of it, threw the rest away. I made a cup of coffee and lit a cigarette and smoked the cigarette out on my stoop. By then, it was evening.

I dressed in a black T-shirt and jeans, put an old pair of Docs on my feet, laced them tightly. I went into my bedroom and opened the bottom dresser drawer, looking for my gun. The gun was gone; I had dumped it in the trunk of LaDuke's Ford after the warehouse job. I thought about my homemade sap and a couple of knives I had collected, but I left them alone. I went back out to the living room, looked through the screen door. The night had come fully now, the moths tripping out in the light of the stoop. My cat came from the kitchen and brushed against my shin. I picked up the phone and dialed LaDuke.

"Jack," I said, speaking to the dead-air whir of his machine, "I'm going down there, to the warehouse. "It's..." I looked at my watch, "It's nine-forty-five. I've got to go down there, man. I've gotta see what's going on."

I stood there, listening to the quiet of my apartment and the rainlike hiss of the tape. My heart skipped and my hand tightened on the receiver.

"LaDuke!" I shouted. "Where the fuck *are* you, man?"

TWENTY-THREE

I STARTED THE Dodge and headed downtown. On North Capitol, between Florida and New York avenues, the people of the neighborhood were out, sitting on trash cans and stoops, their movements slow and deliberate. Later, passing through the Hill, the sidewalks were empty, the residents cocooned in their air-conditioned homes. Then in Southeast, by the projects, the people were outdoors again, shouting and laughing, the drumbeat of bass and the sputter of engines and the smell of reefer and tobacco smoke heavy in the air.

I turned onto Half and drove into a darkened landscape of line and shadow, animation fading to architecture. And then it was only me, winding the car around short, unlit streets, past parked trucks and fenced warehouses and silos, to the intersection of Potomac and Half.

I pulled behind a Dumpster and killed the engine. There was the tick of the engine, no other sound. A rat ran from beneath the Dumpster and scurried under the fence of an empty lot. I lit a cigarette, hit it deep. I had a look around.

The knock-over warehouse sat still and abandoned, no cars in the lot, a police tape, wilted and fallen, formed around the concrete stoop.

Across the street, near the steel door of the second warehouse, two LIGHTING AND EQUIPMENT vans and the Buick Le Sabre were parked behind a fence topped with barbed wire.

I looked up at the east face of the building: A fire escape led to a second-story sash window. Behind the window, a pale yellow light glowed faintly from the depths of a hall. I dragged on my cigarette. Ten minutes later, I lit another. Through the second-story window, a shadow passed along the wall. The shadow disintegrated, and then it was just the pale yellow light.

I pitched my cigarette and stepped out of my car. I crossed the street.

Putting my fingers through the fence, I climbed it, then got over the double row of barbs without a stick. I swung to the other side of the fence, got halfway down its face, and dropped to the pavement in a crouch. My palms were damp; I rubbed them dry on the side of my jeans. Staying in the crouch, I moved across the lot to the bricks of the building.

I touched the wall, put myself flat up against it. My heart pumped against the bricks. I could hear it in my chest, and the sound of my breathing, heavy and strained. Sweat burned my eyes and dripped down my back. I blinked the burn out of my eyes. I waited for everything to slow down.

The air moved in back of me as I stepped away from the wall. I started to turn around, stopped when something cool and metallic pressed against the soft spot behind my ear. Then the click of a hammer and the hammer locking down.

"Don't shoot me," I said.

Coley's voice: "You came back. *Damn*, you know? I was hoping you would."

"You don't have to shoot me," I said.

"You'll live a little longer," he said, "if you keep your mouth shut. You'd like to live a little while longer, wouldn't you?"

"Yes."

Coley pushed the muzzle in on my skin. "You alone?"

I nodded.

"Walk to the door," Coley said.

He kept the gun against my head, put his hand on my shoulder, and pushed me along the wall to the steel door at the wall's end. I looked up, saw the window at the top of the fire escape, saw that it was open—the only way out, if I got the chance. Then we were at the end of the wall.

Coley reached over my shoulder and knocked on the door.

"Listen to this," he said with a chuckle. "My redneck friend Sweet, he's gotten all jumpy and shit since you and your pretty sidekick fucked up his face."

Sweet's voice came from behind the door. "Yeah?"

"It's Coley, man. Lemme in."

"Prove it," Sweet said.

"I'll prove it all over your narrow ass. Open this mother-fucker *up*. Right now."

I stood there, staring at the door, unable to raise spit, not wanting the door to open.

"Open it, Sweet," said Coley. "I got someone here you been wantin' to see."

The door opened. Coley pushed between my shoulder blades, and then we were inside. Sweet closed the door, slid a bolt and dropped it, and grinned. He turned the key on the lock and slipped the key in his pocket.

"My, my," he said. The bruised side of his face had gone to purple and one eye drooped where the socket had caved. He wore a sleeveless T-shirt tucked into jeans. The knife-in-skull tattoo contracted on his tightly muscled, drug-thin forearm as he reached behind his back. He pulled his gun and lightly touched the barrel to my cheek. The gun was a .22.

"My, my," he said again.

"Let's take him upstairs," Coley said.

Sweet stroked at the hairs of his billy-goat beard. "Right."

I walked between them down a hall that was empty, then into a large room crowded with garden tools and machinery. In the center of the room was an oak table and some chairs, where several men were seated. I could see a scale on the table, amid many bottles of beer, but I didn't linger on the setup, and I didn't look any of the men in the eye. Coley kept walking, and I stayed behind him. Once in a while, Sweet prodded me on the neck with the muzzle of the .22, and when he did it, a couple of the men at the table laughed. One of them made a joke at Sweet's expense, then all of them laughed at once, and Sweet prodded me harder and with more malice.

Coley cut left at an open set of stairs. I followed, relieved to be going out of the large room. We took the stairs, which were wooden and did not turn, up to the second floor, through an open frame, Sweet's footsteps close behind me. Then we turned into another hall with offices of some kind on either side, the offices windowed in corrugated glass. Through one open door, I saw an old printing press, and I noticed that the outside windows had been bricked up. The hallway of corrugated glass ended and the room widened, shelved floor to ceiling, with paints, thinners, glass jars, brushes, and rags on the shelves. Then there was a bathroom, its outside window bricked up, and then an open door, where Coley turned and stepped inside. I followed, noticing before I did the window leading to the fire escape at the end of the hall. Sweet came into the room behind me and shut the door.

"Keep your gun on him," Sweet said.

"Yes, *sir*," Coley said, amused.

Sweet went to the door, connected a chain from door to frame, and slid the bolt. Coley held his gun, a .38 Special, loosely in his hand and kept it pointed at my middle. He shifted his attention to Sweet, fixing the chain lock in place. Coley's eyes smiled.

The room had no furniture except for a simple wooden chair turned on its side against a wall. An overflowed foil ashtray sat on the scarred hardwood floor, next to the chair. There had been a window once, but now the window was brick.

"Hold this," Sweet said. He handed Coley the .22. Coley took the gun, let that one hang by his side. "Good thing you were outside, Coley."

"Heard that car of his. Some old muscle car with dual exhaust and shit. Makes one hell of a racket. Not the kind of ride you want to be usin' when you're trying to make a quiet entrance. Not too smart."

"Yeah," Sweet said. "Real stupid."

Sweet came and stood in front of me, not more than three feet away. He shifted his shoulders, smiled a little, his vaguely Asian eyes disappearing with the smile. Alcohol smell came off him, and he stunk of day-old perspiration.

"You see what your partner did to my face?" he said.

I didn't answer. I tried to think of something I had that they would want, something that would save my life. But I couldn't think of one thing. The realization that they were going to kill me sucked the blood out of my face.

Sweet said, "Our friend here looks afraid. What you think, Coley? You think he looks afraid?"

"He does look a little pale," Coley said.

"You afraid?" Sweet said, moving one step in. "Huh?"

I didn't see the right hand. It was quick, without form or shape, and Sweet put everything into it. He hit me full on the face, and the blow knocked me off my feet. My back hit the wall and my legs gave out. I slid down the wall to the floor.

"Whew," said Coley.

Sweet walked across the room, bent over, grabbed a handful of my shirt. He pulled me up. The room moved, Sweet's face splitting in two and coming back to one. He hit me in the face with a sharp right. Then he pulled back and hit me again, released his grip on my shirt. I fell to the floor. I swallowed blood, tasted blood in my mouth. Stars exploded in the blackness behind my eyes.

"Fuck!" I heard Sweet say. "I fucked up my fuckin' hand on his face!"

"Go clean it up," Coley said.

"The guy's a pussy," Sweet said. "Won't even fight me back. I think maybe he likes it. What do you think, Coley? You think he likes it?"

"Go clean up your hand," said Coley.

"Lock the door behind me," Sweet said.

"Yeah," Coley said, chuckling. "I'll do that."

Sweet left the room. When the door closed, I opened my eyes and got up on one elbow. Coley did not move to lock the door. I pushed myself over to the wall, sat up with my back against it. I looked at Coley, who stood in the center of the room, looking at me.

"You know," Coley said, "we're just gonna have to go on and kill you."

I wiped blood from my face with a shaky hand. I stared at the floor.

"The reason I'm tellin' you is, I hate to see a man go down without some kind of fight. That little redneck's gonna come back in here, and if you let him, he's gonna bitch-slap your ass all around. I mean, you're dead, anyway. But it's important, and shit, not to go out like some kind of punk. Know what I'm sayin'?"

I flashed on my drunken night by the river, hearing similar words spoken to Calvin Jeter. Spoken, I knew now, by Coley.

"Anyway, you got a little while," Coley said. "I'm gonna ask you a few questions first, partly for business and partly just because I'm curious. Whether you answer or not, either way, I'm gonna have to put a bullet in your head tonight. Just thought you might like to know."

There was a knock on the door.

"It's open," Coley said.

Sweet walked in, looked with disappointment at the chain swinging free on the frame. "I thought I told you to lock it."

"Damn," Coley said mockingly. "I damn sure forgot."

Sweet looked at me. "Get up," he said.

I stood slowly, gave myself some distance from the wall. I looked at Sweet's right hand: swollen, the knuckles skinned and raw. He walked toward me, the inbred's grin on his cockeyed face. He balled his right fist, but his right was done; I knew he wouldn't use it, knew he would go with the left. He came in. He faked the right and dropped the left.

I moved to the side, bent my knees, and sprang up, swinging with the momentum. I whipped my open hand into his throat, snapping my wrist sharply at the point of contact, aiming for the back of his neck. My straight-open hand connected at his Adam's apple, knocking him one step back. It felt as if a piece of Styrofoam had snapped.

Sweet grabbed at his throat with both hands. I went in, threw one deep right, followed through with it, dead square where his nose met the purple bruise of his face. Something gave with the punch; blood sprayed onto my shirt and Sweet went down. He fell to his side, moved a little, made choking sounds. Then he did not move at all. His hands dropped away from his throat.

"God*damn*," Coley said. "You kill 'im?"

"No. You hit the Adam's apple, the muscles around it contract, for protection. Cuts off your breathing for a few seconds. He'll live."

I heard Coley's slow footsteps as he crossed the room. The footsteps swelled, then stopped.

"What'd you call that?" Coley said, close behind me. "That thing you did to his throat?"

· "Ridge hand," I said.

"Sweet's gonna want to know," Coley said, "when he wakes up."

I felt a blunt shock to the back of my head and a short, sharp pain. The floor dropped out from beneath my feet, and I was falling, diving toward a pool of cool black water. Then I was in the black water, and there was only the water, and nothing left of me. Nothing left at all.

* * *

I WOKE FROM A dream of water.

"Some water," I said, looking at their feet.

Coley's shoes were between the legs of the chair, where he now sat. Sweet's were near my face.

"Get him some water," Coley said.

"Fuck a lotta water," Sweet said.

Sweet's shoes moved out of my field of vision. Then his knee dropped onto my back. I grunted as the knee dug into my spine. Sweet took my arm at the wrist and twisted it behind my back. I sucked at the air.

"Where's your partner?" he said, his breath hot on my neck. "The one with the shotgun."

"He's gone," I said, my voice high and unsteady.

"He's gone," Sweet said, mimicking my tone. He giggled and pushed my hand up toward my shoulders. He held my other hand flat to the hardwood floor. I tried to dig my nails into the wood.

"Where's he gone *to?*" Coley said.

"He split with his share of the money," I said. "I don't know where he went."

Sweet jerked my arm up. I thought my arm would break if he pushed it farther. Then he pushed it farther. It hit a nerve, and the room flashed white. I tightened my jaw, breathed in and out rapidly through my nose.

"Uh," I said.

"Say what?" Sweet said.

"Where is he?" Coley said.

My eyes teared up. Everything in front of me was slanted and soft.

"I don't know where he is," I said. "Coley, I don't know."

Coley said nothing.

Sweet released my arm. I rested the side of my face on the floor.

Then Sweet grabbed a handful of hair at the back of my

head and yanked my head back up. He slammed my face into the floor. Blood spilled out of my nose and onto the wood. My mouth was wet with it; I breathed it in and coughed. I looked at the grain in the wood and the blood spreading over the grain.

"God*damn*, Sweet," Coley said. "You're just fuckin' this man all *up*."

Sweet twisted my hair, yanked my head up out of the blood. My eyes rolled up toward the ceiling. Purple clouds blinked in front of my eyes and I heard the gurgle of my own voice. I felt Sweet push down on the back of my head. I saw the wood rushing toward my face. The wood was black, like black water. I was in the water, and it was blessedly cool.

I OPENED MY EYES.

I stared at the ceiling. It was a drop ceiling tiled in particle-board, with water damage in some of the tiles. Naked fluorescent fixtures hung from the ceiling. The light bore into my eyes.

I rolled onto my side. A Dixie cup full of water sat on the floor. Beyond the cup, a large roach crawled across the floor. It crawled toward Sweet's boots. Past Sweet's boots, Coley's shoes were centered between the legs of the chair.

I got up, leaned on my forearm, and drank the water. I thought I would puke, but I did not. I dropped the cup on the floor and dragged myself over to the wall. I put my back against the wall, sat there. My nose ached badly and there was a ripping pain behind my eyes. I rubbed my hand on my mouth, flaked off the blood that had dried there. Coley was seated in the chair and Sweet stood with his back against the opposite wall. The .22 dangled in Sweet's hand, pointed at the floor. I looked at Coley. Coley moved his chin up an inch.

"Let's kill him," Sweet said. "You said to wait till he woke up. Well, he's up."

"Not yet. I want to get the word first."

"Fuck the word. Let's kill him now."

"Not yet," said Coley.

It went back and forth like that for a while. I started to feel a little better. Time passed, and I felt better still. The hate was doing it. What they had done to me and the thought of it were making me stronger.

I looked around the room: nothing to use as a weapon. Nothing on me but my car keys and a pack of matches. The keys were something; I could palm one, stab a key into Sweet's eye when he came for me. I could hurt him in an awful way before he killed me. Somehow, I would do that. I would try.

"Go downstairs," Coley said to Sweet. "Go down and call him. See what he wants to do."

"Yeah, okay," Sweet said. "You lock that door behind me, hear?"

"Sure thing."

"I mean it," Sweet said. "I'm gonna listen outside that door, make sure you do it." And then to me: "I'll be back in ten minutes. That's how long you got to live. Ten minutes. You think about that."

Sweet walked from the room. He shut the door, and Coley got up from his chair and went to the door. He jangled the chain around in the bolt, made sure Sweet heard the jangle from the other side of the door. Then he dropped the chain without locking it, chuckling as he walked back to his chair. He sat in the chair. His eyes moved to the door and then to me.

"Don't get any ideas about that door," Coley said. " 'Cause this thirty-eight, at this range? You *know* I won't miss."

"I'm not going anywhere."

"Good. That thing with the door, I just like to rattle that little redneck's cage a little bit, that's all." Coley grinned. "You fucked him up pretty good, too. 'Course, he did you right back. He manage to break that nose of yours?"

"I don't think so."

"But it's been broke before."

"Yeah."

"I can see. Where you get that scar on your cheek, man?"

"Who cut off your ear?"

Coley showed me some teeth. "Some brother, in the showers at the Maryland State Pen. Looked at him the wrong way, I guess. All part of my rehabilitation and shit."

"That where you two are from? Baltimore?"

"Yeah. Roundabout that way. Why?"

"Nothing." I looked Coley in the eyes. "You killed Roland, and the Jeter kid, too. Didn't you?"

"Jeter, huh? That's what that boy's name was? Well, I didn't pull the trigger. I take no pleasure in that, though I'll do it if it's called for. Sweet was the triggerman. He likes it, you know. But I guess you could say I killed those boys, yeah."

"Why?"

"We're runnin' a business here, and we got to protect that. Powder right into the projects, straight up. They turn it to rock and then they kill themselves over that shit. But our end, we keep it clean. Now, my boss, the man who bankrolls all this? He favors boys. Young brothers, that's what he likes. Likes to watch 'em on the videotape. He had this idea, why not get them in here and put 'em on tape, use 'em to run powder on the side. I could have told him that shit wouldn't go. One of them got scared and the other one got greedy. We just had to go on and do 'em both."

"Who's your boss?" I said.

Coley laughed. "Aw, go on. What you think this is, *True Confessions* and shit? Uh-uh, man, you're just gonna have to check out not knowing all that. Now let me ask you somethin'."

"Go ahead."

"Why'd you knock us over? It wasn't for the money, I know that."

"I was just trying to save a kid's life. I was only trying to get Roland out of there. He didn't even know who we were."

"He wasn't with you?"

"No. You killed him for nothing."

Coley shrugged. "He would've made me, anyway. Eventually,

he would've done somethin' to make me kill 'im. He was that way. Just *difficult* and shit."

Coley used the barrel of his gun to scratch his forehead. I eased my keys out of my pocket, palmed them, let the tip of the longest one peek through the fingers of my fist.

"But you know," Coley said, "that don't explain why you came back tonight."

"I wasn't finished," I said. "I needed to know the rest of it."

"Now you know," Coley said. "Kind of a silly thing to die for, isn't it?"

"Yeah," I said. "I guess it is."

Coley exhaled slowly, looked at me sadly. "I seen you pull out those keys and shit. Why don't you just slide them over here, man. I'll make sure what gets done to you gets done to you quick."

I tossed the keys to the center of the floor. Footsteps sounded in the hall, louder with each step. Coley got out of his chair, bent over, and picked up the keys. He slipped them in his pocket.

There was a knock on the door.

Coley smiled. "Come on in, Sweet. It's open."

The door opened.

Jack LaDuke stepped into the room, the Ithaca in his hands.

The smile froze on Coley's face. "Goddamn," he said. "God*damn*."

LaDuke pointed his shotgun at Coley. Coley pointed the .38 at LaDuke.

"LaDuke," I said.

"Nick."

LaDuke kicked the door shut behind him, kept his eyes and the shotgun on Coley. LaDuke was wearing his black suit and the solid black tie. I felt a rush of affection for him then; looking at him, I could have laughed out loud.

"Where you been?" I said.

"Office of Deeds, like you taught me." Without moving anything but his free arm, he reached under the tail of his jacket and drew my Browning. "This is you."

He tossed the gun in my direction. I caught it, ejected the magazine, checked it, slapped the magazine back in the butt. I pointed the Browning at Coley. Coley kept the .38 on LaDuke.

"How'd you get in, LaDuke?"

"Fire escape. The window was open—"

"*Damn*," said Coley.

"And then I just came down the hall. Heard you guys talkin'."

"Good to see you, LaDuke."

"You all right? You look pretty fucked up."

"I'm okay. Now we gotta figure out how to get outta here."

"Uh-*uh*," Coley said.

"What's that?" LaDuke said.

"You know I can't let you fellahs do that," Coley said, still smiling, the smile weird and tight. Bullets of sweat had formed on his forehead and sweat had beaded in his mustache.

LaDuke took one step in. The floorboard creaked beneath his weight.

Coley stiffened his gun arm and did not move.

"Let's get out of here, LaDuke."

"Maybe you *ought* to run, Pretty Boy," Coley said.

LaDuke's face reddened.

"And maybe," LaDuke said, "you ought to make a move."

"LaDuke," I said.

His finger tightened on the trigger.

"Know what this thirty-eight'll do to that pretty face?" Coley said.

LaDuke just smiled.

Their eyes locked, and neither of them moved. The sound of our breathing was the only sound in the room.

"Hey, Jack," I said, very quietly.

Coley squeezed the trigger on the .38 and LaDuke squeezed the trigger on the shotgun—both of them, at once.

TWENTY-FOUR

THE ROOM EXPLODED in a sucking roar of sonics and fine red spray. LaDuke's head jerked sharply to the side, as if he had been slapped.

A rag doll slammed against the wall, fell in a heap to the floor, the head dropping sloppily to the chest. The rag doll wore the clothes of Coley. Everything above the hairline was gone, the face unrecognizable; the face was soup.

"I'm shot, Nick," LaDuke said almost giddily. "I'm shot!"

I went to him, pulled him around.

The right side of his jaw was exposed, skinless, with pink rapidly seeping into the pearl of the bone. You're okay, LaDuke, I thought. You turned your head at the last moment and Coley blew off the side of your face. You're going to be badly scarred and a little ugly, but you're going to be okay.

And then I saw the hole in his neck, the exit hole or maybe the entry, rimmed purple and blackened from the powder, the hole the size of a quarter. Blood pumped rhythmically from the hole, spilling slowly over the collar of LaDuke's starched white shirt, meeting the blood that was the blow-back from Coley.

"Nick," LaDuke said, and he nearly laughed. "I'm shot!"

"Yeah, you're shot. Come on, let's get out of here. Let's go."

I went to Coley, kicked his hand away from the front of his pants, where it lay. I reached into his pocket and retrieved my keys. LaDuke stood by the door, facing it, shuffling his feet nervously, one hand on the stock of the Ithaca, the other on its barrel. I crossed the room.

"How many in the shotgun?" I said.

"Huh?"

"How many in that Ithaca?"

LaDuke mouthed the count, struggled to make things clear in his head. "It's a five-shot. Four now, I guess."

"You got more shells?"

He nodded. "And my Cobra. And your extra clip."

"Good. Give it to me." I took the extra magazine, slipped it in my back pocket. "Now listen. There's more of them, and they're gonna be comin' up the stairs. Maybe outside, covering the fire escape, too."

"Okay."

"We gotta go out this door now, see what's what. We gotta go now. We don't want to be trapped in this room."

"Okay."

I jacked a round into the chamber of my nine. LaDuke pumped one into the Ithaca.

"You ready?"

"Yes," LaDuke said, nodding rapidly. "I'm ready."

I opened the door, ran out blindly, LaDuke close behind me. I turned to my left.

A man was coming through the open window at the end of the hall. He was cursing, pulling at his shirt where it had snagged on a nail in the frame. There was a .45 in his free hand.

From the stairway at the other end of the hall, Sweet

emerged from the darkness. Sweet ran toward us, the .22 straight out in front of him.

"You!" he shouted.

I kept my eyes on the man in the window. My back bumped LaDuke's. I heard the pop of the .22, and the round blowing past us, and the ricochet off the metal shelving in the hall.

"Kill Sweet, LaDuke. Kill him."

LaDuke fired the shotgun. Sweet's scream echoed in the hall behind me. Then the .22 was popping and the shotgun roared over the pop of the gun.

The man in the window freed himself, pointed his weapon in my direction. I fell to the side, squeezed the trigger on the nine, squeezed it three times, saw the man was hit, saw him caught in the broken glass. I aimed, squeezed off another round. The man in the window rocked back, then pitched forward, a black hole on his cheek and a hole spitting blood from his chest. The casings from my gun pinged to the floor. I turned around at the sound of the Ithaca's pump.

LaDuke walked between the offices fronted with corrugated glass. He stood over the convulsing body of Sweet, Sweet's heels rattling at the hardwood floor. LaDuke kicked him like an animal. He stepped back, fired the shotgun. Flame came from the barrel and wood splintered off the floor. Sweet's body lifted and rolled.

"Hey, Nick," LaDuke said. Through the smoke, I could see his crazy, crooked smile.

A man in a blue shirt came running out of the stairwell, an automatic in his hand.

I shouted, "LaDuke!"

LaDuke stepped through an open door. Blue Shirt moved his gun arm in my direction.

I dove and tumbled into the bathroom as a vanity mirror exploded above my head. Another round blew through the doorway. The round sparked, ricocheted, took off some tiles. A ceramic triangle ripped at my sleeve. The glass of the shower door spidered and flew apart. Glass rained down and stung at my face.

I looked behind me, saw the bricked-up window. The footsteps of the shooter sounded near the door. I could feel the sweat on my back and the weight of glass in my hair. The Browning felt slick in my hands. I gripped it with both hands. From the hall, LaDuke yelled my name.

Then there were gunshots, and more glass, the corrugated glass of the offices blowing apart. I rolled, screaming, out of the bathroom, looked for anything blue, saw blue and the black of LaDuke's black suit, fired my gun at the blue.

The man in the blue shirt danced backward, shot off his feet, caught between the bullet of my gun and the blast of LaDuke's shotgun. He hit the floor, saliva and blood slopping from his open mouth.

I walked through the smoke toward LaDuke, glass crunching beneath my feet. A steady high note sounded in my ears and blood pumped violently in my chest. LaDuke pulled a fistful of shells from his jacket pocket, thumbed them into the Ithaca. I wrist-jerked the magazine out of my automatic, found the loaded clip in my back pocket. My hand shook wildly as I slapped it in.

"What now?" LaDuke said.

"Out the window," I said. "Come on."

"I say we finish things up downstairs. The rest of them are down those stairs."

"You're bleeding bad, Jack. You gotta get to a hospital, man."

I couldn't tell if he had been shot again. There was an awful lot of blood on his shirt now; blood still pulsed from the hole in his neck.

"You see that turpentine, man, and those jars?"

"Jack."

"Come here, Nick. I gonna show you what we're gonna do now."

He went to the shelved area of the hall, and I followed.

Behind us, from the stairwell, I could hear men shouting at us from the first floor.

LaDuke stopped at the jars and the thinners and the paints. He put his shotgun on the floor. I kept my gun trained on the stairwell. He poured paint thinner into the jars, then ripped some rags apart, doused the rags in thinner, and stuffed the doused rags into the necks of the jars.

I put my hand around his arm, but he jerked his arm away.

"Man," he said, "we are going to light this motherfucker up!"

"Let's go, Jack."

LaDuke smiled, the smile waxy and frightening. The bone of his jaw was jagged and the pink had gone to red. His eyes were hard and bright.

"You're going into shock, Jack."

"You got matches? You always got matches, Nick."

The men continued to shout from below. From the window at the end of the hall, I could hear the faint beginnings of a siren. I found my matches and pressed them into LaDuke's clammy palm.

"Thanks," he said, picking up the jars and cradling them in his arms. "It's all been leading up to this for me. You know that, don't you, Nick?"

"Bullshit. The object is to stay alive. Nothing else. If you got a different idea, then you're an idiot, LaDuke. I'm not going through that door with you, man. I'm not coming with you. You hear me? I'm not."

"See you around, Nick."

He walked down the hall toward the open doorway of the stairwell. I went the opposite way and got to the window. I climbed halfway through the window, then looked back.

LaDuke passed in front of the open doorway. A round fired from below and sparked at his feet. He kept walking calmly with the jars tight to his chest, stopping on the other side of the doorway. He set the jars down on the floor and drew the .357 Cobra from the holster behind his back.

"Jack," I said, almost to myself. Then I screamed his name out with all I had. But he didn't respond. He didn't even move at the sound of his name.

LaDuke struck a match. He touched the match to the three rags, ignited them all. He took one jar and tossed it down the stairs. It blew immediately, sending heat and fire up through the open frame. The men below began to yell. LaDuke threw the second jar, then the third right behind it. Smoke poured up from the stairwell and there was a muffled explosion; the men's voices intensified.

LaDuke pulled the hammer back on the Cobra. He turned the corner and disappeared into the smoke.

There were gunshots then, gunshots and screams. I closed my eyes and stepped out onto the fire escape. It was still night, and two sirens wailed from far away. I went down the fire escape, hung on the end of it, and dropped to the pavement.

LaDuke had driven the Ford right into the fence. There was a hole there now, where the hood protruded into the lot. I walked straight out and crossed the street to my Dodge.

The sirens swelled and there were more gunshots. The spit and crackle of the fire deepened and the screams grew more frenzied. I got in, closed the door and turned the ignition key, and kept the windows rolled up tight. I couldn't hear anything then, except for the engine. I put the car in gear, zigzagged out of the warehouse district with my headlights off. When I hit M, I flipped on my lights and headed west.

I drove across town through empty streets. Fifteen minutes later, I entered Beach Drive and the cool green cover of Rock Creek Park. I touched the dash lighter to a cigarette.

I rolled down my window. The sounds of the guns and the sounds of the fire had gone away. The screams had not.

TWENTY-FIVE

I DROVE TO my apartment and dropped into bed. Maybe I slept. The dreams I had were waking dreams, or maybe they were not. I turned over on my side, stayed there until noon. Slots of dirty gray light leaked through the spaces in the drawn bedroom blinds. I could hear the drone of a lawn mower, and from the kitchen, my cat, pacing, making small hungry sounds. I got out of bed, went to the kitchen, and spooned a can of salmon into her dish.

The *Post*'s final edition was lying out on the stoop beneath a sunless sky, its plastic wrap warm to the touch. I brought the newspaper inside, made a cup of coffee, and had a seat on my living room couch. The burning of the warehouse—the burning and the death—had made the front page. Nothing about violence, though, and no mention of foul play. That would come later in the day, or the next.

I thought of my bullet casings scattered on the second floor of the warehouse. And then there was the matter of my prints. If Boyle and Johnson chose to push it and make the connection, the casings could be traced to my gun. I'd have to get rid of the Browning, and I didn't have much time.

I battered a slice of eggplant, fried it, and put it between two slices of bread, then washed it down with another cup of coffee. Then I took a long, cold shower and reapplied ointment to the cuts in my face, where I had tweezered out the slivers of glass the night before. In the mirror, I looked at my swollen eyes, the area beneath my left eye, black and gorged with blood, and the purple arc across the bridge of my nose. I looked into my own eyes and I thought, That thing in the mirror is not me. But when I moved, the thing in the mirror moved in the exact same way. And I was the only one standing in the room.

I shook some Tylenols out into my hand, ate them, and got dressed. Then I went out to my Dodge and headed downtown.

I PARKED NEAR THE District Building, walked toward the CCNV shelter on D, and cut into the courtyard at the Department of Labor. There was a blind corner there where some men from the shelter gathered to smoke reefer and drink beer and fortified wine during the day. Two men stood with their backs against the gray concrete, passing a bottle of Train in the midday heat. I picked the cleaner of the two, engaged him in a brief introduction, and took him to lunch at a bar called My Brother's Place on 2nd and C. Then I had him clean up in the upstairs bathroom, and when he sat back down at our table, smelling a little less powerfully than he had before, I handed him some written instructions and ripped a twenty in half, promising him the other half upon his successful return. He shambled off in the direction of the Office of Deeds. This man would disappear eventually, become one of the anonymous urban MIA. But looking as I did, even with the benefit of elapsed time, I knew that I would be remembered later on.

I had a slow beer and a shot of bourbon out on the patio and talked to my friend Charles, the bar's dishwasher and unofficial bouncer, an unassuming giant and tireless worker who is one of the few purely principled men left in this city. Then the man from the shelter returned and gave me my information. I sat staring at it, and I laughed, but it was laughter devoid of pleasure, and the man from the shelter asked me what was funny.

"Nothing's funny," I said. "I thought I was pretty smart, but I'm stupid, and I think that's pretty goddamn funny. Don't you?"

He shrugged and took the rest of his twenty. I tore up the written instructions and asked him if there was anything he'd like, and he said he'd like a Crown Royal rocks with a splash of water. I ordered him one and dropped money on the table, then left the coolness of the overhead fan and walked back into the heat.

Back in my apartment, I made a phone call and set the time for the appointment. Then I took a nap and another shower, gathered up the instruments that I thought I might need. On the way out the door, I passed the mirror that hung on the living room wall and saw the thing with the purple nose and the blood-gorged eye—the thing that was not me—walking toward the door.

I PARKED IN THE lighted lot at 22nd and M. It was night, and the heat that had enshrouded the city for days had not receded. Suburban kids locked their Jeeps and Mustang 5.0s and walked toward the New Orleans–style nightspot on the north side of M, the boys clean-shaven and beer-muscle cocky, the girls freshly showered and dressed in the latest cookie-cutter, mall-purchased attire. I lit a cigarette and dangled the cigarette out the open window.

At nine o'clock sharp, Richard Samuels walked across the lot to my car, his fine white hair catching the light. He wore a tie but no jacket, the tie's knot firmly entrapped between the points of his tabbed white collar. He saw my Dodge and then me, and he forced a spring in his step. He opened the passenger door and dropped into the bucket. His face was ridged with lines of sweat.

"Mr. Stefanos."

"Samuels."

"My God, what happened to your face?"

"Your people," I said.

"Yes," he said. "Well."

I dragged on my cigarette, flipped it out, where it arced to the asphalt. "No one knows you're here?"

"No. Of course, you phoned today when my secretary was out. No, no one knows but you and me."

"Good."

Samuels relaxed his shoulders. "I'll tell you, I've had one hell of a day. The police came to me first thing this morning. And the insurance people have been swarming all over me. What with you bringing Vice down on me last week, it's not going to be long before this whole thing blows up in my face, and yours. I'm not waiting around to find out how it plays out. I assume you'll be leaving town, too, after we settle things."

"You're pretty casual about all this, Samuels."

"Just practical." He spread his manicured hands. "I'm a businessman, after all. I've always known when to cut my losses. Surely you would understand. I mean, that's what this is about, isn't it?" I stared ahead. "Now, your partner, the one who you brought along to my office? He didn't understand at all. He let his emotions get in the way of what is, after all, a process of logic. I assume that he died with my men. His emotions were what killed him, isn't that right?"

I gripped the steering wheel, watched the blood leave my knuckles. "How does a man like you get involved in all this, anyway?"

Samuel's wet red lips parted in a weak smile. "Simply put, I saw the demand in the market. In the world I traveled in, in the 1980s, it seemed as if every commercial broker in D.C. was driving around town in his three-twenty-five, a one shot vial of coke lying within easy reach. I thought, Why don't I get some of that action? It wasn't difficult to locate and establish a relationship with a supplier, and soon afterward I was in business. Then cocaine went out of white-collar fashion—for the most part, anyway—and the market went from powder to rock. I simply made an adjustment. My supplier put me in touch with some gentlemen who could deal with the rougher situations, and I moved the powder straight into the inner city. I had the space to run it through—"

"Your real estate holdings. And your profit centers—you make movies; you own the equipment, and the lights. You said yourself, the first time I met you, that you favored control all the way down the line."

"Yes. And I had the manpower to make it work. My own hands never touched the stuff. It was going beautifully, in fact, until you intervened."

"You made a mistake. You had a couple of innocent kids killed."

"Innocent? Mr. Stefanos, don't be naïve. I'm not happy at how it turned out for them, but—"

"Don't. I know all about you, Samuels."

Samuels stared off balefully in a theatrical gesture of remorse. He looked into his lap and spoke softly. "I can't help the way I am, any more than you can change your own proclivities. The decision I made was a business decision, as are all of my decisions. As this is, right now." He straightened his posture. "Which brings us to the real reason we're sitting here."

"Let's get to it, then."

"All right. How much?"

"What?"

"How much do you want? What is it going to take to make you go away?"

"Samuels," I said, reaching beneath my seat, "I think you've misunderstood me."

His eyes widened as I brought up my sap. He tried to raise his hands, but he was too old and way too slow. I swung the sap sharply, connecting at his temple. He slumped forward, his forehead coming to rest against the glove box.

I checked his breathing, then pulled everything else up from beneath the seat. I tied his hands behind his back and covered his mouth with duct tape. A wool army blanket lay folded in the backseat. I arranged Samuels fetally and covered him with the blanket.

I eased out of the lot and headed east.

I PARKED IN THE clearing that faced the river and cut the engine. The lights of the Sousa Bridge shimmered on the river's black water. Through the trees, Christmas lights glowed colorfully, strung along the dock of the marina. Country music and the laughter of a woman lifted off a pontoon boat and drifted in on the river breeze.

I took the blanket off Samuels and sat him up. His silver hair was soaked in sweat, his complexion pale and splotched. I pulled the duct tape away from his mouth, let the tape dangle from his face. His eyes blinked open, then slowly closed. I poured some bottled water on his lips and poured some into his open mouth. He coughed it out, straightened up in his seat, opened his eyes, kept them open as he moved to make himself comfortable. Samuels stared at the river.

"Untie me, please," he said quietly.

"No." I reached over and loosened the knot of his tie. He breathed out, his breath like a long deflation.

"Please," he said.

"No. And don't think of screaming. I'll have to tape your mouth again. All right?"

Samuels nodded blankly. I slipped my cigarette pack from the visor and rustled it in his direction. He shook his head. I lit one for myself. I smoked some of it down.

Samuels said, "*Why?* I don't *understand* this. I can't believe... I can't believe we can't make some sort of deal."

I exhaled smoke and watched it fade.

"I just don't understand," he said.

Some birds glided down from the trees and went to black against the moon. A Whaler passed in the river, the throttle on full, its wake spreading in a swirl of foam and current. I thought of my grandfather and closed my eyes.

Samuels turned in my direction. "Do you ever wonder where dead men go, Mr. Stefanos?"

I didn't reply.

"What I mean is, do you believe in God?"

The woman from the party boat screamed and then there was more laughter, her laughter drunken and mixed with the wolfish shouts of men.

"No," Samuels said. "Of course you don't. Everything is black and white with people like you. People like you can't even see the possibility of a higher power. No, I'm certain that if you were asked, you'd say that there is no God." Samuels's face turned childish, impudent. "*I* believe in God. You're saying to yourself, There's a contradiction here, a man like this believing in God. But you know, I pray for myself every day. And do you think I could have sent those boys to their deaths if I didn't believe that I was sending them to a better place? Do you think that?" He chewed at his lip. "I'm sorry. I'm talking quite a bit, aren't I? I'm nervous, you know."

I stabbed my cigarette out in the ashtray.

"Talk to me," he said, a quiver in his voice. "Why don't you say something to me, please."

I fixed the tape back over his mouth and stepped out of the car. I went around to the other side, opened the door, and pulled him out. He fell to his side, tried to stay down. I yanked him back to his feet. Samuels bugged his eyes, made muffled moaning sounds beneath the tape.

I pushed him along the graveled clearing, his feet dragging, stirring up dust. We got to the bulkhead, where the river lapped at the concrete. Beyond the bulkhead, the Whaler's wake splashed against the pilings and slipped over the rusted window frames of the sunken houseboat.

Samuels's hands squirmed against the rope. I turned his back to the water and kicked him behind the legs. He fell to his knees. I ripped the duct tape off his face.

"Oh, God," he said as I drew the Browning from behind my back.

"There isn't one," I said, and shoved the barrel into his open mouth. "Remember?"

TWENTY-SIX

I BURIED UNCLE Costa in the fall. His grave was next to Toula's, just twenty yards from my grandfather's, in Glenwood Cemetery, off Lincoln Road in Northwest. It was an immigrant's graveyard, unofficially sectioned off, with a special section for Greeks, many of them Spartans, the grounds run down at times, littered with beer bottles and cartons, but clean now and live with the reds and oranges of the maples and poplars on the hills.

A small group attended, old-timers mostly, the very last of a generation, the men who had ruled at the picnics of my childhood, men in white shirts and pleated gray slacks who danced to the wild clarinets and bouzoukis and played cards and drank and laughed, the smell of grilled lamb and fresh phyllo in the air. Lou DiGeordano was there, as frail as I had ever seen him, held at the arm by his son Joey, and a few other men and women, stooped and small, with black marble eyes and hair like the frazz of white rope, men and women I no longer recognized. And

Lyla was there, her red hair long and lifting in the breeze, our hands touching, the touch of two friends.

It hadn't ended suddenly with me and Lyla, as it does not end suddenly between two people who are breaking things off but still in love. We went out a couple of times to our regular restaurants, but the restaurants had lost their shine and the people who served us looked to us as strangers. Lyla had given up drinking and I had not, the change just something else that had dropped between us. We slept together on those nights, the sex needed and good. But the sex, we knew, would not save us. So things continued like that, and one afternoon I realized that I had not spoken with Lyla for a couple of weeks, and I knew then that that part of us was finally over.

The weather did not begin to turn until late September. As the days cooled, I rode my bike more frequently and kept the Dodge parked and covered. Mai went off to Germany to visit her family and Anna returned to school. I took on double shifts at the Spot into October, and in that period there was Costa's funeral and solitary nights and occasionally nights with friends, all of them unmemorable and with the certain sameness that comes with the worn wood and low light of bars and the ritual of drink. My face healed quickly, though when it healed, I noticed that I had aged, the age and a kind of fading in my eyes. My scars had become a part of me now, suggesting neither toughness nor mystery, rarely prompting the interest of acquaintances or the second look from strangers. No one came to me for outside work; I would not have considered it if they had.

In the days that followed the violence in the warehouse, I looked over my shoulder often and listened for the inevitable knock on my front door. The newspaper and television reports stayed on top of the story for a full week and then the next sensational multiple murder took the warehouse story's place. It was always in my mind that Boyle and Detective Johnson knew I was connected in some way. But no one came to interview me and no one came to bring me in. And Boyle continued to come in on a regular basis and sit at his bar stool, his draft beer and shot of Jack in front of him, a Marlboro Red burning in the tray.

Then in late October, on a night when the first biting fall wind had dropped into town, Boyle walked into the Spot at closing time, his bleached-out eyes pink and heavily lidded, drunk as I had seen him in a long while. His shirttail hung down below his tweed sport jacket, and the grip of his Python peeked out of the jacket's vent. He walked carefully to the bar, had a seat on a stool. I stopped the music on the deck and went down to see him.

"Closing time, Boyle."

"Just one round tonight, Nick, before I go home. You got no problem with that, do you?"

"Okay."

I drew him a beer and set it on a damp coaster while he arranged his deck of Marlboros and pack of matches next to an ashtray. Then I free-poured some Jack Daniel's into a beveled shot glass. He drank off some of the beer and lit a cigarette. He knocked back half of the shot.

Darnell's light switched off as he walked from the kitchen. He buttoned his jacket and looked at Boyle. Boyle's head was lowered, his eyes dull and pointed at the bar.

"Hawk's gonna fly tonight, looks like," Darnell said. "You drive down, Nick?"

"Yeah, I got the Dodge out tonight, with the weather and all."

"Mind if I catch a ride uptown with you?"

"Sure, if you can wait."

I nodded toward Boyle and Darnell shook his head. "I don't think so, man. Let me get on out of here. Take it easy, Nick."

"Yeah, you, too."

Darnell touched his hat in a kind of salute. He walked from the bar. I took a few bottles of beer from the cooler and buried them in the ice chest.

"God, I am drunk," Boyle said, pushing his face around with his hand. "Have a drink with me, will ya, Nick?"

"All right."

I opened a bottle of beer and put a shot of Old Grand-Dad next to the bottle. Boyle and I touched glasses and drank. I chased the bourbon with the beer.

"So," Boyle said.

"Yeah," I said.

"Well... I shouldn't be so drunk. But I am. I've been driving around all day, and when I was done driving, I hit a couple bars. You know how that goes."

"Sure. Where'd you go?"

"Out in the country. Frederick County."

I lit a cigarette and shook out the match. I dropped the match in the ashtray.

"Out there in the country," Boyle said, "lookin' for some answers."

"What kind of answers?"

"It's this thing with that partner of yours, Jack LaDuke. How he just disappeared after those deaths in that warehouse. And the Samuels murder—I don't know, it's just been eatin' away at me, you know? I mean, I could have just come to you and all that, but, the way you are, I knew you wouldn't talk."

I put my hand up in protest, but Boyle cut me off.

"Hold on a second, Nick, lemme just go on a little bit."

"Go ahead."

"So I went to talk to Shareen Lewis. Well, she didn't say much of anything. But she did tell me the name of the bondsman— I forget his name right now—who turned her on to LaDuke. So I went to this bondsman, see, and he fills me in on some details on this LaDuke character. I finally found his old man out there in the country, but the old man said he hasn't heard from his son in years. Imagine that, not talkin' to your own kid for years."

"It's something," I said.

"And you?"

"What about me?"

"You haven't heard from him, either."

"No."

"Well," Boyle said, "let me just tell you what I think. What I think happened is—and granted, it's just a theory of mine—I think he checked out in that fire. You remember, fifteen, twenty years back, when all those faggots got caught in that fire down at that movie house, the Cinema Follies? Man, they were just piled up against that locked door. Well, that's the way it looked the morning after that fire in the warehouse. There was a bunch of 'em, piled against the door. 'Course, some of them had been shot up, and there were a few shot-up ones up on the second floor. And we identified a few of them from prison dentals, that sort of thing. The thing is, I think LaDuke was one of the ones in that pile, one of the ones we couldn't identify. What do you think?"

"If he went to that warehouse, he went on his own. I don't know a thing about it."

"Well, anyway, it's just a guess." Boyle walked two fingers over the top of his glass. "Pour me another one, will ya?"

I did it. I dragged on my cigarette and Boyle dragged on his and our smoke turned slowly in the conical light.

Boyle put his glass down, looked into it thoughtfully. "But," he said. "But...if LaDuke died in that fire, it doesn't explain the Samuels murder."

"I don't follow."

"The casings found at the crime scene match the casings found on the second floor of that warehouse. Same gun, Nick. I followed through with ballistics myself. So whoever was in on the warehouse kill also hit Samuels."

I finished my bourbon and put one foot up on the ice chest.

"You know, Nick, we were really close on nailing Samuels, too. I'd say we were one day off. We were working our informants pretty good on the drug angle, man, and we were close. Once we knew he owned both warehouses, after that it was a cinch. But someone just got one step ahead of us. Goddamn, was Johnson pissed off about that. We did find the twenty-two that did Jeter and Lewis, and the man who used it. Guy out of

South Baltimore, just like you said. But we'd still like to clean the rest of this thing up. 'Course, all's we got to do now is find the gun that belongs to those casings."

"There you go, Boyle. Find the gun and you'll have the whole thing wrapped up."

"The gun. The gun was a nine-millimeter, like that Browning you carry." Boyle's jittery eyes settled on mine. "You still carry that Browning, Nick?"

"No. I lost it. The thing is, I was just looking for it the other day, to clean it—"

"Yeah. You probably dropped it in the river or some shit like that, by mistake. Slipped right out of your hands. Funny, you know. If the city could get it together and put up the money to dredge the Anacostia, you wanna know how many cases we could put to bed?"

"Too bad they can't get it together."

"Yeah. Too bad." Boyle closed his eyes and emptied his drink. "Well, I better get home. My kids and all that."

"I'll lock up behind you," I said.

Boyle held on to the bar and got off his stool. I walked with him to the door. When we got there, he put his back against it and wrapped a meaty hand around my arm. He started to speak but had trouble putting the words together, closed his mouth in a frown.

"You're drunk, Boyle. You want me to call a cab?"

"Uh-uh."

"Go home to your kids."

"My kids. Yeah, I got my kids."

"Go on home."

"You know somethin'?" Boyle said. "I feel sorry for you, Nick. I really do. You know...you remember a few years ago, there was this short-eyed motherfucker that was rapin' those little girls in Northeast? Description on him was he was some variety of spic, a Rican maybe, with a bandanna, the whole brown rig. The shit was on the news every night, man—you gotta remember."

"Yeah, I do. They never caught the guy. So what?"

"*I* caught him," Boyle said. "Me and this other cop. We got him in an alley, and he confessed."

"Congratulations. Another good collar for you."

"You didn't read about him being caught 'cause we never took him in. I put a bullet in his head that night, Nick. The other cop, he put one in him, too."

"Go home," I said, pulling my arm away. "That's liquor talk. Save that shit for your buddies at the FOP."

"It's just..." Boyle said. "It's just that I know what's in your head right now. The thing is, I got my kids to go home to. I can go home, I can hold them, and for a little while, anyway, it makes everything all right. I got that, Nick. What do you got?"

I didn't answer. Instead, I opened the door.

"Don't you want to know?" Boyle said.

"Okay," I said. "Why hasn't Johnson pulled me in?"

"Johnson?" Boyle said, a sad smile forming on his face. "Johnson's been there, too, that's why. Johnson was with me when we did that short-eyes. Johnson was the other cop."

Boyle stepped through the open door. I closed it and turned the lock.

I walked back behind the stick and refilled my shot glass. The whiskey was silk; I drank it and smoked a cigarette in the quiet of the bar. The phone rang. I picked it up, the call a misdial. I stared at the receiver in my hand. When I heard the dial tone, I phoned Lyla's apartment. A man's voice greeted me on the other end.

"Is Lyla McCubbin in, please?" I said.

The man put his hand over the phone but did not cover it all the way. He said, "Hey, Lyla, this guy wants to know if he can speak to a Lyla McCubbin. Sounds like a salesman or something. Want me to just get rid of him?"

I heard Lyla laugh, recognized the laughter as forced. I hung the receiver in its cradle before she could reply.

I had another beer, and another after that. By then, it had

gotten pretty late. I thought of my cat, out in the weather, hungry and pacing on the stoop. I dimmed the lights and put on a coat, then locked the place and set the alarm. I went out to the street.

Orange and yellow leaves lifted and tumbled down 8th. I turned my collar up against the wind, walked with my head down, my eyes on the sidewalk.

I passed the riot gate of the shoe store and neared the alley. From the alley, I heard a voice.

"Stevonus."

I turned around.

"LaDuke," I said.

He stood in the mouth of the alley, his face covered in shadow. But the black pant legs and heavy black oxfords were exposed by the light of the streetlamp above; I knew it was him.

I walked to the alley and stood a couple of feet back. The smell coming off him was minty, strongly medicinal.

"Got a cigarette, Nick?"

"You're smoking now, huh?"

"Sure," he said, a slight lisp to his voice. "Why not?"

I reached into my coat and shook one out of the deck. He took it and asked me for a light. I struck a match, cupped the flame. He put his hand around mine and pulled it toward him, leaning forward at the same time. I saw his face then as it moved into the light. He watched me carefully as the flame touched the tobacco.

"Kinda scary, eh, Nick?"

I took in some breath and tried to smile. "It's not so bad."

"Nobody's ever gonna call me 'Pretty Boy' again, I guess."

He was right. No one was going to mistake him for pretty. Whoever had done the work on him had botched the job. His lips were pulled back on one side and stretched open in a ghastly kind of half smile, the gums ruby red and exposed there and glistening with saliva, the saliva dripping over the side of his mouth. Skin had been grafted sloppily along his jawline, unmatched and puckered at the edges, and bluish around the grafted hole in his neck.

"No, Jack," I said. "It's not pretty. But you're alive."

LaDuke took a folded handkerchief from his pocket, the handkerchief damp and gray. He dabbed it on his gums, then shoved it back in his pocket. He dragged on his cigarette.

"How'd you get out of the warehouse that night?" I said.

"When I went down into that mess with my gun, we traded shots. But the fire spread real fast, and then those men knew they weren't going to make it. They ran for the door on the first floor. I guess Sweet had taken the key. Anyway, I kinda woke up, decided that I wanted to live. I booked back up the stairs and ran down that hall. Hell, I was right behind you."

"And then?"

"Shit, man, I don't know. I was going into shock in a big way. The only thing I thought to do was go to my father. So I drove out to Frederick County. I kept my foot to the floor all the way, and I made it. I don't know how I made it, but I did."

"Your father," I said, not really wanting to know.

"Yeah. He did the best he could. Used that horse stitch of his on my face, did some kind of poor man's graft. Wired my jaw together. The main thing was, he stopped the infection, after a couple of days. I don't remember much of it." LaDuke avoided my eyes. "Yeah, my father, he fixed me up."

I felt a chill and pulled the lapels of my coat together to the neck. LaDuke retrieved his handkerchief and blotted the spit from his chin.

"Why'd you come to me tonight?" I said.

"Your cop friend visited my father today. Thought I might warn you."

"Warn me about what?"

LaDuke said, "You took out Samuels, right?"

"Yes."

"How about that gun of yours? You get rid of that Browning?"

"I dumped it over the rail of the Sousa Bridge."

"Good. I just wanted you to know that the law was on it."

"I got a feeling they'll be leaving me alone."

"That's good," LaDuke said. He reached inside his jacket and pulled out an envelope thick with bills. "I came to give you this, as well."

"Where did that come from?"

"Shareen Lewis. My payment for finding her son. Half of it belongs to you."

"You keep it. I don't need it, man. I'm coming into some money, from an inheritance. I'm flush."

"Take it." He pressed the envelope into my hand. "We earned it, you and me."

"All right. I know a kid in San Francisco — he could use the money, I guess."

And then the half of his face that was not gone twisted back into some sort of smile. "We got 'em, Nick. Didn't we?"

"What?"

"We took those guys off the street. I mean, it's something. Isn't it?"

"Yes, Jack. It's something."

He dropped the cigarette under his heavy black shoe, crushed it into the concrete, and began to move away. I touched his arm.

"Where you goin', Jack?"

"I don't know. I gotta go."

"How will I find you?"

"I'll be around," he said.

He turned and walked into the alley. The darkness took him, and he was gone.

I stood there thinking about Jack LaDuke. I looked into the black maw of the alley and blinked my eyes. LaDuke would be deep in that alley now, dabbing at his face with the damp gray handkerchief, in the dark but not afraid of it, because for him there was nothing left to fear. Or maybe he was out on the street, staring straight ahead as he walked down the sidewalk, avoiding his reflection in the glass of the storefronts and bars. Wherever he was, I knew he was alone. Like Lyla was alone, and like me. All of us alone, in our own brand of night.

Leaves blew past my feet and clicked at the bars of the riot gate. I slipped the envelope inside my coat and moved out of the light.

I walked to the corner, crossed the street, and headed for my Dodge. I touched my key to the lock, but did not fit it. I stepped away and walked back to the Spot.

Inside, the room was silent, bathed in blue neon. I went behind the bar. I poured myself a bourbon and pulled a bottle of beer from the ice.

I lit a cigarette. I had my drink.

This one started at the Spot.

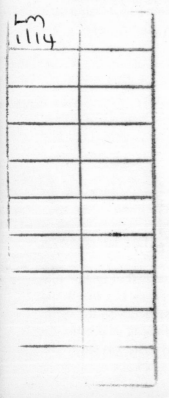